Praise For *Open House*

"A chilling thriller, *Open House* tracks a missing art student who vanished ten years prior and how her disappearance connects with a recent attack during an open house in a small university town. It also showcases the unending loyalty of close girlfriends and sisterhood in life or death."

—*Good Morning America*

"Part murder mystery, part interpersonal drama, a serviceable who-done-it (or did anyone?) with a host of compelling characters . . . this novel has just enough twists to keep its readers along for the ride."

—*Kirkus Reviews*

"Sise captures the insular nature of small towns in this domestic drama, and a series of unpredictable twists makes everyone the culprit for at least a little while. Readers who enjoy suspense fiction with a strong focus on relationships, like that of Liane Moriarty or Jessica Knoll, will be drawn into the McCulloughs' story."

—*Booklist*

"This twisty tale is full of secrets and thrills sure to keep you interested in what is going on through the very end."

—*Book Riot*

Praise for *We Were Mothers*

"Sise offers an astute glimpse into tragic loss, the innermost lives of women, and the highs and lows and societal expectations of motherhood . . . This compelling character study will resonate."

—*Kirkus Reviews*

"Propulsive . . . compelling."

—Booklist

"Sise displays a sly sense of pacing; nearly every chapter unveils a new plot twist, keeping readers hooked. Fans of Liane Moriarty will eat this title up with a spoon."

—Library Journal

"Taut and suspenseful, *We Were Mothers* will keep readers on the edge of their seats until the very end."

—Bustle

"Katie Sise's *We Were Mothers* expertly snaps readers to attention with its grandiose opening . . . Timing, inner discourse and believable fiascos blend together producing fantastic scenes . . . Her observations and vulnerability carry the read."

—Associated Press

"If you can't resist a sharp, suspenseful novel, then *We Were Mothers* by Katie Sise deserves a spot on your reading list."

—POPSUGAR

THE
BREAK

ALSO BY KATIE SISE

We Were Mothers

Open House

THE BREAK

A NOVEL

KATIE SISE

Published by Little A, New York

www.apub.com

Amazon, the Amazon logo, and Little A are trademarks of Amazon.com, Inc., or its affiliates.

ISBN-13: 9781662503870 (hardcover)
ISBN-10: 1662503873 (hardcover)

ISBN-13: 9781662503894 (paperback)
ISBN-10: 166250389X (paperback)

Cover design by Zoe Norvell

Printed in the United States of America

First edition

For every woman who has experienced a traumatic birth

For anyone whose path to creating a family has been marked with loss

For every woman who has battled postpartum mental illness

PART I

ONE

Rowan. Monday afternoon. November 7th.

I became a mystery writer when my dad was killed. His murder flipped me like a switch. The wondering, the imagining, the plotting: all of it is what I do, what I've always done. Or at least, that's what I say in interviews.

But sometimes I lie in bed in the thick, creeping hours after midnight and wonder if that's really the whole truth. We tell ourselves all kinds of stories about our past. And maybe we even convince ourselves they're true. I tell myself and everyone else that I live in the sordid worlds of my novels because of my father's stabbing. That I write mysteries with heroines who solve them because I could never solve his murder.

I have no idea whether these things make me a good writer or a good liar.

I don't remember much about becoming a mother a few weeks ago, only collapsing in the street and hearing sirens as I bled. And then three days ago, I lost my mind and accused our beautiful twenty-two-year-old babysitter, June, of harming our newborn. But June hadn't done anything. Which is why Sylvie Alvarez, PhD, PsyD, is sitting here in my daughter Lila's nursery, making sure I'm fit to take care of her.

Sylvie sips lavender tea on a plush leather pouf, staring at my face while my husband, Gabe, hovers in the background like a linebacker. He's too big for this nursery with its small things, with our small baby. Sylvie's supposed to be one of the best psychologists in New York City, and she's here as a favor because we know her college roommate. Gabe begged her to come for a house call so we wouldn't have to take the baby out in the cold.

I still can't remember the birth. I remember the knives and the blood and the feeling of cold air against my skin when they raced me into the operating room. Gabe has told me most of what happened, but I get the sense he's trying to downplay how badly it went. Not only the emergency surgery, but the part when I woke up from the anesthesia and the doctors set a howling baby girl on my chest and I started screaming at the top of my lungs and wouldn't stop. As Gabe tells it, I started flailing so wildly they had to take away Lila and sedate me again. Sometimes I don't believe Gabe, but I believe that. The only thing I remember about that flicker of a moment was how slippery Lila was, and how trying to keep her safe in my arms was like trying to hold water. The surgical knives were still out, glinting maniacally in the corner of my vision, and I was terrified because she was all I'd ever wanted.

"If you want to talk about what happened with your sitter," Sylvie's saying, her voice smooth like butter. "If you're ready to talk about June. If you remember."

I stare at Sylvie, at the crow's-feet that spike the golden-brown skin around her eyes. I'm perched at the edge of the nursing chair, my body coiled like a spring that could burst free and escape with Lila if I needed to. I kiss the top of Lila's head, my mouth against her dark, downy hair. I want to squeeze her against my chest and bury my head in the curve of her neck, to breathe in the smell of her skin and never stop. But I worry Sylvie will sense something's still terribly wrong with me, and if she thinks I can't take care of Lila then it's all over: they'll take her from me. Or they'll lock me up in a ward and give her to Gabe, and he doesn't deserve her. I know that's an awful thing to say.

"Of course I remember what happened," I say, and in my mind's eye I see June: her heart-shaped face with bright green eyes like sun on ocean water, her tanned skin smoothed by youth and luck-of-the-draw genetics, and her laugh—tinkling, almost. June was so magnetic.

Is, I remind myself.

June's alive. You didn't kill her, Rowan, did you?

I close my eyes, but that makes it worse because June lights up the darkness behind my lids: a flick of straw-colored hair over her shoulder, bracelets stacked on her skinny wrists so that she jangled when she moved from room to room in our apartment carrying Lila. Thinking of what I did to her feels like torture.

"June's okay now, right?" I ask Sylvie, my heart pounding, Lila warm in my arms. Too warm? I set my palm against the back of her neck, like I've seen other mothers do to try to find a fever. "You told me that yesterday," I say, blinking. "That's still true, right?"

Sylvie dunks her tea bag. "Your sitter is fine," she says, like it's nothing.

That open window. What if I had done something to June that night? I was so terrified, so sure she'd hurt Lila. "You remember?" Sylvie asks, prodding me with eyebrows up, waiting.

Gabe looks away like he can't bear to hear the story again. I can feel the shift of his attention like a physical force inside the nursery, a riptide. He doesn't look me in the eye anymore.

Thunk goes something out in the kitchen, and I flinch. Now that I've scared June away, Gabe's mother, Elena, is back. She's banging around pots and pans like she's cooking, but she's more likely sneaking trips to the closed nursery door to listen in on our therapy session. I want my own mother, but she's too far gone, eating stewed green beans in a care facility uptown.

I touch the smooth curve of Lila's fingernail. "I do," I say, because of all the things I can't recall leading up to the birth and the moment I nearly died delivering Lila—beeping monitors, all those masked faces over me—I can remember exactly what I did to June three days ago, the way her slim shoulders felt in my grip, and how her tendons and bones felt like they were made of nothing at all, like a hollow bird skeleton I could smash between my fingertips. I remember shaking her shoulders and screaming awful things into her crumpled, beautiful face:

The baby's gone!

What have you done?

I remember pushing June toward the window as she struggled against me. I didn't want to hurt her, but we got way too close to the sixth-floor window, which was open because I kept worrying Lila would overheat. I can still feel the warning snap of cold from the wind; it was one of the first freezing days of November, the air charged with impending winter, already dark at five, making people like me want to cry for the lack of daylight. And if I hadn't looked down right then to see Lila sleeping soundly in her bassinet, if I hadn't snapped out of it . . .

"The window," I say to Sylvie, needing to fill the silence with words. "The bay window in our living room was open, and I was pushing June toward it because I was so upset, I didn't want to hurt her or anything like that, I was just trying so hard to figure out what had happened to Lila. I remember how Gabe rushed into the room when he heard me shouting, and how he stopped dead when he saw us. June was sobbing, snot everywhere," I say. I'm not sure why I mention the snot detail. Maybe because it was the first I'd ever seen June not look beautiful. "And Gabe asked us what happened, and then June started for the door and Gabe tried to stop her, but she slipped by him."

And then she opened our apartment door, where two neighbors had already gathered in the hallway because of the noise.

She accused me of hurting your baby, Gabe, June had said, and I cringe to remember it. I know Sylvie sees it.

"I remember my thoughts felt disjointed," I say. "It was like I couldn't get ahold of them. And then I looked down, and I saw Lila, and she was okay."

My throat squeezes. Lila stirs in my arms, letting out a sleepy cry that pulls me out of the bloodied past and into the moment. She opens and closes her mouth like a fish, and I know she wants to eat. I'm still too new at nursing to be comfortable doing it in front of Sylvie, but I can't let her go hungry, so I unbutton my shirt and put her on my breast. The latch isn't quite right, and I wince with pain. Heat flames through my limbs.

Mercifully Sylvie doesn't say anything. Neither does Gabe, though I know he notices. I wish he would come to me, rub my back, or maybe get me a glass of water.

"What made you think June had tried to harm your baby, Rowan?" Sylvie asks, her voice so quiet I can barely hear it.

I look down at Lila, at her rosebud mouth moving against my chest, born knowing how to nurse somewhere deep inside her brain, all instinct. I stare at her perfect face. I write for a living, and I still have no words other than clichés to describe my daughter:

Perfect.

Everything.

Heavenly.

Mine.

"I have no idea," I say softly.

Sylvie shifts her weight on the pouf. She doesn't look comfortable. The furniture is gorgeous, but not exactly a great place to set down your body and rest. Sometimes when I glance around everything feels wrong, like I accidentally chose the wrong life—the wrong man?—and now I can't claw my way back to everything that was meant to be.

But that can't be right: I love Gabe, and I certainly love Lila. Everything is as it's supposed to be. And I'll get better, I will. I have to believe that.

TWO

Rowan. Monday evening. November 7th.

Gabe ushers Sylvie out of Lila's nursery.

"Goodbye, Dr. Alvarez," I say to the back of her cream cashmere sweater, and she turns. Her eyes look sunken beneath the overhead lights.

"Goodbye, Rowan," she says.

She doesn't say goodbye to Lila. I stand in the doorway, watching Gabe and Sylvie retreat down the hallway, their shadows lingering, slipping down the walls and over the oak floor before disappearing. I sway with Lila. Even with everything that's happened in the past three weeks since she entered this world, her open-eyed gaze makes me smile: my lips curve when she locks on me, a private grin that means something different than it ever has before.

Gabe's mom appears when Sylvie is gone. She tucks a tight curl behind her ear and studies my face.

"Elena, hi," I say, a little stupidly. I don't know how to talk to her after what I've done to June. I know she thinks I've gone insane, that I'm not well enough to take care of the baby. I can feel it. I hold Lila tightly, not wanting to pass her over.

"Can I hold her?" Elena asks.

I bite my lip. "No," I say. I clear my throat. "I'm sorry," I add, but I don't pass her over, and I don't say anything else.

Elena flushes. "I should go," she says, looking down at Lila like she means the very opposite.

"Thank you for making us dinner," I say guiltily.

Once Elena told me Gabe likes his sandwiches cut diagonally, and I regretted admitting to her that I'd never made him one. I always thought I took care of him in other ways, but now I'm not so sure. Maybe Elena sensed something lacking in me.

"How did therapy go?" Elena asks, her voice a little shaky. I'd like to think she has no right to the answer, but every time I want to dislike Elena I think about her friendship with my mother, how she dutifully visits my mother twice a week, bringing her crossword puzzles. And if my mother's feeling up to it, Elena checks her out of the care facility and brings her to a weekly bingo game in a church basement in our neighborhood, and then they come see us afterward for tea. My mother's only lucid half the time, but she likes visitors, and I'm grateful for it. It washes over me now—that warm feeling of being thankful to someone.

"It went okay," I say to Elena, wanting to give her a little more but too exhausted to get into it. "I just can't believe I did that to June," I say, more to myself than Elena. "She was only trying to help us."

"Maybe you don't need a young woman here, complicating things," Elena says, knuckles white against the leather strap of her pocketbook.

"Elena, please," I say, hoisting Lila higher. "You can't really think any of this is June's fault." Elena's been cold to June since she started her part-time evening hours here, which I felt bad about; it was probably obvious to Elena that we were replacing her overbearing presence with someone we were paying.

Elena opens her mouth to say something, but just then Gabe returns from walking out Sylvie. "Ready?" he asks his mom.

Elena gives me a peck on the cheek, and then they go. I glance around our apartment in their absence, and I hardly recognize it. We have too many versions of all the baby stuff. There's a swing for Lila in the kitchen so we can eat while she sleeps with a fist curled above her head, and another in the living room next to the bay window where I write my novels. There are two matching play mats beneath a half-moon of dangling cloth animals, two turquoise pacifiers, and two bassinets for different rooms in our apartment. When we ease Lila into one of those bassinets, we pray she stays sleeping. Then, when she doesn't, desperation descends on us, a cold breath pleading with her to rest, the visceral urge to get under the covers with her and not wake up so strong it could swallow me whole. Gabe tells me I shouldn't spoil her by bringing her into our bed, and that's when I realize he knows nothing about Lila and me. That scares me, but not as much as it should.

She's here. She's okay.

That's what I tell myself over and over when I hold Lila close—too close; I have to be careful, she's so delicate. I can't take my eyes off her; too afraid if I look away, she'll disappear like dust. When I fall asleep, I dream she's gone. I dream of unspeakable accidents, of doctors and nurses bringing me different babies one after the other and setting them too roughly into my arms, and then pulling back the blanket to reveal a newborn who isn't Lila. In my dreams the police come. They tell me the doctors are so terribly sorry but the knife went too deep, it got Lila where it shouldn't have. I wake screaming for her.

Steady, Rowan. I have to get better, I do.

I try to breathe, to focus on the baby-holding contraptions called saucers, but their neon yellows and greens blur. Lila's only three weeks old and not even close to ready for the saucers, so the plastic animals stare at us from the corners of her nursery with beady eyes and deranged grins. Yesterday Gabe caught his foot against one of the saucers. *Rowan, for God's sake, we don't need people's charity,* he said, swearing beneath his breath, annoyed that I'd accepted the saucers from my friend and that they were taking up so much space, and annoyed at me, in general, for falling apart.

I can see it in his deep brown eyes, the distaste for me. Gabe likes things to be beautiful and serene. Even back when we were young, he'd turn his face away from anything unsavory, and I used to think it was because he was a writer, too, and we're oversensitive, surely. But now I'm not as certain. Now I wonder if it isn't just a tiny bit cruel to be so unwilling to look into dark corners.

Of course we don't need charity, I repeated back to him, even though I've spent a lifetime gathering old things, saying *thank you* when my college friends went on to big jobs and passed along hand-me-down clothing and gently used handbags while I was trying to make it as a novelist.

At least Gabe and I only bought one stroller; at least we haven't been wasteful about everything. While I was still at the hospital, Gabe returned the bulky one we'd originally picked and found a trimmer version that would fit in our apartment's foyer. I think he realized our neighbors weren't going to be okay with a stroller lolling about in the hallway, blocking the fire exit and leaking Cheerios. Our neighbors are fancier than us. At least, fancier than me.

Elena's saying something to Gabe in the doorway, but I can't make it out.

I miss June. I miss what our apartment felt like when she was in it, and that's what I'm thinking about when the idea comes to me: I need to go to June, to find her, to apologize. Why didn't I think of this before?

I move to my bedroom, straight to my bed. I cradle Lila in one arm and push aside the blankets and I get in with her. Then I lay my girl down on the sheets, and she looks so tiny in her white onesie, her skinny limbs startling, fists unfurling. Gabe comes to the door of our bedroom and waits, his shape dark against the warm rectangle of light, his big hand resting lazily on the wooden frame. "Rowan," he says softly, the word heavy with something I can't make out. I wish I knew what he was thinking; I'm sure he can't believe we've gotten to this place: a psychologist making sure I'm okay enough to take care of our newborn. But you never really know with Gabe. Sometimes his gaze crackles with judgment. I didn't used to be so much on the end of that gaze, and maybe it's just that now the person he sees is so very changed: the circles beneath my eyes, hair matted, skin sagging. Red-and-white stretch marks etch me like a bear attack from my lower belly to my breasts. My stomach is still so swollen and I'm still bleeding. I think about my friends who haven't been able to get pregnant, and I'm so grateful to have Lila, I really am. But is this normal three weeks postbirth?

And maybe it's not about the way I look—maybe I should give Gabe more credit. Maybe marriage hardens things for every couple, makes the edges sharper and dulls the surface so it isn't a shiny, perfect thing anymore. Or maybe he's looking at me like this because he's scared. Either way, it's too hard to look at him dead-on, so I glance away, my eyes finding someone more forgiving. "Lila Gray," I say to my little girl, and I can feel Gabe stiffen in the doorway when he thinks I can't see him. *"Li-la-aah Gr-a-ay,"* I say again, adding syllables, letting the words lengthen like yarn unspooled, my voice verging on a coo I didn't think I'd ever get quite right. But I guess it must come with the territory.

"Rowan," Gabe says again, the smallest tremble there this time. I don't look up.

Gray is my maiden name. Gabe and I always said we'd use it for a baby, even back when we were in our early twenties and hunting through lower Manhattan in ripped jeans and T-shirts and Converse, dipping into coffee shops and bars when we felt like it, back when we were writing in the morning, sleeping in the afternoon, and bartending at night.

I fell into a dark spell when we got engaged. I've had them before, when I was little, and as a teenager and in college, too. They're imprinted onto my life like ink stains, and sometimes Gabe uses them against me when he needs to. Once he said he worried about having children with me, because what if I had our baby and then fell again into that deep pit of despair and couldn't climb back out? When I told my mom about his concern, she said, *You've always climbed back out, Rowan.* But now it's hard for my mom to always be cogent enough to remind me of the things I need her to. Her dementia came on quickly—she was mine and then she wasn't.

I used to think Gabe hurled my mental state back at me because deep down he was scared to have children, but maybe he was scared of *me*, and maybe he was partly right; look at the mess we're in now. But aren't we all vulnerable to a mental break? We're all walking around with these big brains that can misfire and split and repress and obsess or hurtle into insanity at any second.

"Do you like her?" Gabe asks. For some ridiculous reason I think about Lila first, instead of the psychologist.

"Sylvie?" I ask, and Gabe nods.

"I do," I say. My fingers touch the translucent skin on Lila's legs. I trace the lacy patterns the blood makes beneath the surface, imagining the vessels and all the perfect systems at play in her tiny body. "Though she's maybe a little too calm," I add about Sylvie.

"Probably part of her job," Gabe says with a shrug. "But yeah. She's preternaturally calm, especially for a New Yorker."

It makes me smile—him understanding me, agreeing. "Do you blame me for what happened with June?" I ask, the words out of my mouth before I realize what I'm saying.

"No," Gabe says right away, like he has to convince both of us of this one thing. "You haven't been right since the birth. It's not your fault. It's been too much—you lost so much blood," he says, "and it was so *bad.*" Tears fill his dark eyes, surprising me. Gabe has cried only once in front of me during our entire relationship, and that was just a few weeks ago in the hospital when I woke up and saw him holding Lila at my bedside. "You just have to get your mind back on track," he says, and then the tears stop and he's steel again, like always. *"Integrated,"* he

says. "Isn't that the word Sylvie used? It was a trauma, what happened to you, just like the doctors said. You went somewhere else," he says. "It's almost like you were someone else, like you forgot who we all were. It was . . ."

He breaks off. He's said too much and he knows it. Guilt floods me. "I'm so sorry," I say. "I'll get stronger. I will."

"It's not your fault," he says again. "You almost died giving birth to Lila." It sounds like a line he's written in a screenplay, or for the various TV shows he wrote for before writing the film that changed his career. It doesn't sound like something I ever thought would happen to us.

We're quiet for a moment. And then I say, softly, "It was a trauma for you, too," because it only seems fair. I pat the empty spot in the bed because I want him to come to us. I want to feel what it's like to let him into my and Lila's secret world, and I want him to belong inside it, because I know deep down he has to or else we won't make it out of this. "Come," I say. I try to sound warm and inviting, but it comes out a little desperate. I look down at Lila. Her toes are like Tic Tacs, and I marvel at how tiny her toenails are, and then I imagine how I'll start painting them when she's three. Maybe earlier.

"What are you smiling about?" Gabe asks, still standing in the doorway.

"*Her,*" I say when he doesn't get it. "I'm smiling about Lila." His face is so still. "Come lie down with us," I say, a shake in my voice that I don't like, the one I get sometimes in meetings with my publisher when we sit down with the marketing and sales teams and I try to be more animated, smarter, lovelier. "Gabe, please," I say, but it's hard to look at him for a meaningful amount of time, not with Lila pulling my gaze like a magnet.

"Rowan," Gabe says. His phone buzzes, and I think Lila and I have lost his attention, but then he shoves his phone deep into the pocket of his sweats and lowers himself into our bed. I see the lines in his olive skin, his dark hair rumpled and sticking up in places it shouldn't. If Lila weren't here, I would reach my hand out to touch his shoulder, his stomach, other places. But Lila's six pounds and may as well be a boulder for all she puts between us.

The heat turns on with a rumble, smelling smokier than it should. I look to Gabe to see if he notices, but he doesn't seem bothered by it. He's looking at me like he's not sure what to do, but then he slides toward us. He's big—six three—and when he comes close the mattress dips and I gasp, worried Lila will roll into the empty space and he'll crush her. None of this happens, but my pulse pounds just the same, and I flash back to the soaked hospital sheets, the gown that didn't cover enough. I shake my head to clear it, but it's still there: the way my body—all of me, toes to teeth—couldn't stop shaking.

Gabe props himself onto an elbow. His gray T-shirt rides up and I can see the curve of his bicep, his forearm flexing. I've always loved Gabe's hands, and I try to focus on them now, to push away the images of the hospital. I touch the swell of Lila's stomach. "I think I remember getting to the hospital," I say. "I keep thinking of the gown."

Gabe opens his mouth like he wants to say something.

"What?" I ask, nervous. The whir of the heater fills the air between us. Our bedroom gets so much hotter than the rest of the apartment.

"There wasn't really time for a gown," Gabe says. "Not until much later. They cut off your jeans and covered you with a blanket."

I swallow. It feels like when you lose a file on the computer and nothing you do will bring it back.

"Maybe you're just mixing it up with later," Gabe says carefully, "after it was all done."

"After what was all done?" I ask. "The birth?" What a weird way to say it.

"Yeah," Gabe says, his body leaning toward us, making the bed dip again. "After the birth."

I inch closer to Lila, wanting to put her onto my chest but knowing I'm supposed to share her with Gabe, too.

"We should sleep while she's sleeping," Gabe says, his eyes roving Lila's face. "She's so beautiful," he says, and I swear he's about to cry again. It throws me. "We could sleep a few hours before her night feeding," he says hoarsely, swallowing back whatever emotion was there.

"Okay," I say. I kick away the blankets, too hot.

Gabe flicks off the lamp and the room goes dark. I feel him settle next to Lila, but it makes me too anxious to have him sleeping next to her. What if he falls into a deep sleep and rolls over? I pick her up and settle her on my chest. I listen to the sound of Gabe's breathing, feeling the solid weight of Lila on me as my own chest rises and falls.

I think of June again, imagining her in her trademark high-necked white tank and boyfriend jeans, dressing nothing like so many other young people in New York City with their partially shaved heads and bleached hair, nose rings and minidresses. June was such a throwback, like an early-twenties version of Blake Lively with long highlighted blond hair and golden skin.

What if I go to her tonight?

I know where she lives, and the neighborhood bars and shops she likes, because I truly listened to her all those times we went out with her and Gabe's screenwriting agent, Harrison. Back on those double dates late into the starry New York nighttime I was someone entirely different: my bestselling novelist persona, I guess, someone smart and maybe even glamorous; someone June might have looked up to. Ever since Lila came it's so different; *I'm* so different. I'm just so scared all the time.

I should be the one to apologize to June. I do so much better face-to-face, when I can explain myself, and really, how much worse could it get if I saw June again? Anything I could ever say or do to her would pale in comparison to what I already did.

My thoughts soften as I lie there, eyes open, counting the cracks on the ceiling, tracing the spiderweb of lines with my gaze. Over and over.

Yes.

That's what I'll do—I'll go to June tonight. I'll wait until Gabe falls asleep, and then I'll slip out and find her. Because it makes sense to tell her I'm sorry in person, to see her again.

Just this once.

THREE

Rowan. Monday night. November 7th.

A half hour later the clock says six p.m., but it may as well be midnight. Gabe is fast asleep, muscles no longer twitching, his whole body gone still. I inch out of bed as quietly as I can, but the friction of my skin makes a *zip* across the sheets. I freeze, Lila against my chest. When Gabe doesn't move I keep going, a gentle slither against the sateen he likes, marveling, as always, at how quiet this apartment is. It must be the way our old building is constructed so solidly, a fortress that blocks out the traffic screeches and human screams below. I'm glad it's quiet for Lila, but a part of me still craves the chaos—I can admit that. You can't live in the city for this long and not be someone who needs the live-wire fray of New York.

I tiptoe across the floor and out of our bedroom toward a dim light in the kitchen. Lila's snowsuit is moon white against our leather couch, and I lay her down gently, making a shushing noise and praying she won't cry out. Her limbs feel too fragile as I guide them into the armholes. I keep having awful moments of envisioning something terrible happening to her—like her bones snapping as I try to fit her into the snowsuit—and my entire body shudders. When I imagine it, it feels so visceral, as if it really happened.

Lila wakes for a breath, but I pick her up and get her snug inside the baby carrier, and then she's back to sleep and we're okay; we're ready. I tiptoe through my apartment toward the kitchen. The fantasy of an apology that absolves me is like electricity in my veins. June will forgive me. I know she will. It's strange how much I want to see her again. I always felt that I understood her; I remember being twenty-two and all the longing that comes with it, the many lives that could be yours and how they're all there for the taking. *Choose wisely,* I always want to tell June, but she has her own mother for that.

In the kitchen I grab my cell. I don't turn it on. I leave a note for Gabe, a quick scratch of pencil against paper so he doesn't worry.

I needed a breath of air. Back soon. Xx R

Even with the note he'll worry when my phone goes straight to voice mail, and I try not to think about how scared he'll be that his unstable wife is out alone with his baby. I try not to think of myself like that, but if the shoe fits . . .

The pediatrician assured Gabe and me it was okay to go out in this weather if Lila was dressed properly, and I put on my own coat, a massive maternity number that may as well be a sleeping bag. I zip it over Lila so we're even warmer, but then I imagine her overheating right there against me and I'm suddenly flooded with panic. How am I supposed to know what temperature the baby's supposed to be? Why didn't I take an infant course?

I push open our apartment's front door and step into the bright light of the hallway, and I think back to the moments after what I did to June—hearing the voices of our neighbor Mrs. Davis and then Mart, the former Broadway star who lives next door to Mrs. Davis, both of them asking if we were all right. I can still hear Gabe reassuring them that everything was *totally fine* as June escaped into the elevator.

June only worked evenings for us for a short time, but everyone who met her liked her. Mrs. Davis hired June to feed and water her cat while she was hospitalized a few days for a procedure, and she returned home delighted to find wildflowers in a vase and a welcome home sign June had hung and signed from the cat. And whenever June and I ran into her in the hallway, Mrs. Davis seemed to relish giving June secret, weary glances if she caught me being paranoid and triple-checking that Lila was buckled into the stroller properly.

I kiss the top of Lila's wool hat. "Here we go, little girl," I say as I put my key in the lock. There's a soft *thud* as it latches, and I hope it's not enough to wake Gabe. I hurry down the hall. There are stairs and an elevator, but our building is so old there's no way the staircase is built to current safety codes; there are intricate iron railings with too much space between the swirls: beautiful, but treacherous for a child or a drunk. If you tipped over the side there's too large a gap between the railings on either side of the staircase—you could easily fall to your death six floors below. I can't believe I never noticed it before I became a mother. I used to strut by it tipsy, wearing three-inch heels, back from a night out with Gabe. But now I zoom past it toward the elevator with my hand beneath Lila's butt even though I know she's supposedly secure inside this carrier thing. For a moment I swear I hear footsteps behind me, and I freeze, imagining Gabe chasing me down, furious. But there's no one.

The elevator dings and Lila and I step inside, swallowed by the tiny box as the doors close. I peer over Lila's head onto the carpet, into the corners, feeling the insane urge to look for evidence that June was just here a couple days ago. One of her blond hairs? An indentation on the carpet fibers from the heeled boots she always wore? In my novels there's always bodily evidence—you can't just wipe someone off the face of the planet. We human beings are too substantial, aren't we? Our digital lives splay across the internet. And real life is messy with its skin, hair, and bodily fluids. You just have to look.

The elevator opens with a shudder. Lila and I pad across a marble floor, past a red velvet sofa with gold armrests. It's kitschy but perfect, dragged home by Mart the Broadway Star from a Midtown theater that was closing. That's what our building is like: a mix of old-school New Yorkers and young(ish) hipsters like Gabe and me. Decadent pink-and-gold wallpaper covers the lobby, and if you move right up close to it, you'll see the pink is actually a parade of tiny flamingos. Light from a chandelier glints across the scalloped ceiling, and a secret doorway opens to a stairway that leads down to the dark bowels of the building, where a billiards room gets dusty waiting for players.

Henri, the doorman, looks up from the *New York Times*. "Good evening, Mrs. O'Sullivan," he says with his smooth Swedish accent. He's in his fifties, handsome, and always telling me I remind him of his Nordic relatives back home. "I still can't believe this dark hair," he says about Lila for the fifth or sixth time since we brought her home from the hospital, staring at the inky wisps snaking out from beneath her hat. He's commenting on Lila's dark hair because I'm white-blond. I force a smile at Henri and try to look normal and under control, because Henri is the first person Gabe will talk to if he tries to reach me on my cell and can't.

"We're just going out for a stroll," I say, so he can relay that if Gabe comes stalking down to the lobby in his sweatpants and bedhead.

"Isn't it a little cold for the baby?" Henri asks.

I stare at him, smelling Windex, which is what I always smell down here because Henri is so meticulous about the glass doors. "I-I don't think so," I finally stammer, trying not to let insecurity spill across my face.

"Then let me get those doors," he says, back to a smile that's practiced and professional.

He pushes the doors open for us, and then grimaces dramatically at the cold air.

I keep going, holding Lila tighter, stepping onto the sidewalk. I start to walk along Washington Street and pass my favorite clothing boutique. I lock eyes with the willowy owner behind the glass. She smiles at me and I smile back. I like easy relationships like that, the kind that exist while shopping within a confined glass box of a boutique. Maybe I was lonely before Lila came? Maybe that's why it's such a gut punch to have her here now, filling me up. I linger for a moment, admiring the lipsticks like silver bullets lined in a row behind a window. The owner drops her gaze. Lila lets out a small whimper, and it snaps me out of my trance.

I start walking along the sidewalk again. I take out my phone and try my friend Artika, who hasn't been returning my calls. My writer friends can be like that: understandably wrapped up in their own stuff. At least my college friends respond to the photos I text with emojis and comments about how cute Lila is.

The phone rings and rings. I'm about to hang up when Artika answers. "Rowan," she says, breathless. "Hang on." Music hammers in the background, and she must put her phone on mute, because everything goes dead for a few beats. Then she unmutes it, and I can hear another flash of music until a door slams and the music fades. *"Rowan,"* Artika says again, the word coming out loose, like she's had a few drinks. "How are you?" she asks, her voice deathly serious. Gabe told her about how I hemorrhaged and nearly died at the birth. He's friends with her, too. They collaborated on a screenplay once.

"I'm okay," I say, trying to make my voice confident. "I mean, mostly. I'm getting much better." What a lie.

Artika goes quiet. She's a crime writer, and she loves a scene, and I imagine telling her the way my fingertips blazed against June's bony shoulders as I pushed her toward the open window, or how it felt like I was burning alive as we hurtled toward that freezing cold breeze together, the words like razors edging up my throat: *The baby's gone! What have you done?* Push, shove, and then my glance falling to Lila sleeping soundly in her bassinet. Realizing I'd done something very wrong . . .

I clear my throat. I can't tell Artika any of that, of course, because all my writer friends would know within the hour and I'd much rather they not. I need her to say something on the other end, to pull me from myself, but she doesn't. She's so quiet I'm sure I've lost her. The cell service is spotty around here. "Tika?" I ask, and I almost disconnect, but then she asks, "How's little Lila doing?"

I slow my pace a little, passing two women in fur coats and red lipstick.

"Lila's great," I say quickly. And then, "She's perfect, actually."

A long pause.

"That's nice," Artika says. I wonder if this is all boring to her. Usually by this point in any conversation, she's already told me a juicy piece of writer news, like one of the young writers we've mentored getting an agent or a mutual friend switching publishers. We're quiet again, and I get paranoid that Gabe told Artika what I did to June, and all at once I wish I'd never called her. I stop on the sidewalk, feeling alone, watching New Yorkers pass me with their own private crises.

"I'm so glad you're on the mend," Artika says in a careful voice, and I imagine her using what I did to June in a future scene, barely masking my identity and putting it all out there for the world to see. We exchange a few more surface pleasantries, and then I get off the phone quickly and try to shake it off. I pick up my pace again, heading down the street in the darkness toward June's.

FOUR

Rowan. Monday night. November 7th.

I'm about to cross Attorney Street when I see Gabe's agent, Harrison, in a knit hat standing outside June's gray-brick Lower East Side building. We've known Harrison for the better part of a decade; he signed Gabe to his agency, WTA, before Gabe had ever written anything really big, which is a rarity. Harrison always says he *saw the future in Gabe's pages*, and he was right. And Harrison is how we know June; they've been dating since the summer.

Harrison arcs his head back to look up toward the windows like he's searching for June among the glittering panes of glass, his body illuminated by the milky glow of a streetlight. I've been mumbling the whole walk here, not giving strangers on the street a second thought as I practiced my apology to June, but I shut my mouth as soon as I see Harrison, worried he's going to spot me and call Gabe. Something about the way the lamplight falls on his gray wool hat, chic trench, and brown leather gloves makes him look like something out of a film noir, as if the rain should start pouring down any minute. He rings the bell a few times, and then switches over to his cell, presumably to call June. He's unguarded in his anguish, his smooth skin drawn into a grim expression I rarely see; he must be very sure that he's unseen by anyone other than New York strangers who don't find anything out of the ordinary, because he would never let himself go like this if he knew I was watching. Harrison is nothing if not exquisitely controlled. When I've seen him talking on the phone with his writers, it's a careful performance filled with what sounds like empathy, and when I see him in a conversation with a producer or film exec I see a cold-blooded shark. But maybe he's truly both of those things; maybe that's just what it takes in this industry. Maybe it's too easy being a novelist, the one everybody speaks to in quiet, encouraging tones, coddling the creative process like a newborn.

"June," I hear him say into his phone, and the desperation in his voice sends heat across my face. He speaks in a steady stream that makes me think it's a voice mail. I catch only pieces of it.

"Are you there, June? I need to see you. I just want to talk to you . . ."

I bounce a little so Lila stays sleeping and warm. It actually feels good to be the one watching. I've been on the receiving end of so many scrutinizing glances lately. I know I should call out to Harrison, but I can't risk him calling Gabe. I think about leaving and trying to give him some privacy, but a breath later he shoves his phone into his pocket. And then he takes off.

I wait a beat, watching the streetlight turn from blazing red to green as Harrison disappears around a corner. I pat Lila's back as I cross the street toward June's, thinking about how if June's home, she's obviously not in the mood to buzz in visitors, at least not Harrison and most certainly not me. But if I could get in the building somehow and knock on her door, she might open it up if she saw me through the peephole. *The element of surprise is a powerful technique,* a writing teacher used to remind me, her gray coils springing.

I stop outside June's building and wait. Teenagers shoot hoops across the street in a lot that looks as if it belongs to a public school. A streetlamp lights them enough that I can make out the perspiration glistening on their faces. New Yorkers pass me—a woman lugging groceries, a boy cruising on a skateboard, another angling his phone to take photos of the graffiti marking June's building. I avoid their glances, hoisting Lila higher so I can press my lips against her cheek. I'm creeping along the edge of dread as I wait and watch, feeling like a stalker for doing something like this.

Finally out of June's building comes a man talking on his phone and nudging along a bucket filled with gray water. "Excuse me," I say pleasantly, trying to look like I belong here as I slip past him into the warmth of the hallway. I think I've made it, but then I hear his voice.

"Forget your key?" he asks, and I turn to see him holding open the front door like he decided not to leave. His eyes are all over my face. He mumbles goodbye into his phone and disconnects, looking even more suspicious of me the longer he stares. A tiny bit of water sloshes over the bucket onto the linoleum. "You new here?" he asks. Chilled air rushes inside as we stare at each other. Lila lets out a squawk that's enough to draw his attention to her. He shuts the door and his features soften. "I'm visiting June Waters in 4D," I say, a quiver on my lips. I've never been here before, but I know June's apartment number from the résumé she left with us as a formality. "June is our babysitter," I say, gesturing to Lila.

"I see," he says, nodding like it all adds up. "Go on up then, elevator down that hall."

I go before he can change his mind, feeling his eyes on my back as I tread over the dingy floor. Lila's stirring, definitely waking up now.

We ride the elevator and get off on the fourth floor. Outside June's apartment, 4D, is a lone pair of green rain boots and a yellow umbrella. A crumpled piece of paper lies on the welcome mat. "We're just gonna knock softly," I say to Lila. I lift my hand to knock and hear a dog barking. I had no idea June had a dog. I knock harder than I mean to, and the dog goes nuts. Lila starts crying a little, and I bounce her against me, promising her I'm gonna take her out of the carrier in just a second when we get inside. I try to force a half smile onto my face because I'm sure June will look through the peephole and I don't want to look as insane as I feel. But it's hard with Lila crying, which gets louder the longer we stand here.

"Help you?" someone asks from an apartment down the hall. I turn to see an elderly woman with snow-white hair poking her head out the door.

"I'm fine!" I say. "Just visiting."

"Hello?"

The dog is barking so loudly it takes me a second to realize this *hello* came from the doorway of June's apartment. I turn to see a guy somewhere in his early twenties. He's holding a tiny squirrel-like dog that won't stop barking.

Lila wails. Milk rushes into my breasts so fast they feel as if they've caught fire. An overhead bulb is dying, making the guy's features look shaky and scattered.

"Hi," I say. I need to get Lila out of this carrier. "Is June home? Can I come in? I'm Rowan, June babysits for me? This is Lila—"

Lila's sobbing with a breathless hitch to her cry I've never heard before, and then all of a sudden I'm crying, too.

"Are you okay?" the white-haired woman asks.

"I'm okay," I answer. And then to June's roommate, I say, "I'm so sorry," but it's hard to get the words out.

The boy's face pales. "Just come in, Mrs. O'Sullivan," he says, and that tiny detail—him knowing my last name—confirms to me that this is indeed June's apartment and that I'm not walking into a murderer's den with my newborn. The door shuts behind us, and everything inside June's apartment looks wavy through my tears. I unzip my puffy coat and get Lila out of the carrier as fast as I can. "Shh, it's okay, baby," I tell her. "I'm right here." Once I get her snowsuit off I pick her up and spin around to face the boy. June's told me his name before, but I can't remember it. Lila's still crying, only settled a little from before. "Seth, that's your name, isn't it?" I ask tentatively. I should have introduced myself. I'm nearly sure I have his name wrong the longer we stand there.

"Sean," he corrects.

"I'm so sorry," I say again. "Is June here?" I ask, but Lila's crying so loudly I'm not sure he hears me. She's obviously hungry, and a panicky feeling races through me. "I really need to nurse her," I say. Why didn't I plan for this?

He stares at me. People nurse in public in New York City, but most do it discreetly, and I doubt Sean's seen a thirty-four-year-old woman nurse her baby at close range. "I could nurse in a different room," I say, gesturing to a closed door. "Or if you have a blanket, I can cover up." I rip off my hat and hold it there, ashamed. The dog is still barking, Lila's still crying, and I have that all-over itch I get when the fire alarm goes off in our apartment because we cooked and forgot to open a window. "Please," I say, and then I apologize again, and then I think about how I shouldn't apologize for my newborn being hungry. Sean moves toward a closet and comes back with a fuzzy blue blanket, the kind of blanket you have when you're in your early twenties, when no one has ever made you get rid of things that look too shabby but are actually perfect.

"Thank you so much," I say, taking the blanket and sinking onto the sofa. I drape it over us.

"Boomer, shut up," Sean says to the dog. He keeps barking.

Mercifully Lila latches on the first try. I feel the pinch of pain followed by a release of something when the milk lets down (oxytocin?) that floods me with relief. Lila's on me and she's eating; we're okay. I glance around the apartment, feeling myself relax, my body still and warm, like this all makes sense now, like this is the perfect place to nurse my baby in front of a strange boy. Hormones are nuts.

Sean's still standing, trying not to look in my direction. His eyes are fixed on a fish tank in the corner. It's an odd choice for such a small apartment because it takes up so much space, but it's kind of cool. Half a dozen goldfish circle neon-colored castles in water that's a shade too murky. Sean bends to put down the dog. "It's the only way he'll be quiet," he mutters. The dog runs over to my feet, sniffing my boots. I feel bad I didn't take them off at the door, but Sean's wearing a beat-up pair of Adidas, so maybe he doesn't care.

The apartment is finally quiet. My hand goes to Lila's back, her tiny ribs palpable beneath her onesie. "Is June home?" I ask softly. There's a cracked door to a bathroom, and then two closed doors off the tiny living room, but I can't imagine any circumstance in which June would be here and not come out to see what the commotion was. Unless she's sick or something? My stomach knots when I think about her hiding behind one of the doors, inches away from us, not wanting to see me. Scared.

"June's out," Sean says matter-of-factly. His gaze goes from the dog to my face, and I see that his eyes are hazel with a golden glow. The black pupils are tiny, as though he was in the dark and then turned on all the lights when we showed up. He's cute, five nine or so, with broad shoulders and a big neck like a wrestler. His uneven white skin is flushed at the hairline like he's upset, which makes me think maybe June told him what I did to her and he's nervous to have me here.

"I'll give her a call," I say, fishing for my phone with my free hand.

"Don't bother," he snaps.

"Oh," I say, nodding like that makes sense. I'm not sure what to do. I need to feed this baby, and June not being here seems like less of a problem now that she's eating. And maybe June will show up if I hang around a little.

Sean's staring hard at my face. I look away, but then I feel bad, like maybe he doesn't know where else to put his eyes because of the nursing. I force my gaze back to him. "Would you mind if I stayed until the baby's done eating?" I ask. I need to give Lila twenty or so minutes before I stuff her into that carrier again. This need seems bigger than my imposition, and that makes me wonder if becoming a mother will finally be the thing that exorcises my politeness.

"Suit yourself," he says, sounding like a fifty-year-old man. He can't be more than twenty-five.

"So how do you and June know each other?" I ask, trying to act casual, as if all of this isn't bizarre. I shift my weight, my right leg already falling asleep. Sean's standing near a red plastic microwave. In the tiny kitchen, design magazines are stacked next to Hello Kitty salt and pepper dispensers.

"June and I met on Bumble," Sean says. He comes closer, taking a seat in an armchair across from me.

"Oh," I say. I really hope I didn't show up here to find June living with a boyfriend while she's dating Harrison.

Sean's features soften a little. "It's funny, really," he says. "June and I went on a few dates. So random. And it didn't work out *like that*. But I'd been looking for a roommate for this place." He sweeps an arm around as if he's Vanna White and this apartment is a new puzzle. "We'd only gone out like four times, once to a Midtown bar, once to Bowery Ballroom to see Phoebe Bridgers, Welcome to the Johnsons, the Bronx Zoo . . ." He's animated now like he really wants to tell me these things. "But I knew she'd be a great roommate. Though I kind of got the idea she thought the zoo was an odd place to go on a date," he says, looking genuinely perplexed, like he still hasn't figured out why.

"The Bronx Zoo is magical," I say.

Sean's light brown eyebrows go up. They're too thin for his face. "Right?"

I nod. "I can't wait to take Lila when she grows up."

"It can be romantic, too, though," he says, his face darkening. "It's not just for kids." It falls flat between us, too awkward for this already strange moment.

"Oh, definitely," I say, nervous.

Mercurial moods have always scared the crap out of me. My dad and a lot of his drinking buddies were moody, alternating between sweet kittens when they first got drunk and angry beasts somewhere after ten or twelve beers. And then weeping after sixteen. (I used to count.) And even when my dad wasn't drinking or only slightly buzzed, he could be set off for hours by someone saying something the wrong way, and there was no getting him back until something or someone else reset him. That someone was never me; sometimes it was my mom, with a compliment or a good meal. (Or maybe sex? I was too young to know how any of that worked, and he was killed and gone before my sixth birthday.) He never hurt me physically, but he was a monster to live with those years. His moods were poisonous, and the unpredictability of it all was enough to set my teeth on edge even when he was downstairs and I was hiding in my room. I could feel him pulsing through the hot pink walls of my bedroom like a presence. My mom never married again, never even had a boyfriend. Why would she?

Once, soon after I'd turned five, a police officer came to our house to find my dad because of a broken window and petty theft in town that night. I don't know whether my father had done anything—that wasn't the part that killed me. It was when my mom stood at the front door and lied to the police. There she was, her pale pink nightgown fluttering over the outline of her body, lying to the officer at our door, telling him my dad had been home the entire night with her. But he'd been out—he'd only just come home, drunk; I'd heard them slamming around the kitchen when he returned. The way she'd lied so easily for him—how could she do that after all she'd doggedly tried to teach me about the truth?

I kiss the top of Lila's head, lost in my thoughts.

"I took June to the Bengal tiger exhibit," Sean is saying, snapping me back.

He waits for me to say something. When I don't, he goes on: "They're stunning creatures," and I think *literature major*. Confidently using creative adjectives only comes with practice. "June loved them, actually," he says.

And you love her, I think. I need to call her—I need to at least try to accomplish the one thing I set out to do on this trip.

"So where did June go?" I ask.

I wait, but Sean doesn't answer. He shrugs, as if all of it is beside the point, which annoys me. I go for my phone again, wrenching it free from my pocket and holding it in my clammy hand. Sean just watches me. I'd forgotten I'd turned it off, and it's awkward trying to get the grip right and power it on while I'm clutching Lila against me. I finally do it, expecting a flood of messages from Gabe, but none come.

Sean crosses his legs. I really need a drink of water, but I worry I've asked for too much already, and I need him not to get sick of me and kick me out before Lila's done eating.

"How do you know June?" Sean asks flatly, less friendly now.

If Sean is secretly in love with June, or somehow being strung along by her, I don't want to tell him I know June through Harrison. Maybe he doesn't even know June's dating Harrison. My brain feels like it's not working right; I haven't had to juggle this many balls since Lila's been born. A few months ago I could've navigated this social situation easily, but ever since Lila came my mind doesn't feel as sharp, as capable.

"I met June through a friend of my husband, Gabe," I finally say.

"Harrison?" Sean asks. His face falls; he's like a stage actor with how quickly emotions twist his face. "That's the friend you met June through," he says, suddenly all knowing, like he just figured me out.

He stands up and goes to the fridge. I half think he's going to pull out a lock of June's hair, but that's just me and my imagination. *You get so carried away,* my mother used to tell me. *Use it for your writing: not for your life.*

"Yes," I say. "Through Harrison." June works for an agent named Louisa at WTA, which is where she met Harrison. But June must not tell Sean a lot about the details of her life, because wouldn't he already have heard about all the times June, Harrison, Gabe, and I have hung out as a foursome?

Sean retrieves a Lean Cuisine from the freezer. He unwraps it, and then it takes forever for him to break down the cardboard box and peel the plastic off the top. He pops the container into the microwave and beeps a few buttons. I use the moment his back is turned to fire off a text to June:

Was in the neighborhood and stopped by your apartment. Any chance we can talk if you're close by?

Sean punches a final button and the microwave whirs to life. Another beep sounds from somewhere inside the apartment, and Sean's head snaps up. I get Lila onto my shoulder to burp her, and then Sean comes back to sit, eyeing me suspiciously. I pat and rub Lila's back, alternating between the two like I saw someone do on YouTube, smiling at Sean and preparing my escape. "I promise I'll be out of your hair in a minute," I say.

Sean ignores that. "Harrison is a pretty major player," he says.

At first I think he means Harrison's a major player with women, which isn't really true. Harrison is an old-school romantic, actually, and falls way too hard.

"His client list is really impressive," says Sean, which makes me realize he means Harrison is a major player in the entertainment world, which *is* true. It makes me wonder what Sean thinks of all of us adults; maybe he mistakenly thinks we have it all figured out. "June tells me everything about work," Sean says. "Even stuff she probably shouldn't."

He smirks, and I wonder if he means June told him some intraoffice gossip about Gabe. He holds my gaze far too long, golden eyes hard, reminding me of how I write my killers.

Lila's already sleeping again as I pat her back, and I realize I can be home in thirty minutes if I power walk, and then I can nurse her on the other side.

I just need to get out of this apartment.

Sean watches me as my eyes search the apartment for a clock, and when I see an old black digital one with bright red numbers and a thin layer of dust on top, he says, "That clock's five minutes fast." He grimaces, like something hurts. "You know June, she's always late."

"Just by five minutes," I say about June, and then I try to smile because it came out like I was trying to defend her.

"And that's why I set the clock like that," Sean snaps. "To help her." It's weird, because obviously June has a phone and can see what time it really is.

"I'm always helping her," Sean adds, like an afterthought.

I've got Lila up on my shoulder, burping her. I can feel her diaper full through her pajamas, but I don't want to change her in front of Sean—I just want out. "I should go," I say. "It's getting late, you must have plans."

"You can stay," Sean says. His smirk is gone now, his face impassive.

"No, it's all right," I say, standing with Lila. I gather the baby carrier up around my shoulders and start to slip her inside.

"Let me help you," he says, coming toward us. I don't want him standing so close, but he's right there, touching the straps of the carrier. I know he's trying to help, but I'm so anxious my fingers start to tremble as I try to snap us in. I haven't had a man this close to me besides Gabe and my OB in a very long time. "A woman I used to work for had one of these carriers," he's saying, his hands right on the hip straps. "Trust me, you're wearing it too low. It'll give you back pain if you don't fix it." He adjusts the hip straps and then hoists the shoulder straps back and tightens them so Lila is riding higher. "It should be like this," he says. I'm so surprised by how much more comfortable it is that I stop feeling weird about what he's doing. "Safer for the baby, too," he says. "You really need to watch the instructional videos on these things," he says, like he's the smartest and I'm not. And I suddenly don't care. It feels so much better not to have the strap pressing into my hip.

"Thanks, Sean," I say.

He adjusts one final strap. "Just trying to be helpful," he says.

"You're definitely that," I say as he steps back and admires his work on the carrier. I wonder if he's really in love with June, and what it must feel like to live with someone who doesn't love you back. I wonder how mad it makes him.

Ding.

I hear the same sound again, the one I heard when the microwave was going. An icy feeling passes over my skin when I realize it was more of a chime sound, like a text coming through. My eyes sweep the apartment. Sean's phone is still on the coffee table, but this sound came from one of the bedrooms.

I pretend not to notice the sound, and Sean does the same; he just smiles at me. And I know I shouldn't do what I'm about to—

"Can I use your bathroom?" I ask, my eyes holding his.

"Yeah," he says. He clears his throat. "Of course."

I edge a little closer toward one of the bedroom doors, clearly moving in the wrong direction. Sean doesn't stop me—he just eyes me like I'm a criminal, like I might steal something. I take a couple steps until I'm at the makeshift wall, guessing that this room would be June's. Sean still doesn't say anything. I break his stare, and then I carefully open the bedroom door.

"That's June's room," Sean says behind me. There's satisfaction in his voice, almost as if he wanted me to open the door. I can feel him inches behind me now, but I don't turn. My heart pounds as my eyes adjust to the dark of June's room. It's bare bones and immaculate. There's a small dresser in the corner with a jewelry box and framed photos on top, and a mattress on the floor that makes me feel inexplicably embarrassed. A phone sits on the mattress, glowing with my texts and a few others.

"That's not the bathroom, *obviously*," Sean says.

"I'm sorry," I say, and I mean it. I turn around to face him, deciding to not even pretend. I need to get my baby out of here—I've pushed this far enough. "I-I'm really sorry," I stammer, making like I want to leave.

He blocks me with a box step, his eyes narrowing. How foolish could I have been to do something like that with Lila here? "I shouldn't have done that," I try to say calmly, meaning it for more than one reason. "I heard the phone, and I'm just really eager to see June. To apologize."

"To apologize?" Sean asks, thin eyebrows up again. "For what?"

I bounce Lila, wanting out of here so very badly. "There was this one day when I was overtired and I snapped on her," I say. An understatement. "Again, I'm *really* sorry, Sean," I say. I try to make my voice brighter when I add, "I'm sure I'll see you around," and then I inch toward the door.

Sean laughs, taking me by surprise. "Probably not," he says.

I force a smile. I turn and walk across the tiny apartment with Sean on my heels, the tiny hairs on the back of my neck standing at attention.

Sean slams the door behind me. Relief washes over me as I disappear into the stairwell.

FIVE

Rowan. Monday night. November 7th.

Back home, I open the door to my apartment as softly as I can, but all the lights are on and right away I know I'm caught. "Rowan?" Gabe's voice. *"Rowan?"* He's coming closer.

"Hi, sweetie," I say before I can see him.

"Where were you?" he snarls, barreling into the foyer. His gaze goes to Lila. "Are you okay?"

I yank off my puffy coat, barely able to get out of it but not wanting to ask him for help. He steps toward me like he needs a closer look at Lila, like he wants to make sure she's all right. Is that really what he's doing? "Do you seriously think I can't take care of our daughter?" I ask.

His eyes dart back to mine. "I asked if *you* were okay."

"But you're staring at Lila like you're trying to figure out if she's still breathing," I say. Anger prickles my limbs, burns through my abdomen.

"You aren't supposed to be alone right now," he says. He's scared of me, of what I could do. I can see it all over his face.

"Really?" I ask. Sirens blare outside, one of the few sounds that make it through our windows. For a fleeting moment I worry I've done it—that I've lit us all up with whatever this feeling is inside me. "Says who?" I ask.

"Says every doctor who's treated you in the past three weeks," Gabe says.

I do everything I can to hold my tears back. "Lila and I needed fresh air," I say.

The sirens come louder now, gathering fury, vibrating through my bones. And then I get my first swell of confidence that I *do* know what I'm doing with Lila. But it flickers away as soon as it comes, and I'm stuck again in purgatory with Gabe's accusing stare. I haven't seen him look at me like this since that first hairline fracture in our marriage when I had my dark spell. We'd been married only a few months then, and there were all those therapy appointments I could barely get myself to because I was so depressed and panicky, so Gabe had to come. At the first few appointments, we used to hold hands in the waiting room, hip bones glued together. And then months later I held brainless magazines instead, and the inches of puffy blue waiting-room cushions became increasingly visible between our bodies. When I started going by myself, I could tell how relieved Gabe was, not just because I was getting better but also because he didn't have to take off time from writing to bring me there.

Even when I got better, it wasn't the same between us. Everything frayed in a morbid, drawn-out unraveling: the quiet bed, the lack of letters, the cocktail party at a friend's loft when Gabe got too drunk and cut into me too nastily, shouting something about how I should go home, something about how I wasn't *needed* there, which made no sense in the context of a cocktail party (who's truly *needed* besides a bartender) and that's how I knew he was wasted; because he was never imprecise with words. Neither am I. Words are our currency; our trade. Words are our whole world, or at least the keys to it; the entire way we make sense of things.

Gabe runs his fingers through his inky hair. I can see things happening on his face: how fear is morphing into relief that we're okay.

"I left you a note," I say to smooth it over, to nudge everything in the direction it's already going.

He nods, taking this in. "Your phone's going straight to voice mail," he says, but his words have gone soft.

"It was low on battery, so I turned it off in case I needed it. But I left you a note," I say again, smiling like it's all okay, like it's maybe even his fault for not checking the note. "Lila loved the cold air," I go on, as if we're a normal married couple having a normal conversation about our newborn. "She slept so soundly in it, like they always say winter babies do." Who says this?

Gabe's hands are in his hair again, a gentle pat to his scalp like he always does when he needs to think. "Come sit?" he finally asks me.

"Let me wash my hands first," I say. I go to the sink and pump the soap, the scent of cucumber too strong as I scrub. When I was pregnant with Lila, I threw up the first eighteen weeks each time I smelled anything pungent. I kept waiting for it to stop when I hit the first trimester mark, but it just kept going, until finally the nurses stopped trying to convince me I probably only had a few more days of it. Other friends with kids would tell me, *Eat crackers when you first wake up. Leave them on your bedside table, so you won't even have to lift your head.*

All that wisdom other women have for you when you're pregnant— they're bursting to share it. Will I be like that, too, when this post-partum part is over? Will I be practically glowing as I bend my head toward a pregnant woman in the park and tell a story about Lila and me? That picture looks so idyllic, but I feel so far away from anything like it, because here I am in my kitchen with a suspicious husband, my left boob killing me because I need to nurse from it, and blood probably spotting my underwear like it did the last time I tried to take a long walk.

"Should I take her?" Gabe asks me. I'm trying to bend toward the faucet with Lila still in the carrier. I want to say, *She'll just start screaming,* but instead I say, "I need to nurse her on the other side."

"Rowan," Gabe says, gesturing toward my midsection. I look down. I must have pressed my belly against the sink and not realized how wet my clothes had gotten. The skin around my cesarean scar is still so numb I can't even feel it.

"I'll change later," I murmur.

Gabe's sweats hang low enough that I can see a thin strip of his boxer briefs. We stare at each other, and then the doorbell buzzes and I flinch. "Who's that?"

"I called Harrison," Gabe says.

"What? Why?" I ask.

"Because I was *worried*, Rowan," Gabe snaps, and for the first time I feel bad. And not for the first time I worry that Gabe doesn't have enough close male friends. Why does he run to his agent at the first sign of trouble? There are a few guys Gabe goes out for drinks with, but they're industry people to whom he'd never air his dirty laundry. Harrison knows all kinds of things about us, from me losing my mind on June to the time Gabe and I had a rough patch financially when a film Gabe produced tanked and he couldn't recoup the money. Gabe never breathed a word of that to any of our couple friends, and he swore me to secrecy. And then he decided he'd only ever write and direct, so that our money was never on the line again. Which was fine by me; I just never understood the deep shame he felt about it, like he'd committed a crime.

I follow Gabe to the door and he opens it, and I see Harrison in the same sharp brown coat and gloves I just spied him in outside June's apartment. I imagine Sean up in that apartment, seeing Harrison's face on the intercom, maybe getting some kind of smug satisfaction when he didn't let Harrison inside. Sean, keeper of the gate, June's dissatisfied best friend.

"Harrison," I say. His wavy blond hair is mussed from his wool cap. I smile, because deep down I like Harrison. There was an inconsequential flicker of time when I was drawn to him, the first night Gabe,

Harrison, and I met, when I stood beside Harrison and stared into his dark blue eyes and imagined putting a hand against his blond stubble. But then Gabe came to stand beside us, and when I met Gabe, that was that; I was done. *Gabe*, the man around whom gravity doesn't pull in the same way. It folds in on itself, intensifying until you're in his orbit and it's the only place you've ever wanted to be.

"You're home," Harrison says kindly. He looks at Gabe and says, "Your lost love is found." Then he turns back to me. "And how beautiful is this baby? Even more beautiful than when I saw her in the hospital. Though I guess in the hospital she was covered with all that slime."

I appreciate him trying to make a joke instead of looking at me like I've done something wrong. "That *slime*," I say, smirking, "is filled with healthy bacteria." We grin at each other while Gabe stands there looking annoyed.

"I have to feed her on the other side," I say, needing to get out of the foyer, to disentangle myself from our threesome. But then Harrison's face changes, and he raises his eyebrows like he always does when he's about to ask me or Gabe something verging on serious.

"Have you seen June?"

The question hangs in the air like something sour. "Or talked to her?" Harrison adds, and then runs a hand over his boyish blond curls. Beads of sweat glimmer near his hairline.

"I haven't," I say. I meet Gabe's dark eyes and see them staring back at me. And then I decide to just say it. "I haven't seen or talked to her since that night I had my break."

Gabe's eyes widen. Maybe because I haven't called it that before. Was that what it was? A mental break? Why hasn't anyone been able to put a name on it? My OB ran through a checklist with me for postpartum depression, and it didn't sound like I had that, and Sylvie said she was sure that I had postpartum anxiety and PTSD from the birth, and that we didn't need to get caught up on labeling it, we just had to treat it.

"And I would love to talk to June," I say, "but Gabe's not really letting me out of the house."

Harrison can take complicated stuff; it's how he's built. "I see," he says calmly, like a husband holding his wife and baby hostage is normal. And then he shrugs a little. "I can't seem to get ahold of her," he says. "I saw her that night, after everything happened here. She was obviously upset, and she stayed the night." He says this without judgment, like he's somehow able to be on both my and June's sides, and I believe him. It's what makes him so good at his job. "But this morning she ran out of work distraught, and she's been out of touch since then, which is really unlike her because she's Gen Z."

He tries to smile like it's all funny. But it's obviously not. His voice drops a notch when he says, "I'm a little worried."

I open my mouth to say something, but all at once I have this crushing image of June lying on her back in the street outside her apartment. I see it like a mirage: those same teenagers I saw shooting hoops, but this time passing the ball over June's body, the traffic light changing. June lying there like a corpse, almost like she's too drunk to move. In my mind I look closer—*Maybe she is a corpse? Maybe she's dead?* I shudder but Gabe and Harrison don't seem to notice anything. "I-I'm sorry," I finally stammer, trying to squeeze the image from my mind. What is wrong with me? "I really need to go feed Lila."

I leave them alone in the foyer, hurrying with Lila toward my bedroom. In the dark I turn on my phone to see a text from June.

Saw your text and Sean told me you stopped by. Can we meet? Tomorrow? I'd like to talk to you. Can it be just us?

SIX

Rowan. Tuesday morning. November 8th.

The next morning I'm standing in line buzzing with nerves in a chic coffee shop called Switch. Last night while Gabe was busy entertaining Harrison, I snooped in his phone and saw his meeting scheduled at Paramount, and then quickly texted June back to tell her I could meet at 10:15. It was almost too easy, like I'd dreamt it, and now I'm exhilarated standing here: a free woman in a coffee shop holding a beautiful baby, surrounded by purposely distressed brick walls and gorgeous baristas who look like aspiring actors and probably are. I feel full of energy and powerful, too, like the person I was before I got pregnant, the one who wrote up storms in these kinds of places.

"Can I help you?" asks a twenty-something with a purple streak in his red hair.

"Yes, thank you," I say, scanning a menu on the wall lettered in neat handwriting with chalk. "I'd like a decaf almond milk latte, please."

Because my daughter is sensitive to dairy.

I look down at Lila and a strange feeling comes over me. I want to ask the boy: *You see her, don't you? I didn't make her up?* It's the most unsettling sensation, as though Lila is too good to be true, like she's only a figment of my imagination. I take a deep breath and touch the tip of her nose, grounding myself with the feel of her skin. I look around for June, but she isn't here yet. I want to buy her a coffee but I have no idea what she drinks, so I settle on a blueberry muffin and hope she likes it. I've only ever seen her with the water bottle she always carries, a stainless steel one with a fancy design that closely matches her phone's case. June is the kind of person who always looks stylish, down to little things like her fingernails and toenails being painted, or the stacked rings that looked effortless but never are. Those things take thought, and June gives them that. And not to be weird, but her legs are also always tanned and shaved, even in late fall, and they never look streaky like mine did when I tried self-tanner in college. It's sort of remarkable.

Maybe I'm just getting old.

I switch my weight from one leg to the other, hardly believing how much better the baby carrier feels now that Sean fixed it and it's not cutting into my hip anymore. I scan again for June while the barista makes my coffee, listening to snatches of conversation and the grinding of beans. Hipsters dot the tables. I like this neighborhood; Gabe and I rented here once for a year in our midtwenties. It's filled with artists.

I take my coffee with a smile and a thank-you. I head toward an empty table by the window, carefully lowering myself onto a creaky wooden chair. I get lost sitting there, watching New Yorkers pass in a blur and seeing the city I love, snuggling Lila. She was up for an hour before we started our walk here, so I'm pretty sure she's going to sleep deeply. I rub her back, feeling the curve of her spine beneath my hand, the points of her shoulder blades. It's hard to believe someone so perfect is mine.

I scan the scene beyond the coffee shop's glass windows. I once read that green is the easiest color on the eyes, but along these city streets there aren't evergreens dotting the landscape with color. Here, when autumn plummets toward winter, it's all white and black and gray, concrete and puffer jackets and black pants. I let my eyes relax, zoning out until a familiar face jolts me into focus.

Sean.

We're only a block from his and June's apartment. I look away from the window so we don't catch each other's eyes through the glass, but then I see him slowing down.

No, no. Please don't come inside.

But there he is, pushing open the coffee shop's door and sounding the old-fashioned *ding*. I have no idea if he's here because he saw me in the window, or if he was already planning to stop here because this is where he gets his coffee before he goes off to do whatever it is he does. For a brief second I imagine what his day job might be (ticket counter in the theater district? PR assistant? Receptionist at a veterinary clinic? Chimney sweep?).

I stare down at the knots in the wooden coffee table, not wanting him to see me because I don't want him to be here when June arrives. What if he tries to join us? I can sense his lumbering body weaving slowly between the tables, and I know I've been spotted. I lift my chin and meet his gaze. "Hey, Sean," I say, smiling.

He doesn't smile back. He stops in front of my table, looking smug, like he knew I'd be there. What if Harrison's right to be worried, and something bad happened to June, and Sean was the one who texted me from June's phone, tricking me into meeting here? That's how I would write this scene. "How are you?" I ask, trying to sound pleasant even though my heart is pounding.

He only stares. I will myself not to break the silence.

"What are you doing here?" he finally asks, sounding vaguely suspicious.

Where is June? I look around once more to make sure I haven't missed her, but the coffee shop isn't really that big. I can't lie to Sean, because June could be here any minute, and then I'm caught anyway. "I'm meeting June," I say matter-of-factly.

Katie Sise

"Really?" Sean asks, dubious. "She decided she wants to see you?"

Heat comes to my cheeks. So he *does* know exactly what I did to her. And why shouldn't he? Maybe he's June's confidant after all, just like he told me last night.

"Yes. Apparently she did," I say. I remind myself that I'm a grown woman with a baby and a husband and write-ups in the *New York Times Book Review*: things I can hold on to. I don't need to melt beneath his stare. I meet his eyes and hold his gaze, accusing as it is.

"She told me things about you last night," Sean says in a hushed voice, staring at me like I'm a wild animal under his observation.

"That's nice, Sean," I say. "I'm so glad you had a chat about me."

He ruffles. "You and your baby are lucky to have June," he says. *You and your baby.* It comes out like an insult to both of us.

"Her name is Lila. And it's been nice seeing you," I say, making my voice sound like I have a backbone, like I'm done with the conversation and he should leave.

"Are you even allowed to be out by yourself?" he asks.

It lands like a slap. My stomach goes queasy; my face stings. Lila, as if sensing me, stirs and whimpers. Tears burn my eyes until my vision blurs.

"What did you just say?"

I blink away my tears. For a moment I wonder if I said those words myself, crazy as that sounds. But I'm sure it wasn't me—it was someone else. It was—

June.

I turn to see my gorgeous babysitter standing next to our table with a hand on her hip, her cheeks pink from the cold. Her dirty-blond hair is piled into a messy bun, and she's wearing earmuffs and somehow making them look cool. She tugs them off, looping the plastic around her wrist, never breaking her glare. "What are you doing here?" she asks Sean, a harsh snap in her voice. I can't believe she's on my side—it's in the air between us like a bolt of lightning. Sean goes quiet. When he finally mutters "I'm getting coffee, June," his voice is so meek it's almost sad. June stares hard at him, and inside that glare is exactly what she thinks of him: I can see why she kept telling me she wanted to find her own place; I can see that she knows he loves her, and that it probably once felt innocuous but now turns her stomach. Worst of all: I can see she pities him.

Sean withers beneath her stare. He knows, too.

"I'll see you later, Sean," June says, a small note of manufactured cheer in her words. He doesn't head to the register for coffee. He just leaves the café, empty-handed. *Ding* goes the bell again, and then he's gone.

June sits. "I'm sorry about him," she says, unwinding a fake cashmere scarf. "I used to think he meant well and was just overbearing. But now I'm not so sure. Sometimes he worries me."

"You should be careful, then," I say, but June only waves her hand at me like I'm overreacting. Lila being born has shifted the dynamic between June and me. We used to be the wife and girlfriend of two close friends who like to go out together at night, and that was all; it was never an even playing field because of our age differences, but it was closer than this. Now me caring about her comes out in more awkward, maternal ways, and I don't think June likes it. I watch her eyes flicker away from me to the menu on the wall. "I got you a muffin," I say. "I wasn't sure if you drank coffee."

"Thanks," June says. She takes the muffin and unwraps it hastily like she's hungry, but then she doesn't take a bite. Instead, she looks down at Lila and asks, "How's she doing? I love her little dress."

I grin—a real one—I can't help it. This morning I put Lila in a corduroy jumper with a lace collar, and she looks more beautiful than anything I've ever seen with my own eyes. I'm about to say some version of this, but then June starts crying.

"June," I say, my throat tight. "I'm so sorry. I'm so very sorry for what I did to you." I give her hand a squeeze and let go. "What I did was so terrible, and there's no excuse," I say, my words coming quickly. "I think something's wrong in my brain. Or at least, there definitely was in that moment. I just, I can't even explain it." June's eyes have a shadow of dark circles, the first I've ever seen on her face. She blinks, takes me in. I have no idea what she's thinking. The coffee shop is so loud I'm not worried about anyone overhearing us, but I still lower my voice to say, "I was sure that you had hurt the baby, and I was so terrified I couldn't even think straight. I don't know if I had some kind of mental break or something, or what it was."

June stops crying. She nods, seeming suddenly curious. And why wouldn't she be? Most people her age aren't privy to maternal mental health gone awry. "I'm very, very sorry, June," I say. "It's all I can say, even though I know it's not enough."

June sniffs. "I'm sorry, too," she says, her gaze going into her lap.

"You didn't do anything wrong," I say. A woman with a broom bumps into our table and mumbles an apology. I pass June a napkin and she wipes beneath her eyes. She misses some of her mascara, but it looks pretty smudged there beneath her lids; I've seen her wear it like that sometimes when she had plans at night after working for us: a sweaty dive bar or a dark club, a drink on the High Line overlooking the river. I imagine June sweeping through New York and taking things that aren't hers without even realizing it. I imagine the way other people's boyfriends and husbands must look at her.

"Are you . . . ," June starts, but then she trails off and I wait. "Are you getting some good help?" she finally asks. "Like a therapist, I mean? Or some medicine at least?"

It surprises me. It's a mature thing to ask; I don't think it's what I'd be focused on when I was her age. "I am," I say. "A trauma therapist named Sylvie whom Louisa recommended, actually. Though I don't know what good it's doing." I shake my head. "I still can't really remember the birth. Last night I dreamt of that day I collapsed and someone called an ambulance." I still remember that, at least—looking up into the sky and seeing the clouds like bloated white sheep, and then open-ing my mouth to call out for help and feeling cold air rush inside it.

June looks down at Lila. "Thank God she was all right," she says, but then she shakes her head too quickly, as if she's said something wrong.

I don't tell June about the rest of the dream: how I saw my dad step out of the ambulance and look down at me, bloody on the ground, just like I looked down at him so many years ago. *Doughy, small blue eyes. Angry.* I blink him away and focus on June. She almost looks scared, like she's waiting for the story to get worse.

"June, listen," I say, trying to wave my hand like it's less of a big deal than it is. I'm probably putting her off becoming a mother with all of this. "I'm okay now," I say. "Well, I mean, I think I am. Nothing like that has happened again, what happened with you that night." I brush off the returning image of June dead in the street—that wasn't quite right, either, how real it felt when it certainly wasn't. "I've felt more like myself," I say. I take a sip of my latte, wanting so much for what I've said to be true.

June nods. I can tell she doesn't believe me. Smart girl.

"Rowan," June starts. And then she says, "I need some time off from working for you."

"Oh, of course," I say.

She nods and her gold earrings catch the light, a little glitter near her jaw. "I want you to know it's not because of what hap-pened," she says.

I'm not sure how that can be true, but still I say, "Okay, sure."

She holds my gaze. "I care about you and Lila so much," she says. "It's more that I need to get away for a little while, and I'd been feeling like that even before everything happened. I'm going upstate to my parents' house."

"Oh," I say. I didn't realize her parents lived in New York. Which is because I've never asked. "Where did you grow up?"

"Harbor Falls," she says, taking a piece of muffin.

I nod like I know the place. How did I never ask her this on one of our nights out with Gabe and Harrison?

"It's near Saratoga," June says.

I smile stupidly because I've been there once, and sometimes the ring of familiarity is enough to cheer you. "Gabe and I went to the racetrack a few summers ago," I say. "It's gorgeous up there."

"It is," she says, but something's changed on her face. I decide not to press her about her family, her upbringing, no matter how guilty I feel for not already knowing.

"I'm sorry, June," I say.

"I know you are," she says, "and I am, too, that everything happened. I really am."

"You didn't do anything," I start to say again, but she's rising from the table.

"I should go," she says, unwinding the earmuffs and slipping them onto her head. A gold watch I haven't seen her wear before catches the light, and then she puts her puffy jacket back on and it's gone. I think of the watch my dad was killed over, a gorgeous antique number he inherited from his grandmother, and the way diamonds glistened along the wristband in a delicate cascade over my mom's wrist. It was maybe worth twenty thousand, and I think of him bragging about it to his bar buddies, and then I remember each of their scraggly faces: seven of them. All rebels, all drunks. Each with his own secret desperation and reason to want the watch. We never found out which one of them did it; they splintered after my dad was killed and scattered like dominos. Only one was arrested, but he was let go because the timeline didn't make sense. There had been robberies in our neighborhood before, so it could have been someone random, but we always assumed it was one of my dad's friends because they were the only ones who knew about the watch.

I watch June gather her things and put her muffin back into its petite brown bag. I rapid-pat Lila's butt because I don't know what else to do. I don't want to stand up and try to hug June, because I don't know if she would even want that.

"Will you be okay getting home with Lila?" June asks, staring at Lila's beautiful face.

"Yes, of course," I say, thinking how glad I am that when June leaves I won't be sitting here alone. I'll be with my daughter. "We'll be fine. Thank you for meeting me," I say, but she's already edging away from us.

"Goodbye, Rowan," she says.

I watch her weave through the customers and open the door. She heads west along the sidewalk, and then abruptly heads north, crossing the middle of the street and barely missing the edge of a taxi. The driver blasts the horn. My eyes go a few feet ahead of her trajectory to the other side of the street and I see Sean standing on the sidewalk. I squint to be sure it's him. Was he really standing out there the whole time in the cold, waiting for June? Watching us?

I can't see June's face, only the back of her dark blond head, but she's hurrying toward him. I can't exactly tell, but Sean looks full of fear for her, or is it anger? We're too far away for me to be sure what it is I really see on his face. And then the strangest thing happens: June sinks into his embrace.

My stomach goes cold. Sean puts his lips into her hair, against her neck like a lover would. And then they walk away into the swell of the city, out of my sight.

I have no idea what to make of it.

PART II

SEVEN

June. Five months ago. June 3rd.

I'm standing outside a bar called Welcome to the Johnsons waiting for Sean Cassidy, hopefully my soon-to-be roommate, and soaking up the feeling of people watching me. I don't know what went wrong to make me like this. I guess I'm hoping if everyone is busy noticing how beautiful and full of light I am, then maybe they won't see my gaping dark holes.

Sean stumbles down the front steps, and I smile just enough to let him know he's the only one I have my eye on. He meets my gaze and I feel a zing straight through me, a shot of something cool and crisp that wakes me up: the sense that something exciting and good might happen at any moment. There's this memory I have of my dad holding my freckled hand as I stepped into a plastic baby pool. A gasp came from deep inside me when my leg slipped into the freezing hose water, and my God, I loved that feeling: the shock that gripped my shoulders and shook me back to life. I still need it: the zip over my skin, the thing that reminds me I'm alive. But I'm twenty-two now and I need more than cold water.

Sean hurries across the hot pavement to where I've been waiting for him next to a parking sign and a rusted bicycle with a basket holding bread. I wonder where this is going to go, and the wondering is such a lovely feeling.

"That guy was such a dick," Sean says to me. He's talking about the bartender.

"Yeah," I say, though he wasn't, not really. He was just thirty-something and aloof, probably because we're barely old enough to be in a bar and still look like kids to him. "Let's go," I say, because Sean is just standing there on the sidewalk perusing the city like it's a film set and he's the director.

"Yeah," he says, still standing there, "we should go." We're buzzed, but not drunk enough to make an easy decision that we won't think twice about until tomorrow. Neither of us wants to suggest another drink, but going to Sean's apartment means something else entirely, so we kind of just stand there and let New York swirl around us like a cloud of perfume.

A woman perched on top of a milk crate waves a sign with a politician's face on it and yells at us to vote. Her purple acrylic nails are like wine stains against the white paperboard. Her tiny terrier looks miserable lying there next to a water bowl.

"Do you think she's all right?" I whisper to Sean. I've only been in New York for a few weeks. My barometer for other people's mental health isn't fine-tuned yet, but I have the creeping suspicion that the longer I'm here, the better it'll get.

Sean ignores my question. "It's too muggy for eight o'clock," he says with a scowl on his face. I don't think he has any idea where this is going.

"We're too drunk for eight o'clock," I say with a laugh, and then I link my arm through his so he gets the right idea. But his scowl doesn't budge. I've never really met anyone who gets so bothered by such small things. It makes me wonder what he'd do in a real crisis.

"*Sean,*" I say, the word drawn out like I'm trying to flirt, though that's not quite it. It's more like I'm trying to win him over, like there's a prize to be had. I remember in high school feeling like I had to win the whole thing, like I had to make the boys want me and the girls want to be me. It always surprises me when people call that kind of behavior shallow. To me it feels deeper than a pit of snakes.

"It's only *June*," Sean says, like this heat is a harbinger of worse things.

"My month," I say with a smile as we start walking. I still love all thirty days of June just like I did when I was little. It's always been my lucky month: the month good things happen to me. Even my mom was more affectionate than usual on the first few days of June, opening my bedroom door and letting in streams of golden light from the hallway. She'd say, *Happy June, my sweet Junebug,* and on the good mornings, she'd bend to kiss my cheek. On the mediocre ones she'd leave a glass of tea for me on my bedside table, always something decaf like chamomile or peppermint, and even now the scent makes me think of mornings on the cusp of dreams and tangled sheets. On bad mornings, when her demons were circling and she wanted to be anywhere else but in the house with Jed and me, she'd come in without even a whisper, opening my shades with the *screech* of metal rings against the curtain rod. Or she'd stay in bed, and my father would get us ready for school.

"Should we go somewhere else?" Sean asks me.

We stop at a traffic light. Swarms of New Yorkers cross the street from the other direction and traipse along the sidewalk, close enough that we can catch snippets of their conversations. Everyone is too close here, and I love it. No one can ignore you, because they're right there in your space, sharing your sidewalk square, making eye contact to decide which person is going to slow down and crush themselves against a metal pole so the other person can pass first through a makeshift construction tunnel.

"Are you really up for another bar?" I ask, the way a parent would: like it's not the best idea. I'm stalling, wanting to go back to Sean's place but not wanting to be the one to say it.

We linger in the warm air. A dogwood tree arcs, catching fading orange sunlight between its white flowers. Different languages prick my ears and a woman laughs. Spring in New York is as magical as everyone says it is. It doesn't really matter that I'm sleeping on a pullout couch, or that my roommate is so concerned I'm bringing germs inside that she makes me leave my shoes outside the door and wash my hands with hospital-grade antibacterial soap before I even say hello. *Rules of the house!* she always says, but not in that appealing, self-deprecating way some people have about their flaws. She's my brother Jed's friend from college, and she rents the couch to me for two hundred bucks per week on the unspoken promise that I'll be out of there as soon as possible. I think she was once in love with Jed, so I guess now I'm the beneficiary of that love, even if it maybe makes her a little sick to have me there. *You look just like him,* she said when I arrived with my mom's old flowered suitcase. And then she doused me with hand sanitizer and showed me the couch and told me to keep my things in a slim closet by the door. She's doing me and my brother a favor, but I need to find a real place to live, stat.

"Let's go to your place," I finally say to Sean with a burst of bravery. "I wanna see it."

Sean looks dubious. I can't figure him out, sexuality wise. I think he's straight, mostly because we met on Bumble, but he doesn't seem that interested in hooking up with me—we haven't even kissed. I know he has an extra bedroom, because he mentioned it last week when we were surrounded by Bengal tigers at the Bronx Zoo. One was sleeping in a tree, looking like he was about to fall out, when Sean said, "Sometimes I sleepwalk. It makes me worried about having a roommate, but I do need to get one at some point."

And then I wondered for the rest of the Bronx Zoo tour if he was considering me as a potential person to room with. I've been out with him three times total (this night makes four) and I feel like I could do it—I could live with him. So now I need to figure out the best course of action: Do I hook up with him (if he even wants that) or do I steer us toward something platonic and hope he wants a roommate who chips in with rent?

I can't mess this up.

We head down Attorney Street and I feel the flutter of excitement again, wanting his apartment to be glamorous, but also wanting it to be crummy enough that I could see myself living there. I haven't even found a job—I'm working off savings I earned waitressing second semester senior year while living with my parents—and as of this morning my savings account has eight hundred dollars in it.

"That's my building on the right," Sean says.

It's gray brick and kind of dull, but who cares? "It's a cool vibe here," I say as we get closer, and I can see him puff up with pride. "Is that an elementary school?" I ask.

"Yeah," he says. Rainbow-colored cones are set up in a circle on the basketball court. Near the free throw line is forgotten chalk in a heap next to a Ziploc bag and a duffel.

Sean puts his key into the first door, and then the second. We're in. And there's no doorman, which usually makes apartments way more affordable. My heart picks up speed. This could work; I could maybe pay for something like this. And I need a roommate—I'd be way too scared to live alone—and Sean is the only person I know living in the city, because barely anyone from my college came here. And most importantly, Sean seems to get nicer the more I get to know him.

I swallow down the feeling that I don't know him well enough—it's what my dad would say if he knew I was trying to live with someone I barely knew, and he'd be right: I don't even know the basics about where he grew up. But people have sex with people they just met, and is this really that much worse? Don't you just have to go with your gut sometimes? I know some things, like how Sean went to Georgia Tech and knows a brother of one of my friends from high school (so he isn't making the whole thing up, because I checked); I know he's smart and that he does something with computers from home. He doesn't even go to an office or get out of his workout clothes, which he says is the best part about being a freelancer.

The lobby floor is grimy, and the building itself a little decrepit, but not too bad so far. We pass silver mailboxes and a man in navy pants and a matching shirt that I think is a uniform. "Hey, Paulie," Sean says, and the man smiles at us both. Sean doesn't introduce me.

"I'm on the fourth floor," Sean says as we get on the elevator. We ride in silence, and it's kind of awkward. Sean is a terrific conversationalist when he wants to be, when he's on a topic he cares about. But good luck guessing what that might be, and if you don't get it right, he acts half-bored. Or maybe I'm boring him, but I don't think so. When people complain about me, it's not usually because I'm dull.

"This way," Sean says in a singsong voice when the elevator doors open. It looks like there are only four apartments per floor, which gives it a homey vibe. The apartment across from Sean has a pair of beat-up Nikes outside, but Sean's welcome mat is clean. He opens the door to 4D and we step inside.

I suck in a breath—and, okay, so it's not glamorous. Sean said it was a two bedroom, but it's clearly a one bedroom with a makeshift wall sectioning off half of the living room. Not that I'm complaining—I'm not fancy, I just need somewhere to live.

"I love it," I say, because I do. And it's obvious so does he. He looks around the place like it's heaven. "It's awesome, right?" he says. "But I really want to get a dog."

"I love dogs," I say, and never have I been so grateful to not be allergic.

"You do?" he asks, beaming.

I can't see any windows because of the wall that's been put up. It gives me a claustrophobic feeling, like I'm in a closet and can't breathe. New York is so open out on the streets, but then everyone has these tiny apartments.

"Do you have one?" Sean asks.

A window? I almost say. "A dog?" I ask, trying to focus on him and not the apartment. Quickly, I add, "I don't have one now, but we had a chocolate lab growing up."

"Is he dead?" Sean asks, and the wording is so off-putting it breaks up my smile.

"Um, yeah," I say. "He died right before I went to college."

Sean takes a step into a small kitchen that was probably remodeled in the eighties. (It's only inches away from the entry door, so we're pretty much already standing in it.) On the counter is a red microwave and porcelain Hello Kittys that I think might be salt and pepper dispensers. Sean opens a white fridge and retrieves two beers, cracks off their tops, and passes me one. "Thanks," I say. He must set his fridge really cold, because the glass is icy against my fingers.

"To great apartments," Sean says, and I smile even wider, because I wonder if he's thinking what I am. I'm nervous, so I try to remind myself that he's the one who mentioned he was looking for a roommate.

"To great apartments," I say as we clink bottles, and I think about how perfect this place is. There are no nice things around, but there's no mess, either.

"I like things neat," Sean says as if he read my mind.

"Me too," I say. And then I almost utter the words—they're right there in my throat, climbing higher . . .

Are you looking for a roommate?

But I'm too nervous—I don't want Sean to reject me. Instead I move toward him. Somehow, in some way, it just feels easier. It's a rejection I could handle if it happened, though I don't expect it to, because when I comb my memory I can't come up with a single instance a guy has stopped me from making the first move. I press against him and drop my beer to my hip. My other hand goes to his shoulder, and for a quick breath it feels like we're slow dancing. "Sean," I say softly. I'm five eight and he's five ten or so, but I'm wearing wedge sandals so we're looking dead into each other's eyes. "Do you want this?" I ask, because even though I can already feel him pressing up against me like he does, there's something else there, too: a hesitation, or a tiny kernel of doubt.

His breath is coming faster now. "I do," he says, but his voice catches.

"You're sure?" I ask. "Something's not wrong? Is it me?"

"It's most certainly not you," he says, and then he bends to put his beer on the coffee table. The living room is so small it feels like we can reach out and touch every surface. I put my beer down next to his, and I stand there, my toes scrunching against my sandals. I like Sean enough to kiss him, but I'm not sure how much else I really want to do with him. Maybe that should be a warning, but if it is I'm too tipsy to heed it.

Sean closes the space between us. His hand goes behind my back and pulls me close and I revel in it—the moment right before the kiss happens, my favorite moment, the one I would live inside if I could. Those precious seconds before any kiss I've ever had are always better than the actual kiss that follows. Maybe that's how I'll know when I've found my person: when the kiss itself trumps all.

This one doesn't.

We're only kissing for a second when I know for sure that this isn't going to work. His kiss is too hard, too much all at once, and I can feel myself shrinking back; I feel every possibility of something between him and me slipping away like low tide. "I'm so sorry," I say, and Sean lets go of me right away. "I shouldn't be kissing you," I say, my heart racing, needing to find the words that will work, the ones that will hold us together just enough to not lose everything I want and need from him. "I need a friend right now," I say, because that's truer than anything. "Not this. I'm so sorry." And then I add more partial truths. "I'm really mixed up. Lost, really. And trust me, these are all my issues, it's not you." Sean's wide hazel eyes narrow with hurt. He's backing away from me slowly. "I hope, I mean, what I really need right now is someone I can trust. Someone who has my back. A friend, you know, to do this with, to live in the city with, to go places. Back to the tigers, maybe," I say, forcing a smile.

Sometimes I'm not sure how much of what I say is real. In moments like this it's like reading a script—I know exactly how to make my face look; I know exactly how much waver to add to my voice.

I'm not sure whether that makes me a good actress or a good liar.

EIGHT

Rowan. Wednesday afternoon. November 9th.

The day after I see June in the coffee shop, Gabe and I are at the pediatrician's office with Lila. Wall decals of grinning jungle animals leer at us, and everything smells antiseptic like the hospital. The nurse checks Lila's temperature with a thermometer on her forehead. I have no idea if my OB communicated my mental state with our pediatrician, but I imagine he did: Do doctors do that? Call each other? I bet they do when they think a baby's safety could be at stake. And I'm the only one who knows the state of my mind well enough to know that Lila's safe with me, aren't I? Gabe told me his mom used to fly off the handle when he was little, and one time when Elena was drinking, she told me that of all the things she's ever regretted, she regretted her temper the most. I wonder if my dad would say the exact same thing if he hadn't been killed so long ago; would he have regretted all the ways he tortured us? I don't know if Gabe's fully forgiven Elena for her temper and all the things it meant for them, and whenever I ask him about any of it, he says he doesn't remember much about being little, just being shuttled back and forth between his parents after their divorce. He loves and trusts his mom enough to let her care for Lila, and

I don't think he sees any point in drudging up years-old transgressions. And it's not like we leave Lila alone with anyone—I'm always there.

"We'll just need her undressed for her weigh-in," the nurse is saying.

"Can I do it here?" I ask, unable to recall if it's the right thing to lay her down on the paper. I'm assuming they change it for each new patient.

"Sure!" says the nurse, smiling at Lila. "She's just gorgeous."

"Thank you," I say, relaxing into the normalcy of it all: a kind nurse, an appointment with a pediatrician, and my daughter alive and well. *Just one normal day after the next*—that's my plan for getting back to myself. Whatever jigsaw puzzle piece came loose needs to stay permanently back in place.

"*Rowan*, your shirt," Gabe huffs.

I look down in the middle of lowering Lila onto the table and I catch sight of what he's talking about—the snap of my nursing top has come undone and my breast is almost entirely exposed. "Oh," I say, but then I lose my balance a little and let go of Lila too soon. She falls only half an inch onto the exam table, but it's enough to make me gasp. "Lila," I say as she starts crying. "Oh no." I feel the nurse's gaze boring into my back.

"Is she all right?" the nurse asks, and I want to die.

"Yes, I think so," I say, scooping her back up into my arms. "Who cares about my stupid shirt?" I hiss at Gabe, who's standing there with his mouth agape.

"Take your time," the nurse says, her kindness somehow making it worse. "When she's settled down I'll weigh her," she adds, voice easy.

Lila does settle down; she even stays quiet as I lay her gently against the paper. Her eyes look up at me, studying me. "I'm so sorry, Lila," I whisper, but there isn't reproach in her little gaze. She looks at me very seriously, like she's trying to tell me something. *I love you, too,* I try to say softly, but no sound comes out. I carefully take off her onesie and tell the nurse we're ready.

"Diaper needs to come off, too," the nurse says.

I take off Lila's diaper and it's dry, so my inclination is to save it and use it again, but then I second-guess myself and hand it to Gabe to throw into the trash. He does, avoiding my gaze. I force a smile at the nurse and pass Lila into her arms. On closer inspection, I see her scrubs are covered with a parade of Disney characters. Lila is happy until the nurse lowers her down onto the scale, and then she starts to cry, kicking her tiny legs.

I step forward. "Can I pick her up?" I ask.

The nurse writes down Lila's weight on a pad of paper, and the seconds her pencil spends scrawling the numbers feel like an eternity with Lila crying louder on the scale. Finally, she says, "Of course," while still writing numbers. Before she leaves she says, "Dr. Templeton will be right in."

I sit down with Lila in an uncomfortable gray plastic chair. Gabe stays standing. When the nurse is gone, he asks, "Are you okay?"

"Yeah," I say. "Just nervous."

"Why are you nervous?" Gabe asks. His hands go into the pockets of his jeans. His light blue button-down is a little wrinkled, and I wonder what the nurse thought of us. Maybe she just saw new parents trying to get it right, or maybe she saw something worse.

"I don't know, exactly," I say. "It feels nonspecific. I haven't really stopped feeling a little nervous since Lila was born."

Gabe looks at me, and I think he understands, but then he says, "But Lila's fine. Are you nervous about something else?"

"No," I say. "*I'm nervous about Lila.* That she isn't really fine or that I'm going to do something wrong."

"Something wrong?" he repeats.

"Do you seriously never worry you'll do the wrong thing with our baby and something bad will happen?" I ask. "Is that just one of the gifts of being a man? Because I think every mother who ever lived has thought it."

Red comes to his cheeks. "Do you seriously think men don't worry about their children? How about how worried I was the night before last when you took Lila out for a stroll?"

I laugh—I can't help it—and it comes out hard and bitter. "Oh, that's rich," I say. "I'm specifically asking if you've ever worried that you could do something to Lila by accident that would cause harm to come to her, and you give me an example of a time you were worried that I had our baby and something bad would happen to her. That's typical."

"What's typical?" he growls.

I'm holding Lila across my chest, swaying faster and faster. "*Me being the problem* is typical for the undercurrent of our marriage," I say.

We're quiet, and maybe there it is: the truth, sharp edged and hard to swallow. I stare into his brown eyes, and I know I love him—I can feel it in every ounce of me—but what if Gabe and I don't love each other deeply enough to get through all the things we need to? Surely there are gradations of love in marriages, and how would anyone ever know where their marriage stands with nothing else to compare it with?

In the periphery of my vision, the jungle animals on the wall seem to be coming nearer, closing in like Lila and I are their prey. I want Gabe to tell me that I'm a good mother. But he only shakes his head as if he can't bear to be in the room with me, and then Dr. Templeton enters.

"Hello, O'Sullivan family," she says in a soft voice, smiling at the three of us. I wonder if she sees how much Gabe and I hate each other in that moment, maybe the most we ever have. Gabe slaps a smile onto his face for the pediatrician, and then my phone rings. I scramble for it in my pocket, but it's hard to wrench it out while I'm holding Lila in the other arm. "I'm so sorry," I say. Why is my pocket so small? I can't get the phone out. "I should've turned off my ringer. I'm really sorry." I finally free my phone and see a number I don't recognize with a 518 area code. I silence it.

The doctor sits on a stool with wheels. The mauve cushion goes *pfff* as she rolls closer to us. "Lila's not gaining weight like she was last week," she says.

My heart ratchets up a notch. "Oh no," I say. "Is that really bad?"

"Babies are supposed to be back to their birth weight by the time they're two weeks old," she says. "And at the appointment last week, Lila was. But this week she hasn't gained. She's actually lost an ounce. Which does give me cause for concern. We can get you working with a lactation consultant to build up your supply, if it's even a supply issue. I don't think it's a transfer issue because Lila was gaining well at first."

"Transfer?" I repeat, my mind scanning for a definition in this context, coming up blank. "What does that mean?"

"It means Lila's ability to actually transfer milk out of the breast. And again, I don't think that's the problem here. Sometimes babies are just so sleepy they're not getting as much as they need, and it's just important that we get to the bottom of it. I'll give you the card for the lactation consultant we work closely with, and you should have her come today if possible or by tomorrow. It may just be that you need to pump additional breast milk after feedings and give Lila that extra milk in a bottle to be sure she's getting enough ounces. We need her to be drinking twenty-four ounces per day, and whether she gets that from the breast or bottle is fine. So let's see what happens when you start to pump, and the lactation consultant can help with all that. Do you have a breast pump?"

My phone buzzes with the missed call alert. I ignore it.

"I do have a pump, a good one I think because a friend recommended it," I say. My heart is going so fast I feel like I'm going to pass out. I almost lean into Gabe, but I'm still so prickly at him that I don't. Dr. Templeton must sense how awful I feel, because she says, "That's great. So start pumping today for ten minutes after your next feed. See how much milk you get, and give me a call and let the nurse know.

And then feed that bottle of milk to Lila, nice and slowly. Do you have infant bottles?"

"Um, yes, we do," I say. At least I read enough stuff to know I was supposed to have a pump and infant bottles on hand. How do people do this who don't have access to all the information they need or anyone to help them? I probably should have read more; it's just that I always found those parenting blogs so overwhelming with all the car seat reviews and product recalls and recipes for pureeing your own baby food. It seemed like a bunch of extra stuff was thrown in with the necessary stuff, which is great if you want to read all of that; it just strikes me that maybe there should be one resource with the vital stuff. "I should have taken a breastfeeding course," I say to the doctor.

She taps a pen against her clipboard. Gabe still isn't saying anything. He read zero books and took zero classes, so I guess there's not much he could add. "Did your OB recommend a class?" she asks.

"Um, I think so?" I say. "He had a poster up about a breastfeeding class, but I kept focusing on those childbirth classes. I went to one of those instead." *Some good it did me,* I almost add, but I'm not exactly ready to joke about how bad the birth was.

Dr. Templeton nods sympathetically. "Even the hospital doesn't push the infant care class if the parents don't want to take it," she says, but then she gives me a wave. "But we don't need to focus on that. I'm here for you and Lila now."

It brings tears to my eyes. "Okay," I say, "thank you."

Now Gabe's phone starts vibrating. The doctor turns to him, noticing. He doesn't apologize; he just acts like it isn't happening.

"We'll turn off our phones next time," I say, embarrassed for what seems like the twentieth time during this appointment.

Gabe shoots me a look, but he takes his phone out to turn it off. I glance at his screen and see the same 518 number. "Where's a 518 area code from?" I ask the doctor, which is a strange thing to ask in the middle of Lila's appointment, but I'm too exhausted and jittery to have any filter.

"Albany," the doctor says, seeming unbothered by the interruption. "I went to college at SUNY." She smiles at me, prettier by the minute. Kindness is like that.

"Must be a sales call," Gabe says, turning off his phone. "We don't know anyone in Albany."

"Yes, we do," I say. I hear the satisfaction in my voice at knowing something he doesn't, and it makes my stomach turn. Why am I being like this, so small and petty? "June's family is from around there," I add, gentler.

His eyes narrow, but I can't read the look. He almost seems confused. Either he didn't know June was from there or he's wondering why anyone in her family would ever call us.

"June is our babysitter," I say to the doctor. I smile. Maybe a part of me wants the doctor to ask me about her. I want to know if Dr. Templeton knows how nuts I went, and if she's concerned.

But she doesn't ask—not a single thing about me or my mental health. She gets down to business with Lila's exam, and I stand there watching my baby, soaking her up, soothing her when the chill of the stethoscope presses her bare skin.

I almost feel like a normal mother.

NINE

Rowan. Wednesday evening. November 9th.

Early that evening we meet with a lactation consultant who brings a massive silver baby scale. She weighs Lila before her feed and after, and then tells me Lila's only taking in an ounce from each breast. And of course that's not enough, so I start sobbing. All I want is Lila to be okay, and plus it's dark out, which makes everything scarier and uncertain. I never feel okay at night, not really. Not since that night nearly three decades ago when someone broke into our home and did things to my dad I hadn't dreamt anyone could; you don't have those ideas when you're five. Even when my dad hurt my mom, he did it with grabs and twists and yanks—not a knife.

The lactation consultant puts me on an elaborate pumping and feeding regimen that my brain isn't equipped to follow, but she tells me I can call her any time of the day or night, which makes me cry again. She leaves around eight, and we get Lila into her bassinet next to our bed around nine thirty.

I turn off the lights in my bedroom. The moon is nearly full and high in the sky, and I stare out the window and pray we're all going to be okay. I still pray; my dad was the one who taught me. We'd kneel next to the bed, our hands clasped and our heads bowed reverently.

I still wonder why he never prayed for himself. Maybe if he had, he wouldn't have caused all the trouble he did for us. Even bragging about the watch: What kind of person needs that to fill them up? Maybe most people do. But then what was the point of all those Sunday masses he took me to? The coveting of that watch, the bragging: Wasn't that hubris or greed or all the other sins we prayed not to commit? So much of who he was makes no sense to me.

Gabe's in the kitchen making tea. He's never been a heavy drinker of alcohol, but the smell of chamomile reminds me of when he swore off booze for six months because he realized hangovers were getting in the way of his writing (we're both early morning writers). We drank tea every night those days, curled up together in bed reading books. We had less sex without the booze, but we read and cuddled more, which was infinitely better. It's not that I don't like sex—I do—it's just that I felt so close to Gabe then, and I relished the feeling of it, all curled up with our books and screenplays. Every night after dinner I'd set out my stack of advance copies that publishers asked me to blurb, and Gabe and I would ignore our phones buzzing with texts from friends to meet them out. We'd climb into bed and I'd pass the books to Gabe so he could take a look, too, and help me decide which ones to say yes to. He'd carefully unfold the letters from publishers tucked into the pages politely asking me to lend a quote for the jacket and profusely complimenting my work. Then he'd tease me with blurbs I could write that verged on ridiculous. Gabe had more of a silly side back then, especially if he knew it would make me laugh. But mostly we were quiet those nights, squirreled away with those advance copies and reading them cover to cover. (There's something about an advance copy of a novel that neither Gabe nor I can resist—there's a thrill to finding a treasure before the rest of the world gets to see it.) When Gabe picked up alcohol again after those six months, things shifted a bit between us, not to anything all that bad: just different. We spent our nights out with friends again at dive bars, laughing, a little buzzed but never sloppy (the six-month abstinence was a reset that stuck). Gabe and I are only-children, and our friends back then were like surrogate siblings. But somewhere around turning thirty, most of them had broken up or gotten married and had children and moved out of the city to idyllic towns in New Jersey or Westchester with names that ended in *dale*. When we did see them it was a little forced; they all seemed so stressed as they tried to entertain us on their patios, the women asking their husbands how much longer the grilling would take as they shifted toddlers on their hips, or the husbands asking through gritted teeth where the pacifier was when a baby was crying over the conversation we were trying to have. We understood, of course; we wanted a family of our own, too. But we felt like we couldn't keep up on those sunny suburban afternoons, listening to conversations about sleep schedules and potty training. After a while we all drifted apart, and then it was just us again and a few scattered writer friends and college friends who didn't live in New York anyway.

I wait in the bed for Gabe to finish up in the kitchen, curling my legs to my chest. Instead of running through all the things I want to say to him, my mind's pleasantly blank. I can hear the kettle whistle, and I know Lila's sleeping deeply enough it won't wake her. There's this feeling I have when we get Lila down for the night: it's mostly exhilaration, like a momentary brush with freedom, but it's always followed by a sinking feeling that no matter how tired I am, and no matter how much I need a full night's sleep, there's no way I'll get one. Lila will be up in an hour or two to nurse, and then after that feed I'll get three hours or so until she's up again—if I'm lucky. And I *am* lucky to have Lila. I'm just so exhausted and scared of myself it's hard to think straight. Why didn't my old friends ever talk about *this* feeling? Wasn't it the crux of it? Or did they never feel this way?

"Rowan," Gabe whispers when he comes in.

My eyes have adjusted to the darkness of our room. I can make out Lila's figure in the bassinet, the gentle rise and fall of her stomach. Gabe comes toward the bed with two steaming cups of tea, and as he nears Lila's bassinet I say, "Careful! Can you see?"

"I'm not going to spill the tea on the baby," Gabe says, and I get it, I do; I understand why his frustration with me is festering.

"I'm just trying to help," I say, but he and I both know that's a lie. I'm not trying to help; I'm doing exactly what he thinks I'm doing, which is trying to make sure he doesn't spill tea on the baby. I can feel myself turning into something different; someone I don't recognize.

Gabe swerves around the bassinet and puts the tea down on our bedside table. I think he's going to be cold with me because I made a big deal about the tea, but he surprises me by getting into our bed and kissing me on the mouth. It takes my breath away, same as any tender kiss on a moonlit night would, and a shiver runs over the skin on my arms. He puts a hand on my chest, lowering me onto the bed with a gentle push. His hand goes to my still-tender stomach, and he carefully avoids the fresh scar. Then he slips his fingers under my pajama pants. There's a breath when I think I know what he's going to do, but then I'm all wrong.

"Rowan," he says, his voice a low, baritone hum in the warm air between us. "I'm worried about you. About us."

"Me too," I say into the dark. His hand is back on my stomach, rubbing a small circle near my navel.

"What are we gonna do?" he asks. He sounds like a little boy, and it makes me want to take care of him, something I haven't felt for him in forever. I push myself up so I'm sitting against the headboard. He does the same, and our bodies are close but not touching. He reaches to grab his tea, takes a sip, and then puts it back on the bedside table. He turns to me and says, "I'm sorry for being a prick."

I want to tell him he hasn't been one, but in fact it's almost the perfect word for what he's been: an uptight, unfeeling prick. Like I said, we know how to use language.

I suck in a breath and then I say words I know might send us spiraling in a direction I'm not ready to go. "I feel like you don't love me the way you used to," I whisper.

The words hang there like Christmas lights, twinkling and dying out when he says nothing. His hands go into my hair and then move to my neck, circling my throat like a promise, something he needs me to understand. My heart is a trapped bird beating against my ribs. How bad is our situation, really? How do I not know what he's going to say?

"Rowan," he says, and he leans closer until I can feel his mouth against my collarbone, kissing me. I let out a moan that takes me by surprise, embarrasses me. "You know how I feel," he says, breath against the skin of my breasts.

"I don't," I say, wanting him to contradict what I've said. But maybe that's what he's trying to do now. He pushes me gently down to the bed and keeps kissing me. I don't know where this is going—we haven't even gotten the clearance from my OB to have sex yet, and plus Lila's sleeping right there in the bassinet. "Didn't you hear what I said?" I ask against his lips. I need him to argue with me, to fight for me—I know my world through words, not actions.

He stops kissing me, his breath coming fast, the smell of chamomile tea everywhere. "I heard it," he says. "But how can you believe that could be true?"

I disentangle myself from his arms. "Because everything feels different. And I'm scared you don't like who I've become." It sounds so juvenile, but I don't know how else to say it. "I'm scared that this incarnation of me, being a mother, being unwell, that I'm going to lose you to it."

He lets go of a long breath, his whole body quieting down, like he's giving up, which isn't what I want. I wish I had just shut up and kept kissing him.

"This is an impossible situation," he says, finality in his voice, like he's just summed it up for us.

"I love you," I say firmly, but there isn't any time for him to say it back because my phone rings. I scramble for it, not quite believing I forgot to silence it. It's that same 518 number I saw in the pediatrician's office.

"Hello?" I answer. Gabe's hand is still on my hip, fingers curled over the bone. I want it to stay there.

"Rowan O'Sullivan?" comes a jovial voice on the other end.

"Yes. This is she," I say.

"This is Art Patricks," the voice says.

I'm quiet for a moment, certain I don't know anyone by that name.

"Can I help you?" I ask.

"I sure hope so," Art says, his voice a slow drawl. "Certainly would make my life a little easier." He sounds almost friendly but not quite.

The phone's dim light catches Gabe's face, just inches from mine, staring.

"I got your number from June Wallenz's employer, Louisa Smith," Art says. "June babysits some evenings for you, yes?"

My pulse goes nuts. He could be a lawyer. Maybe June's decided to press charges against me?

"We have a babysitter named June," I say carefully. "But she told us her last name is Waters."

"Oh, right," Art says, a laugh in his voice. "*June Waters*. Her stage name, isn't it? I do believe she told me that one this past Christmas." His words sound tinny on the phone. He's quiet for a beat, and then his voice is harder when he says, "It's not her real name, though. Did you know that?"

"Um," I stall. I lock eyes with Gabe. Did we seriously not check June's license or any form of identification before hiring her to watch our baby?

"I'm a close friend of the Wallenz family," Art goes on. "I'm also a police detective. And June never made it to her parents' house this morning as planned, which is why they called me. And I certainly know young people, how their plans change and so forth, and the local law enforcement won't take it seriously with June barely being missing. But it's unlike June to text her father the night before with an arrival time and then disappear into thin air and leave her father waiting for her on the train platform. I pinged her phone and can't get a location, which happens when a phone's battery is dead. I'm sure you can imagine their concern, being a parent yourself." The whites of Gabe's eyes are glowing. I put the call on speaker so he can hear the rest.

"Well, I certainly hope she's okay," I say. "But I wasn't the last person to see June. Her roommate, Sean, was waiting for her after we went our separate ways."

Gabe's lips part. I can see the questions on them: *Who's Sean? When did you see June? Why?*

"The last person to see June?" Art repeats with a chuckle. "You really have been writing too many of those mystery novels, haven't you, Rowan?"

My skin goes icy. Did he google me before the call? Gabe's face has folded, and I don't know whether it's because he's worried about the route the call has taken or he's trying to figure out why I saw June and Sean.

"Let's back this up then," says Art, still sounding eerily happy, like this is a game. Is this a game?

"Is this a prank?" I ask.

"I can assure you it's not," he says, stoic now. "When was the last time you saw June?"

I swallow. "Yesterday morning," I say.

Gabe's eyebrows go up, but he says nothing.

"Was she babysitting for you?"

The phone is on the bed between Gabe and me now, lit up like a warning. *Slow down,* it tries to tell me, but I don't listen: I press the accelerator and fly faster over treacherous ground. "I saw June yesterday morning in a coffee shop," I say. "We had a long talk, during which I apologized for my behavior."

"Your behavior?" asks Art.

"Yes. I apologized for something I had done—the way I'd treated her while she was babysitting. I wasn't right, postpartum hormones and all of that, and I apologized to June."

"What was it that you'd done?" Art asks.

"That's not your business, Mr. Patricks. It's mine. And if a real detective, not a family friend, wants to come question me about it, I'll be happy to answer any questions with my lawyer present." I let out a chilly laugh. "Jeez. I guess I *have* been writing too many of those mystery novels."

Click—the line goes dead. But it was Art who hung up, not me. I stare at the phone, and then I look up to meet Gabe's eyes. I brace myself for a fight.

TEN

June. Four and a half months ago. June 17th.

Two weeks after that night I botched kissing Sean, my dad is lugging a box of miscellaneous crap from his car to the doorway of my new apartment building, and I'm practically bursting out of my skin anticipating them seeing my place and meeting Sean. My mom's standing just outside their Toyota Camry with her green eyes narrowed and seeming even more skittish than usual. She's glancing from my stacked cardboard boxes to the glass door of the building, and I'm pretty sure she's thinking about how someone could rob us. She's always considered herself an unlucky person, which would never make sense to an outsider, only to my brother and me.

"Mom, you okay?"

That's not a question I usually ask her, but we're so out of our norm it feels all right. We never came down to New York City when I was growing up, even though it was only a few hours south of our town.

"I'm fine, Junebug," she says, and indeed her using my nickname is a sign that this is a good day for her; that she's truly all right, maybe just a little nervous. Maybe she's just not sure about all this, even though I explained to her that Sean and I met for coffee a few times during the past two weeks and ironed out all the details of living together (I also used those coffee talks to make it abundantly clear to him that it was all just-friends and platonic).

My dad puts a shower caddy next to the building's front door. My heart is full when I see it, because I know my mom put this together for me; there's the strawberry shampoo and conditioner I like, and the kind of loofah no one I know uses, but some people must because they always sell them in the checkout section at Marshalls. I want to thank her, but she always shuts down when I get emotional, so instead I gesture to the chain-link fence and boarded-up window I can tell she's fixating on, and I say, "Mom, I know this street might look understated, but it's actually a highly coveted neighborhood."

My mom smirks. She doesn't like when I sound smarter than her. "Understated," she repeats, a little too snarkily. But I smile anyway. For the first time I can ever recall, her trademark peasant blouse and cutoff jean shorts look all wrong, and a small, guilty part of me sees her how any sophisticated New Yorker might: as an out-of-date suburban woman who doesn't live here. It's the cruelest thought I've had in years.

"June, you're gonna do just fine here," my dad says, picking up on our tension and trying to snap it like always. He lowers the next box of my stuff onto the concrete with his back rod-straight because that's what a physical therapist told him to do after he got injured years ago in a racing accident. It always makes my chest tighten when I see him move like that.

"Just remember what I said," I remind them, and then I lower my voice. "The actual apartment is really small. But it has potential."

My mom's eyes are puffy—she must have cried this morning. I just need her to get through meeting Sean, who's waiting for us upstairs. I glance up to the fourth-floor window and I swear I see a curtain move, but I can't imagine Sean would just be standing up there watching us.

I'm more nervous by the second. When I called my mom and dad last week to tell them about Sean asking me to be his roommate, my dad got really territorial about the whole thing. *How long have you known this boy, June?* he asked me, and then he tried googling Sean, but not much came up because Sean is the only person my age without any social media accounts.

"I'm just not sure she needs all that stuff," my mother says as she watches my dad carry the boxes to the door. The packing tape on one of the boxes has come undone, and a gymnastics trophy peeks out, the plastic gold gymnast striking a pose so flexible it borders on crude.

My dad says, "Well, then, *she* can throw it all away." He grunts as he lifts the next box, forcing a toothy smile in my direction. "Can't ya, June?"

I smile back. "Sure can," I say. I'd rather them not fight here. I glance sideways at my mom. "Unless you want to keep some of it?" I ask.

My mom rolls her eyes. "I don't want to keep your old trophies and artwork, no," she says. She hasn't said it rudely, but the words themselves are painful coming from any mother's mouth, and they land just like she knows they will, and I can't help but flinch no matter how much practice I've had at her slights.

"Oh," I say. I take a breath. I try to tell myself what I always do, that maybe she just doesn't have a filter. And she came here, didn't she? To this foreign city that makes her uncomfortable.

My mom stares at the elementary school across the street. "Reminds me a bit of your old school," she says, gesturing toward it. She's skinny, but she's also almost fifty, and the pale white skin on her arms is starting to go a little looser. Wrinkled, even. And the only thing similar about my elementary school and this one is the red bricks, so I know she's just searching for something to say. She always does that in lieu of an apology.

"Yeah, it does," I lie.

"Are you two going to help me, or just stand there looking nice?" my dad asks us. He's dripping sweat. It's at least eighty, and the sun heats up the New York sidewalk like a griddle.

"Sorry, Dad," I say, moving to get a box out of the back seat.

My mom stays put as my dad and I carry the final boxes.

"Ready?" my dad asks when we're done.

"Ready," I say. And then I buzz Sean's apartment, my nerves spiking.

"Yeah?" Sean says gruffly into the intercom.

"It's me," I say back. "It's June."

My parents exchange a look.

"Come up," Sean says, and then the doors buzz. My dad snatches the handle and yanks it like a bomb will go off if we don't open it in time.

"Yikes, Dad," I say as he shoves the boxes into the vestibule and lunges to open the second door.

"Shouldn't this Sean person come help you bring up your things?" my mother asks. "Isn't he your *good friend*. Weren't those your words?"

"Mom," I say, frantically gesturing to the intercom. And then I whisper-hiss, *"He can probably still hear you."*

Embarrassment passes over her face for a split second. "Let's go," she says, holding open the door so I can follow my dad with a box that's too heavy for me. I muscle through it, feeling my lower back straining. My mother makes a *humph* sound when I almost fall, like this whole thing is a debacle I've dragged her and my dad into.

We take the elevator in silence. When it opens, my dad shoves his two boxes into the hallway and pushes them over the floor.

"It's the other way, Dad," I say, pointing toward 4D.

Sean swings open the door. "Hello," he says formally. He regards us curiously, like we're animals at his beloved Bronx Zoo.

"Care to help?" I ask as I nearly crash into him with my box.

"Oh," he says, and then he reaches out his hands to take my box like the idea hadn't occurred to him. Maybe my mother is right.

"This is Sean," I say.

"I'm Nick," my dad says.

"Joan," my mother says, not really meeting his eyes.

"It's nice to meet you," says my new roommate, and then he disappears inside his apartment with my box and my dad.

"Cool place," I hear my dad say from inside. My mom gives me a look like she might bolt, but she doesn't. She follows me inside, and if I just saw my mother through other New Yorkers' eyes, I'm now seeing my apartment through hers. The kitchen tiles are dirty, and the sink is filled with dishes. The wall that separates my bedroom looks cheaper than it did that night I was here: almost flimsy, as if it could fall down at any moment. It makes me sure Sean put it up himself, and then I entertain a morbid fantasy that Sean put it up while we were going on all those pseudo dates so that he could eventually trick me into moving in here. My heart pounds and I try to smile at my parents, but suddenly everything seems wrong.

My dad glances around and says, "This place reminds me of an apartment I had in college." My dad is the kindest person I know, and he's trying to make Sean feel at ease, like they're bonding. But it has the opposite effect on Sean, who seems to take what my dad has said as an insult.

"Did you go to college in New York?" Sean asks snottily, like that's the only way my dad could possibly have ever had an apartment like this.

"Oh no," my dad says with a chuckle. "I went to community college in Albany. My buddy and I shared an apartment just like this. But then we got a bearded dragon named Stanley, and we had to feed him live crickets, and the crickets kept escaping into the building, and eventually we got kicked out." He laughs again, nostalgia on his face. Sean smiles at him like it's dawned on him that my dad isn't the enemy.

My mom is standing extremely still, surveying the place. I don't know what she's thinking, but I know it's not good.

"Hey, is that a mechanics magazine you have right there?" my dad asks, gesturing to a magazine resting on a flowered sofa.

"Well, it's *Popular Mechanics*," Sean says, but there's no trace of snobbery left in his voice. "But sure, I mean, it's about how things work. I love stuff like that."

"I'm a mechanic," my dad says.

"That's impressive," Sean says, nodding. "The inner workings of machinery is something I've loved since I was young," he adds. He's never told me that before, and it makes me smile despite my mother standing there with her beautiful scowl.

"My dad can fix *anything*," I say, not caring that I sound six.

"Actually, me too," says Sean. "That's why I got into computers. It's similar, the inner workings of something, the back end that no one else sees. I thought about being a surgeon for a hot second there. I think I'd love slicing into someone and seeing how it all works."

No one says anything. "Oh, wow," I finally manage. If my father is concerned for my well-being after what Sean just said, he doesn't let on.

My mother exhales; she's clearly over this conversation. "Is that June's room?" she asks, gesturing toward the flimsy wall. "May I see it?"

Sean turns and seems to see my mother for the first time. My mother is insanely gorgeous, but as she's gotten older it's the kind of beauty that sneaks up on you. It wasn't like that when I was little, when her beauty grabbed people by the throat, back when she was the queen of SlimFast and Everything Else in Harbor Falls, New York. She did that diet shake way past its prime, and the same with the Jane Fonda videos, but it never mattered that her vibe was a little out of date, or that her house was tiny, or that in the winter, when her garden was dead and the sun set at four, she often shut her bedroom door and wept. Out on our lawn she held court over all the other mothers—and even some of our male neighbors—who surrounded her like she was the arbiter of how to be incredible. Because she was. I used to stand there, age five or six or whatever ages little girls are, waiting for the bus at the end of our driveway in the tangerine morning light; and my mom would be there in the driveway, too, an inch too far away and sipping tea that smelled like mint gum. Every once in a blue moon she'd get close enough to run her hand over my hair, and I could never tell if it was meant to be affectionate, or if she was smoothing away an imperfection on my blond head. I think she was trying to give me space and let me do my own thing with the other kids, but space was the very last thing I wanted from her. And then the space started to feel impenetrable, and that's when I knew we were in trouble, and that it would take an act of God to break through to her, to make her love me like I needed her to. My brother, Jed, had it worse. He didn't even try to win her back from the deep depressive episodes she fell into; and that made her give up on him entirely.

"Sure, Joan," Sean says now, staring at my mother. Her name sounds odd on his lips. "Silly me. I should have given you a tour right away," he adds, as if there's really anything of note to see.

We follow Sean into my room. The four of us can barely fit inside together it's so small, and the shape is odd: it's like an obtuse triangle. "Well, I can't say I've been in a room shaped like this one ever before," my father says. Jed and I used to call him Captain Obvious when we were little. I miss Jed and our camaraderie; he comes back east for Thanksgiving and Christmas, and sometimes we talk on the phone, but he's five years older than me and we don't have much in common.

My mother lets out a laugh spiked with arsenic as she glances around the teeny odd space. "Well, here you go, June," my mother says, and I can feel the air change like it always does when she's about to tank me. "Is it everything you've dreamt of?"

"It actually is," I say, and even though I'm staring at my feet and I can't meet her eyes, I know that I mean it wholly and truly, that indeed this city is turning out to be everything I've ever dreamt of and there's nothing she can do that will change that. And to Sean I say, "Thank you so much for letting me live here."

I turn back to my mother. "I suppose that's all, Mom?" I ask, sadness wringing me like a washcloth. I need her to go. "Dad can bring up the last box? You didn't plan to have dinner with me or anything like that?" I ask, knowing full well she hasn't given a single thought to taking me out for a meal.

She bristles. Even Sean goes quiet. His eyes dart from her to me.

"I guess that's all, June," she says. And then she does the thing she always does; she turns and walks away from me. When I was little and she was having a bad day, it felt as if we were magnets with the same polarity and she couldn't get away from me fast enough. If I was in one room in our house, she was in another. But then sometimes, out of nowhere, for weeks at a time she was healthy—strong—and not depressed out of her skull, and she'd hold me. And those moments were what I lived for. Her love was the ultimate dopamine hit—intermittent and unpredictable—and now I look for it everywhere.

"Thank you for moving me in," I say to my parents.

My dad wraps his arms around me. My mother watches from a cool distance before she comes toward me, kissing the top of my head.

"Good luck, June," she whispers.

ELEVEN

Rowan. Wednesday evening. November 9th.

June is gone," I say to Gabe, still staring down at my phone after Art disconnected us. I don't know why I say it like that. She's not gone, of course; she could be anywhere beautiful girls find themselves in New York City: in the theater district at a new show, at the farmers' market in Union Square, in Cobble Hill shacking up with a new love. But she feels gone to me as I grip the phone, sweat against the plastic case, my fingers finally releasing it. The screen still glows as it drops onto the bed.

I finally look up at Gabe. His thick eyebrows almost connect. He has a baby face when he's concerned, all wide brown eyes and pursed lips.

"What do you mean, she's gone?" he asks.

"You heard the detective," I say. "Do you think something terrible happened to her?"

Gabe comes closer to me, puts a hand on my knee. We're facing each other now, sitting cross-legged on our sheets. My back aches with the awkwardness of it.

"You saw her," he says.

I nod, mortified.

"Didn't you think you should run that by me?" he asks.

"I took Lila to meet her in a café to apologize," I say. "I'm sorry I didn't tell you, I really am."

Gabe shakes his head. "You can't just do this now. We have a daughter, *together*. She's mine, too."

"I know that," I say.

"You've always done this, Rowan. You've always played outside the rules, or at least bent them when it suited you. You can't now; not where Lila's concerned."

I nod, chastened. It's fair.

"What did he say before you put me on speaker?" Gabe asks.

"Just that June said she was going home to her parents and she never showed. Her father was waiting for her at the train station."

Gabe is quiet. He almost never says anything right away when he needs to think. It's the opposite of what I do. "Gabe," I push. "Don't you think that's bizarre?"

Another beat of thinking. "I mean, it doesn't sound good," he says. "But we don't know their relationship. Maybe she doesn't like her parents. Wasn't her mom difficult?"

"She told you that?"

"Yeah," he says, nodding. "I think she did, actually, once." He looks away and fumbles for his phone. "We should call Harrison," he says.

"Call Louisa first," I say.

TWELVE

June. Four months ago. July 6th.

I can feel the air fizzing as I walk through the chic hallways of Williamson Talent Agency to interview with talent agent Louisa Smith. I clutch the glossy white folder with my résumé tucked inside, and a sharp pang of longing lodges in my chest as I pass the glistening photos of actors and movies lining the walls. I want people to see me and know that I can be someone special—someone like the actresses lining these walls, someone good.

"This way to reception," says a girl with two messy buns. Her Doc Martens thud against the oak planks as I follow her down the hall. She's walking just enough ahead of me that I know she's not looking for a conversation. She opens a glass door into a large lobby with potted plants and a sleek reception desk where three women wear headsets and take calls.

I approach the reception desk and smile bigger than I mean to because it's all so exciting: I can't believe that only two weeks of being Sean's roommate led to something like this interview. I still have to get the job, of course, and it's only an assistant position, but still: WTA is a prestigious boutique talent agency, representing actors and screenwriters and on-air hosts.

A woman with a severe red bob looks up and returns my smile. "Can I help you?" she asks.

I wish I could tell her I was here as an actress to see my agent. "I'm June Waters," I say instead. I love my stage name so much more than my real one. At some point I'll have to show them my license if I do get the gig, but I'm pretty sure stage names are appropriate for making appointments. "I'm here for an eleven a.m. interview with Louisa Smith," I say. I imagine myself sitting down for my interview and Louisa deciding right then and there that she wants me as her client, not her assistant, and then maybe saying something like, *There's this audition for a contract player on a soap opera coming up, and I think you'd be perfect* . . .

I know that makes me sound like a jerk. But daydreaming is a thing I do a lot. My biggest fantasy is that I make it to Los Angeles and a month later my mom calls and tells me she's finally on the right cocktail of medicines for her to see everything clearly, and that it's just too hard to be this far from me. And then, over shepherd's pie and without much fanfare, she tells my father that they simply must move to the West Coast; *We can't be without June,* my mother would say. In Los Angeles, in this particular daydream, I am successful enough that I buy us a house with a garden so beautiful her eyes mist when she sees it.

"Oh sure," the receptionist says sweetly. "Why don't you take a seat and I'll let Louisa know you're here."

"Okay," I say, still smiling. "Thanks."

I sit on a plush seat and try not to squirm. In the waiting room it's just me and an older actor I recognize from a crime show. He's reading *Entertainment Weekly,* and he doesn't look up at anyone.

I watch the receptionists carefully. I really feel like I can get this job if I'm just charming and sharp enough. Youth and beauty are currency all over New York City, and certainly in places like this, and I have both in spades. I'm not bragging—the rest of me is crap, mostly. You've got to use what you have, and I'm certainly not some numbers whiz or anything like that.

I got this interview because one of Sean's clients is WTA; he built their new website last year. Sean's a few years older than me, and he's already done web design for companies so big you've heard of all of them. (It's kind of surprising because he's not that stylish as a person, but the sites he builds are gorgeous.) He emailed one of the directors at WTA, who told him there was an assistant job open. And *presto*, here I am.

I'm getting tenser the longer I sit here in the lobby. I try to take a deep breath and think of ways to make Louisa like me during the interview. I glance out the window and spy steel buildings and clouds—I can't see the ground from where I'm sitting. WTA is perched on the top floor of a slim glass building in Midtown, and even the elevator is ten times nicer than my apartment.

I love calling it that: *my* apartment. Even when I say it to myself I hear a lilt in my words. For twelve hundred dollars a month, Sean's place is mine, too. And if I get this assistant job—Sean guessed it would pay a little more than forty thousand a year—I could afford the twelve-hundred-dollar rent each month and even put a little away into savings. And hopefully still have some left over for fun.

I have barely anything left in my savings account; I really need to nail this interview.

A girl wearing a chic trench enters the lobby. She's sucking on a lollipop, which I doubt any regular person would do: she must be an actress. Her bangs are blunt cut and she's cute and funky like Zooey Deschanel.

I just know that the faster I get noticed—the faster I get my break—the faster I'll finally start to feel okay.

Better than okay . . .

Somewhere along the way, maybe when I was twelve or so, I saw the way the world gazed upon celebrities and influencers and the like, as though they were beautiful just for being in the spotlight. It was almost like the spotlight itself bequeathed grace, softening edges, drowning mistakes in adoration.

And now I want it more than anything.

The receptionist grins at the girl with the bangs and ushers her into the hallway. The lobby feels so still when she's gone. People with a big presence can do that.

"June Waters?" says a female voice. I look up to see another receptionist with jet-black hair shaved on the sides. She locks eyes with me and says, "Louisa will see you now."

Oh my goodness. "Thank you!" I say, way too excitedly. *Please, be cool, June.* I take a deep breath and follow her through a glass door with the WTA logo into a conference room. There's a long chrome table and windows overlooking the skyline. It's all the things: sophisticated, chill, and edgy, and my stomach twists into knots when I imagine the actresses and writers and film people who have meetings here. "Thanks," I say to the receptionist, who doesn't seem much older than me. She's wearing white sneakers and a lemon-yellow minidress. The vibe here seems more casual than I usually dress. I try to offset my looks and be surprising by dressing more conservatively: a puffed sleeve rather than a plunging neckline. And I only post photos of myself in the aforementioned classic looks, because it's kind of like a calling card. I actually wish I could post this insanely cool conference room, but I'm sure they'll check my social media and I don't want to look too green and wide eyed.

"Do you like working here?" I blurt to the girl.

"I do," she says, pulling out one of the two dozen chairs surrounding the rectangular table. "Sit here," she instructs me. "Louisa's really smart and good at her job," she adds.

"Thanks," I say, sitting down too hard.

"And the hours here are good," the girl says.

I want to ask her what she does when she's not here, but instead I ask, "So what do you want?" which comes out all wrong. I feel heat on my cheeks, and I try to explain myself. "I mean, what are you going after, like are you an actress or a writer or something?"

The girl laughs, but it's good-natured. "Nope," she says. "I was babysitting for a while, but that sucked, so I just looked for a job with adults. Adults act like children, too, sometimes, but I seem to be better equipped to deal with that." We smile at each other. "I want to go to law school," she says. "I'm studying for the LSATs."

"That's amazing," I say. "I could never do that. I was extremely bad at school."

The girl laughs again, and it makes me smile despite myself, despite the pain of what I've admitted to her. I want to say, *Do you know what it's like to have to go to school every day since you're five years old and suck at it?*

It's like having a day job you're terrible at, with no possible way out, because you're required by law to go to it. I only got one A my entire career: in an English class that was based on participation and journal responses to the stuff we read. Graduating from college—my dad was the one who said I had to go, and I know I should be grateful, and I'm sure I will be someday—was like breaking out of jail. A suitcase slung over my shoulder and a deep sigh of relief; *finally free.*

"I'm Kai Chen," the girl says. "And I know your name. Do you need water or anything before Louisa comes?"

I shake my head. "I don't think so," I say. I'm so freaking nervous.

"Good luck today," Kai says. "Maybe I'll see you around."

She leaves and the room feels colder. I glance through the windows of the conference room into the hallway: I can see heads moving above the blurry part of the glass, and a forehead and nose of one really tall guy. I studied everything I could find about Louisa (and all the other agents at WTA) so that she'd know I'm serious about the job.

The door swings open and I straighten, smile already in place. But it's not Louisa. It's a wildly handsome blond man somewhere in his thirties, who says, "Oh, hello. I'm looking for Louisa."

"Me too," I say, which makes him laugh.

His long fingers tap the doorway. His suit is perfectly tailored—he's more dressed up than the two other male employees I passed in the hallway.

"I'm Harrison," he says, but I already know that. Harrison Russell: the agency's top books-to-film agent. He represents screenwriters and novelists whose books get turned into movies and TV shows. Louisa represents actors, and her client list is one of the most diverse I've seen out of any of the agents I studied this week—which makes me want to work for her even more—and one of her actresses is on *The Young and the Restless*, which my mom would love. She used to convince my dad to change the channel on the tiny TV above the desk in his shop to play that soap opera every afternoon she worked there.

"I'm June Waters," I say. "I'm here for an interview for Ms. Smith's assistant job." I don't know why I say *Ms. Smith* instead of *Louisa*, but it feels more polite, and when he smiles at me I'm glad I did it.

"Well, good luck then, Ms. Waters," he says. There's a lilt in his voice when he says my name, and it gives me a small thrill. I smile back at him, holding his eyes a little longer than I should.

"Tell Louisa I'm looking for her," he says. Then he raps his knuckles twice against the glass door.

"I will," I say, like I already work here, like it's in the bag.

My phone buzzes while Harrison's still standing there. I can't believe I forgot to turn it off. "Oh my gosh," I say, fumbling for it. A text from Sean flashes across the screen.

When are you going to be home? I'm making us pasta!

Annoyance cuts through me. I press the side button and wait for what feels like an eternity until my phone lets me swipe it off. I almost hit the emergency SOS option by accident, but I finally get the thing to power down.

I look up at Harrison. His teeth are so white, so straight. "I'm really sorry," I say. "At least that happened before Louisa got here," I go on, taking a chance at being casual with him.

"The fact that you're embarrassed by it already puts you miles ahead of the rest of the kids your age who interview here," Harrison says.

Kids. I'm most definitely not a kid, and maybe he sees it on my face, because he corrects himself.

"*Young adults*, I mean," he says. He shifts his weight, still in the doorway, not leaving me yet. "Good luck today," he says kindly. "Louisa likes cats and gluten-free food, if you're looking for conversation starters."

I laugh, not expecting it. "Don't we all," I say. Harrison laughs, too, and then Louisa shows up in the doorway, eyebrows up.

"Am I interrupting something?" she asks, which makes me even more nervous. To Harrison, she says, "I didn't realize you had the conference room."

"I don't," Harrison says, gesturing to me. "This young woman is June Waters, and she's all yours."

Something prickly passes between them, but then Louisa rolls her eyes and it seems mostly over. Harrison gives me one last perfect smile and leaves us alone. Louisa doesn't smile, and it sets me right on edge again.

She looks at me—really looks. "You know," she says, still in the doorway. "I really do need an assistant." And then she grins, and that's the moment I get a feeling like this is going to happen—like the chilly version of her I just saw wasn't intended for me and if I'm lucky, maybe it won't ever be.

Louisa shuts the door and comes to sit at the conference table. She's holding a folder like I am, but hers is chock full of stuff. There's a cup of white pens with the WTA logo splashed across them in red and she takes one, opening the folder to reveal a few blank sheets of paper. She takes the paper out and tells me, "I'm old-fashioned. Still a note taker. If I don't have a pen in my hand and paper, I don't feel quite right."

She might be trying to make me feel more comfortable, which I appreciate, but I can't relate to what she's saying. I haven't used a pen to write anything in ages because my phone is so much faster to type on, and now I'm too nervous to come up with a response to what she's told me, so I say something completely mundane. "This room is beautiful, with the view of downtown?"

It comes out like an awkward question. *God.* At least I'm interviewing to be her assistant and not one of her actors. Because saying something that dull would probably have me crossed right off the list.

Louisa glances out the window. She's beautiful, somewhere in her mid- to late thirties with brown skin and eyes, black-framed glasses that catch the light, and hair that's pulled into a bun at the nape of her neck. "You see that bakery down there," she says. "You should stop there on your way out."

"Do they have good gluten-free options?" I ask, regretting it as soon as it leaves my mouth. Heat comes to my cheeks. I'm a fake—it's official. I haven't eaten gluten-free a day in my life.

Louisa's eyes light up and I feel worse. I try to tell myself it's not a lie: I didn't say I was strictly gluten-free, I just asked about options.

"They do!" she says. "The gluten-free banana muffins are to die for. And there's this bread made from almond flour, no oats or anything like that."

"I'll try it," I say, knowing I won't, because I don't really have the kind of cash where I can just buy expensive baked goods. I'd bet the amount Louisa spends on a snack would cover what Sean and I pay for dinner. Pasta with tomato sauce, tuna fish, mac and cheese, tofu scramble—it's amazing how little you can spend on that kind of stuff at the grocery store compared with what the New York eateries charge.

"So, June," Louisa says, staring at me. "Tell me a little about yourself."

"Oh," I say, my hands smoothing my skirt even though I'm trying not to fidget. "Well, I should be honest and tell you that I want to be an actress."

Oh my God. What have I done?

Louisa's eyes widen.

I let out a breath. *Oh no.* "I know that probably makes you not want to hire me," I say quickly. "But I wanted to be honest about it. Actually, I didn't realize I was going to tell you that before it came out of my mouth—that's actually more honest. But lately, well, especially since getting to New York, I feel more like a fake. I keep saying things I think other people want to hear."

I've lost this now, this thing I wanted so badly. It's like a fistful of flowers dropped on a roadside, something so beautiful you promised yourself you'd hold on to until you got to a safe place but you couldn't do it.

Louisa doesn't say anything.

"I *do* want to be an actress," I say, more thoughtfully this time. "But I also need a job and I'd like it to be one that I care about and that I'm good at. I'm really interested in seeing behind the scenes of the business, even though, of course, I wish I could be acting right away. But I'm really interested in WTA and I'm really impressed by what you all do here, particularly what *you* do here. So while I don't want your job, I'm actually pretty organized and I think I could be a great assistant to you so you can do your job better. I like details. I like knowing what makes people tick, and I also genuinely like to see other people do well, like you and your clients."

Louisa is so quiet I'm not sure what to do. I'm suddenly exhausted, as though telling the truth has zapped me of everything I've been holding tight in my chest the past few weeks.

"It's funny you say that," Louisa says slowly.

"Which part?"

"The part about feeling like a fake here in New York," Louisa says, "especially among all of this." She gestures into the ether of the conference room. She sits taller, and a tiny gold necklace twists over her collarbone. "I had a fertility treatment this morning before coming here," she says. She glances out the window to the same clouds I saw before, but now they're tinged with gray like a storm's coming. "And I'm wiped and irritable from the hormones. But I have to come to work and be all the things I'm supposed to be for my clients. So, I'll tell you what, June. Let's keep this interview going and we'll go over some things. Because it might be really nice for me to have an assistant who's honest with me and whom I can be honest with."

"We can have a code word for when you don't feel well," I say.

"A code word," she says. "I like that."

"Maybe *gluten-free banana muffins*," I say.

Louisa laughs. "No way," she says. "Because I eat those way too often. We'll get mixed up."

I laugh, too. "I should probably continue the honesty thing and tell you that I eat a lot of bread."

She smiles, but then she goes quiet. "I went gluten-free because I read on this woman's blog that it was the only thing that helped her get pregnant. I know that's totally crazy. The woman wasn't a doctor or anything."

"But sometimes there's true stuff on the internet among all the insanity," I say.

"I think you're right," Louisa says, her smile back. She clears her throat, then twirls her pen. A slim gold band decorates her ring finger. "Let me tell you a little about this job," she says. "That seems only fair, since I've told you everything else." She waves a hand in front of her. "If you worked with me," she says, "you'd work in a cubicle right outside my office. There are three assistants in that area—mine, another assistant for an agent named Roger Cleary, and then of course one for Harrison, whom you've already met. Some of the job is keeping me organized, but most of the job is answering phones and using your judgment to know which actor needs what from me at any given moment. You seem like you're pretty emotionally intelligent, so I have a feeling you're going to pick up on that quickly. Some of the job is knowing what's most pressing at any given point. A producer who's trying to get in touch with me about an actor of mine misbehaving on set is one thing, and very different from an actor who shows up on set high on a substance, which I would need to deal with right away. I don't have many actors like that, actually, and my clients all have my cell, so you won't be dealing with too many emergencies, because they usually just call me. Most of them think they're my top priority—and in a way that's true—so they're not shy about calling my cell. But you're my first line of defense a lot of the time, especially if I'm dealing with another client's crisis or in a meeting and can't answer my cell, and I'll need you to use your judgment on when you should interrupt me in a meeting or on a call and when you shouldn't. Oh, and every once in a while I get scripts to consider and I like a younger person's opinion on them. Are you a reader?"

"I am," I say, nodding vigorously. "Thrillers, mostly. Some rom-coms. Commercial fiction." It's the only area of my life where I'm book smart—literally. "I love to read, actually. Books and movies are my drug." Maybe it's a weird thing to say after what she just said about her actors. "And it's my only drug," I add firmly. I really can't believe all the strange-but-true things I'm saying today.

"Good," she says, smiling, and I smile, too. I feel okay with her. Even comfortable.

"Tell you what, June," she says, all businesslike again. A phone rings in the hallway beyond the glass of the conference room, and someone laughs. "Why don't we try this. Under one condition."

"Anything," I say, holding her gaze. I want this job so badly my blood has gone hot.

"At least in the beginning, I don't want to talk about your acting career," Louisa says. "Give me a few months to get to know you. I talk about acting careers all day long with my clients, and I really do need an assistant who can do this job well. But I like to see people succeed, too. In a few months from now let's talk about where your career is, and where it could potentially go. Now of course, if you're doing a performance somewhere, you should tell me and I'll come see it. But first we work, and we work hard. The hours aren't terrible. I'm usually in a little before nine, and I'm done by seven. But I'd like you to be here in the morning by eight thirty so you're in before me. Sound all right so far?"

My heart thumps. "It sounds perfect," I say.

THIRTEEN

Rowan. Thursday morning. November 10th.

The next morning I'm standing outside the oak doors of a town-house on West Eleventh Street and thinking about how Sarah Jessica Parker lives right near here. Once I saw her watering the garden in front of her townhouse. I've always loved SJP and actresses from her generation; they're the reason I write. My mom and I used to curl up with shows like *Sex and the City* and *Ally McBeal* and binge-watch them when I was in my teens. We loved TV and books—we loved stories. We loved my mom's enormous king bed. I slept in it most nights and it was heaven.

The thing not everyone realizes is that writers should watch a lot of television and movies, because the art of story is laid out for you in bite-sized pieces: either a two-hour film or an hour drama usually gets the job done—beginning, middle, end. Watch the way it works:

Opening conflict. Introduce your characters.

Main character is actionable and drives the plot forward.

Obstacles galore. Emotional conflicts everywhere. Setbacks.

Twist—three or four, if you've got them.

All characters hurtle toward a boil, and then boom: unexpected consequences.

Twist again.

Revelation: the truth surfaces.

Resolution.

Every character wants something on every page. When you figure out what that is, and how all the characters' motivations and scheming fit together, you have a story. Tweak it lighter or darker until you know what you've got: drama or comedy. For some writers the line blurs, but for me it's always a drama.

There's only one doorbell, which makes me think Sylvie owns the whole townhouse and uses a room inside for her psychology practice. It's freezing out and so very gray, but we only had to walk a few blocks from our apartment with Lila, and she seems content in Gabe's arms. Gabe rings the doorbell, and someone buzzes us in right away. Gold-framed pictures line the charming foyer. A wooden staircase arcs up the right side of it, and Sylvie comes out a curved oak door behind the staircase. "Come in," she says, a wry smile on her lips. "You must be freezing."

Gabe's holding a sleeping, snowsuited Lila against his chest. It's sort of amazing how much she sleeps during the day. I know I'm supposed to do something to turn that around so that she sleeps better at night, but I just don't see how it's possible to wake a sleeping newborn. All the books make it sound like you just snap your fingers and they'll wake up, but Lila sleeps so deeply that none of the advice I've read seems to work. I've tried taking off her clothes or putting a little cold water against her feet, but it's a total joke to think that would wake her unless she's already on the tail end of a nap. And it's the same thing for her feeds; all the baby books tell you to try to keep them awake while they nurse, but have you ever tried to keep a sleepy baby awake on your boob? Good luck.

Every time I mess things up with Lila I miss my mother so acutely it hurts in a spot right behind my breastbone and doesn't go away until I fall asleep or cry. I need to bring Lila to the care facility to meet her, but I don't know how I'm ever going to convince Gabe that it's a good idea.

Gabe's mom keeps stalling on bringing my mother to see me, telling me she hasn't been well enough. And it's true—when I've called her, she seems way more out of it than usual. So I'm going to have to go there myself, but Gabe was so nervous when we talked about it with the pediatrician, that she would catch something in that place among all those people crowded together during the winter. I feel a stab of guilt when I think about meeting June in the café: What if Lila caught a virus? Last night after Art called, Gabe told me we had to be more careful, and I thought he meant with Lila, because of the germs she could pick up in a public place. But he corrected me, saying, *We have to be more careful with June, Rowan. How much further do you want to push her?*

It made me feel so awful when he said that, like I was a predator. I tried to explain that June didn't seem mad at me or even like I was bothering her; I tried to explain that it was just an apology and that she was the one who texted me to meet. And then Lila woke up and we started the whole nursing and pumping routine that the lactation consultant taught us. Gabe barely looked at me while we counted ounces and sanitized pump parts and tried to get Lila to take the milk from a special infant bottle without throwing it all back up. And then it was midnight and we passed out. At three a.m. we did it all over again, and at that point I didn't bother looking him in the eye, either.

"Follow me," Sylvie says. We climb the curving staircase and trail after Sylvie into a second-floor kitchen. I'm getting the idea that this whole place is hers. It's breathtakingly beautiful, all moldings and doorways and prewar charm. "I've got to ask a favor," she says, and I wake up a little because it's not what I expect her to say. "One of my clients is in crisis and I need to make sure she's been admitted to Bellevue. Would you mind waiting here while I make a call for a few minutes?"

Sylvie is booked through next year, or at least that's the message we got when we tried to make an appointment on our own; she's definitely not taking new patients. She's what you'd call a trauma therapist, and she's supposed to be the best, and we got in with her only because of

Harrison's colleague Louisa Smith at WTA, who went to college with Sylvie and called in a favor for us when I snapped and freaked out on June. All this is to say that, *yes*, we are very willing to wait in her townhouse's well-appointed kitchen while she makes a call.

"Of course, no problem at all," Gabe says, and my heart breaks a little, because his usually confident smile falters. He looks more desperate than I've seen him in a long time. He needs this thing with Sylvie to work. So do I.

Sylvie disappears through yet another door behind the kitchen. Townhouses in New York are like this, so many secret rooms and entranceways and unexpected twists, attics with stained glass windows as decadent as the ones in old churches, libraries tucked behind bedrooms, second staircases, panic rooms.

I love secret things.

We sit on pale wooden stools at a thick marble island. A crystal bowl of limes and lemons sits next to a chic black coffee-table book about Tom Ford and a vase filled with blue hydrangeas. Copper pots and pans hang overhead. My head is tipped back staring at them when my phone buzzes. "It's Dave," I say softly to Gabe, who puts his hand on mine and squeezes. It feels like an apology for last night, for how mad he got at me, the things he said. Maybe I shouldn't look into it that much, but isn't that kind of what marriage is? Increasingly subtle apologies for larger transgressions?

I look at Dave's number and feel myself relax a little. Dave Larson is my literary agent and pretty much family at this point. He's been with me for a dozen years or so, ever since I sent him something I wrote my senior year of college. We didn't sell that first novel, but he stuck with me. "How are you?" he asks when I answer my phone. His voice is so careful. Everyone's is lately.

"I'm all right," I say. "Well, I'm at a headshrinker right now, but besides that I'm just fine." I trust Dave with my deepest confidences and my entire career. This is not a typical experience for all writers and their agents, but it is mine.

"Should I let you go?" he asks.

"No," I say quickly. "We're just waiting. I'll hop off when she comes and gets us."

Dave's quiet a moment on the other end of the line.

"The pages you sent me, Rowan," he finally says, but then his voice trails off. It makes me nervous. I swivel on Sylvie's counter stool, more uncomfortable by the second. I think back to the writing frenzy I was in last week. I pressed send on that email to him having barely reread my work. Lila had fallen asleep in her bassinet and I felt a starburst of energy, the itch to write so strong I chose it over brushing my teeth/showering/cooking or any of the other items on the long list of things I'm supposed to do when the baby sleeps. I don't think it's mania or anything diagnosable, but it's almost like a fire in my feet that spreads through me right into my fingertips, and then I need to write right away or else.

Or else what?

I'm not sure.

"These new pages are very unlike you," Dave says, his words soft.

"Oh," I say, trying to exactly remember the work, the feeling of it. There was a thick forest with wild threats at every turn, and a family of four who went deep inside it. Only three of them made it out.

"I like it very much, don't get me wrong," Dave says. "The writing itself is beautiful. I just, it feels so stream of consciousness, so unlike most of your writing. Some of it . . . some of it doesn't really make much sense, Rowan, so I thought maybe you could let Gabe take a look at it."

He's never suggested this—not once in a dozen years.

"What does Gabe have to do with this?" I ask. It's a strange thing to say with Gabe sitting right next to me, but like I said, Dave and I run deep. Gabe knows this. He barely turns to look at me, he's so focused on rubbing Lila's back.

The line is quiet again. And then Dave says, "Rowan, how about you take some time. For you and the baby. No one is expecting new work from you."

"Okay," I say numbly, embarrassed.

"Do you need anything from me?" Dave asks. "Is there anything I can do for you? Anything at all, you know I'm here for you."

I do know he's here for me. But what I need is my mind back, my postpartum hormones to level out, and my nipples to stop hurting so badly when I nurse—among other things—and that's not something he can do. (I'd also like a phone call or a text from June, telling me she's okay. I texted her last night and tried to sound calm and cool. I started with how nice it was to see her in the café, and then when she didn't respond I came out with it and asked if she was all right. She didn't text back.) "There's nothing I need from you," I say to my agent, trying to keep my voice from letting on how bad I feel.

Sylvie's opening the door, back again. She looks sheepish.

"I've got to go," I say into the phone. "My therapist is here."

We hang up. Sylvie compliments Lila's beauty and then tells us to follow her. I must be somewhat less paranoid, because I feel less like Sylvie is trying to figure out if I'm a fit mother and more like she might be trying to help me. We follow her through the door behind the kitchen into an office with neutral furniture and soft edges—pillows with tassels and a circular, tufted white coffee table. I scan the diplomas on the wall. I wonder if June's boss, Louisa, goes out to drinks with Sylvie, and if Louisa spills her problems. I don't picture Louisa with her doting husband being the kind of person who has too many problems, but what do any of us really know about each other? Practically nothing.

I've always liked Louisa, but she only represents actors, so we haven't had much interaction with her at WTA. Sometimes we see her out and about at WTA events and parties. When I called her last night about June there was so much worry in her voice. *Are you okay, Rowan?* she asked me, as if I was the one who'd gone missing, and then Gabe took the phone away to tell her what we knew about June. But Louisa hadn't seen June at all, not since the day before she went missing, when she abruptly told Louisa she needed some time off. Gabe said Louisa sounded kind of pissed, like June leaving came out of nowhere. But I'd bet it was hurt, not anger. Maybe, like me, Louisa had become attached to June.

"Sit here, Rowan," says Sylvie, gesturing to a beige settee. And then she surprises me: she motions for Gabe to sit on a different sofa, far enough away that I couldn't reach for his hand even if I wanted to.

"Let's talk about the birth," she says. She takes a seat equidistant from us, like the tip of an iceberg. She folds her hands in her lap and waits for me to start talking.

FOURTEEN

June. Four months ago. July 6th.

All these bodies swirling and writhing beneath the earth . . . *Good God.*

The hot chaos of the subway station is enough to take your breath away, but I'll have to get used to it, because now that I officially work at WTA starting tomorrow, I'm pretty sure this is the subway train I'll take to get there every day. I descend the final steps to the dank belly of the station where men, women, and children bump into me over and over. No one else seems to find it entirely disorienting, which I don't understand, because it's at least ninety degrees down here and we're packed in like caged animals. I try to take a deep breath and focus on getting closer to the edge of the track, but I'm all over the place and still on such a high after leaving Louisa. I keep replaying it in my mind—it's like a daydream that actually came true, the way she seemed almost proud walking me down WTA's hallway to fill out some paperwork. *This is June, my new assistant,* she said to Kai, who sat behind the front desk and looked genuinely happy to hear the news. What if this turns out to be a great thing for me? What if these people are kind, the sort of people who want to see you do well? What if this is the place that starts everything for me?

A PSA comes bellowing through the subway station—something about keeping New York safe, and warning us: *If you see something, say something.* Violin music plays nearby, but there are too many people in the way for me to see the musician. I'm edged up against a skinny guy with a mohawk when a deep rumble vibrates through the station. A woman pushes up against me with an umbrella, even though I've checked the weather six times today and no one predicted rain. The rumble picks up strength and now I'm pretty sure it must be the train. I move a little faster, trying to politely elbow past people to see if it's the F train, which Sean told me is *the best train in the city.* It seems like it's maybe the only convenient train from anywhere remotely near our apartment, so he might just be saying that to pump himself up. He does that a lot; he has all these convenient theories that reinforce his choices. Last night he tried to tell me vegetarians don't get enough B_{12}, which makes their hair fall out, and which is why he eats hot dogs every day. I feel like there might be a middle ground there, but I didn't say so because I'm trying to play nice with him. He's helped me so much, and it's not like I can offer much in return besides trying to be a good roommate. I know some people are just helpful like that, but he's on a different level. He sat with me for nearly an hour last night going over the whole New York City MTA travel map, explaining all the different neighborhoods and their vibes.

God, it's packed down here. I'm almost through the crowd. The rumbling has turned into screeching as I push through the final group of people, but then suddenly I'm standing too far over the painted yellow warning line at the edge of the track. The subway train careens toward me. *"Crap,"* I say beneath my breath, trying to back up, but it's useless. There's a mother behind me trying to shepherd her toddler closer to an enormous stroller covered with plastic, and I'm too scared I'll knock them over. A newborn stares at me through the crinkled plastic with big brown eyes. "Excuse me," I say to the mother, who's speaking rapidly to the toddler. She turns and I say, "Help." My hair is

sticking to my sweaty skin and wrapped around my neck like a tenta-
cle. The woman tries to back up, but there are too many people right
behind her. I'm so foolish. Why did I try to cut in front? The woman
is swearing beneath her breath now, and she makes a small amount of
headway moving backward, but now her stroller won't budge. I can't
move because I'm too scared I'll push into her stroller and somehow
hurtle her kids toward the train.

I take a breath.

The train's headlights are bright now, shining directly into my eyes
and straight through my brain. Seeing me. Can the conductor even stop
this thing in time if I lose my balance?

Stop being dramatic, June. You're not going to fall.

I straighten as tall as I can. There are still a few inches between me
and the edge of the track. As long as someone doesn't push up against
me I'll be okay.

Closer, closer.

The train is practically screaming at me—racing down the track at
forty miles an hour or so—when I feel a sharp bone against my back.
Someone's elbow.

No.

My toes dig into my shoes like I'm trying to grip the cement
beneath me, the yellow line too far gone now. *Vooooom* goes the train
as it wooshes past. The silvery cars blur in front of me, only inches
from my face. The bony elbow against my spine presses harder—*please
don't push me*—but then finally it falls away. Tears prick my eyes as the
train slows and comes to a creaking, breathy stop. The doors let out a
gasp as they crank open. The driver yells at everyone to let passengers
exit before they try to board. My legs shake as I step over the gap and
board the train.

I hold on to a smooth metal pole and think about how everything
is sharper here, more dangerous. This city isn't for ingenues; it's for
sharks. And I am not a shark. (At least, not yet.) I ride the train and

let my mind wander, thinking about all the ways this city is going to change me. I think of how out of place my parents seemed when they were here, and I wonder if me living here will make me less and less like them. How much of *where* we are determines *who* we are?

The doors open again on Fourteenth Street. Passengers push out, and an orange plastic seat becomes open, so I take it. My legs are sticky against it. I close my eyes and think of my mom holding the garden hose in her delicate grip and watering mums while the other parents looked on. They always watched her. And they seemed so lost and tired compared to her. Sometimes the other moms would wander over, sipping mugs that had things like *forty-ish!* on them, and they'd ask my mother about the bake sale at school or about her flower boxes or about the weather. They just wanted to be near her and hear her talk, and I didn't judge them because I understood perfectly what that felt like. And my mom didn't seem to judge them, either, or if she did she never said anything to me or any of her friends. She didn't have many friends, which took me a while to notice. She was social in the middle of a group, but she never took it to the next level, never invited anyone over for coffee. She could be friendly only for short bouts of time; otherwise it exhausted her. She read; she did Jane Fonda; she drank SlimFast; and when she felt up to it she worked the desk at my dad's auto body shop and photoshopped the stuff they hung on the wall. *Bathroom this way! Pay before you leave!* My dad was once a professional race car driver—there are pictures of him up in the shop, photos my mom framed and hung. She loved him back then: the thrill of him, who he was when he was performing in that way, at the top of his sex appeal, winning everything. I know that's a strange thing to say about my parents. But I can feel it like an undertow; anyone could figure it out if they bothered to get to know either of them. Then, when my mom was pregnant with my older brother, Jed, my dad got hurt and couldn't race anymore. He started drinking way too much, and by the time he got sober he'd already pissed and gambled away a lot of their savings. Then they had me, and I'm not sure my mom has ever forgiven Jed and me for tethering her to my dad like a noose.

I love my father so much it hurts my brain to think of it.

The doors open at Delancey Street and I'm out of the train again. I'm through the turnstiles and I'm on the stairs; I'm a phoenix rising into the steamy air of New York City, breathing like I've been born anew, on my way to the ramshackle home I'm trying to build here and fighting for scraps of the life I want.

On my way to Sean.

FIFTEEN

Rowan. Thursday morning. November 10th.

The birth?" I ask, squirming against the cushions on Sylvie's sleek settee. I'm trying to get comfortable, but I can't. "You need to take Lila's snowsuit off," I say to Gabe.

"Won't she wake up?" he asks me. A clock on the wall ticks so loudly I can count the beats. The clock seems an odd choice for a psychologist's office, but maybe it's me: lately all my senses are on fire. Motherhood has struck me like a tuning fork, and now the world feels electric; all the things I used to hear, touch, and taste were so bland compared with this.

"Maybe," I say with a shrug, like I'm a casual mom and not a terrified one. "But that's better than her getting too hot."

Sylvie glances from me to Gabe. I wonder what she thinks when she looks at him. Does she find him sexy? Most women do. He's got the right mix of dark and artistic combined with a powerful current that feels a lot like desire. When that desire is directed at you, you melt. Or at least, I did. I knew the moment he wrapped his arms around me and took me to bed I'd forget anyone else I'd ever been with. Being his wife has meant many things, and one of them is this: I'm always ready for him. I've never once turned him down. My body reacts to him in a way that doesn't feel normal given the number of years we've been together. I could leave him if I had to—I don't know what that must mean about us—but I'd never find someone who I want the way I want him.

"I'd like you to take me through what you remember about giving birth," Sylvie says. She's perched forward on her chair, looking less relaxed than I thought she'd be. "Anything you can think of," she's saying, "and you can start with sights and smells and sounds and we'll work into it."

"I was just thinking about how heightened all my senses feel since Lila got here," I say carefully.

"You're wired to protect Lila from the bear approaching your cave at night," Sylvie says. She swipes a delicate curl behind her ear and crosses her legs. "All of that is built deep into our limbic systems."

Are you a mother, too? I want to ask. Instead I study her face as though the answer's written there, but she mistakes the way I'm looking at her for confusion. Her speech is slower when she says, "When I say limbic systems, I'm referring to the part of our brain that's wired for taking care of our young, and for fight or flight."

I smile weakly; I obviously know what a limbic system is. Gabe is nodding along to Sylvie, which I find ironic because he'd roll his eyes if I said something like that to explain my anxiety.

"I know what a limbic system is," I say, and it comes out snottier than I mean it to. "Hippocampus, amygdala . . . the places for forming and cataloguing and attaching emotional content to memories, ironically," I go on. I'm sort of trying to make a joke, but mostly wanting her to know I'm not a total amateur at this therapy thing; I've been trying to get my brain under control for more than half my life. I was only sixteen when I had my first dark spell, the time my mom dropped me off at sleepaway theater camp deep in the Adirondacks armed with bug spray and my diary when I should have packed condoms. I bunked with two Jessicas who fought over our eighteen-year-old assistant director, and three weeks in, when they found out I was the one he was sleeping with, they mutinied. The rest of camp was agony, especially when the guy found some other girl to strip down and press against a tree. But it wasn't his rejection that hurt the most; it was the quicksilver change in the girls—the way they loved me at first and how fast they turned. *From love to hate.* It's common enough, isn't it? There were knives in the air between us every time I climbed into my bunk at night, and when we changed out of our pajamas in the morning, their eyes furtively swept my body as if they were trying to see what I had that they didn't. It was like they were trying to picture what I'd done with him. And it hit me in the gut: the aching realization I'd given away my virginity and any chance at friendships all in one shot. But maybe the Jessicas weren't to be trusted, anyway. *Not worth your time,* my mother told me when I arrived back home a teary mess, my period late. *You'll find your people,* she kept saying as I cried during the car ride back to New Jersey. Eventually I did find my people, but as a teenager it was too hard for me to sense which women were the good ones—friendship was too nuanced for me to really understand back then. When I started bleeding a month late I knew deep down it wasn't my period, a gush of blood too powerful to be anything other than what it really was. I imagined my summer washing away: the rabid jealousy of the Jessicas, the starlit nights beneath the cover of trees with the guy's hands all over my body, and even the time I had four beers and peed my bed and was too mortified to tell anyone, so I had to furiously wash my sheets in the sink. I was too much of a child to handle any of it, and it pushed me into my first dark place. It didn't lift until I joined a swim team that winter and made new friends.

"I need Gabe to let me see my friends again," I say to Sylvie, who's watching me like she can see my camp memories projected above my head. I'm specifically thinking of my friend Kim who lives on the Upper East Side and works in fashion and has eight-year-old twins and a darling towheaded four-year-old. Kim had so much advice for me when we used to meet for tea when I was pregnant, though now I can't recall much of it. It felt so helpful at the time, but none of my friends ever warned me about how hard breastfeeding was: the nipple and engorgement pain, the worry over the baby not getting enough milk, mastitis. I'm terrified that we'll go to Lila's next appointment and the pediatrician will weigh her and tell me she hasn't gained enough, that something is wrong with her and me and we can't make this thing that I thought would be so natural work. It's not natural, at least not for me, but still I want it so badly. I'm sure this is why women used to raise babies among aunts and mothers, so they could spot when there was a problem and help right away and give advice and take care of both the baby and the new mother. But even as I think about it, it feels too simplistic; it's another era, and it's not coming back, because now we value different things: independence, autonomy, careers that take off in the right cities. So now we have lactation consultants, and thank God for them, I guess, but there's nothing like your own mother/aunt/sister. Things could be way worse, I suppose. My mother could be dead.

"And how do you think seeing your friends might help?" Sylvie asks. She taps a finger against the arm of her chair. Her manicured nails are cream colored, and they glisten beneath the overhead lights like pearls. She doesn't wear a ring and I wonder if she's married; there aren't any photos up of kids or a husband, only a lone photo of Sylvie with people who look like they're probably her parents.

"Because isn't that what friends always do?" I ask, annoyed by her question. Lila squirms in Gabe's arms. *Take off her freaking snowsuit,* I try to telegraph to Gabe. Sylvie stares at me like this is a Jedi mind game. And then she waits. And I guess it works, because I say, "I know you want me to talk about Lila's birth, but I don't really remember it." I've said those words so many times it makes me sick to say them again now, but Sylvie only nods, like it's a starting point. I don't have the heart to tell her that it's not a starting point if there's nowhere to go after it: only darkness, an absence of memory, life lived and forgotten in a posttraumatic fugue. "I was very sedated," I say.

Gabe finally decides to take off Lila's snowsuit. I swear I see sweat lining the back of her hair, but I keep my mouth snapped shut. Sylvie's wall clock keeps on ticking, and I watch the way Gabe flinches when Lila's zipper creaks. She's so tiny inside that thing, and then Gabe slips her out like a fish. He props her up on his shoulder and grins when she doesn't wake up. That grin makes me love him again; it makes it so obvious we're on the same team, that we love Lila more than we've ever loved anyone including each other. It doesn't hurt the way it should to admit that; it just feels big and expansive, a love I want to live inside.

I exhale.

I need to get better—I need to try this. My memory feels like a porcelain bowl of water: everything and nothing at the same time, and not exactly something you can hold on to or shape the way you'd like, but still—my lips part to make words, something I know how to do better with a pencil but can do well nonetheless. "I remember before the birth, at the sonogram appointments, how Gabe and I used to watch the sonogram screen like it had the answer to everything. I can't really remember what we saw. It all feels blurry now. I have those pictures somewhere . . ." I sense Gabe turning away from me. In any room his eyes find a window, but there isn't one inside Sylvie's office. He busies himself smoothing Lila's terry cloth pajamas. Wonky yellow ducks on the feet of her jammies gape at us. "And the afternoon of Lila's birth I remember bleeding and ending up on my back in the street, and the ambulance being so bumpy, and I must have passed out, because the next thing I remember is waking up to see all the blood, the doctors' faces, how scared they all were. I remember hearing someone say, *The baby is out,* and I remember they tried to let me hold Lila, but I didn't feel completely there. I felt like I was underwater and losing touch with what I knew reality to be—I felt like I was holding her, but then still reaching for her somewhere else. I remember seeing a silver table with knives on it and scissors and maybe even the thread they used to stitch me up." My voice is edging higher. "Why didn't anyone put that all away?" I ask, my hands sweating against the sofa now. "Lila was so slippery," I say, sounding way more hysterical than I mean to, but I can't seem to help it. Those knives. "And I was so scared I'd drop her, and she'd get hurt, and I think that's why I started screaming. And then they sedated me. And that's what I remember."

A flash of memory comes to me: I see myself in a white nightgown with tiny blue flowers, blood on my fingertips. I haven't thought about the nightgown in years—I used to wear it as a young child. Anxiety floods me—it feels so real, as if I've gone back in time and inhabited my tiny helpless body. "There's this part of me that thinks," I start, my gaze holding Sylvie's, "that some of what happened at Lila's birth reminds me of my dad dying. The knives and the blood, I mean." After I say it, I freeze up.

Sylvie's nodding slowly. "Keep breathing, Rowan. I'm right here with you, and you're safe now, here in this office with your family and with me. It's safe to remember."

I don't say anything for what feels like a few minutes. Gabe's still patting Lila, sneaking glances at me. Finally, Sylvie asks in a gentle voice, "You were in the house when your father was killed, is that right?"

I hear Gabe suck in a breath. "W-what?" I stammer.

The clock ticks. Bile rises in my throat. And then, because I am polite and have been taught to answer questions posed to me by doctors, I say, "Yes. I was there. I was in my bedroom." My fingertips prickle in a way they usually only do when I feel the urge to write, and then the prickle turns into a burn that spreads like wildfire over my skin.

"What else do you remember?" Sylvie asks.

"I was five," I spit back, not wanting to give her the real answer.

She nods, calm as a saint, making me feel like a liar, like I'm trying to fool everyone with my act, like maybe I was there and killed him myself. Tears scorch my eyes, and when they run over my face I don't bother trying to wipe them away. How does she know what happened to my family? At some point during our last session, I told her my father wasn't around, that he'd been killed when I was little, but I didn't say it was murder or that it happened in our house. Did she google him? Did she google me?

"You seem offended," Sylvie observes.

Gabe pats Lila so quickly I almost scream at him to stop. The clock keeps up its rabid timekeeping—*tick tock tick tock*—and my brain starts to feel like it's misfiring. Something seems so incredibly wrong; it's like I can't stay in this room, like a part of me is back there in our old shabby house and my mother is screaming bloody murder. I can feel the hot August air on the back of my neck—the way my nightgown stuck to my flat chest. We didn't have air-conditioning; we always left the windows open at night, and I swear the smell of my mom's backyard roses is filtering through the window, but that can't be right, because you could only ever smell those from the back of the house and my bedroom was in the front.

"I *am* offended," I say to Sylvie, wanting to snatch back my past and bury it six feet below the earth where only I can find it. "I don't really know you well enough to be doing this with you, don't you agree?"

She gives me a small smile. "This is therapy. My only goal is to help you move forward."

"By speculating on my past?"

"Traumas from our childhood hold power over our present," Sylvie says. "Especially those for which we never received any professional help. The big ones like death and abuse, but so many others, even things that as adults we might perceive as small can be traumatic for a child. So when you mentioned the knives on a table during your birth triggering you to dissociate and feel, in your words, that you were losing touch with reality, it seems natural to me that you've observed this event was a look-alike for another traumatic event in your childhood. It doesn't get much more traumatic for a five-year-old than the murder of her father in her own home, while she was present, wouldn't you agree?"

My heart pounds. I need to stall—I'm not ready to do this in front of Gabe. The truth is that I *did* see the knife, and I've never told anyone that, because frankly: I never told anyone anything. My mom said I would just go stone-faced and silent when the police tried questioning me. That night my dad died, the knife was on the floor right near his shoulder, too muted for me to catch sight of at first. It was there like an afterthought, like someone had forgotten a run-of-the-mill kitchen knife on a cutting board. It was barely bloody, just a few specks of something I didn't recognize as parts of my father's body.

"How do you know about my father?" I ask Sylvie.

She stares at me. I wait, ready to hear her admit that she looked into me: maybe she read my interviews, how I answer every journalist who asks me why it is I really write mysteries with some variation on the sick satisfaction I get when I expose the real killer, something no one could ever do for my father and my family.

"Gabe told me," Sylvie says plainly.

I whip my head around to look at my husband. His cheeks are flushed—maybe from embarrassment?—and he's bouncing Lila just slightly in his arms. Her tiny face is tucked into the warm skin of his neck. He looks at me, but I only see sadness. I turn back to Sylvie.

"I didn't see my father killed," I say. I should just tell her about the knife. "There was a scuffle, and then me running down the hall to see my mother on the phone with nine-one-one while my father lay at her feet." I turn to look at my daughter, but my eyes won't stay there. I look down into my pale hands, my nails that I painted bright red on the bathroom floor last night when I couldn't sleep. "I did see the crime scene, and I remember every inch of it."

SIXTEEN

June. Four months ago. July 6th.

I stick my key into the lock and twist. One smooth turn and then *clank!*—the key takes the clunky jump it needs to unlock my apartment each time. These little quirks are what make the apartment feel like my home: the pea-green paint peeled in a star shape in the corner of the bathroom; the way it always smells like bread because the old woman down the hall bakes a loaf each day; and the way the radiator comes to life every hour or so with a sound like it's the Wild West and bullets are being set free inside a saloon.

Inside our apartment Sean's standing in our crappy kitchen wearing an actual freaking apron. There's a laugh fizzing on my tongue like Pop Rocks, and thank God I swallow it down, because in the split second it takes me to process the scene I realize he's not trying to be ironic with the apron. He's completely serious, standing there with a butcher's knife raised like he's about to take off a chicken's head. Half-split garlic cloves are everywhere—on the cutting board, the counters, the scent wafting through the apartment in a cloud so thick I'm surprised I can't see it. We don't have a kitchen table because our apartment is way too small to fit one into, but our coffee table is set with antique china and meticulously arranged silverware in what I know is the correct order because of my waitressing days.

"Sean," I say, whistling appreciatively. "Holy cow."

"Yes," he says, setting down the butcher's knife. He's got a thing for knives. He always carries around a Swiss Army knife like a Boy Scout. "Literally: *holy cow*," he says, pointing to the food. "That's meat sauce you see, one hundred percent grass fed." There's a heaping pile of pasta sprinkled with parmesan. (I would never, ever tell him that I hate parmesan—I would rather eat dirt than speak those words out loud in this moment.) I watch him move to the old-fashioned record player he keeps near his aquarium. "You're late, June," he says, taking a Johnny Cash record out of its sleeve. I've noticed he uses my name when he's annoyed at me.

"Am I?" I ask, not sure how I can be late coming from an interview I had no control over.

Sean places the needle onto the track as carefully as you'd set down a newborn. Johnny Cash's "I Walk the Line" starts playing, soft and oh so solemn. "You said you'd be home by six," he says, not looking at me.

I said I'd probably be home around six. But when he looks up at me, I smile instead of saying anything. The music makes it easier.

"Sit," he says, gesturing to a spot on the floor.

I crouch down in front of our coffee table—but in doing so I feel too much like an obedient dog, so I get up and walk to our sink. I try to take some control back as I wash my hands, gently swaying to Johnny Cash. I'm happy to be a cooperative roommate, especially after Sean went to all this trouble to make dinner, but I also don't like the way he sometimes makes me feel like a windup doll he can control. I flash another smile over my shoulder as I dry my hands. "The table looks divine," I say. "And the food smells amazing." The compliment clearly pleases him. His face is so insanely readable.

I move back to the table, but this time I grab a pillow from the couch to put under my butt before sitting down on the floor. It's embroidered with a kitschy **HOME IS WHERE THE HEART IS**, and as soon as I sit on it Sean is bending toward me. "Not that pillow," he scolds, his face darkening. He practically rips it out from beneath me and sets it on the couch as carefully as he handled the record. It's weird. Or maybe I'm weird for sitting on one of his throw pillows. I don't know, I wasn't really brought up in a fancy enough way to be sure of myself with stuff like that. "Sorry," I say quickly. "My tailbone has just really been bothering me."

He glares at me like he doesn't believe me, and he's not wrong; I keep finding myself in a tangle of white lies when I'm with him.

"My mother made that pillow," he says in a monotone, and I realize I've never asked him about his parents, and he's never brought them up. "Use this one," he says, tossing me the kind of pillow that's too hard to be comfortable.

"Thanks," I say, trying to position it beneath me, already sliding off the curve.

Johnny Cash talk-sings at us as Sean sits on the floor across from me and admires the gorgeous table setting. "Wait, we need candles," he says. He goes to get up, but I don't want candles—I don't want this to feel romantic at all.

"I have good news," I blurt. "Sit. Don't worry about candles."

"Fine," he says with a sigh, suddenly dispassionate about the whole thing. He sits and considers me with a suspicious look on his face, like I'm about to say something that will set fire to this bizarre game of house we've been playing.

"Louisa Smith gave me the assistant job on the spot today," I say, so happy about my news I can't do anything but hold it out in my hand like treasure.

Sean's mouth drops so far, I almost laugh. And then he says, *"Shut up,"* like a preteen.

"Swear to God," I say, hand on my heart.

"Wow, June, that's amazing!" he says. He sounds like a little kid on Christmas, and it feels so genuine I give him my first real laugh in days.

"Thank you so much for getting me the interview," I say.

"It was nothing," he replies with a gracious wave. "We have to do a toast."

"Okay," I say, still grinning.

He pours us each three inches of cabernet from an already-uncorked bottle on the table. We raise our glasses, and it all feels so adult.

"To you," he says. I'm about to take a big sip when he adds, "And to us."

The wine sours a notch as I force myself to repeat the words. "To us," I say, and he looks so pleased. I start to drink along with him and the wine burns down my throat. I cough. I swear I can feel it land all at once inside my stomach in a dark red pool. And then Sean says, "Tell me everything, my pretty little thing."

My mother always called me pretty, like it was the thing she was most proud of. Sean moves closer and a tiny voice inside my head starts to scream, but I stifle it, smiling at him, wanting more than anything to make this work.

SEVENTEEN

Rowan. Thursday morning. November 10th.

We have options available to us, Rowan," Sylvie is saying as I sweat. "There are evidenced-based therapies specifically designed for the treatment of PTSD." She turns to Gabe, but he's not looking at her. She says to him, "For our next session, it might be helpful if you stay at home with Lila and I work with Rowan alone."

Gabe is staring hard at me. I see so many emotions written on his face, but mostly fear and love. And those are really the only big ones, aren't they? Everything else is mostly just an offshoot.

"Fine," I say, my eyes still locked on Gabe. My husband; my protector; the person I thought I'd be with forever. Why do things feel this broken? I turn back to Sylvie and ask, "Do you know our babysitter's missing?"

Gabe lets out a grunt that sounds like exasperation. "She's not *missing*, Rowan," he says. "You make it sound like she's been kidnapped."

"Maybe she has," I say. "She's still basically a kid. A kid we brought into our sick lives and tortured."

There I go. Somewhere dark. No coming back.

"Do you believe you tortured your sitter?" Sylvie asks.

Oh my God. Therapy. "Didn't you hear what I said?" I snap. "Is this really all about me? I just told you June was missing."

"Yes, but I'm your therapist. I'm not the police."

I exhale. Gabe says, "We didn't torture June. We employed her."

"I think Gabe liked that she worshipped him," I say. I don't meet his eyes, but I feel them boring into the side of my face.

"What is *that* supposed to mean?" Gabe asks, his knee bouncing up and down in the corner of my vision, and this time it's not for Lila. He's nervous.

I turn to him now, feeling slightly sorry for myself, and for him, too. Maybe even for Lila, that this family she's been born into already has cracks. "Come on, Gabe," I say. "Can't you even admit to that, at least?" What is it with him being so unable to admit when he's done something? "I'm not even saying it's wrong," I say, "only that it's true. It's natural to enjoy someone worshipping you."

"June didn't worship me," he says. "If anything, she seemed to worship *you*."

The air is very still. I sniff to break the silence, to hear my body make some kind of noise signaling my actuality, to know I'm really *here* and that this isn't another bad dream.

"That might be partly true," I say. June worshipped me the same as anyone who values talent. It's not everyone, but it does exist: people who are so fascinated to learn you make your living singing/drawing/sculpting/painting/writing/acting, people who want to be close to you, to see if it's as magical as they think. It isn't, of course. "But I think June felt sorry for me by the end," I say to Sylvie. "Can I hold my baby, please?" I ask Gabe.

Sylvie crosses her legs again.

"Rowan, please, she's so quiet," Gabe says, his hands so big on Lila's tiny bottom.

She *is* quiet. For now.

"Fine," I say. I feel like such a brat in this room. Maybe everyone does in therapy? I'm not used to everything being about me outside my work life. (And I can admit that it's like that in my work life: it's all, *How are you feeling about this novel, Rowan? Do you need more time? Should we extend the deadline? I don't want to get in the way of your process, Rowan. Do you like the cover? Are you happy with marketing?* It's a person from the publishing house making sure the hotel is perfect when I go on book tours, and it's a gentle email reminding me about my speaking engagements that month, and it's how any uncomfortable conversations are had through my agent. Dave deals with anything unsavory, not me.)

But I'm not like that in my personal life. I'm not perfect, but I'm a good friend, a good neighbor. I don't litter and I call people on their birthdays. And I'm certainly not a diva in my marriage. Gabe is the center of our universe, the eye of the hurricane, the volcano about to erupt. He can't separate his creative genius from the person who needs to unload the dishwasher.

"Tell me about June," Sylvie says. "I've met her once, briefly, at WTA, and I've heard a lot about her from Louisa, but mostly professional things. Louisa was happy with June as an assistant, but I should be transparent and tell you that I know Louisa was displeased when June started dating Harrison."

I nod because I understand why Louisa would feel that way, but I don't say anything. It feels a little off that Sylvie's bringing up the personal connections at play here. Though I guess she's only seeing me as a favor to Louisa, so maybe it's all out in the open anyway, and more casual than it would normally be.

Gabe won't look at either of us. He's staring down at Lila's head, clearly wanting nothing to do with this conversation.

"June was very beautiful," I say softly.

"Was?" Sylvie says.

I shrug again. I can't help it. "She could be dead," I say.

It's the first thing I've ever said to Sylvie that seems to surprise her.

"Dead?" she repeats. "What would make you say something like that?"

"I don't know," I say. "Just a feeling. Not like I can necessarily trust the things I feel, lately."

"Why don't we start there?"

"With June being dead?"

"No, Rowan. With you not being able to trust the things you feel."

Tick, tock goes the clock, like something out of one of Gabe's movies. Sylvie doesn't look at Gabe, only me. She asks, "Why don't you tell me more about those dreams and fantasies you've been having about harm coming to your baby?"

"Okay," I say slowly, wanting to talk about anything but this. I think of a particularly awful nightmare I had last night about Lila and me on a too-small boat careening into a deep navy sea, the wood of the sailboat splintering beneath our bare feet, the creeping knowledge that we were going to sink filtering through my half-awake state. I woke with hands flailing for a life preserver for both of us. Gabe was nowhere; he wasn't in the dream, and he wasn't in the bed when I fully woke up. He came back at midnight and told me he couldn't sleep, that he needed to get out, to walk the streets.

I open my mouth to try to put the nightmare into words, and a swell of dread rises within me.

EIGHTEEN

June. Three months ago. August 2nd.

On the first Tuesday in August I'm sorting through screenplays in my cubicle outside Louisa's office. We've settled into an easy working pattern, and the longer I'm here at WTA—three weeks and five days but who's counting?—the easier it is to slip through the office like every interaction isn't the biggest deal in the world. I mean, of course I want my big break to happen here, but I also really enjoy working for Louisa: our easy banter and our jokes, how we talk about our lives to each other, and how we stay in the office working later than almost anyone else.

Louisa gives me loads of acting business advice, and she got me a discount with an acting coach she knows. I start classes with the woman in three weeks. I knew I truly, deeply liked and cared for Louisa one weekend morning when I was at a sidewalk sale on Spring Street and bought a pair of earrings for eighteen bucks that I just knew she'd love. She squealed when I gave them to her and wore them to work four days in a row. And then I saw a picture she posted from the weekend with her therapist-friend Sylvie, and Louisa was wearing them then, too, and she had a huge smile on her face, which made me think: *Please get pregnant soon, please let that be the news you have for me one Monday morning . . .*

I add the three screenplays I read in the last two days to piles with my sticky notes. Sorting screenplays into four piles—*bad, medium, pretty good, you have to read this!*—is my new job, and I absolutely love it. It turns out I can read a 120-page screenplay in around two hours and have something intelligent (or at least, semihelpful) to tell Louisa. Sometimes I even take them home with me. I feel so important carrying them on the subway, all the pages bound and topped with a blue cover marked *Williamson Talent Agency*. Plus, telling Sean I have to work each night is a great way to get him off my back. He's increasingly suffocating, like a bad smell you can't figure out, so most nights I tuck in early and lock my door. And it turns out I love reading screenplays—getting swept away, imagining them as movies playing through my mind (and, admittedly, sometimes imagining myself playing the lead)—and then reporting back to Louisa in the morning. I like it even more than going out drinking. Who knew? It's the kind of thing my parents would be proud of, if I had those kind of parents. I just don't think my dad would even understand this world of talent agencies, so I keep the details short when I call home. Mostly we just talk about the weather and my dad's shop. But maybe I'm underestimating my dad; maybe I should tell him more. My mom sounds a little off lately, like she's about to tank. I really should take a weekend trip up to see them and check.

As I file away the latest screenplay, Kai pops her head over my cubicle.

"Heya," she says. We've been out for cheap dinners three times during the past few weeks. It's sealed us as office friends.

"What's up?" I ask with a smile. Having a friend has already made me feel more at ease in this city. Before Kai, I really just had Sean and Louisa, and New York City isn't really the kind of place where you meet other women at bars and exchange numbers so you can go get coffee together or go to the gym.

"My friend is throwing down in Williamsburg on Saturday, do you wanna come?" Kai asks.

"A party?" I ask. It's only taken me these few weeks in New York to realize there aren't house or apartment parties the way there were in college and anywhere else I've lived. Everyone here seems to meet at a bar or restaurant.

"Yup," says Kai. "A proper party. At their loft."

Loft. I love that word. I imagine buying one when—*if!*—I get my big break. "Sure," I say, smiling, and then Harrison Russell rounds the corner with his head down, looking at his phone. He pops his gaze up when he sees Kai and me and smiles. He pays so much attention to me. Kai's kind of aloof with him—maybe because she has a serious girlfriend and isn't charmed by him, but more likely because she knows it's better to keep things professional at work, and I'm sure that's a smarter way than mine: I keep halfway flirting back when he makes jokes with me, because he's cute and he's not married, and I kind of can't help it.

"Hello, Harrison," I say. WTA is a first-name-only kind of place. Even when recognizable actors come in, we still use first names; our higher-ups coach us to act casual with them and never starstruck. Last week I rode the elevator with an actress I've loved since I was little and she starred in my favorite Disney show, and I felt like I was going to pee my pants, but on the outside I was calm as pond water.

"June," Harrison says, staring down into my cubicle. There's an adorable dimple in his smooth skin, and his eyes are the darkest blue. He always gets this look on his face like he's delighted to see me. It's really sweet, and frankly, it makes me feel so good. "Working hard, I trust?" he asks. He has a formal way of speaking that I love.

Kai's out of Harrison's sight line, and I catch her roll her eyes. "Gotta go," she says, and then she takes off down the hall. I watch her slip through a doorway and disappear.

"I *am*," I say to Harrison. "Well, I'm reading right now." I gesture at the next screenplay I'm about to start, something someone submitted to us to consider for one of Louisa's actresses. Sometimes I catch myself thinking of Louisa and me as an *us*, and it gives me a little buzz.

"I wish my assistant was an industrious reader like you," Harrison says.

I grin. Harrison's assistant is a sixty-five-year-old woman named Madge who meticulously runs his whole show and has worked for him forever. So no matter what he says, I've been at WTA long enough to know he'd never give her up, and that even if she were an industrious reader, he's way too much of a control freak to hand over scripts to an assistant. I smile and let these things go unsaid.

"Have you had lunch yet?" he asks.

My heart picks up. "Um," I stall. He's never asked me anything like that before, nothing that could even hint at the idea of us hanging out beyond the glamorous perimeter of WTA. I feel the furious urge to lie, but the truth is I just ate. And I don't have enough money to buy lunch twice, even if the likelihood is that he would pay. Plus, I would feel ridiculous asking Louisa to go to lunch twice in one day.

"I just got back, actually," I say. His eyes are so bright in this light. He always looks like he's up to something, like he's toying with an idea for an adventure he might include you in, if you're lucky.

"Oh," he says. How old is he? Early thirties, maybe? "Well, then how about coffee after work. I'd take you for a drink, but I'm sober."

My blood starts moving faster. He's asking me on a date. Coffee is a date, right?

"I would like that," I say, my words careful. I'm so nervous I can't breathe right. I'm definitely interested, but I'm not sure if I'm not supposed to see anyone outside the office like that. But maybe he means as friends? I mean, I go out with Kai, so what's the difference?

A whole lot, probably. What if Louisa gets mad?

Or what if Harrison wants to take me out because he thinks I have something special and the agency should represent me?

He smiles his perfect grin and I smile back, wondering where in the world this is going to go, and hoping it's somewhere good.

"Great," he says. "One of my writers, Gabe O'Sullivan, has a table reading at eight. So if you're still free after that coffee we could grab dinner, too, and catch the reading."

Gabe O'Sullivan. Writer of the blockbuster movie *Enemy* among a bunch of others. And a table reading? That's when actors get together to read through a script start to finish, and it's the kind of thing only insiders get to see. There's no blocking (when the director moves them around), it's just a first read to hear what everyone sounds like together and to get a feel for the play or film script. I've never been to one, of course—I've only read about them in my acting books. "Is it a new play?" I ask. "I thought he only wrote movies."

A relaxed grin settles on Harrison's face. He likes talking about his clients. A lot of the agents here are like that; they don't seem comfortable in the spotlight the way the actors do, but they like championing someone else. Louisa says that for some agents (and I think she'd put Harrison in this category) it's partly ego—they get a rush negotiating the deals and going to power lunches that Louisa says are exactly as you imagine them to be: producers, directors, actors, and writers all sitting around a table talking about projects that may or may not come to fruition.

I would still give anything to be at that table.

"Gabe writes everything," Harrison says, leaning farther into my cubicle, confident now. "The man is a force."

"A force," I repeat. "I like that."

He waits. I study his face, seeing only the slightest bit of nervousness left on it.

"I'd love to see a table reading," I say, grinning, putting an end to any doubt he might have. I can't keep the excitement out of my voice, and I know he hears it. He's smiling, too.

"It's a date then," he says. "Come to my office when you're done working. Don't let Louisa keep you too late."

A date. I shove down the wish that he'd called it a business meeting, or whatever you'd call it when you take out a person you think might be right for your agency. But you never know—this could all lead anywhere. The point is that someone like him wants to hang out with someone like me. And that could be a very good thing.

NINETEEN

Rowan. Friday morning. November 11th.

After a particularly sleepless night, I'm outside the care facility waiting to introduce Lila to my mother.

June is still gone.

I know this because I called the detective last night around seven, right after I got Lila down for the first time. *Just looking for an update, Mr. Patricks,* I said to him in a voice chiller than I'd intended, and after he gave me a bit of a hard time about being uncooperative on our first phone call, he told me that June was now officially a missing person and her case had been turned over to the New York City Police Department.

The wind picks up, whistling over the silver metal railing along the ramp that zigzags toward the entrance of the gray cement building marked THORNDALE SENIOR LIVING. I'm so on edge my teeth hurt. And it's brutally cold, so if they keep me out here waiting another minute I'm just going to have to brave the germs and head inside. On the phone yesterday I told the nurses my concerns about bringing in such a young baby, and they suggested I arrive during the residents' rest period when everyone would be inside their rooms and Lila would be exposed to fewer people. They said they'd send a nurse out and she'd take me right to my mom.

When I told the pediatrician about my mother's condition and asked about bringing Lila to the care facility to meet her, she said, *If it were me, I'd visit my mother. You'll never forgive yourself if something happened to your mom and she never met your little girl.*

I didn't tell the pediatrician about bringing Lila into a café to meet with June. Because that just feels stupid and naïve the more I think about it. And I *can't* seem to stop thinking about it: it's like an insane loop of doubt and self-punishing thoughts ever since Lila's been born. I can't stop berating myself for all the mistakes I've made; I'm practically counting seventy-two hours since that café date, trying to listen carefully for any sounds of a sniffle, feeling for any elevated temp. And now after I take her inside to meet my mom I'll just have to start the clock all over again.

The worry feels endless.

Finally a nurse comes out. "Can't be careful enough!" she says in a cheerful Irish accent, pointing to her green surgical mask.

"Thank you," I say. "I really appreciate it."

"Come inside before you catch your death," she says. The turn of phrase unsettles me. It sounds off-kilter coming from someone so young.

I hold Lila tightly as we head through the glass doors. I've got one of those breathable muslin blankets to drape lightly over her head as we walk down the halls—I figure it has to be better than nothing, and it's not like I can put a mask on a newborn. But the halls are mostly empty. The linoleum is squeaky clean, and I've never been so grateful for the smell of Lysol. We pass a room with an elderly woman keening. She quiets down for a moment, and then asks, "Where is my brother? My brother, Jack? Where is he?"

"So how's the baby?" the nurse asks as we walk toward my mother's room. She's all sunshine, seemingly unbothered by the crying woman, who looks to be in her nineties. Her brother is probably dead.

"Um," I say, a lump rising in my throat. Thank God other people are tougher than me so they can do these types of caretaking jobs while I just make up useless stories from the safety of my apartment. "The baby is wonderful," I say. I peek beneath the muslin and kiss the top of her dark head.

"And how's your recovery going?" the nurse asks. "I had terrible postpartum depression."

It startles me. Not that she's so forthcoming (which I appreciate) but that she's already had a baby. She looks early twenties. "Well, I'm not really sure what's wrong with me," I say, figuring I owe her honesty like she gave me. Wouldn't the world be such a better place for parents if we all did this? "My therapist seems to think I've got PTSD from having such a traumatic birth, and I definitely have postpartum anxiety—I can feel it coursing through me like a dark, frantic river—but I wouldn't call it depression." I don't feel hopeless—it's the opposite, actually: the hope I feel for Lila and me and our future together is enough to crush me; it's a blinding light, an expanding balloon, a palm opening to hold mine. It's all the things that might be.

"Hmmm," says the nurse as we pass an orderly pushing a cleaning cart packed with Windex, tissues, and tiny shampoo and conditioner bottles. "I'm sorry to hear that your birth was traumatic."

"I almost bled out," I say.

I can see her red eyebrows rise. "Really?" she asks. "Your mom didn't tell me."

"She doesn't know," I say, surprised she thinks that anyone would ever tell that to my mother in the state she's in. "We didn't want to upset her," I add.

"Your mother can handle more than you think," she says.

I remember the last time I came here; my stomach was so big I couldn't get comfortable sitting beside my mom in the bed, so they brought in a recliner. "But she gets so agitated when she's confused,"

I say to the nurse, "and I guess I figured it could work the other way around, too, like if we upset her, it could make her worse."

"I don't think it works like that," the nurse says. "But you'd have to ask her doctor."

We walk the rest of the way in silence, and in the doorway of my mother's room, the nurse says, "Good luck," and I can tell by her eyes that she's smiling behind her mask. She swings open the door for me. "Mrs. Gray," she says softly to my mother, "you have visitors." And then she leaves us alone.

"Mom," I whisper, but she doesn't turn. She's sitting very still on the edge of her bed, looking out the window to one of the semidecent views the facility offers for slightly more money: a small pond is visible just beyond the parking lot. Her profile is backlit by the winter sun, and I can make out the sharp features I've loved my entire life: the strong forehead sloping down to a tiny nose, high cheekbones, skin stretched but still remarkably unwrinkled by age. Her tiny lips always look pursed these days, like she's unsure of what exactly she should do about this predicament we've found ourselves in. "Mama," I say, something I haven't called her since I was a child, but it comes out just like that, like I'm a little girl again and I need her more than anything. I whip off the muslin blanket from Lila and my fist tightens around it until it's sweaty in my grip. Lila's perfect head peeks out of her carrier beneath my jacket, and the way I love her—somehow even more in this moment, and in each new moment—is nearly too much to take.

Finally my mom turns. There's always this instant, a small breath of air before I know whether she'll be lucid enough to know who I am. I bite back the urge to say, *It's me.* Or even: *It's us.* Because sometimes that makes it worse.

But then my mom smiles and I see she knows exactly who we are, and the relief that floods me could fill a sea. "Rowan," she says, the word as magical as birthday candles. Her skinny, veined hands go to the sides of her face. Her knuckles seem more knotted and pronounced each time I come, but none of that matters now, because she says, "Lila," and the sound of it makes me gasp. I've never loved my daughter's name as much as I do hearing it from my mother's lips.

"Lila," I say to both of them, like it's a melody I've waited to play.

My mother just stares, and then I'm zipping off my coat and tossing it onto a chair and going closer, closer and my mother is taking in my baby like she cannot believe any of it is real. The moment feels suspended in time, held in place by golden seams that promise not to bust until we're ready to leave this place.

But then it's over. Everything I thought was happening was only my own magical thinking, because my mother looks into the doorway behind me like she's searching for someone, and she opens her mouth and I can see her about to ask whether or not I've brought my father. "Mom," I say, but I'm too late.

"Where is he?" she asks. Bingo. Every time.

Please don't leave us now; please don't ask about Dad.

New tears burn my eyes. "Mom?" I say carefully. I want to take Lila out of her carrier. I want my mother to hold her, to coo over her, to tell me that she's perfect and that she's beautiful and so meant to be. I want my moment back.

"Gabe isn't coming," I say, trying a different tactic. "Neither is Elena."

"Gabe?" my mom asks. She only looks a little confused, not totally gone, but sometimes this happens right before a big episode. It's almost like a gentle slip, and she either snaps back into shape or we lose her entirely.

"You remember it's just Lila and me today, no Gabe or his mom," I say, keeping my voice light, trying to breeze over this, trying to come back from it. "I was hoping it could be just us."

My mother's blue eyes are on fire. They bore into mine.

"Rowan," my mother says carefully. She looks like she's trying to understand something. But then she asks, "Are you all right?" and I think of all the nights after my father died when we buried ourselves under the covers and she held me tightly and asked me the same thing. I think of the books she read to me. I think about how I learned the arc of story from those books, the delicate beginnings, the murky middles, and the dramatic and cathartic endings. Even children's books follow the rules, and when I write, so do I.

"I'm fine, Mom," I say, giving it everything I have even though I've never been this tired, this scared, or this hopeful. I carefully unfasten the baby carrier and ask my mother, "Do you want to hold your granddaughter?"

The air in the room goes still while I wait for her to answer.

TWENTY

June. Three months ago. August 2nd.

I can barely focus on scripts for the rest of the day, so instead I organize Louisa's filing cabinets and listen to her taking phone calls in the background. At least a dozen times I think I'm going to tell Louisa about Harrison asking me to go to the reading, but each time I chicken out. At six twenty she gets off a call with an actor who's upset about his billing on a new TV show, and she says to me, "June, you're a lifesaver. I'm going to feel so much more organized."

"But are you sure we shouldn't scan all of this?" I ask her. "What if this place burns down and you lose all your stuff?"

She waves a hand. "You must think I'm so old-fashioned."

"I do!" I say, and we both laugh. And then we hear a knock, and we're still laughing when Harrison opens the door, and that's the very moment when I wish more than anything I'd already told Louisa about him taking me to coffee and Gabe O'Sullivan's reading tonight. I know right then that not telling her was the worst choice.

"Hey," Louisa says to Harrison from behind her desk. It's obvious she thinks he's here to talk to her. She's smiling pleasantly just like she usually is at the end of the day when we're working together; evenings are her favorite time.

I'm sitting on the floor, papers everywhere. I'm facing Harrison, and he takes one look at my face and figures out I haven't said anything to Louisa about tonight. Agents are master readers of other people's faces and voices—it's uncanny, really. Louisa spends half her day sniffing out potential problems and defusing them before her clients even know anything was afoot.

"So I mentioned this to June earlier," Harrison says slowly, "but she thought she might be working late, so we never really firmed it up."

I'm marveling at how he's playing this. He smiles at Louisa, and it looks so different from the way he smiles at me. "Gabe O'Sullivan has a table reading at Playwrights Horizons," he says.

"That's nice," Louisa says mildly. And then she's quiet, waiting for him to say more.

"I thought I could take June," Harrison says, "if she's done in time. I thought it might be nice for her to meet some of the people at Playwrights and to see a reading in action."

Louisa stiffens. She hasn't taken me anywhere, and I don't know if she's being territorial and thinking that she should be the one to bring me to industry events, or if she's feeling bad because she hasn't yet (not that I've been expecting it), or maybe that she's unhappy because this sounds like a date and office romances—while not forbidden—are frowned upon.

I watch her face until I can't anymore. "I can finish all of this before I go," I say a little desperately, gesturing to the papers stacked in rectangular piles on the floor.

"Don't be silly, June," Louisa says.

I turn to look at her again—to really look, to somehow telegraph that she's my first choice and that if she's not okay with this I won't go.

"You should go," she says, smiling a modest and very fake smile. "Harrison's right." The smile fades into something more practical. "It would be good for you to go to Playwrights and see a reading. You're reading such a wide variety of scripts these days, by writers of very different calibers. But the ones chosen to be performed at Playwrights are top notch. You're sure to see something good."

"Oh, this O'Sullivan script is genius," Harrison says. "It's unlike anything he's done before. Very quiet and unsettling."

Louisa's back is up again, and I think, *Shut up, Harrison, now's not the moment to be an agent.*

She looks at me and only me. "Have fun tonight and soak it in, June. It's always good to see writing and acting performed at a high level. And this is a great idea," she says, twirling her ergonomic chair until she almost loses her balance. She recovers. "Really, I should start taking you to more things," she says with a wave. "It's just, you know most of my clients are in films and not plays, but there *is* a film festival coming up next month that we could go to together . . ." Her smile is forced not because she doesn't mean what she says: it's because she has to say it in front of Harrison. The tension in the room is so thick it makes me sure they've had bad blood in the past.

"I would love that," I tell her, meaning it more than anything, but also very much meaning this next thing I say: "But I also like just hanging out here with you. It's more fun than I had in college."

This makes Louisa burst out laughing. "Okay," she says. "Well, that makes me happy." We grin at each other like we're the only ones there, like Harrison isn't a part of us and won't ever be, and like that's for the better. He shifts his weight. His shadow passes over one of my piles.

"Well then," he says, pulling Louisa and me apart with his deep baritone voice. "Let's get going." I can feel the weight of his gaze even though I'm still locked on Louisa. I turn around and he smiles. "The night is young, June," he says, but it's like he's saying it to Louisa, to push the envelope and make it sound even more exciting than it maybe even is, to get in one little jab before we go.

"All right," I say. "I'll just get my stuff."

Louisa gives me one more smile, but this one is wistful, the way I've only seen my mom look at me before I leave the house, like each time could be the last time and there's really nothing either of us can do about it.

"Goodbye," I say.

"Have a good night, June," Louisa says, but I'm already out the door, a zap of electricity across my skin, the one I'm always looking for. A smile cracks on my face.

"Let's go," I whisper, quiet enough that only I can hear it.

TWENTY-ONE

Rowan. Friday morning. November 11th.

My mom's wide blue eyes are on Lila now, not me.

"Of course I want to hold my granddaughter," she says. I sit in the chair beside her unmade bed. The white covers are spotted with yellow sunflowers. It surprises me that it's already eleven a.m. and that an orderly hasn't been here to tidy her room, especially when the staff knew I was coming. There are tissues on my mom's bedside table, and crumpled balls of paper nearly topple over the edge of her tin wastebasket.

My hands are shaking against Lila's body as I take her out of the carrier. Her brown eyes are open, looking up at me, which surprises me because usually when she wakes she cries out to nurse. The lactation consultant told me I'll know she's satisfied with enough milk when she seems awake but relaxed, hands unclenched. But right now I see her little fists balled tight as ever. I need to nurse her straight away, as soon as my mom is done holding her, and all the things I want this moment to be make me fluttery with anticipation. "Lila," I say to my little girl, "are you ready to meet your grandmother?"

My mother makes a noise that sounds like a gasp, but sometimes even regular things my mom does make me nervous, like any slight neurological twitch could be the signal that another dementia episode is upon us. I pass Lila over faster than I mean to, but my mother is ready, her arms strong and sure as she takes my baby and cradles her, like this is the thing mothers are meant to do, that this is, in fact, what our arms are meant for.

I don't cry.

I stare at my mom and Lila, my heart full to bursting. I love them so deeply I can hardly take it; it's like staring into sunlight or diving into a black hole, so much feeling and power I can almost glimpse creation itself.

"Gray," my mom says, shaking her head. "You are so very beautiful."

I freeze again. My jaw is so tight I'm worried it'll break.

"No, Mom," I say, frustration rising within me no matter how saintly I want to be in my mother's presence. "Her name is Lila. Lila Gray."

My mother looks up at me. "Oh, right, of course," she says. And then. "Rowan, this baby is just heavenly."

"She is," I say. "I love you, Mom."

"And I love you."

Lila stares up at my mother. She opens and closes her mouth and I know she's hungry, and I have to sit on my hands to keep them from taking her back.

Just let them enjoy this moment, I think, and my rational mind knows an extra few minutes without milk won't matter in the grand scheme of things, but my body thinks something different: my chest has filled with milk, and I can feel some leak out into my bra, and all I can think about is those drops adding up to an ounce going to waste, and then I say, "Mom?" and my mother says, "You want to nurse her, don't you?" and the feeling of being understood by another mother, especially my own, is enough to fill me with everything.

"Yes," I say, confidence swelling within me. "I do."

My mom passes Lila back into my arms and says, "But we should talk, Rowan, we really should. Don't you think? We should talk about everything that happened."

I told my mom on the phone about my new therapist wanting me to go back there, to remember what happened with my dad. I glazed over it quickly because I didn't want to upset her, but I wanted to gauge her reaction before trying to descend on her here in her room and force it upon her. "Okay," I say, watching my mom, nervous. We never talk about this.

"Go ahead, darling," my mother says. "I'll be all right. I can handle it if you can. You know I'm here for you, even though sometimes I'm not . . ."

These moments are the most painful part of her illness—when she knows what's happening to her mind, when she's clear enough to understand how often she's not.

"What do you remember about what happened to your family?" she asks.

TWENTY-TWO

June. Three months ago. August 2nd.

Outside WTA, a persimmon sun sinks between steel buildings. The sky is smoky lavender streaked with yellow; it's chilly for an August evening. Steamy gray fumes rise from a subway grate, and the silver fleck of a candy wrapper flutters in front of Harrison and me. Hordes of people buzz past in a mix of suits/uniforms/gym clothes/going-out-clubbing outfits, talking to each other or to someone else on their phones. Languages swirl around me like a cyclone.

"I love this city," I say to Harrison as we stand there taking it all in. He lights a cigarette.

"Do you?" he asks, inhaling.

"Yeah," I say, watching an elderly woman pull a cart full of groceries. "I do. It's got a grip like a vise on my heart."

Harrison's eyebrows go up. "Really?" he asks with a smile. "I like that."

We walk west toward the Theater District. I hate smoking, but Harrison's a handsome smoker, all long fingers and dramatic gestures. He tells me about his day, which is what he often does at work. I can't deny that I find it exciting, to be in on this world, to know that a certain actress just signed on to a film, or that Harrison is in the middle of packaging a film with one of Louisa's big-name actors and how that's going to make one of his screenwriter's careers, and how all of it fits together like a puzzle created by the top dogs in Hollywood. Puppeteers, really, all of them: making and breaking careers with a snap of their fingers.

"So he's got a new pilot that's perfect for Hulu," Harrison's saying as we walk past a pharmacy. "And they've already bought one of his spec scripts before, so he's on their radar."

Oh, what I wouldn't give to be one of WTA's actresses. Is it possible, in any universe, that Harrison's thought that, too? The problem is I have zero credits. So for someone like Harrison or Louisa to send me in for an audition, to risk their reputations in that way: I would have to be so singularly extraordinary, and I just don't know if I am. I'm deeply scared I'm not, and that I'll fall flat on my face in this city I love, and that I'll never actually get a break and make it. And I worry one day I'll be unhappy with my life and look back on all of this like a dream.

"That hot dog smell makes me want to barf," I say as we near a deli with outdoor tables covered in plastic red-and-white checkerboard.

"Oh, that's too bad," Harrison says, slowing down in front of the deli, the hot dog smell stronger than ever. "This is where I'm taking you for dinner."

We laugh and keep walking.

On Sixth Avenue, Harrison gestures at a coffee shop called Frankie's and says, "I was thinking we could hit this coffee shop. It has food, too, so we could grab a bite and still be on time for Gabe's reading." He checks his phone. "Well, we might have to hurry a little . . ."

"Sounds good," I say, and we head toward it and duck inside, and then his hand is on the small of my back like this is what we always do, like we always touch each other.

I look up at him and catch his blue eyes, and that's the moment I know for sure that he wants this to be romantic. And his eyes are questioning, like he wants me to let him know if I want the same thing. Do I want the same thing? It's hard to disentangle what I want from what I *really* want. In some ways it feels like a letdown: if he wanted me to be one of WTA's actresses, he wouldn't be putting his hand on my back and looking at me like this, because he's not like that. He's never once dated one of the firm's clients, and I know that because both Louisa and Kai told me. Kai didn't phrase it quite as nicely as Louisa; Kai said Harrison's pious and won't date clients, but that assistants have been fair game, and that none of them work at WTA anymore, and that one of the women won't return Kai's texts, even though they used to be friends. Which makes me feel like a fool, but then I asked Louisa where most WTA assistants landed next, and she says they generally get better jobs at other agencies, and that turnover is high at the assistant level. Louisa didn't realize why I was asking, so I didn't push any further than that, but now I'm getting the sense that Kai's been exaggerating for the sake of drama, which is annoying.

"You first," Harrison says, guiding me past a crush of tables. It's tiny in here. Intimate. More dinner than coffee, that's for sure.

"Well, *this* is romantic," I blurt, glancing around.

Harrison freezes. His mouth makes a grimace, like when you eat something too bitter. "I'm so sorry, June," he says, and it comes out genuine, like he's mortified. "We can go somewhere else."

I smile at him—it feels so refreshing to see him like this, the professional confidence I see at WTA nearly disappeared. "No, it's perfect," I say, and then I take his hand. I know I'm setting something into motion and can't possibly know the outcome, but I do it anyway, and everything between us shifts to something new. We hold on to each other's hands, maneuvering through the tight spaces between diners, and then sitting at a table in the corner with a candle lit beside a vase of daisies. My mom always loved her daisies in August, and I think of her now and what she'd think about me going out with someone who I imagine is at least ten years older. I brush aside how blazing mad she'd be, and the way she'd stuff it down at first and act like she didn't care, and then resign herself to the larger fact that I'm always disappointing.

Harrison and I stare at each other, and the rush of cold I feel when I think of my mother makes me want to take his hand again, so I do. "I'm not seeing anyone else," he says, too quickly. "And I've been imagining asking you out to dinner since the first week I met you. And I'd like us to . . . well, to do more of this . . . if that's what you wanted, too. And if it doesn't work out, I would never let it get in the way of your work at WTA. I'm an adult and so are you."

I take a breath. His eyes are on my face and I know I look beautiful, and I know that doesn't sound quite right for me to say, but it's the truth and it factors into me having the courage to utter the words I say next.

"Would you let it get in the way of me one day being a WTA actress?" I ask, giving his hands a gentle squeeze.

He pulls away.

The waitress sidles up to our table with a notepad. My heart pounds in my ears, dulling even the sound of the other diners chattering around us. There's a cold, hard rock forming in my stomach.

I've said the wrong thing.

TWENTY-THREE

Rowan. Friday morning. November 11th.

I'm staring at my mom as I nurse Lila, unsure of where to start, stalling like I usually do whenever we talk around the edges of this big hulking darkness that befell us so many years ago. My mom fiddles with her pearly pink rosary beads, her lips shaping silent prayers while she avoids my glance. While I was growing up, she always had rosaries stashed in different places: in between the pages of books, in the top drawer of her bedside table, and at least two tucked beneath her pillow. She ran her fingers over those beads every night as we fell asleep together. One of her doctors told me that she's likely to go back to the habit with increasing frequency as her mind fails, almost like a touchstone—something so ingrained it's harder to lose. The same doctor told me that one of the hallmarks of her condition is the desire to sink back into the past, which is maybe why she's so willing to talk about my dad now; but I'd bet it's more likely she's willing to revisit something painful to help me, because isn't that part of being a mother? I would do it for Lila.

"You know, it's funny," I say as Lila gets sleepy on my boob. I run a finger along her cheek to wake her, and then I take a deep breath like the lactation consultant taught me to do to perk her back up enough to finish the feed, but these tricks don't work as well as I need them to. Lila is already sleeping, her beautiful red lips an oval against me. "Oh, Lila," I say, exasperated. "Please wake up."

My mother lets out a girlish laugh. I look up to see her staring lovingly at the both of us. "What is it?" I ask.

"When you were little," she says, "I couldn't wake you up for the life of me. You fell asleep at the breast every time."

"I did?" I ask with a smile, the first time I've ever felt lighthearted about the feeding issue.

"Oh yes," my mother says.

"So what happened?" I ask my mom. "Did I lose weight? Did you have to take me to the doctor?"

My mom shakes her head. "It was different back then," she says with a wave. "We didn't have so many appointments like you all do now." She's crystal clear, and I wish it could always be this way. "You woke up around six or seven weeks. And you stayed a skinny little thing no matter how much I fed you."

I think of my mother back then, likely surrounded by her friends supporting her. Her own mother was gone, but my dad's mother adored her and always sided with her any time she argued with my dad, which was often. My grandma lived with us on and off for years. And then when my dad was killed, my grandma sort of lost it (understandably) and disappeared for months. We saw her again only once, and then she died the year after. *Tragic,* my mother always says with a shake of her head, which I took to mean that in a way, we lost both my dad and his mom on the night he was murdered.

"You saw Dad's friend flee out the back, right?" I ask. I'm not sure why this is what I start with when I already know it to be true, but it seems a good, easy starting point.

My mom is taken aback, which doesn't make sense when she was the one to bring it all up. "Y-yes," she stammers, which sets me on edge. I don't want to push her into something that stresses her, if stress is indeed a trigger for an episode. "I saw a midsized man streak across the lawn," she says.

"But they were all average sized," I say about my dad's friends. Not a notably tall or short one among them. Not a sober one, either. They were all drunks back then. And since that night, one got sober, and no one sees him anymore.

"Yes, that's true," my mom says. I notice for the first time that her gray button-down shirt is askance, the buttons all wrong. It makes me sick to think of someone else supervising her shower and selecting her clothes when she can't. But what can I do? Even if Gabe wanted to try my mom living with us, I'm not sure I could safely care for her, especially now that Lila's here and I can barely take care of the two of us.

"The cops were so convinced it was Johnny who did it," my mom says, talking about the one who got arrested for it, but there's no life in her voice.

"I remember Johnny," I say easily, like his name isn't weighted with death and betrayal. He's the one who eventually got sober. When my dad was alive, Johnny was my mother's least favorite of them all, the one who steered them to darker places: vandalism one night, petty theft another, arson a year later at a bar (payback for the owner forbidding them to enter). They were never convicted of anything.

We always assumed it was one of my dad's friends who came to steal the diamond watch. First, because they'd all been out with him that night, so every one of them knew he had been rip-roaring drunk and unlikely to even wake up when they slipped inside our house to get the watch, and they all knew he never remembered to lock the doors when he came in from a bender. And second, because my dad's friends were the only ones who knew he kept the watch in an opaque blue vase. Don't ask me why he told them his hiding spot; I'll never understand that. I assume it's because he considered them his brothers, but even family can turn on you—everyone knows that. And none of them ever came forward with anything to help the police solve the crime. They all came to the funeral parlor with bloodshot eyes and heads dipped low. I remember that old Catholic church that smelled like oil and secrets, and the way my dad's friends wore ill-fitting suits and didn't sing along to the verses even though they'd heard them every Sunday since before they could speak. I remember how everyone at the funeral stared at me—*his young daughter*—like they were trying to discern if I would ever be okay.

On the day my dad died, he cleaned the watch in front of my mother, and it was gone when the cops searched the house. The cops surmised (as best they could; I suppose it was a guess, really) that the single stab wound was inflicted out of self-defense. The lead detective told us it didn't look as if the perpetrator came there to kill him; more likely, he'd come to steal the watch, and when my dad found him mid-robbery, my dad went after him, and the man stabbed him and fled.

"Sometimes I wonder how much you remember about your dad, about what he did to me," my mom says carefully.

I almost say, *And to me, too,* but I sense she's trying to get at something other than the things I know about, so I shut my mouth and wait. But she doesn't say anything more, and so finally, I say, "I remember him doing things to us that were so terrible, yet so subtle, they were hard to put a finger on. Do you remember that cookbook we used to love to make pastries with? Do you remember how he used to hide it?" He always hid things that might seem unimportant to anyone other than my mom and me: rosary beads, children's books we loved, the form she was supposed to sign and send into my kindergarten. He mind-gamed her (and me) in small but distinct ways that reminded us that he was the boss. He'd hide my mom's checkbook and berate her for not paying an electric bill; he'd brush by her too quickly, knocking her off balance and mumbling a near-gleeful apology. Sometimes he didn't speak to her (or me) for days, only to drown us in a deluge of words when he finally opened his mouth to apologize, gaze watery, forehead creased.

I was so glad he loved that bar so much; I was so glad when he was gone. It wasn't only because I hated him, it was because I loved my mother so intensely.

"Oh yes. Those things he used to hide," my mom says slowly, shaking her head. "He'd turned into such a bastard. He wasn't like that when we got married. He drank too much then, but he was still hopeful."

It feels like such a trick: that someone could turn this way. And not like the tricks and twists you prepare for in a marriage—infidelity, sickness, financial ruin, and the like—but something more insidious: a turn of the tide, an angry pot on the stovetop boiling over, a well-timed slap hurtling toward your neck.

"I remember how drunk he'd get," I say, "and how he'd come home and then he'd . . ." I look down at Lila. I'm not sure any of us are ready to go where I'm about to. "I think, what I remember," I start, unable to meet my mom's eyes. What I remember is everything I could hear through the walls: his moans and rhythmic thuds, the sound of the headboard, the bedsprings. I remembered all the things you put together as an adult when you start making those same sounds, and I remember her protests.

"I think he always came home and made you have sex with him," I blurt. I look up to meet her eyes. They're bright blue and icy cold. "Mom?" I plead, and then I reach for her hand. It's hard to cradle Lila in just one arm while she nurses, and my mom squeezes my hand and lets it go again. "You couldn't have wanted that," I say. "Right? I just, I can't imagine any universe in which you'd want to sleep with him when he was drunk like that, but if you did, you know I don't judge you. He was your husband."

My mother starts to cry. Tiny sobs that shake her frail frame.

"Oh, Mom," I say, "I'm so sorry. We don't have to do this."

She waves her skinny fingers and says, "No. We can. God, Rowan, especially if it would help you now. We can go there, of course we can.

I just, sometimes I can't really believe that was our life, that those were the first five years of your life. I can't believe I put you through that."

I shrug like it's nothing, which she and I both know isn't true. But I can surely understand it—she was married at twenty-two. How was she to know what was coming?

"He was filled with so much anger," I say, because that's what I always come back to when I think of him.

"That's for sure," my mother says, straightening. "He never hit you, I always console myself with that."

"Never," I say, and it's the truth.

"You're right that I didn't want to have sex with him," she says, and my heart sinks somewhere lower than even the past few weeks have sent it. "Perhaps the trauma of that night he died, Rowan, perhaps the things you don't remember . . ." She trails off, and then says, "I worry your therapist is right. She's good, isn't she? Supposed to be the best?"

I nod. Lila starts to suck again, and I encourage her with a circular rub on her back.

"Perhaps that night has been buried so deep," my mother says, growing agitated, hands trembling. "Perhaps it's causing you to forget other things."

"About what happened to Dad?"

"That, and . . . Rowan, I don't know. I'm confused about some of what I do know, what I've heard, what I remember . . . I'm worried I'm not the one to help you with this because of my mind going, but then I'm your mother, so, who else?" Her eyes go to her rosary beads.

My cell buzzes. It's Gabe. I'm sure he's worried—he barely wanted me to come here today, and he's going to be really annoyed that I canceled his mom driving Lila and me at the last minute so I could come here by myself. I almost don't answer the phone, but that feels unfair, so I do.

"Hey," I say. "I'm with my mom. She just met Lila." There's a smile in my voice, curling the words and lifting them higher.

"Rowan," Gabe says, and then he clears his throat. "You should head home soon. There will be cops coming by to talk to us about June. They found . . ."

His words stop. I can hear him breathing.

"Gabe? Are you there? They found *what*?" I ask. Lila stirs, finally waking. She clamps down too hard on my nipple and I squeal. I don't know how, but her gums feel like daggers even though she doesn't have teeth.

"They found a spot of blood on the floor outside of our apartment," he says. I feel dizzy even though we're sitting. I put a hand to my mouth like I want to stop myself from throwing up. Gabe goes on: "Mrs. Davis called the cops, convinced she saw a tiny spot of blood by the elevator, and she was right. I don't know if they really think it's June's blood, or if they're telling me about the blood to freak me out, but they're coming by to question us at five p.m.," Gabe says. He clears his throat again. "Because the neighbors told them about you, about what you did to June."

My hands tighten on the phone. "I didn't *do* anything to her," I say, my words accelerating. "I just accused her of something. I had a mental break or something! I just yelled at her, Gabe, you know that."

"Yeah, but our neighbors heard everything," Gabe says. "How bad it was . . . *your screaming*."

"You sound like you're accusing me of harming June," I say, feeling my mother's eyes all over me.

"I'm not, Rowan," Gabe says. "Of course I'm not. Just, please, come home."

TWENTY-FOUR

June. Three months ago. August 2nd.

We recover.

I don't know how it happens, but we do.

Harrison looks at the menu and orders quiche, and politely tells the waitress we're in a bit of a rush. I get a salad. We both get decaf lattes. The waitress scrams, and Harrison says, "June, I'm sorry. It just took me by surprise. I didn't know you wanted to be represented by us."

"Really?" I ask, and he immediately looks embarrassed. A part of me feels bad for him, but the other part of me thinks, *How thickheaded do you have to be to think I don't want to be represented by an agent at WTA?*

Is he playing me? He knows I want to be an actress; I told him that weeks ago at work. So how could he not think I'd want this? I stare at him, waiting for him to say something, to answer me.

"A lot of people who work for WTA have creative aspirations on the side," Harrison says, "but it doesn't mean they're actively searching for representation by WTA."

"You sure about that?" I ask, as respectfully as I can.

"I'm sorry," he says again, and this time he actually looks chastened.

"Please don't take this the wrong way," I say, "but from my perspective, there are so many power players at the top in charge of who gets what. And then there are people like me, lowly creatives who aren't superstars yet and have zero power. So I guess, well, at least don't insult us all by pretending you think we don't want it more than anything. Who in her right mind wouldn't want to be represented by WTA?"

He says nothing—not even another apology—but he's listening.

"I have an audition tomorrow," I say, diving in deeper, sinking my claws into the pulsing truth of what my heart really desires. "It's for a black box theater in Brooklyn. I'm auditioning for Cecily in *The Importance of Being Earnest*."

"Oh," he says, and he almost looks annoyed, like I'm derailing where he wanted this night to go. But then a tentative smile returns to his face. "I didn't realize you had traditional theater training," he says.

"I do," I say, which is only partly a lie. Starting next week I take an acting course at HB Studio, which is one of the oldest and most respected acting studios in the city. And this past weekend I read Uta Hagen's *Respect for Acting*, and I *am* starting to feel more like an actress, even if I've only done plays in college. Also, last week I met with a modeling agency that Louisa is concerned is a scam but that I think may be legit. The problem is they're asking for thirteen-hundred dollars to pay for my headshots (which I *do* need), but Louisa says that if they're a legitimate agency then they should encourage me to find my own photographer outside their company, one with whom they're not affiliated. And then she gave me a lecture about kickback schemes, which was a massive buzzkill.

"I'll come see you if you get the part," Harrison says.

"I'd like that," I say.

"Are you doing a lot of auditioning?" Harrison asks, toying with his napkin.

"I am," I say. "I'm waiting to hear about a part in an indie film."

I smile and sip my water. Oh, how I love that word: *indie*. June
Waters: *indie actress*. Could anything be more wonderful?

"It's a crazy business," Harrison says. "But it's kind of perfect.
Addictive, in a way."

I shrug. "And there's nothing else I want to do," I say. "I don't have
a plan B."

"Maybe there won't be a need for one," Harrison says. The twinkle
in his blue eyes has returned, and it's lighting me up. He's got a little
boy quality to him, like he's always right there on the edge of something.
Trouble, maybe.

"Maybe not," I say, exhilarated.

The café stirs around us. Diners come and go; waiters clear plates;
a jazzy Nina Simone song plays. I feel full of possibility as we sit there
quietly. There's something about being with Harrison, same as when
we're in the office together: he's got a good vibe, he's pleasant and easy
to be with. It's comforting without being boring. We're companionable
together, even when we're not talking, and I'm surprised I'm not more
nervous. The waitress brings our food over, and we're pretty quiet as we
start eating.

"What are your parents like?" Harrison asks me halfway through
his quiche.

"Oh well," I say, wiping my mouth with a starchy gray napkin. "My
dad's a mechanic. He's easy, sort of simple in a really good way. I get
him, what makes him tick. He pretty much just wants to make sure my
brother and me are fine and that his shop is doing well. He used to be
a race car driver and now he loves horse racing. He used to gamble but
doesn't now, he just goes to Saratoga in the early morning to watch the
horses run the track before going to his shop. He loves those horses—
have you ever been to the racetrack?"

Harrison shakes his head, takes a sip of water.

"They're even more gorgeous up close," I say. "Like powerful
machines, all tight and sinewy and explosive when they race, and some

are treated like royalty, bathed to a sheen, but I think it was conflicting for him because he knew some were being treated terribly and exploited for profit. I was too young to understand any of that when he used to take me to the racetrack, up until I was twelve or so and then it was just so early I wanted to sleep in instead. He'd get up at five a.m. to go," I clarify, so that Harrison doesn't think I'm some spoiled brat who couldn't be bothered to get out of bed. "Because he had to be in his shop by seven thirty. Looking back, I wish I made more of an effort to hang out with him at his shop, or just figure out ways to keep doing things together."

"You could still do that. The next time you're home," Harrison says.

He's right. I should. "I owe them a visit," I say. I shake my head, slow down a bit. "And then my mom, well, she's trickier. We don't have an easy relationship. She can be very cold with me, and she's really prone to depression, so sometimes she couldn't get it together enough to mother us and she just took to her bed." I let out a strangled laugh. "Sorry," I say. "*Took to her bed.* That sounded so old-fashioned. And sorry I'm going dark on you here. But she's complicated. And some of the ways she withheld love probably have to do with the ways in which I seek it."

Harrison's eyebrows rise. "That's pretty astute for someone your age," he says, and somehow the way he says it doesn't come out insulting toward all young people; it comes out like he thinks I'm a marvel. "It took me a long time to work out my stuff with my parents," he continues. "And they're gone now, so I'm glad I did. It's amazing the influence those early years have on your entire life. My mom cheated on my dad—she had several affairs, actually, and a bunch of times I knew what was happening, and it nearly killed me," he says. The waitress sets down a bill and smiles at us. She must have heard what he said, but she doesn't let on. Harrison puts his credit card down quickly and she takes it.

"I'm so sorry," I say when she leaves.

"Yeah," he says. He looks at me and I hold his eyes. "I remember this dress she used to wear when she wanted to look beautiful, attractive, and it weighs me down how often I think back on it. It feels like carrying around a loaded weapon I never wanted in the first place." He looks away. "She *was* very beautiful," he says, and then he shakes his head like he's trying to set free the memory of her and what she did. "One of the things I like about New York is how forthcoming people are about their pasts. So don't apologize for going dark. Wasn't even that dark."

"I could go darker," I say, trying to make him smile, because when I think of a boy growing up knowing those things . . .

"So could I." The corner of his full mouth lifts into a smirk.

The waitress appears again, thanking us and setting down the check. "Thank you for dinner," I say.

He signs it, and I think of all the actresses he's taken out for a meal. "I'll take you somewhere nicer next time," he says when the waitress is out of earshot.

"Next time?" I repeat playfully.

"Next time," he says, confidence in his voice, the same confidence I hear at work, one of the things about him I'm drawn to.

I want to kiss him. And he wants to kiss me. He's the first person I've wanted to kiss since that misguided mess with Sean.

We leave the restaurant, and outside the night is dim. Taxis and delivery trucks and bicycles zoom by, but I feel quiet somewhere deep inside me. Night in New York does this to me, but so does Harrison. I take his hand as we walk, and it feels so good. He's warm, and I'm not sure whether that's because he's nervous or that's just how he always is. I guess if this keeps happening, I'll find out. We walk along the street and I think about him undressing me, staring at me, really seeing me. I think about where it will happen: My bedroom? No—*no way*. I can't take him to my apartment. Not because it's small and kinda crappy but because I can't bring a guy home with Sean there. I get a chill just thinking about how awful that would be.

Harrison and I walk silently toward the theater's neon sign—**PLAYWRIGHTS** in yellow, **HORIZONS** in orange—emblazoned over steel planks and wide glass windows. But no matter how excited I am, I can't shake Sean. He's a hulking presence, a storm cloud hovering in my thoughts.

Belonging—that's what it is. Sean thinks we belong to each other, and I haven't figured out how to tell him he's desperately mistaken, and I'm not sure what he'll do to me when I do.

TWENTY-FIVE

Rowan. Friday afternoon. November 11th.

Lila wails inside her car seat. I'm stuck in a clogged line of traffic on the way back downtown from my mom's. Rain pounds the windshield. "Oh, Lila, sweet girl," I say, gripping the steering wheel, barely inching forward. "I'm so sorry." Panic is a hard knot in my chest and I'm desperate. My rational mind knows we're safe—that Lila's strapped in, that we're going from one secure location to another, and that that's not the case for many mothers and babies across the globe—but my body won't listen to my rational mind: it's like there's a disconnect, like Lila's sobbing makes me insane and nothing will bring me back from the brink until she's in my arms and I can settle her.

She screams louder and I sob. What is *wrong* with me? I should have let Gabe's mom come, but selfishly I wanted the moment to be just my own mother and me, without Elena lurking in the background. Gabe had a meeting at WTA, and he'll be furious when he realizes I canceled Elena and drove Lila myself, which just makes me feel even angrier. Why couldn't he have rescheduled his meeting and come with me to see my mom? If he were here, at least I could have climbed into the back seat and comforted Lila. How much I hate him in this moment burns through my veins like hot liquid—it makes my tears come harder. I'm clenching the wheel and then I say it, too, just like my mother did:

"*Gray.*"

My heart skips a beat.

What if I'm slowly losing my mind just like she did?

"I mean, *Lila*," I correct myself. Wipers slash through my vision, *chop chop chop.* "*Lila Gray O'Sullivan*, I love you so much," I say, tears hot on my skin as she screams. "It's okay," I say, and then I say it again, over and over, until I know she's not the only one I'm reassuring: I'm saying those words to Lila, of course, but also to myself, and maybe even to my mother.

I grip the wheel tighter. Cars inch forward and I follow them through the pelting gray rain. I turn on the radio to see if the music will help calm Lila, but it doesn't.

She only cries harder.

TWENTY-SIX

June. Three months ago. August 2nd.

Moments later Harrison and I walk into the rehearsal room at Playwrights Horizons holding hands, which feels right. We're on the precipice of something, so why not let everyone know it? And I feel so much more powerful to be here as more than just an assistant at WTA: to be here as someone Harrison just took out to dinner. I could be anything: an actress, a love interest. My chin is up a notch, and not even the humidity can get in the way of my hair, which rolls easily over my shoulders in blond waves. Thank God I'm not wearing something stupid.

The room we walk into is cavernous but simple: light oak flooring, a long table set up with folding chairs and Poland Spring water bottles at each station. There's a stage several yards behind the table, but I get the feeling the actors won't be using that tonight. Only two actors sit in the chairs at the table so far—a beautiful forty-something woman and a bald man, both of whom look vaguely familiar but not enough that I know their names. There are some big-name actors at WTA, but there are these kinds of players, too: the kind of working actors who earn a consistent living but slip under the radar. They play guest stars on your favorite TV shows and they work on Broadway; they sell yogurt on commercials, and they have contract roles on soap operas. I'm just surprised there aren't more of them scattered around the table. It's almost eight.

"Harrison," says a petite blond making her way toward us. She's got an earthy look to her, all silver rings and turquoise.

Harrison smiles at the sight of her, and says, "Eleanor, meet June." He turns to me. "Eleanor is the casting director for Gabe's play." He doesn't tell Eleanor who I am, and maybe that's because neither of us are very sure—*his friend, a WTA assistant, his date?* I smile at Eleanor and shake her hand. "It's so nice to meet you," I say. And then I thank her for having me, which seems to endear me to her, because she asks, "What can I get you, June? Water? Coffee?"

"Oh, I'm fine," I assure her. She tells us to enjoy the reading, and then she races off toward the bald actor, who's asking for the Wi-Fi code. "Should we sit?" Harrison asks, gesturing to the dozen or so seats that form a small audience section and face the table.

I nod yes, but just then a tall dark-haired man moves into the doorway and my heart goes very still.

"Who's that?" I ask before I realize the words are leaving my mouth. My voice is a whisper, but Harrison must have heard me, because he says:

"That's Gabe." And he says it with a little laugh, like I've asked something silly.

I clear my throat, but I can't say anything. I need a minute; I need Gabe O'Sullivan not to come over here. I don't even fully understand the feeling inside me, only that this man is big and hulking and dark-haired and perfect, and that if I can't stop myself, then the strange feeling inside me will be my undoing. I know all of this lightning-quick, like a taste of sugar, a bird shot out of the sky. And a part of me accepts it, like when you stare down a massive wave and tuck under to the peaceful part of it, knowing you'll see the sunshine again once it passes if only you can time it right. But I can't time this right. I don't even know what it is.

Gabe's shoulders take up nearly the entire doorway as he scans the room. He sees Harrison, and then me, and his dark eyes hold mine until something slick curves inside my stomach, an unraveling. It's not like I've never had that happen before when I've seen a guy in college or passed someone in New York City in a café or on the sidewalk, but this time the current is too strong and too dangerous. I can feel his mouth on me like it's already happened: on my jaw, my neck, and my mouth. I can practically taste it.

I nearly lose my footing.

I break Gabe's stare. I look down at my feet. The pale wood floor is still there, holding me up.

"Gabe," says Harrison, who doesn't seem to notice anything amiss. Or if he does, he's a very good actor, because his hand is suddenly on my back, steering me toward Gabe. *Don't do this to me,* I try to telegraph to Harrison, but of course that doesn't work. So I say to myself, *Turn back, June.* But my body isn't listening. And it's not like I can stop walking midstream anyway, because how awkward would that be?

So I don't turn back. I look up as I move toward this man, this creature, and I lock on his gaze again. He's watching me walk across the room, his eyes on me, not letting go, until something happens that I should have expected and didn't:

A lithe, white-blond, ethereal woman appears in the doorway behind him.

Rowan O'Sullivan.

I recognize her from an article I read about mystery writers, about all the things female suspense writers get asked about their killers and crime scenes that male writers never do. Her quotes were smart and forward, quippy but weighted. She takes in the room with a small smile on her face, her hand on her very pregnant stomach. High cheekbones; a necklace glittering at her collarbone; and red nail polish—I catch it as she tucks a wisp of hair behind her ear. Her lips part and she says something to Gabe that I can't make out. He slips an arm around what's left of her waist, but his eyes never leave mine.

I can feel Harrison tighten beside me, an animal recognizing a threat as we move toward them.

"Gabe, Rowan," Harrison says in a deep voice as we get closer, so close I can smell Gabe: like the woods, but a little wet and musky, too, like when the sun sets and leaves you freezing cold.

"I'd like you to meet June," Harrison says. His voice is all business, and I try to snap back into shape, into the person I was just trying to be five minutes ago: *June Waters. Potential actress; person of interest.* I've never, ever been the kind of person interested in another woman's boyfriend or husband, and I won't start now.

Rowan smiles, her lips pale and delicate. Gabe drops his arm from her waist and extends a large warm hand. I take it in mine, and I'm so nervous I can barely breathe. Any confidence I had a moment ago seems to have evaporated in their presence; they're both so very golden, like the actors who come into WTA, or the people I pass on the street and fall in love with every day: New Yorkers, all of them, artistic and edgy. I let Gabe hold my hand a beat too long and wonder if this city, these creative people, will be the end of me.

He is magic. It's in his gaze, his eyes locked on mine, the way he feels in the room. I pray his personality is terrible and spoils the spell of this moment—because wouldn't that be so much easier?

Gabe O'Sullivan. Rowan O'Sullivan.

Married, expecting a baby.

I turn away from them.

"Let's sit," I say to Harrison. He blinks at me. He knows.

"Good luck tonight," I say to Gabe. And I mean it.

TWENTY-SEVEN

Rowan. Friday afternoon. November 11th.

*A*n *NYPD police detective is here in our apartment.*
It's hard to think those words, to even understand them.
We're not at the precinct because we're not under suspicion
of having done anything, but Detective Louis Mulvahey is here with
a solemn face like we're at least guilty of something, and maybe he's
right. He's well over six feet and somewhere around my age with a close-
cropped haircut and a hole in his earlobe that he probably regrets. He's
sitting in the living room, looking down at a notebook. I think of how
many times I've written this scene in one of my novels, and it strikes
me as so ridiculous that I almost laugh.

It's only five p.m., but dusk has spread like a bruise and plunged
us into darkness. Lila's in her bassinet, and my body is my own for the
moment. I watch her tiny stomach go *up, down, up, down,* and the
craziest thing is that I know I'll miss her in my arms within the hour,
and I'll pray for her to hurry and wake up so I can hold her again.
This strikes me as more insane than everything I've done the past few
weeks: that I can love this small person more than I've ever loved anyone
on the entire planet after only knowing her for four weeks. After my

mom's, when I could finally park the car and get her wailing body into the safety of my arms, it felt like the biggest relief I'd ever known. And when she nursed hungrily, feverishly—I'm not sure I've ever felt that grateful for my body.

The detective flips his notebook pages. We're sitting across from him, and he's been going at us easily for about a half hour, mostly getting background information on June's employment here, asking nothing urgent or scary or accusing. But I have a feeling he's working up to it. How could he not be?

Like I said: I've written this scene before.

"So, just to review, Mrs. O'Sullivan," the detective says slowly, acting dumber than he is. I've told him at least twice to call me by my first name. "You met with June in the café to apologize."

"I did," I say. My eyes are still on Lila. Gabe shifts his weight on the sofa beside me. I can feel the four of us edging toward something, but I'm ready for it. "And like I said, I saw her leave with her roommate, Sean. And that's the last time I saw her."

"We can't seem to get ahold of Sean," Detective Mulvahey says. "We've left several messages, but his phone is going straight to voice mail. You haven't heard from him, have you?"

"I haven't," I say, getting impatient now. "Look, what I did to her was wrong," I say, pushing the detective toward the place he wants to go, guiding him, because the waiting is worse than whatever he's planning to dish out. "I'm sure she was frightened," I go on, and I give him all my focus now; I need him to understand that I would never hurt her. "I wanted her to know it wasn't her fault," I say.

The detective nods. And then he smiles, and it's unnerving the way his skin dimples, as though the smile is real, which of course it isn't. "You see, that's the thing," he says, his words still so slow it makes me want to scream.

Just tell me how bad I've been.

He taps his pen against his notepad.

This is how I'd write you, I think: *Slow, but ever so smart. And maybe crippled by your indecision and inability to trust your instincts. Because I have to give you a flaw, you see: that's how writing characters goes.*

He stares at me. No way he could guess what I'm thinking unless I'm wildly underestimating him. I don't break his stare.

"Your neighbors were very clear about how frightened June seemed when she left your apartment," he says, "so you can imagine our reason for concern."

"Oh yes," I say, nodding. "I'm sure June was *very* frightened. She's such a sweet girl, and relatively new to the city, and I had a mental breakdown right in front of her. I *screamed* at her and accused her of hurting my baby. You'd be scared, too, yeah?" I ask. "I'm not hiding what I've done, Detective."

The number of times I've had to say it out loud to people—to admit how far gone I was, what I did . . . "Is there really no mercy for mothers who've come undone?" I whisper, almost to myself.

Gabe freezes beside me. But then a beat later he jumps in, saying, "Like I said over the phone, *for the reasons I detailed*, my wife has had an extremely difficult postpartum period and we would appreciate some sensitivity."

I stare at Gabe and realize we've both written this scene before: *Suspicion. Guilt. Love. Hate.* Throw in a missing person and a detective and you have the tools of our trade. How sick is it, this desire to solve the unthinkable? To make sense of all the bad in the world? To even think we could solve any of it seems the biggest crime of all: the sheer narcissism of it, controlling your characters' every move and tweaking scenes to your liking, bending breathing, pulsing characters to your will. Because they *aren't* fake to us: that's the secret, really. Our characters are sometimes more real than the people we know in real life.

The detective scrawls more details into his notebook. Then, to the back of his hand, he casually says, "There's less mercy for anyone, new mothers included, when a young woman is missing."

Guilt spreads over me like a rash. *"We have no idea where June is,"* I say. "But have you questioned June's boyfriend? Harrison Russell?" I turn to Gabe in time to catch the look on his face. How far does he think I'll go to protect us? Do I *need* to protect us? Did we do something?

I think of all the times I've imagined June dead. My body gets hot just thinking of her, but no—*no*. I'm getting carried away again. I would never hurt June.

TWENTY-EIGHT

June. Three months ago. August 2nd.

Moments later everyone in the theater takes their seats. We're all staring at the actors surrounding the long table, sipping their waters and clearing their throats, fluffing their hair and unwinding flimsy summer scarves worn only for the sake of drama.

Gabe's play is about to begin.

Harrison and I are next to each other on folding chairs. My stomach is wound into coils. *Breathe,* I tell myself, avoiding Harrison's glance. Gabe's in the row in front of us, and I can still smell his woodsy smell. When he puts his arm around his wife, my toes curl inside my sandals and my stomach twists tighter.

I have to get out of here.

When I was twelve, there was a woman who kept coming into my dad's shop. I understood exactly what she was doing: she was flirting with my dad, trying to get him to stray, or at least to *want* to stray, as if him wanting her would fill her up in some way. I never understood it then, but shouldn't I have? All I ever wanted was my mother's adoration, and is that really so much different? Love is love in all its deadly forms, and we all want it like something primal. The woman's act went on for months, but it didn't work. My dad was too desperately in love with my mom, or too mired in his own loyalty to even think about it.

I hated that woman.

"Thank you for coming," says Eleanor, the earth-mother casting director. She's standing to the side of the seated actors. "We are so thrilled to hold our first table reading of Gabe O'Sullivan's new play, *Stay*, here at Playwrights, and simply ecstatic to work with such a talented writer. I think you'll see tonight that the work is in good hands with these talented actors, and with our director, Lanesha Carlson." Eleanor gestures to Lanesha, who sits on the other side of Gabe wearing an effervescent smile.

Rowan squirms in her seat, sending her white-blond ponytail swinging. Wisps of hair fall free over her delicate neck. Her slim shoulders lean toward Gabe, pressing into him.

"Welcome, Lanesha, to Playwrights Horizons," Eleanor says. And then she turns to all of us and announces, "It will be our first time working with Gabe and Lanesha, and we are so very excited."

I look down to see Harrison's long fingers drumming softly against his leg. I look back up at Eleanor, whose eyes have fallen on Rowan. "And because this room holds more talent than any other room in New York tonight," Eleanor says breathlessly, "I'd like to say hello to Rowan O'Sullivan. I just spoke with Rowan, so I know she's in the middle of a manuscript that will likely be yet another *New York Times* bestseller." Eleanor lets out an awkward laugh, like she didn't really plan on saying any of this and is wondering how it's going over.

Gabe turns to look at his beautiful wife. A shadow falls over his features for a nearly imperceptible second, and then he smiles at Rowan, aglow. At first I think I misjudged the shadow, but then Harrison whispers, "Just let the man have his night to himself," and it confirms what I think I saw: jealousy between writers and lovers.

"Without further ado, let's begin," says Eleanor, who looks relieved to be done talking. She sits on the other side of Lanesha.

I expect the lights to dim but they don't, and I feel a sliver of disappointment because I want so badly to hide in the dark. But instead there's glaring fluorescence and no reprieve. Anyone who looks at my face can see how wretched I feel, and I try hard not to stare at Gabe. But the words are coming now from the actors, beautiful words, words Gabe wrote for them to shape their mouths around. The play is about a young woman who takes care of her brother ages ago during an unnamed war in a country that could be anywhere. It's like Gabe chose purposely to leave everything nonspecific so that the audience could focus on the relationship between the siblings. The play praises familial love—the romantic interests are only sidebars, flitting in and out of the story—and it leaves me aching. And it also leaves me thinking maybe I want to get more involved in theater. As I listen to the storyline it strikes me that this narrative is perfect for the theater, but it would never be picked up as a big film. I know I'm still such a novice in this world—but already I understand this. Maybe I need to try to see more works by playwrights; maybe they're telling really different stories.

During the play Gabe is very quiet. I expect him to jump in, maybe to correct how the actors said the lines he wrote, but instead all night he defers to Lanesha, allowing her to be the one to call for a pause when a scene is through so they can quickly discuss, and then they tuck their heads together and talk about things like adding another beat to a scene that fell short and felt incomplete. And during these quick dashes of collaboration, Lanesha types on a laptop as Gabe's low voice rumbles. And then the scenes begin again, and everyone is silent and reverent.

Everyone is reverent except me. Life around me seems to slow down and stretch out as I slip inside the skin of someone I hate, someone I never thought I could be.

But I haven't done anything, I try to console myself, *and this will pass; it's nothing, only infatuation and entirely meaningless, a thing without substance or anywhere to go.*

Gabe turns around only once, about an hour in when the actors take a break to go to the restroom or smoke cigarettes, and he looks first to Harrison.

"It's genius, man," Harrison says, much more casually than I hear him speak at work. A moment of brotherly energy passes between them, but then Gabe turns to look at me.

"Do you like it so far?" he asks.

Rowan is still facing forward, looking down at her phone, like nothing else exists but that glowing screen.

But *this* exists—this energy between Gabe and me, and I want to slap her and say, *Keep him away from me, whatever you do: keep us apart.*

"I love it," I say, my voice coming out easy and confident and separate from how my body feels.

A grin etches Gabe's face, wide and sweetly natured. "You do?" he asks. I'm surprised at the excitement in his voice, that me liking his play could put that feeling there.

I laugh, wondering what else I could make him feel.

Harrison shifts his weight.

"I *do*," I say. Our exchange doesn't make Rowan turn her head. *Wake up,* I can't help but think. Gabe's holding my eyes and still grinning when I go on, "I wonder if you're exploring familial love now that you're expecting a baby." His eyes widen a little. I ask, "Do you think that has something to do with your desire to write about something other than romantic love?"

"I'm sure it does," Gabe says, and this finally makes Rowan turn. Her features are so beautiful, like an Icelandic princess with wide blue eyes and high cheekbones. There's a smattering of freckles on her nose, but otherwise her skin is clear and milky white. She scrunches her freckled nose now, and says, "Neither Gabe nor I have siblings, isn't that funny?" She turns and smiles at Gabe, then back at us. "So I wonder if he isn't exaggerating the potential of a typical sister/brother bond, but I guess I'm not the one to answer that. Do you have a brother, June?"

"Um," I say, even though it's not the kind of question to which anyone should answer *um*. "I do," I say quickly, trying to sound confident again.

"And would he stay at your bedside and nurse you back to health, forsaking all others including a once-in-a-lifetime romantic love?" Rowan asks.

I'm nervous right away. I wait a beat before I answer. Her eyes hold mine.

Then I say, "No *way*," and everyone laughs, including Rowan.

"Have you ever seen a reading like this before?" she asks. "It's so fun to see work in its early stages."

Gabe flinches.

"Um," I say again, stupidly nervous. Rowan's eyes are still on me, and I wonder if she sees a silly, naïve girl who could never hold Gabe's attention like she does, who could never contribute anything meaningful to this conversation about *table readings* and *early work*. "I haven't," I say. "But I read a lot of scripts for work. And it doesn't get much more *early stages* than that."

Rowan's pale blond eyebrows go up. "Really?" she asks. It's not snarky, it's just like she doesn't believe someone as young as I am could be doing anything other than getting coffee at WTA.

"Yup," I say, embracing my youth with a flick of my hair and a tilt of my chin, trying to use it like a weapon instead of a curse. "I read scripts before they go to Louisa. She has me clear them for her."

Harrison's been too quiet during all of this, but he jumps in now. "Louisa adores June," he says. "June started as an assistant, but now she's Louisa's right-hand woman, and her gatekeeper for new talent, really."

I'm still Louisa's assistant, it's not like I got promoted, but I decide to keep that to myself.

"Wow," Gabe says. I don't know whether he's really impressed or faking it because he likes where this conversation is going, but it does the trick: now it's three against one. Rowan withers, but only slightly. She shrugs, and it comes off as if she's bored with the three of us.

I roll my ankle. *Careful, June.*

"It must be a lot of pressure to be the first eye on screenplays," Rowan says, which makes me nervous, because I hadn't ever really felt a lot of pressure about it. "I mean, you know, you have to be sure you don't miss the next big thing and all. Because the next big talent is doing something unlike anything you're watching on TV after work right now."

"I don't watch TV after work," I say, thinking I'm winning.

"Oooo," Rowan says, and right away I know I've miscalculated. "See, that's your biggest mistake," she says. "You *have* to watch TV. It's WTA's bread and butter." She laughs. "You work at a talent agency, not a literary agency."

All of us go quiet.

An actress singsongs something far away, high and lilting, and one of the male actors responds with a punchline. But it's just the four of us inside this moment, and Rowan has gone too far—she's been too unfriendly. It would have passed muster between men, it would have been considered ribbing or fair play or whatever, but between two women that have just met—it does not pass. It comes off as what it is: a woman who has sensed a threat.

She's right, though, isn't she?

Isn't that exactly what I am?

Eleanor calls for the actors to take their seats—the play is about to pick up where it left off. Harrison gives my hand a quick squeeze, but it falls short. Nothing about him touching me is enough.

Gabe doesn't look at Harrison before he turns around, only at me. He gives me a small private smile that lights me like a fire. Rowan turns back around and powers down her phone. I have no idea whether she feels guilty, and I don't care. Because it makes it easier, really, to imagine all the things I want to do.

TWENTY-NINE

Rowan. Friday afternoon. November 11th.

The detective leaves, but not before telling us he'll be back in touch.

I change Lila's diaper, but she's fussier than usual so I strap her to me and pace my bedroom, trying to settle her. I hear Gabe's low voice—he must have called someone. I creep to my bedroom doorway.

"You should be ready for this," he's saying to someone. He must be talking to Harrison—he must have called to warn him. And I feel bad about throwing Harrison into the mix, but surely the detectives have already realized that Harrison and June were seeing each other. I'm surprised they haven't already questioned him. *What's going on here? Where is June?*

I like Harrison—I like his personality, how easy he is. Gabe is impossible in a way that Harrison isn't. There was a time, oh so long ago, when the three of us, in our twenties, were at an industry party. The slate was clear: I hadn't met either of them until that moment right around eight p.m. when they were both standing at the bar nursing gin and tonics. Harrison had been courting Gabe as a client, but they hadn't signed anything yet. And then I sidled up to the bar right next to

Harrison and caught his light eyes first. "Excuse me," I said with a smile, and then I saw Gabe, and that was that. It was over before it started.

Harrison has only mentioned that night once. It was years later, and we were drunk, and he said, *"I saw you first,"* as if that was the thing that mattered, as if I didn't have a say. But I'd thought about it, too, and about how different things would be if I'd chosen Harrison. What would my life be like if that night I slid across the sleek leather of the fancy banquette and beckoned Harrison to follow? What if, beneath the table, he put a hand on my skin?

But it never would have happened that way, not with Gabe there, and that's the part that seemed to stick with Harrison for all those years. Or at least that's what he said to me half a decade later when we were drunk. *To think I was the one who invited him to that bar,* he'd said with a bitter laugh.

We all make our choices and send our fates spiraling. I'm married to Gabe and Harrison has June. *Simple, simple.* I do wonder, though, if that's why Harrison parades his lovers past Gabe now. Do we double-date with him and his girlfriends because we're all friends or because he's got something to prove, dangling these beautiful women in front of Gabe? Why was his first date with someone as gorgeous and vibrant as June to one of Gabe's table readings? Was it really just a coincidence?

Lila's finally nodding off. I go to the top drawer of my bureau, my fingers against the beaded antique knob. I want to find those sonogram pictures from the prenatal appointments I was telling Sylvie about. Maybe they'll trigger a memory of Gabe and me in those early days, so hopeful about our baby.

I open the drawer and see it's empty, or at least empty of the clutter that usually fills it. There's only my diary tucked in the back corner on top of two notebooks, which makes no sense because the drawer is usually overflowing with whatever I deem important in the moment: notes, handwritten cards from friends or from my agent or editor, knickknacks my mom gave me, and certainly all my sonogram pictures. Where did all my stuff go?

I yank out the diary and flip through the pages. It's a new one, and I'd barely written anything in it. The rest are stored in a box at the top of my closet. Maybe I should go back and read the early entries from my pregnancy. This one only has two, and I'm immediately uncomfortable as I start reading. The entry dated two weeks before Lila's birth says:

> *I really don't feel well. Something just isn't right. I'm so winded, first of all, which the OB says is normal, and he didn't look concerned at all. But then there's the dizziness and how often I'm contracting. I can feel my stomach tighten like a fist, and sometimes it goes on for what feels like minutes. My friends say they're just Braxton Hicks, but my OB is sending me in for a nonstress test. I go tomorrow.*

And then I'd written something the next afternoon, which reads:

> *Good news! After a very eventful morning, we're all doing fine. Doctor monitored me for an hour and I'm definitely contracting. So I was admitted to the hospital and received my first dose of betamethasone. I go back tomorrow for the second. They give it to anyone who could deliver early, because it helps develop a baby's lungs so they can avoid the NICU, if possible.*

I put the diary back and take out the notebooks. One is filled with book ideas and notes written in pencil, my favorite way to write. The next is blank. I flip through it anyway and find Lila's birth certificate. I open it up and suck in a breath. How can this be right?

Lila Grace O'Sullivan.

We always said we'd use *Gray* for a baby—we were decided on that before I went in to give birth. Why did Gabe make a last-minute change? Or could it be a clerical mistake? Maybe someone misheard him?

Lila's fast asleep now against me. I take the birth certificate and head out to the living room. Gabe's still on the phone, still talking in a hushed voice.

"I have to go," he says when he sees me. He disconnects the call.

"Gabe," I say, waving around the piece of paper. "The birth certificate, it says—"

"Where did you find that?" Gabe asks, all accusing, like I've gone and snooped in the writing pages he's so secretive about. "I've been looking everywhere for that," he says.

I roll my eyes. "In my top drawer," I snap. "Why is Lila's middle name Grace on this? Did you do that?"

Gabe flushes red. He's mad. "Rowan," he says, and then there's something more on his face—he's not only mad, it's more complicated than that. "We need to talk about June," he says. "There's something I need to tell you."

THIRTY

June. Three months ago. August 3rd.

I'm in my cubicle at WTA the next morning, staring at the cloth wall where I've tacked some photos of Jed, my dad, and my mom— like we're some happy family—all individual shots because I didn't like the ones of the four of us. I barely had any to choose from anyway, because who prints out photos anymore? They live on our phones, destined for nothing.

My eyes bounce over the faces in my family. I can't focus on anything, not the slope of Jed's nose or the guitar in my dad's hands or the warmth in my mom's eyes as she looks over her garden (that's why I chose that photo of her, of course). I try writing everything down in a journal I keep in my desk drawer that I mostly use to write notes for myself on my screenplays, but the journal is for my eyes only, so I figure why not try to parse what I'm still feeling after last night. It doesn't work. I'm barely here when Louisa comes in, a sleep-deprived shell of myself, a shadow.

"You're early," she says. And then she holds out a GF croissant from the bakery we love. She always buys me stuff there.

"I couldn't sleep," I say.

"Oh," she says. "Something bothering you?"

Yes. Something's bothering me. I exhale. I wish I could tell her, but I can't.

"I guess it was just last night," I say, and I try to smile. "The excitement of it all." It's not a lie. It's as close to the truth as I can get without telling Louisa what passed between Gabe and me, how wrong it was. I replayed it all night in my bed, sweating into my sheets. I swear it was there for him, too. During the second half of the reading, I could feel it pulsing in the air between us even stronger—I could feel it in all the things he said. I could feel that it wasn't nothing.

"June?" Louisa says gently. "Come sit with me."

I follow her. I think about how I was hoping Gabe's personality would suck, and how it was the opposite of that. He felt so virile to me, a man at the top of his game, on top of the entire world, even. *Virile.* That's not a word I've ever used before. It's the kind of word I've read in character descriptions in my scripts for work; it's the kind of word Rowan O'Sullivan probably uses when she writes her novels.

"Here, love," Louisa says, pulling out the chair opposite her desk, the one where the beautiful actors sit when they come to meet with her. She sits, too, and we stare at each other. It's surprising how comforting her gaze feels. "June," she says, her elbows on the desk, her entire pose comfortable to make me comfortable, even though I know her well enough to know she's nervous. "I know this is your first time working in an office," she says. "And when I was your age, I wish people had been straighter with me and not talked in circles. You remember what we promised each other that first day we met?"

"That we'd be honest with each other," I say.

"Exactly," Louisa says. "And I was caught off guard last night when Harrison sprung your evening plans on me, but I thought about it some more last night. This isn't a massive agency with compliance rules and contracts; office romances aren't forbidden unless you date your direct supervisor, which Harrison isn't. I just—if it's anything more than friendship—and you don't have to tell me anything about any of this, I'm just giving you the heads-up if it's heading in that direction—I just want you to be smart. You have to know that any office romance can complicate things for you."

"I'm sorry," I blurt, my stomach so sick.

She shakes her head. "Please don't be sorry," she says. "I just want to talk through it with you. I want you to proceed cautiously, that's all. And there was this time, and I hate to bring this up . . . Harrison was once involved with an assistant, and it went south quickly and dramatically. It was back when he wasn't sober yet, and people do change. And if I'd made the decision to get sober, the last thing I'd want is people poisoning a love interest I had with stories from my past. But I care about you and I'm telling you what I know. The assistant no longer works here, and she doesn't even work in entertainment anymore. I think she moved back home to Nebraska, far as I heard. And the specifics of their relationship or how it ended isn't something Harrison and I have ever talked about, but the young woman was very shaken."

I don't even know how to take that.

"I'll keep it platonic, friendly," I say, and it comes out easy. Maybe if I hadn't met Gabe, I would have had a lovely and romantic and uncomplicated evening with Harrison, and it would have felt like a loss to leave it all behind. But that's not what happened. "Honestly, Louisa, I'm so mixed up that I'd have to take it super slow and just-friends at first anyway," I say. "Trust me. I'm kind of a head case right now."

But how am I going to explain that to Harrison? Why would he ever go for that? Is the pleasure of my company really scintillating enough to make up for the fact that I just want to be all slow and friendly about things at first? Doubtful.

"I do trust you," says Louisa. Tears well in my eyes. "June," Louisa says, and her hand goes across her desk to lightly rest on mine. "I've made you cry, I'm so sorry."

"It's not your fault," I say. "And I appreciate you looking out for me. I like this job and I don't want to mess anything up."

"And to be clear, of course people have had office romances here," Louisa says. "You know about Sharon and Cassie," she says, talking about two women who are entertainment lawyers at WTA and who got married last year. "But there's an age difference and power imbalance between you and Harrison. And as a woman who's been working in this industry a long time, I want to tell you that this isn't a good idea."

I nod. I'm still crying, which is not what I want to be doing.

"I just feel this knot in my stomach about it all," I say. I wish I could tell her how I felt meeting Gabe, and how that hadn't happened to me before, and that I couldn't sleep last night because all I could do was picture his face.

Could I tell her that?

No. I couldn't. Louisa's married. Won't she only see it from that perspective? How terrible a woman has to be to want what's not hers?

I think of my dad with that woman, how loyal he was. The woman was beautiful—but it didn't matter to him; he did what was right. I'm just scared I'm more like my mother, so messed up with the constant searching for something—the feeling, the want, the adoration.

I'm worried it's going to kill me.

THIRTY-ONE

Rowan. Friday afternoon. November 11th.

What about June?" I ask Gabe, petulant as a toddler. We're in the living room. Lila's on me, finally asleep, and I rub circles on her back as Gabe paces. I ease onto the sofa, but Gabe doesn't stop moving.

"What's wrong with you?" I ask. "And what's going on with the birth certificate? You could have said something before if you didn't like the idea of using *Gray* for Lila's middle name."

"I *did* say something," he says, exasperated, still pacing like a madman. "I'm sorry if you don't remember, but we talked all the time about using *Grace* for Lila's middle name."

"I'm sorry," I say, but I don't sound sorry at all. "I don't remember."

He looks away, toward the bay window and out to the gray bricks of the neighboring building. There aren't many stellar views from the sixth floor. *"You don't remember,"* he says into the dead air of our apartment. He turns back to me. "And now here we are." He rakes his dark hair with his hands like he's furious, and then he starts to cry.

"Gabe," I say, startled. I lean forward to get off the couch, which is harder because Lila's on me and it takes so long that there's an awkward beat where he's just standing there crying and I can't get to him. "I'm so

sorry," I say as I finally get up and move across the floor. I press against him, Lila between us, and we sway together like a ship going down. "I'll try harder," I say. "We'll do the thing Sylvie was talking about—the special therapy for PTSD." Gabe cries harder and I can't believe it. "And I love the name Grace," I say quickly. "So don't worry about that. *Lila Grace* is a beautiful name."

He pulls away. He looks at me, but everything feels different. Usually when Gabe looks at me—or at any woman, really—he's a vortex: he can pull you into his dark stare with hardly any effort at all. It's who he is. It's part of his charm, his charisma. But now? I see terror in his gaze, in his bloodshot eyes and the set of his shoulders.

"You're scaring me," I whisper.

He puts his big hands on my arms. *"Me too,"* he says. "You're scaring *me*, Rowan."

"Where are my sonogram pictures?" I ask, not ready to let go of this. "Did you take them?"

"Rowan," Gabe says, dark lashes fluttering. He sucks in a breath, his broad chest heaving with it. "June came here that night."

I shake my head just slightly, trying to get between his words. "What? Which night?" I ask.

"After you went to see her in the café with Lila, the day you snuck out to apologize to her." I flinch at his choice of language: *snuck out*, like I'm a teenager, a prisoner. "She was so upset that night when she got here," he says.

"Because of me?" I ask.

And then after I say it, it dawns on me that he just lied to the police—we both just told the detective that we hadn't seen June since I met her in the café.

"Well, sort of, it's hard to . . ." His voice trails off, and I want to shake him. He clears his throat, looks down at our little girl between us. He's more matter-of-fact when he says, "Your meeting really upset her. She's come to really care about you, and . . ."

I hold up a hand. "I didn't do anything other than tell her I was sorry, and she told me she was taking some time to get away to go to her parents, and we talked about Lila a little, and that was *it*. That and her roommate, Sean, came, and then he was waiting for her outside, and . . ."

"Did you tell the police that?"

"About Sean? You heard me tell the police that. I just told the detective about Sean waiting for her and how they left together."

Gabe nods his head too quickly. What's *wrong* with him? "Right," he says. "I remember that. And hopefully they're pursuing Sean as a lead. But then she came here that night, incredibly upset, and . . ."

"And you didn't tell the detective?" I ask. My heart is off now, skipping beats. "What if someone hurt her, and you're withholding information they need to find her?" Lila is so hot against me I feel like I could pass out. "Do you have any idea the kind of trouble you could get us in by lying to a cop?"

Gabe puts an arm out to touch us—me? Lila? I'm not sure—and I yank my arm away. "Rowan," he says, "do you have any idea the kind of trouble we could be in if they find out I saw her last?"

"But you don't even know that's true," I say. "She could have left here and gone out with a friend. You could be lying *to the authorities* for absolutely no reason."

"I doubt she went back out with friends," Gabe says. "She'd just gone out for drinks with Kai. You heard the detective—the day she disappeared started with you meeting her in the café, then she went off with Sean, and then much later: drinks out with Kai. As far as the detective knows, Kai is the last person who saw her alive."

He sounds like a character in one of the TV shows he used to write for, recounting a timeline, catching up the audience.

"But the truth is that you were the last person we know who saw her alive," I say slowly, the words physically painful. *Alive.* How are we having this conversation? How is this real? "And we're telling the cops that, Gabe; we have an obligation to June—to protect her."

Gabe's eyes go blank, and then, like a robot, he says, "I didn't do anything to June."

"Then why are you lying?" I ask, more furious by the second. "You have to go to the cops—or call that detective right now, Gabe—you have to tell him."

"But what if she's dead?" Gabe asks, and my blood goes icy. "What if she's dead, and there's no way we can help her because it already happened, and it looks like I was somehow involved in it because I was the last person to see her on the night she disappeared?"

I put a hand to my forehead. I need to sit back down—I can't just stand here in the middle of our living room, unmoored. "I don't get it," I say, inching back in the direction of the sofa. "Why would June ever come to our apartment if she was so upset by me? And where were Lila and I during your little meeting? In my bedroom?"

My bedroom, not *our* bedroom. Pronouns are one of the verbal indicators of how a character views her surroundings; her territory; her lover; her family—the things that belong to her. And because he's a writer, too, Gabe catches it.

"You and Lila were sleeping in *our* bedroom," he says slowly, the emphasis like a prickly slap on my wrist. "I told June to keep her voice down, and she did."

"Thank heavens you thought of that," I say, rolling my eyes. "God forbid your heart-to-heart woke me up."

"This isn't a joke," Gabe says, stepping forward, making the oak floor creak beneath him. Time seems to slow. Standing in the living room like this, staring at each other, reminds me of our wedding, when we stood just like this during the opening notes of our first dance, about to show off the ballroom lessons we'd been coerced into taking by Gabe's mother. Neither one of us wanted to do it, so why had we bent so easily to Elena's will? And now it's a decade later and we're uncomfortable for way worse reasons; for a darker twist we never could have seen coming.

"Do you think I don't know how serious this is?" I ask. And then because I can't bear to stand here a moment longer, I leave him there alone and go sit. I take Lila out of the carrier and get her settled in my arms, gathering my courage to say what I'm about to. "You're lying to me about something, Gabe. Why in the world would our twenty-two-year-old sitter seek out *you* in her time of need?"

Guilt floods me for asking him what I'm about to right in front of Lila.

"Were you sleeping with June?" I ask, my skin on fire. Time seems to whip past me and then slow, leaving a long space in which I ask myself: Would I leave him if he had sex with her?

Yes. I would. But the answer doesn't come as easily now that Lila's here, which scares me. There's so much more at stake now, and my heart thumps against my ribs. Could I really have missed something as big as an affair? Me, the solver of mysteries?

Gabe looks down at Lila and his face is angrier than I've ever seen it. I feel a sick satisfaction for being the one to make it so. Isn't that one of the cruel things marriage does to us? The one-ups and resentments; the agony of battle, of climbing back on top, of losing and winning and never being on the same team the way you were when you first fell in love.

"How could you even ask me that?" he growls, but he doesn't meet my eyes.

"Because something isn't right here," I say. I can sense Lila's starting to wake up, and nothing makes me sicker than dragging her into this. "June coming here, you lying to the police. None of it makes sense. If you didn't sleep with her, then you did something else, and I want to know what."

"All I ever did to June was care about her and try to look out for her because no one else was," Gabe says.

"Oh my God, Gabe, get off your high horse for once. Really, do try."

"Screw you, Rowan," he says, and it takes the breath right out of me.

My phone rings. I look away from Gabe, and with trembling fingers I swipe the bar to answer it.

"Mrs. O'Sullivan," says a deep male voice. I'm pretty sure it's Detective Mulvahey, but for reasons I can't yet put my finger on, I don't want Gabe to know.

"Yes," I say crisply, businesslike.

"This is Detective Mulvahey," the voice says. "I'm very glad I caught you."

Here's the funny thing: it's the sound of fake kindness in his voice that tips me off that he knows we lied to him. Or at least, that Gabe did. "We finally got access to that video footage from the entrance of your apartment building," he says into my ear. I avoid looking at Gabe as he goes on: "And it's fascinating, really, because we found out that in fact you did see your sitter again. Or at least, she was trying to see you. June Wallenz arrives at your apartment building at ten twenty p.m. Tuesday night. She talks to Henri Andersson, who gestures for her to go inside. He watches her ass as she walks into the building, which I was none too fond of, having daughters myself. And here's where it gets really interesting: there aren't cameras inside your building, only the one on the front door. And would you believe: *June never leaves your building.* Your doorman, the lascivious Henri Andersson, tells us there's a back door out to a garden and an alley behind the building, but we don't have much reason to think June would use the hidden back door of your building and exit into an alley in the middle of the night. Henri's memory of the night aligns with the footage: he let June up and never saw her come down, and he just assumed she did so while he was in a back office or using the bathroom. But here's the strangest thing of all: you and your husband told us that neither of you had seen June since you saw her in the café that morning."

There are so many of my bodily systems betraying me—I swear I've peed myself hearing everything he's just told me, and blood is so hot on my face I think my skin will melt—but I still gather myself enough to speak up and defend myself.

"And that's still true for me," I say into the phone. I look up at Gabe. He's standing very still, his eyes on me.

Mulvahey's quiet on the other end of the line, and if I were writing his inner monologue, I'd be debating whether to believe me, and the implications of such. Because if I were him, and if I believed the wife and suspected the husband of foul play, I'd secure the connection by extending a verbal olive branch, a trick, a sleight of hand to get the unsuspected wife on my side.

"Is your husband within earshot?" he asks softly.

Bingo. The olive branch.

"Yes," I say simply. To think I'm on the phone with the person who may undo my marriage . . .

I blink at Gabe. *Is that what I'm doing here? Am I choosing my sitter over the father of my child?*

My heart is thudding inside my chest. Is there another way out of this?

I need to slow this phone call down, but I don't know how to do that. I think of the scene spooling out before me, but I don't know how to rewrite it to save both June and Gabe. A part of me thinks what most wives would: *there's no way my husband killed a young woman.* But haven't I written enough novels and read enough true crime to know it would be a mistake to assume that? We have no idea what we're capable of; we certainly have no idea what someone else is capable of.

I shake my head to clear it.

"Rowan," says the detective, and I wait for it. I know it's coming. "Did your husband lie to us about not having seen June?" he asks into my ear.

Gabe is staring at me, his big shoulders hunched, his chin tilting as he takes me in. He could have slept with her—I would be a fool to think otherwise. And if that's all that comes to light with me telling the truth, then so be it. And if it's worse, then I'll deal with it. But I couldn't live with myself if I lied about June; there have been things I've been willing to do to get ahead, rules I've bent, ways I've lived outside the lines of what normal people do. But not this. "Yes," I say calmly. A secret exchange. Not because I want to burn Gabe, but because I won't let June be in harm's way or not be found because of our lies, Gabe's lies. And could Lila and I really live our life with someone without knowing what they were guilty of?

My midsection has gone numb again, and my neck feels like it'll break from the force of holding the phone so tightly against my shoulder while my arms cradle Lila.

"Are you worried you're in danger?" the detective asks.

"No," I say, even though Gabe's glare is full of something dark and heavy. I look away from my husband, down to the shape of my baby girl tucked against me.

The detective clears his throat. And then he says, "We have a warrant to search your apartment building and your apartment itself. I'd like your husband to be unprepared for our arrival. Our team will be there shortly. Is there somewhere safe you can go with your daughter?"

Isn't there?

Yes, of course there is. I have a mother.

"I'll be fine," I say.

And then I get off the phone and look up at Gabe. I swear I don't think he'd ever kill June; I believe that. But what if he's lying about something that would help the cops find her?

We just need to find June. And then we'll get past whatever this is. Together.

"What was that all about?" Gabe asks, dark eyes flashing.

THIRTY-TWO

June. Three months ago. August 3rd.

I don't see Harrison for the next few hours at work, and it makes me want to shrink up and lie on the carpet. I can't stop thinking that I did something wrong at the reading, some social or romantic transgression, or that Harrison sensed the attraction I had for Gabe and now everything between us is over.

I'm trying not to overreact, and everything seemed okay last night when we parted at the subway (quick hug, no kiss). But I'm still nervous. Something doesn't feel quite right, like I hurt him in some way, like I committed some slight.

I'm obsessing over both Harrison and Gabe so hard that I start to feel sick. And then, at four p.m., out of nowhere Harrison peeks his handsome face over my cubicle. I stifle a gasp. I want to press rewind and go back to last night at the restaurant when it was just me and him and I'd never met Gabe.

Harrison smiles at the sight of me, his cherubic face lighting up.

"Hi," I say, smiling despite myself.

"Hi," he says, grin going wider. "Last night was fun."

"It was," I say. Among other things.

"Do you want to do it again?" he asks.

Do I? My heart is going too fast. A part of me feels like I *need* to do it again. I need him to take me out and help me get rid of this massive pressure on my chest; I need to go out with someone who isn't taken.

"Um, yes, I do," I say, and then I think of everything Louisa told me. "I'd like to go out and also to take things really slow, like glacial pace." I try to make a joke, but his face folds a little like he's embarrassed. And then Kai is coming toward me, scowling when she sees him.

The second Harrison sees Kai he's smiling again, confident. Any hesitation that was on his face is gone.

"Tonight?" he asks, soft enough that Kai can't hear him.

"I have that audition," I say.

"Ah yes," he says. "For Cecily." And then he bows his head dramatically and says, *"But pray, Ernest, don't stop. I delight in taking down from dictation. I have reached absolute perfection. You can go on. I am quite ready for more."*

I laugh. "How do you have that line memorized?" I ask.

"I played Ernest a long time ago," he says, not acknowledging Kai, who's stopped right next to him.

"I have to talk to you *later*," Kai says conspiratorially to me. She loves office gossip; she knows everything about everyone, and she loves telling me.

Harrison stiffens. And then Kai walks away, swaying her hips dramatically like she's trying to make a point.

"You know, it's funny, that part is right from my audition section," I say to Harrison.

He adjusts his tie, a perfect royal-blue number. "You'll do great," he says.

"Did you used to want to be an actor?" I ask. Does everyone?

"A long time ago, yeah," he says, "but I also wanted a paycheck."

He's trying to make a joke, but there's a look that passes over his face that tells me he doesn't like not getting what he wants. I've met a few of these failed actor types at WTA who became other things—writers, casting directors, costume designers—and they seem to go a few ways: with some of them, you can feel it like a boil beneath the surface, the wanting of a thing that never came to pass. Others seem to move on to something else and not look back.

"Tomorrow then?" he asks.

"Tomorrow," I say.

"Dinner?" he asks.

"Lunch?" I ask back.

"Oh, right," he says. He snaps, then points an index finger at me and says, *"Glacial pace."* We both laugh, and it feels good. His eyes are twinkling again and I *do* like him; I have to remember that.

An hour later Louisa shoos me out of WTA so I can make the 6:20 audition in Park Slope, Brooklyn. By 5:28 I've refreshed my makeup in WTA's bathroom, and now I'm waiting by the elevator bank. When the doors open, out steps a striking woman I recognize from Louisa's social media pictures as her psychologist-friend Sylvie Alvarez. Louisa talks all the time about Sylvie, almost like she's some kind of guru: *Sylvie says this; Sylvie says that.* Sometimes I think the stuff Sylvie tells Louisa sounds like crap, but if it works, if it makes Louisa feel even an ounce better about not being pregnant yet, then I'm grateful for it.

"Hi, Sylvie," I say as she's about to walk past me. We have a backdrop of movie posters and closing silver elevator doors, and it feels like something out of a meet-cute. I know I'm gonna miss the elevator by standing here, but the thing is, Sylvie's not on Louisa's calendar today, and Louisa has a five thirty appointment with an actress who makes WTA tons of money and can be really demanding. I don't want Sylvie knocking on Louisa's door during the meeting—it's too possible it would annoy the actress. And I'm not there to stop Sylvie from doing so, because Louisa did me the favor of letting me go early.

Sylvie looks at me and it's obvious she has no idea who I am.

"I'm June, Louisa's assistant," I say.

Sylvie puts a hand to her chest. "Oh! I've heard all about you," she says, with a warmth that makes me sure she's heard good things. It lights me right up.

"Louisa's in a meeting at five thirty," I say. I don't mention the actress's name, because I've learned that being discreet is one of the keys to being successful at WTA.

Sylvie loses her smile. "Oh," she says. She comes off as so statuesque even though she's only an inch taller than me. "I was hoping to take her out tonight," she says, as though I've said something that would prohibit her from doing so. She puts a hand toward her mouth and leans toward me like she has a secret. "You know she's turning forty tomorrow, right?" she asks.

I gasp way more dramatically than I would have liked. But I can't believe Louisa is almost forty—she looks younger—and I can't believe I almost missed her birthday. I'll have to figure out something I can get her tonight. Sylvie leans back and smiles; it comes off a little evil—like she's happy to have known this fact when I didn't. But the truth is that Louisa never makes anything about herself, so there's no way she would have mentioned a birthday to me, because she wouldn't have wanted to make me feel obligated to make a big deal about it or purchase something.

"I'm so glad you told me," I say, which is a grand understatement. I admire the delicate gold triangular studs that mark Sylvie's earlobes; she's wearing the kind of floor-length floral wrap dress that Saks sells for one of my paychecks, and she looks like a million bucks in it. She kind of comes off like a grand dame mixed with a mean girl. "But still, Sylvie," I go on, because another thing I've learned is that to placate anyone with an ego it helps to use a first name. It's almost as if they like the sound of themselves so much it's a balm to their ears. "I wouldn't knock on Louisa's door, okay? I'd wait for her in the lobby and have Kai at the front desk send her an email that you're waiting for her. This client can be higher maintenance than some of the others."

Sylvie's back to smiling, but this time it looks forced. It's been sort of enjoyable telling her she can't do something. I bet that doesn't happen a lot.

"Thanks for the advice, June," she says. It comes out kind of condescending, but maybe I'm just being sensitive. And who cares either way, because I'd bet twenty bucks she's no longer planning to interrupt Louisa.

I smile back. "You're welcome, Sylvie," I say.

Sylvie stares at me a beat too long. Then she proclaims, way too wisely for my liking, "At your age, it feels so good to finally be able to wield some power, doesn't it?"

My mouth drops. "Dang," I say, shaking my head a little. "You must be one heck of a shrink."

I say it just genuinely enough that she can't honestly tell Louisa I've been rude to her. I turn and walk into an opening elevator, and I don't look back. I can feel her eyes on me.

THIRTY-THREE

Rowan. Friday afternoon. November 11th.

Before I go to my mom's I stop by Harrison's. Just Lila and me, no Gabe.

I knock hard on Harrison's front door. At least Gabe's starting to let me go places. I got out of the apartment tonight by telling him the phone call was just Mulvahey checking up on my details (which was as truthful as I was willing to get with him), and that all of this with June was too upsetting, and I had to get out of our apartment and go back to my mom's. I told him everything at the care facility had been so good with my mom and Lila, and that I needed that moment again right now—not this. Gabe pecked my cheek and let me go, but his eyes held the kind of sadness that comes from the person you love accusing you of betrayal of the worst kind. And now that I've said it, I don't know how to take it back, or if I even should. The truth is, I can't say for sure that Gabe would never sleep with June. But maybe Harrison knows something I don't.

Harrison opens the door and I step into his airy, spectacular SoHo loft. There are no bedrooms, just a massive rectangle with a gorgeous kitchen and a high ceiling crisscrossed with wooden beams. I put down the oversized bag I packed with everything from diapers and baby paja-mas to my laptop and breast pump, and I say, "You look awful."

He shrugs a broad shoulder. He looks so young when he's upset, his full lips pouting like a child's.

"I'm worried about June," he says, helping me out of my coat. "The cops are coming by later to question me."

"That might be partly my fault," I say.

He's so close to me, helping set my arms free. His hands on me are strong and confident. "Oh, really?" he asks, like he's trying for light-hearted but not quite getting there.

Harrison notices things that Gabe doesn't, like how I would obvi-ously need help getting out of a coat like this when I have Lila strapped to me. He hangs my coat on a rack, and then he shuts the door behind me. He locks the chain. Jazz music is playing on his speakers; he used to tell me if he wasn't representing writers, he'd be repping musicians. I follow him to his living room. I need to put Lila down—I need a break from carrying her around. Even with the carrier in the right position my back is starting to scream. Harrison helps me unload a blanket from my diaper bag and we both kneel and spread it on the floor. I carefully rest Lila on it. I can't believe she doesn't wake up.

"She's so beautiful," Harrison says.

"She really is," I say. "I keep marveling at her. All the things every-one says about motherhood are actually true. And then some."

His face darkens as he stares at her. "But it's hard, too, right?"

"Yeah," I say. "It is. But I keep thinking how amazing it is that she's *her*, that the magic of her means that any other month I'd gotten pregnant it would have been with a different baby, not her. It's strange to recognize that."

"Life is complicated," Harrison says, his gaze still so dark. "Do you believe all of us were fated for each other somehow, to be in each other's lives? Or do you just believe that about Lila?"

It surprises me. "I guess I believe we're all in each other's orbits for a reason," I say. "Not even something metaphysical. Just that obviously we were all drawn to each other."

A car honks outside, and I imagine the SoHo streets swarming with shoppers.

"Well, I for one am starting to regret that June was a part of my orbit," Harrison says. His wavy blond hair is mussed like he was just outside in the blustery cold.

"What do you mean?"

"Where did she go, Rowan?" he asks sharply. "What happened to her? Do you think all of this is real?"

"I don't know what happened to her, same as you," I say, shaking my head. We're both still just kneeling on the floor by Lila.

"She was always looking for attention," Harrison says, his forehead creasing like he's trying to concentrate, to figure this out. "And I thought that maybe . . . is there a chance she's pulling something over on us? A trick?"

"They found blood in our building," I say. "And there's video footage of her going in and not coming out. So yeah, I'm pretty sure this is *real*."

Tears are in my eyes now. Harrison wraps his arms around me and helps me to my feet. "Oh no," he says, giving me a hug. It feels good to be this close to him. It's been so many years that he's been the one looking out for us, mostly for Gabe but also for me. He's been the one steering our ship, creatively and financially, and I trust him. "What if she's dead?" he asks, and a slight tremor goes through him. Finally he backs away and he looks unsteady as he makes his way to the sofa. I sit beside him. Maybe too close. But there's always this thing between us, whenever we're alone, which isn't often. I don't think it's sexual attraction or anything like that, but it's almost like a rope connecting us, drawing us closer.

"Gabe's lying to me about something," I say. "I know he would never hurt June, it's not that, it's just . . ."

Harrison's eyes are the color of deep blue denim jeans. And they're bloodshot. "Do you think Gabe and June were hooking up?" he asks me. I can see it in him—the fury. At least a part of him believes in the possibility of it. I can't tell if that's why he's so agitated. I hope so, because if I didn't know better, a part of me might think he was drinking again.

"Are you okay?" I ask.

"I need to know," he says, and I can see the shake in his hands, the jealousy at the thought of it happening: his friend/client, his girlfriend. "I need to know if June was messing around on me—and on you—with Gabe. I need to know if Gabe would do something like that to me."

"I don't think so," I say, because I really don't, no matter how much a fool it might make me. "I counted on June and I trusted her with Lila. I know she's young and I know people make mistakes, but I asked Gabe and he was furious at me for even thinking it."

Harrison snorts. "Gabe. Of course—of *course* he'd be defensive about it, like it was never even possible."

"I believe him," I say.

"Good for you," Harrison says with a laugh that comes out too crude. "It must be nice to be with someone you trust."

I take a minute. And then I ask the thing I'm scared of. "Do you think it's possible?"

He considers me. Says nothing.

"Do you think it's possible that he would cheat on me?" I ask, my voice getting too high, too pathetic.

Harrison turns away and looks out a black-framed window. Then he swivels his head to face me dead-on. "I do," he says, and my heart stills.

I swallow, trying to get myself back to okay. "Do you know something I don't?"

"No," he says with a sniff. "It's just a hunch."

A *hunch*. A pretty big thing to say about someone else's marriage, but I asked for it. We're quiet—it's one of the only times I've ever heard Harrison betray Gabe, and by the time I recover, the moment has broken apart and thrown us into different corners.

Harrison looks around his immaculate apartment. "I should pick up before the cops come," he says, his voice low. "I should be ready." He reaches out a trembling hand to touch my face. I grab his fingers and give them a small squeeze. It's always there, really. The alternate life—the split-second decision, the lingering question:

What would have been?

But it's different now that Lila's here. And that's what I'm thinking as I gather my baby and make my way to my mother. Everything is as it's meant to be. Isn't it?

THIRTY-FOUR

June. Three months ago. August 3rd.

Forty minutes later, after an uneventful subway ride, I'm standing outside a squat cement building waiting to go in and audition. I don't want to show up too early—I'm nervous enough without having to wait alongside other actresses. It's only my fourth time in Brooklyn, and I absolutely love it. (I once told Sean that I'd like to live in a Brooklyn neighborhood called Williamsburg, and he acted like I'd punched him in the face. It's becoming impossible to navigate a conversation with him; there are landmines everywhere.)

It's hot out and sticky, too, and the sky is white-gray and kind of scary, like it's holding on to trouble. I glance down at the paper I've printed, going over my audition lines silently in my head, my eyes closing as Brooklynites swirl around me.

CECILY

I think your frankness does you great credit, Ernest. If you will allow me, I will copy your remarks in my diary. Oh no. You see, it is simply a very young girl's record of her own thoughts and impressions, and consequently meant for publication. When it appears in volume form I hope you will order a copy.

Dear God, let me perform this scene well. I'm just such a newbie, I'm not even sure whether I'm supposed to do an English accent, but when I googled it last night it seemed like I should, and I just pray my accent doesn't suck too much.

A big, bulky door swings open. Out trots an elfin girl who doesn't look at me as she brushes past. I should really go in, but a part of me wants so badly to bolt. I imagine just turning around and going back to Sean, but that almost sounds worse than botching this audition and making a massive fool of myself. I've barely done any classical theater like this; most of the stuff we did in college was contemporary.

Still. I used to get the leads . . .

Now another guy barges out the door. He's carrying a headshot, which I don't have—*yet*. I've got to get on that; it's just so expensive. Like fifteen hundred for a good photographer.

I check my phone to see if there's anything from work Louisa needs, but there's nothing.

6:13.

I have to go inside. I make myself do it: I pull open the heavy door and go into a tiny lobby. Only one other actress is there, and she looks nothing like me, which is a relief. She's a short brunette who doesn't even look up as I enter, which is maybe for the best. She's studying her lines. And she has a headshot, too.

I wait my turn.

A bald man comes to the lobby and calls in the other girl. And as I wait, I can hear her saying Gwendolyn's lines—and she's definitely using an English accent, so that's good. And at least we're not auditioning for the same part—I'm pretty sure I'd be thrown off if I could hear her saying the lines I'd practiced into the still of the night. What else could I do last night in my room? I certainly couldn't sleep.

It's quiet in there when she's done. I can hear a low voice, maybe the director giving her feedback. She sounded pretty solid, actually, like a real actress. Confident. Which I'm not.

I suppose I could fake it. I've faked plenty of things since I've been in New York, so what's one more?

The girl is out the door and the bald man is back, saying, "Are you June?"

"I am," I say, smiling. He looks me over.

"Come in," he says too sternly, like I'm not supposed to be there and somehow inconveniencing him.

I follow him through a door into a black box theater not dissimilar to what we had in college, though this one is literally painted black: the walls, the four rows of bench seating, the stage itself.

"This is Michael," the bald man says about a guy who's maybe thirty, sitting in a chair. "He'll be reading Algernon."

"Hello," I say.

"Hi," he says back, already much friendlier than the bald man.

"And I'm Charles," says the man. He gestures around. "This is my theater. And so far I am displeased with the actors that have read for Cecily. So perhaps you will save the day." He forces a smile, and I realize the unfriendliness I thought I saw before might just be social awkwardness, for which I have a massive soft spot.

I turn my smiley glow upon him. "I certainly hope so," I say.

I stand on my mark, an X of blue tape. And then I think about what it would be like to land this role, to have Louisa come see me play Cecily, maybe Harrison, too, and maybe even Gabe. Why not? Why wouldn't I have them here watching me bathed in a spotlight I've only barely earned, soaking up their attention like I deserve it?

I take a breath.

I open my mouth.

And then I nail my audition.

The lines come from somewhere deep within, just like they've done before when I hit my performances correctly at school. It's otherworldly when it works, a force that churns inside you and comes out like a golden stream of light. You're connecting with the material because you've made it a part of you: you've joined with the character and made her your own. It doesn't matter that Oscar Wilde wrote her in 1895, because she's alive in *you*. You are *her*. You've shed your skin and it's glorious: the ultimate escape.

Charles is beaming when I finish. "Joan!" he says.

"June," I say, a snap in my voice because I know how good I've been.

"June," he says quickly. *"June."*

Michael is smiling from his cheap, crappy folding chair.

"That was magnificent," Charles says.

"Thank you," I say. It was.

"Do you have a headshot for me?" he asks.

"Nope," I say. "But my Instagram has plenty of photos of me." I smile, knowing that not having a headshot doesn't matter now.

He laughs. He knows it doesn't, either. "How about a résumé?"

I shake my head. Louisa said she would help me with one, but we've been so busy lately.

"All right then, how about you fill out a contact sheet here, and that way I can get in touch with you this week."

"Okay," I say. "Thank you so much."

I'm brimming with something so powerful I feel like I could lift off of the oily black stage floor and fly far away from here, over the rushing swells of the East River, back to Manhattan. My fingers are barely my own as they fly over the contact sheet with a stubby pencil. I say my goodbyes to Michael and Charles and hurry out of the theater and into the lobby and onto the street. I'm breathing so fast I could faint. I stand there, pressing my back against the bricks, barely able to believe what's just happened.

I did it.

My hands are shaking as I power on my phone. A text from Kai parades across the screen.

I don't love you dating Harrison, if that's indeed what you're doing. He's way older than us. And he's kind of intense, don't you think?

My heart pounds. But I barely have time to even process it because a sharp voice calls my name.

"June!"

I turn back to the theater—did I forget something? But it didn't sound like Michael or Charles, it sounded like . . .

Shit.

It sounded like Sean.

I turn, scanning a group of people across the street. There's a couple pushing a boy on a tricycle and a delivery man carting a half dozen plastic bags with stapled receipts waving like flags. Beyond them is a dog walker running half a dozen dogs, and then, standing there in a tattered orange baseball cap and gym clothes, is Sean.

"What are you doing here?" I shout in disbelief. I can't help it. "Is everything okay?" He knew I had an audition in Brooklyn, but I don't think I ever told him the name of the theater. And it's a thirty-minute subway trip here from our apartment.

He's wounded that I've said this—of course he is. Immediately I try to smooth it over. "Hang on!" I call across the street. I dodge a taxi as I cross Seventh Avenue to get to him. I just want this interaction to happen as far away from the theater as possible—and from what just happened inside it. I want Sean separate from this night.

"Everything's fine," Sean says when I arrive on his side of the street. I'm out of breath from sprinting and postaudition nerves.

"Oh," I say, trying to understand what's going on here. "Then why are you here?"

"Why am I here?" he repeats.

"Yeah," I say, trying to mask how annoyed I am.

"I'm here because it's getting dark out, and I didn't want you to have to come home from Brooklyn all by yourself. You barely know the subway system, June."

I stifle the grimace on my face; I try hard to make my attitude more palatable. I've signed a lease for one year with Sean. I could break it—of course I could—but not without financial penalties.

"How chivalrous," I say, even though it's *not*. It's controlling. And I'm really starting to get fed up. "But Sean," I say carefully. "Please, next time, shoot me a text so I have a say in it, okay? If you're trying to be helpful, I appreciate that. But it's seven o'clock. It's hardly pitch black out and plus I know how to take the subway. I'm not eleven."

His jaw drops. "That's very ungrateful, June," he says. "Maybe I'll just be done helping you, and you can see how you do all by yourself." And then he turns and walks away.

"What? Wait!" I call out. Did he seriously come all this way just to huff off back to Manhattan because I called his bluff? "Sean, come on," I say, trotting after him in my heels, which is hard. A few sidewalk slabs later one of my shoes catches on a crack and I lurch forward. I think I've caught myself, but then my ankle twists and I go down. "Ouch!" I cry out.

Sean turns and I watch it happen: his anger melts into an easy, gooey expression that turns my stomach. He's going to help me; he's going to be my rescuer, which is all he's ever wanted to do. I don't even think he wants to touch me. I'm not kidding when I say nothing about us feels romantic: it's something so much more twisted. Maybe I do need to break that lease.

I spit. I'm on my hands and knees, and my ankle is screaming at me, and I don't think I've ever been pissed or humiliated enough to spit, but apparently there's a first time for everything.

"Oh, *June*," Sean says.

He's coming toward me. I can hear the squeak of his sneakers even above the sounds of Brooklyn, which makes me feel like maybe I'm imagining it—or maybe he's driving me so insane I'm tuning in to his frequencies like an animal would. I find myself feeling like that in our apartment all the time: once I *smelled* him outside my door before he even knocked.

"Leave me alone, Sean," I say. I'm still on my hands and knees, and tears burn my eyes.

"There, there," he says, bending, his sweatpants-cloaked knees too close to my face.

"There, there?" I repeat. "Are you for real?"

"June, you're upset," he says. "You've had a fright."

"A fright?" I can't even with this guy. "Sean, *enough*," I say. "Enough with all the concern for me. I'm completely fine. Stop acting like I'm a child. I don't like it. I never even liked being a child in the first place."

"Me neither," Sean says. He brushes dirt off the thigh of his sweatpants. They're so thin I can see the deep line of his quad muscles.

"Well, then we have that in common," I say. "Now help me get up."

He does.

"Let's go home, June," Sean says. "We should get ice on that."

I follow him, limping toward the subway in angry silence.

THIRTY-FIVE

Rowan. Friday afternoon. November 11th.

My mom isn't okay when I get to her room. Something's clearly gone down before I get there—an episode of sorts. The nurse tells me my mom has had a rough day, and that I shouldn't expect her to be lucid, and also that Gabe's mom is coming later and still planning to take my mom to bingo. "Sometimes Elena needs to see your mom for herself to realize she's not up for it," the nurse tells me before she leaves us alone.

I can tell by the way my mom is lying there in her bed with her hair a mess and tears streaking her face that it's been bad. Sometimes when she's confused she lashes out, and I'll never get used to how scary it is when it happens. She's so tiny I'm not worried about her hurting Lila or me, only herself.

I want my mother back.

I sit with Lila at the edge of the bed. My mom is sleeping, and I don't want to wake her, so I hold Lila and watch the dark sky. There was so much good my mom gave me, so much of herself she poured into making us as okay as we could be. I never once doubted her love, and I used to think that was magical because I knew something so different with my dad. But now that Lila's here I realize the word *magic*—or any other word, really—can't begin to describe what's between a mother and her child. It's the first thing that's ever defied my ability to write about it.

My mom stirs. Only her reading lamp is on. They always leave it on for her at night in case she wakes and doesn't know where she is. I reach out a hand and pat her leg gently as she wakes up. "Mom," I say softly, cradling Lila with the other hand. Her eyes flutter open. "Rowan," she says, which floods me with relief, but she looks so scared it doesn't last long.

"I'm right here," I say.

Lila's sleeping deeply on my chest, and there's a hazy warmth to the room even though it's freezing outside tonight. The dim light reminds me of when my mom and I would curl up in her bed each night. "Mom," I say carefully.

She tries to pull herself up onto her elbows but it's too awkward— she can't quite get her body right. So she rolls onto her side and props up her head with a pillow. "Sweetheart," she says. "I need to talk to you. I've been asking them to send you to me all day. They kept telling me how busy you are."

"Why didn't you call me?" I ask softly. The low lighting inside her room makes me want to whisper. "I would have come."

"I know, dear," she says. "I couldn't find my phone. I think I've misplaced it."

I'm sure it's in her desk where it always is, but I don't say that because I don't want her to feel bad.

"I was thinking, sweetie, about everything that's happened to you. And I want to tell you something, and whatever you decide to do with that information is okay with me. All right?"

I nod, unsure of where she's going, surprised she's this lucid.

"I think the truth may be more important to you than protecting myself. And Ken, well, he's dead and gone now anyway. Heart attack, you remember?"

"Ken Conroy?" I ask, confused. He was one of my dad's friends, and the only person named Ken whom we both know.

She nods. I didn't know he was dead; she never told me, and I don't make it my business to keep track of my dad's friends. I tried to bury them the same time we buried my dad. I remember the exquisite agony of running into one or two of them in town at the deli buying sandwiches and Coca-Cola, or at the Hollywood Video renting movies for whatever family they had left. Most of them disintegrated, folding in on themselves, getting into scrapes with the law and leaving wives and children.

"It's just that," my mom starts, then pauses. "I know you're working with that woman Sylvie. And that she says you'll figure out why you had that break and snapped on your sitter, and you'll put all those pieces together yourself, with Sylvie, safely. But I want you to know that I've done some reading on PTSD, here, alone, on my phone. There's just so much alone time here."

Guilt floods every cell. Couldn't I have her live with us? Couldn't I get her out of this place?

Where is June?

I shudder. I want to talk to my mom about what's happening at our apartment right now—I can practically see the uniformed cops swarming it with dogs and flashlights and forensic equipment. Will there be sirens? Will our neighbors pour into the hallways? Will they find something?

My mind runs in a loop, but I focus on my mom because it's so clear she needs to say this.

"And what I've read as I've researched is that any mind is capable of shutting down and repressing the memory of a traumatic event. And I know how traumatic Lila's birth was. It's just, Rowan, your mind has already had practice at shutting down and forgetting."

I pat Lila's butt, my eyebrows up. "What do you mean?" I ask. I think of the knife and what I remember about my dad's bedroom that night.

231

"I was carrying on with your father's friend Ken," my mom says, like a foot smashing a hornet's nest.

"*What?*" I ask. If I wasn't sitting, my legs would have given out. "Carrying on? You mean having an affair?"

"Yes," my mother says, matter-of-factly, like we're talking about something else. And there's no guilt in her eyes, only fire, like she has to tell me something and this is only the tip of the iceberg, and also like this is no longer about her but about something much bigger.

"Really?" I ask, incredulous. I'm never much surprised by people's affairs. But this is different; this is my mother.

"Yes," she says again. "And Ken killed your father."

My heart stops. It skips so many beats I swear I'll die right there. I can't speak. I can only stare at her beautiful face squinting at me, taking me in.

"Mom," I finally say, my hand still against Lila's back. "Why didn't you ever tell me?"

"Because you already knew," she says, and she leans into me and takes my hand. "You were there. You saw it."

I'm not sure where I go in that moment. The room feels fuzzy, the edges of the bed blurring, shadows dancing over the walls. A car honks somewhere nearby and it feels like a slap.

"You were just a bitty thing, Rowan," she says. "You were only five. At first I thought we were both pretending not to know. But then I realized you'd been so traumatized that you'd blocked it out. And I was too scared to put you in therapy, too scared of what you'd remember and reveal to a therapist or to the authorities. I loved Ken and my heart was broken, and I worried that not only would Ken go to jail but somehow I'd be implicated in what happened and I'd be taken away from you. Your father was dead and nothing was bringing him back, and I'd seen it with my own eyes—it was self-defense. I didn't need a jury to find Ken innocent, not when I knew there'd be so many ways a trial could go wrong."

My blood pumps faster. I try to play the scene in my mind, but I can't get it right.

"What happened?" I ask. "That night? What did I see?"

"It was the oldest story, that's the sad part," my mom says, shaking her head, looking regretful for the first time. "Your father was who he was—I won't blame him for what I did—but I fell in love with Ken. That's what it was—*love*. Strange as it sounds. I'd never stepped out on your dad before, and it took me by surprise, swept me off my feet, all the things you hear about people feeling in a marriage that shake them awake and make them stray. And I did. Ken wasn't married, didn't even have a girlfriend, which made it easier to rationalize. Your dad came home one night and caught Ken in our house and he knew. I never slept with Ken in our home, but that night Ken had come to talk to me, he was desperate, it was late, I let him in. He was drunk, ranting on about wanting to run away with me, having it be just us, and you, of course: he knew I'd never leave you. Your father came in during his impassioned speech. He lost his mind and they fought. And that's when you came downstairs into the kitchen to find out what was going on. I tried to pull your dad off Ken, which worked for a moment, but then your dad grabbed a knife and chased him upstairs. We all went up. There wasn't enough time to keep you from seeing it—I knew your dad was capable of killing Ken with that knife, and I knew I had to try to stop him. But when we all piled into the bedroom, it was Ken who'd gotten control of the knife. You and I both saw him stab your dad. Once to the stomach and it was over."

I pull Lila up and put my lips against her head. I can't believe what I'm hearing, and yet, deep down I know it like a hard shiny kernel of something real; I understand this story like words I could write on a blank page and know them to be mine. But I can't see it—yet. I can only reimagine the scene, but I'm not sure if part of what I'm seeing is true memory or if I'm coloring in the lines with what my mom's telling me.

"What did I do?" I ask. "What did I do when I saw Dad stabbed?"

"Nothing," she says. "Neither one of us did anything for the first few seconds, we were so deeply in shock. Ken and I tried putting pressure on Dad's wound, but it was no use. You just stood there, and all I could think about was how I'd ruined your entire life. I couldn't look at Ken again—not after what I'd done to you. That night was the last night I ever saw him alone. I'm so sorry, Rowan. You'll never know how sorry I am."

"The watch?" I ask, but even as I ask it a memory comes back: I swear I can see her handing it to Ken.

"I told Ken to take it and to lose it," she says. "I was thinking so fast. I told him I'd tell the police there was an intruder and that they took the watch. You were practically catatonic at that point. I wrapped you in a blanket and called the police, and when they came, I told them you were sleeping in your bedroom and never saw a thing." She leans forward and puts a hand on me. She doesn't touch Lila. She is only my mother in this moment, nothing else.

"Will you ever be able to forgive me?" she asks.

My heart slows down. "I think I already have, a long time ago," I say.

We sit there saying nothing, gazing at each other through a haze of what we've just said. There were always words between us, but there aren't any more for this moment. Even Lila goes still, no more squirming against me. I hold my mom's hand and it feels like an hour passes, and eventually her eyes get heavy. "Sleep, Mom," I say. "I'll be here when you wake up."

When she starts to doze I take my laptop from my bag. I open it, my fingers hovering over the file marked *November pages for Dave*, thinking that if I've just survived a night like this one, then certainly I can handle reading old pages that seemed to scare my agent. I click. The work comes to life, glowing like a beacon in my mother's dark room.

Chapter One

Josephine

Moth wings beat against my bedroom window, trying to get into the light. Two tiny babies sleep on ivory sheets beside me—a boy and a girl. They are mine.

Piano music filters from the apartment next door and I imagine a woman weeping as she plays a baby grand. When the music stops, I imagine her rising from the bench and clawing at the walls, shredding wallpaper into bits that gather beneath her fingernails.

"Where is he?" she screams. "Where did he go?"

This woman—who is she?

I close my eyes and try to forget her, but she is there, pressing against my skin, freeing it from the bone, trying to get out.

THIRTY-SIX

June. Three months ago. August 4th.

The morning after my audition I'm standing outside Louisa's apartment with coffees and a slew of paperwork. I'm in shorts and a tank because it's so hot. (New York City's in the middle of a heat wave, and there are advisories for children and the elderly blasting on my phone's notifications every hour or so.) I raise my hand to knock on Louisa's door, nervous about what I'll find inside her apartment. She sounded awful when she called me at my cubicle this morning at eight thirty, her voice wobbling and unfamiliar when she asked if I wouldn't mind bringing her a few things from her office because she needed to work from home today. I don't know whether she's going to want me to stay or go, so I brought screenplays to read if she wants company. It's her fortieth, like Sylvie told me, so I have a box of chocolates from this place she loves near work and a necklace I found for ten dollars at a street sale last night that I know she'll love, a simple piece of white coral on a thin gold chain. I'm hoping she went out last night to celebrate and that she's just really hungover. Though that doesn't really sound like Louisa.

The door swings open. It's James, Louisa's husband. I've met him twice at WTA when he's been by to bring her flowers or lunch.

"Hi, James," I say carefully. "Is Louisa all right?"

James's face is drawn, lines etched from his eyes to his hairline. "She isn't, not really, but she will be," he says. He tries to smile, but it doesn't work. "She said I could bring you back, if that's okay with you?"

"Of course," I say, because all I want is to see her.

We walk through the living room into a long, slim hallway lined with a smattering of carefully curated beautiful things: photos of James, Louisa, and other family members; some random vintage ads for perfumes in ornate silver frames; and a few pencil drawings of birds. James knocks on a door, and Louisa's quiet voice says, "Come in."

James gently pushes open the door. "Let me know if you guys need anything," he says before leaving us alone.

I creep into Louisa's room and see her sitting up in bed. Her eyes are bloodshot and there are still tears on her face.

"Are you okay?" I ask, going to her.

She shakes her head slowly, her eyes on me. "I had another miscarriage," she says, her voice so soft it breaks me.

My hands cover my mouth. "Oh no, Louisa," I say through my fingers.

"I was going to tell you about being pregnant today. Because it's my fortieth, I don't think I told you that, so I thought it would be fun to celebrate by telling you and Sylvie and a few of my close friends."

I start crying. "I'm so, so sorry," I say.

"Me too," Louisa says, patting the bed beside her for me to come sit. I do. "The miscarriage started last night," she says. "And I think, you know, I think it's all done. I have an appointment at my OB in a few hours to make sure. No one ever tells you what a miscarriage is like. I mean, the details of it. You know miscarriage exists because people talk about it somewhat, but no one tells you the details. It's crazy, June, it's almost like giving birth, and I just don't know why no one ever tells you these things, so you're prepared, and so you could know what to do, and so it wouldn't be so terrifying and traumatic because maybe you'd be more ready, if that's even possible . . ."

She starts sobbing. I wrap my arms around her and hold her tight as she cries. I've never wanted something so badly for someone else, something I can't even come close to giving her, and I've never seen grief like this up close; I've never felt my body so consumed with how someone else feels. Maybe it's the whole point of being here on this planet; to be close to each other and love each other. Maybe I don't need to rise to the highest point in the pop culture heavens or have a million Instagram followers to feel happy.

I cry harder into her shoulder and my tears are about her and so much more: some of it just plain gratitude for how she always makes me feel—loved and included. That she would choose to tell me about an early pregnancy, that I'm that important to her . . . I swear Louisa makes me feel more special than anyone has in forever. This is the real kind of special: the kind I should be searching for, not the fake kind that comes with being an adored actress, the kind I've been chasing.

Maybe it's just this.

THIRTY-SEVEN

Rowan. Friday evening. November 11th.

It's still only early evening, but my mom's room is pitch black except for the glow of my laptop, and she and Lila are both sleeping soundly. The cops haven't called me yet, and my fingers shake each time I check my phone.

In the dark I reread my writing over and over. The pages that follow that first section from Josephine detail two women: one who knows a tragedy has happened and is on the brink of insanity trying to get everyone to believe her, and another who stands by and watches carefully, at first observing the mad woman with curiosity, then empathy, then desperation. Suddenly the second woman's life becomes about helping pull the first woman from the depths of madness. The storylines of the two women dovetail—at first they're barely acquaintances, and then they become so deeply involved in each other's lives that they're ultimately the only ones who can save each other.

My heart beats erratically as I fly through the chapters, unsure of the problem my agent had with the pages. Certainly they're more fragmented and metaphorical than what I usually write: it's as though I was writing about a feeling rather than the plot-driven stuff that's my bread and butter. There's also an allegory of a lush, deep green forest the first woman enters with her family: four go in, and only three come out. Some of it is stream of consciousness, as Dave said. But some of it is *good*, and the insidious, dark feeling of it reaches a hand into my brain and twists. There's something *here*, an undertone of warning and danger. When I write my novels I write circles around the things that scare me, the things I can't—or won't—face in myself or in others. I have a creeping feeling that I'm getting closer to understanding what it is I was trying to say. I remember the night I wrote this—it was like I was in a delirious frenzy. Rain was pelting the window in a rhythmic *tap-tap-tap* that lulled me somewhere deep, almost sleepy but too wired to pull myself away from the keyboard. And then around midnight I fired off the pages to Dave in an email and powered down my laptop.

But now that I'm in them again, there seems to be a sense of me trying to claw my way out of something. My entire body feels like it's cramping up as I read the pages over and over. I squeeze my fists and release them, knowing I need a break from this. I put the laptop on my mom's desk and sit with Lila in the recliner opposite my mom's bed. I'll just watch her sleep for a bit, and then I'll leave her a note and I'll go.

After a while I close my eyes, just for a moment, but before I know it my thoughts are taffy, all stretched out and dreamy, and then I'm sleeping. In my dreams I look down to see a little boy wrapped in a swaddle. I carefully take him from a nurse, and this time no one tries to take him from my arms like in all my other dreams. Ghosts stand around my hospital bed, but they don't seem scary at all.

I look down at the beautiful baby. "Gray," I say, gathering him to me. I weep onto his smooth, unearthly pale skin.

THIRTY-EIGHT

June. Three months ago. August 4th.

We've been working side by side for two hours when Louisa gets up to go to the bathroom. I freeze, listening for sounds of her crying, scared she's going to be bleeding and that I won't know how to help her. I know it's nuts for her even to be working today, but I also know that me being here and us working together is taking her mind off what happened. Or at least that's what James whispered to me in the kitchen when we took a break to make Louisa lunch.

Louisa seems okay when she comes out of the bathroom. Maybe it's really over—the physical part, at least. She stands at the edge of the bed where she's working. I've been working at a little dressing table. My phone buzzes with a text from Harrison.

Haven't seen you yet today. All ok? Lunch still on? If you're free, I'd love to see you.

Hey! I text back. I'd completely forgotten about lunch today. I'm so sorry. Something came up. I'm working at Louisa's today. Can we raincheck for tomorrow?

I stare at my phone, but Harrison doesn't text back.

"I've got a favor to ask of you, June," Louisa says. She's so distracted and unlike herself that I have to focus extra hard on what she's been telling me today so I don't miss anything. "I've got one of Gabe O'Sullivan's scripts with notes," she says.

My heart squeezes like a fist at the sound of Gabe's name. I don't like it—especially when I've done a good job forgetting him today. (Which makes me think I maybe have some shred of decency left.) "Normally I'd just messenger it back to him," she says. "But I don't want to use the company messenger service from my home address. Can I let you go early today and you can drop the script at Gabe's building with the doorman on your way home?"

Oh God.

Yes? No? "Of course," I say, because how else can I answer this question without explaining that I should be staying far, far away from Gabe O'Sullivan?

"You sure?" Louisa asks, an eyebrow up. She's not distracted enough to miss something strange on my face.

"I'm sure," I say confidently.

"He's a terrific writer," Louisa says. "And have you read his wife?"

My heart pounds. I read her writing last night for the first time. It was terrific. "I read her debut novel last night in one sitting," I say. "After I met them both at the reading, I was curious."

"They're both so magnetic," Louisa says. "And that first novel of hers is a stunner. They're expecting, you know, so just imagine the talent genes." Louisa looks out the window of her bedroom to her view of Central Park. I wonder if she's thinking about Rowan being pregnant, and how lucky she is. "The O'Sullivans are both just so incredibly talented," she says, distracted again. "I mean, you'd hate them if you could, but they're just so lovable, the both of them."

I force a smile.

She looks back at me. "I'm getting pretty tired, June. I think I should probably rest. How about you take that script down to Gabe's place?"

THIRTY-NINE

Rowan. Friday evening. November 11th.

I'm a madwoman racing Lila and myself back downtown.
It's too dark, too hot, and I imagine the car dying and skidding off
the road and the police coming to find us overheating and delirious. Lila's asleep in her car seat—thank God for that—and down the
West Side Highway I go, gripping the wheel with sweat slicking my
palms and worried I'll lose control and drive us both into a guardrail.

Fifty-Seventh Street.

Forty-Second.

Thirty-Fourth.

I try to hold the wheel tighter, but I can't stop shaking and sweating—I can't seem to get a good hold on the car. I brake too hard for
a red light and we lurch to a stop. I look into my rearview mirror to
catch Lila's reflection in the infant mirror we've set up, and I can see
her beautiful face, but not the rise and fall of her chest. I hope she's
all right—her neck is strained at the worst angle, and for a moment I
consider getting out of the car and trying to fix her. But the light turns
green and someone behind me blasts the horn. I hit the accelerator and
we start again, faster, faster, and I'm so scared I'll lose consciousness and
slip away and they'll find me dead or dreaming on the side of the road,

dreaming of babies, dreaming of him again. I roll down the windows, needing the air on my skin, needing to feel connected to something outside this claustrophobic box. My phone rings. I expect it's Gabe, but when I look down I see it's the detective. I don't answer.

The yellow and white lines blur as we pick up speed. I keep going until I exit into the Meatpacking District, passing retail shops with window lights illuminating beautiful things.

I take Washington Street to the parking garage and swing inside, hoping there won't be a line of cars waiting. There isn't. The attendant takes my keys and I thank him and gather my baby and our bag and then I'm booking down the street, Lila against me. I race past Horatio Street and Jane Street and turn left on West Eleventh, sprinting to the townhouse on my right. The muscles in my legs are like water as I try to climb the front steps. I pound the door and ring the bell over and over. When the big oak door finally swings open I say, "Help me."

Sylvie's fingers rest against the wooden doorframe. She looks so calm, like this has happened before. "Rowan," she says softly, "what can I do for you?"

"I remember," I say.

She stares at me, her dark eyes bright.

"I remember a little boy," I say, the words metallic in my mouth, choking me as they burst free. "My little boy."

"Come in, Rowan," she says, and I do.

FORTY

June. Three months ago. August 4th.

My God. I'm here. Right inside Gabe's apartment building. It's old-fashioned and gorgeous, with a gold ceiling and a decadent chandelier from an era when movie stars slipped in and out of New York buildings and had love affairs and no one was on social media. There had to have been more secrets back then. Or at least, more secrets kept.

I scan the lobby and die a small death when I see a doorman positioned off to the side. My heart pounds, my fingers are tight against the script. What if he just takes it from me and brings it to Gabe himself? Isn't that how doormen work?

"Good afternoon," says the man.

I try to force a smile. I want to see Gabe so badly it feels like a physical presence, like I could put my hands inside myself and rip it out and show someone the thing throbbing in my palm. And it makes me so shameful that I can feel this way about someone who isn't available. At Louisa's, when we were hugging, I felt so sure that I'd figured it all out, and now I'm coveting a married man. But it's okay, I think, to have a little crush, to want to be near someone. Right? I'm not going to act on it. It's just that hole I keep talking about. It felt full at Louisa's, and now here it is again, empty and waiting.

"Um, hi," I say to the doorman. "I'm June Waters." I sound fake even to myself. How will I ever make it here?

"How can I help you?" asks the doorman. He scans me, and then grins so appreciatively I'm sure his face will split in two. Ew.

"I'm here to see Gabe O'Sullivan." There we go: that wasn't a lie. I *am* here to see Gabe O'Sullivan and give him a package.

"Is he expecting you?" the doorman asks. I really should just leave the script with the doorman. I know I should, but I don't. I can't make myself say the words.

"Um," I say again, stalling. Is Gabe expecting me? I don't know— but probably not. Louisa told him she'd have the script messengered to him, which would mean either any random low-level person like me or a messenger service.

"Yes," I lie, and I find myself warming up to it—to being someone else. Someone Gabe's expecting to see. "He's expecting me."

"Then just a moment," the doorman says. He lifts a phone receiver that looks like it's from the nineties and presses a few buttons. "I've got June here for you," he says into the receiver, like he and I are old friends on a first-name basis, even though he probably just forgot my last name. I kick myself for not picking something more memorable than *Waters*. Wasn't that the whole point?

The moments I stand there waiting for whatever Gabe decides on the other end of the line are agony. Is he going to ask me to go up to his apartment? Is he going to come down here to the lobby? Is he going to tell me to just leave the script with the doorman?

I tap my sneakered foot, wishing I'd worn something different today. The doorman is still staring at me. He stares at me while I wait one beat and then two; he stares at me while he listens to Gabe, while I turn away and count cracks in the floor near my feet. I wish he wouldn't look at me like this, but I have no control over the wrong stares. It's kind of awful, isn't it? How you can want the stare of someone so very much—and then feel sick to your stomach when it's the wrong man.

"Gabe will be right down," the doorman says.

Gabe will be right down.

I turn away and let my eyes settle on a framed black-and-white photograph of a woman wearing a cap-sleeved leotard and smoking a cigarette. It takes up nearly the entire wall. Beneath it sits a plush velvet bench with gold armrests that swirl like vines. The floor beneath me is brown-and-white checkerboard tile. This building feels like a different world.

The elevator doors open and then there's Gabe, walking toward me. He's smiling, and the words *rakish grin* trail through my brain, and I realize I never really understood that phrase until this moment.

"June," he says softly, not even acknowledging the doorman.

My insides do something strange, and I feel unsteady on my feet. I swear to God I don't know the last time I felt like this. Maybe once or twice when I was a teenager, but not since. I clear my throat.

"Hi," I manage to say. He stops in front of me. Only a few feet separate us now.

"Whattya have for me?" he asks casually, and he looks at me like he's ready for this, for whatever this is going to be, like he's been waiting for me. Sometimes actors are like this—so charismatic you melt within moments of them coming into the office—but not usually the writers. They're broodier and almost always less socially adept. Some of them won't even come in for meetings—they just want to do it over the phone. So it's hard for me to figure out whether this is just what he's always like with women, or if it has anything to do with me. Maybe I'm trying to figure out what I'm always trying to figure out: Am I special enough to be an actress? To be someone Gabe wants to be around? I wouldn't ever even need to kiss him. I just want to be near him.

"I have a script," I blurt. The lobby seems suddenly darker, as if a bulb burned out. Or maybe my eyes aren't adjusting right from the sun.

Or maybe I'm about to faint because this man is now standing so close to me I can see the lines etching his olive skin, the faint stubble on his jaw. "From Louisa," I say. Why can't I say anything interesting?

"I'd have you up to my place for a cup of coffee, but my wife is writing," he says. Still smiling, but it dims a little.

My wife.

Rowan O'Sullivan is probably writing her next mystery novel. Probably keeping him on his toes with her brilliant mind. Probably the perfect match for him.

But would he be looking at me like this if that were true?

"I love your building," I say. *I don't love your doorman,* I think, because I can still feel the man's eyes on me.

"Do you?" he asks.

I nod.

"Hey then," he says. "How about I give you a tour of the billiards room and the secret staircase. There's a garden out back, too, and we can go over the notes on my script together. I mean, if you have time," he adds.

My heart hums. I read Gabe's script at Louisa's and made my own mental notes on both his story and the feedback and notes so far. That he might want to hear what I have to say about the script . . .

"Okay," I say quickly, a jolt of energy running through me.

He reaches out a hand, and I almost give him mine. But then I realize he wants me to hand over the script. I do.

"Let's go, June," he says.

I can feel the doorman's eyes boring into my back as I follow Gabe toward leaded glass windows and a black iron door.

FORTY-ONE

Rowan. Friday evening. November 11th.

I'm rocking Lila inside Sylvie's office, swaying to the clock, feeling Sylvie's eyes on me. I look at Lila's little socked feet and run my fingers over her toes.

"I remember him," I say again, still only looking at Lila. I need Sylvie, but I need Lila more, and Sylvie's so quiet, innately sensing it.

"I remember a little boy," I say, finally meeting Sylvie's eyes. "Lila's brother. Her twin. We named him Gray, and they tried to let me hold him, and they tried to tell me he didn't make it, but I already knew that because I was his mother. I knew it first, before anyone else. I think I knew it the moment I started bleeding on my walk that day, and I think I knew it all the way to the hospital in that ambulance. I definitely knew it when they were slicing into me. I could feel him gone."

I look back down to Lila. "And then," I say, "I didn't know it at all. The things that have been fuzzy in my memory: the sonogram appointments, the birth, all those things have been me trying to forget him, to lock him away. Because remembering him is so painful I'm not sure I . . ."

My voice trails off, not because it's too hard to say the words but because I think the words are only for Gabe, Lila, Gray, and me. The truth is that I loved Gray; I still do, I always will, and so does Gabe, and he's out there mourning our son without me, and I need to go to him.

"Why didn't you tell me?" I ask Sylvie.

Sylvie's eyes are kind now, there's less agitation in her frame. I never had anything to compare it to because I only ever knew her as a woman with an impossible case: *me*. But now something's broken open, and she seems easier with me. "From my understanding," she says carefully, "from what the doctors told me, they kept trying to tell you in the hospital that Gray didn't make it, but you couldn't take it in. You panicked; you dissociated. You were not well. You weren't ready to accept what had happened, and the doctors feared that continually retraumatizing you with the story of what happened to Gray would get in the way of the healthy bond you were trying to create with Lila. A decision was made to allow you to leave the hospital with Lila in the only way you seemed to be able to: as Lila's mother, not as a mother who had lost her baby. With proper help, your doctor and I believed you would remember in your own time, safely. And you have, Rowan."

I put Lila on my shoulder and pat her gently.

"I need to get back to my family," I say to Sylvie. "Gabe lost his son, too, and I haven't been able to be there for him, to help him with how awful he must feel, or with anything. I've only blamed him, mostly in my mind, for not being attentive and loving enough for me or being everything I need, or for being distracted. Meanwhile I haven't done anything for him or anyone else during the past few weeks except forget Gray and scare everyone I love."

"That's not true, Rowan," Sylvie says firmly. "The truth is that you've done a beautiful job feeding, loving, and taking care of your surviving baby, creating the kind of bond every mother hopes for. And that's a monumental thing."

My feet tap the floor. I can feel my body coming back to itself, being mine again. And then I think of something that makes more sense now. "Is this why Gabe hasn't let me see my friends?"

Sylvie nods. "So many people can't bear to witness PTSD this severe up close. The last thing we wanted was your friends breaking down in front of you and you not understanding why. We also tried to stall you on seeing your mother because, though we spoke to her about Gray dying and you blocking out his memory, we knew there was a chance she'd become confused and accidentally tell you about him. But then when you'd gone a few weeks without remembering, we were willing to take that risk so you could see her. It seemed very important for you to see your mom, and not worth the damage caused by keeping you away and Lila not meeting her. Elena, of course, was able to keep it together. And the entire reason Gabe brought June in to help is because he was sure she'd be able to keep a professional distance and respect what we were asking of her, which was for her to help you with Lila and not remind you of the baby you'd lost, and to let you come to it in your own time. The ultimate acting job, really, and Louisa was also sure June could do it. And I think June did do it, actually—I think she handled all of it remarkably well for a young person, until of course that day you accused her of hurting Lila. But perhaps now you understand why your mind was so shattered and confused by the memories it was trying to repress. Perhaps now you can understand why you lashed out at June, why you were so sure your baby was hurt."

"What happened to him?" I ask, the words nearly unbearable to say. "To my son. Do you know?"

"Gray's placenta detached, which your OB told me occurs more frequently during twin pregnancies. Your OB is updated on everything we've been doing here, and he'll be ready for your call when you are. After you speak with him, I hope you'll come to me, and we can process it together. The sad truth is that so many women lose babies during miscarriages and stillbirths and most don't receive the proper help for it. It is a *trauma* to lose a baby, no doubt about that. But often we brush it under the rug as normal, just a fact of life. And it may be a fact of life, but the women I see here, and some of the men, too, depending on how far along the pregnancy was and if they were present for the miscarriage, are extremely traumatized."

"I'll keep coming," I say, knowing that I will. "I want to remember him and mourn him and I want the sonogram photos back and maybe photos of him when he was born, if we have any, and I want to frame them and have them in our home and tell Lila about him and never ever forget him again." I'm sobbing now. "I need to get to Gabe," I say, and then my phone rings. It's the detective again. He's the last person I want to talk to, but what if he needs my help? What if June needs me?

I pick up the call.

"Mrs. O'Sullivan," he says, his voice low and gravelly, and there's so much static on the line it's hard to hear him, and he goes on about something I can't make out, but then the line goes crystal clear and he says, "I need you here to identify the body."

My heart pounds so ferociously I'm sure it'll beat free of my chest. "No," I say. *"No."*

"We found June inside the billiards room in the basement of your apartment building," he says into my ear. "Can you hear me?" he asks. I shake my head furiously. There's static in my ears and I'm sure it's my blood going haywire, and the detective is trying to tell me something, something about June, but his words are too staticky and I can't process them.

"Please, please," I say, because I need a minute, but he won't stop talking.

"Are you okay?" he's asking me, his voice finally cutting through the static. And then, "Rowan, just come back to your apartment building. I need you here immediately."

FORTY-TWO

June. Three months ago. August 4th.

I t's crazy, sitting here with Gabe in the back garden, his dark eyes so intense. Ivy climbs up a stone wall. A pile of sticks and rocks in the corner looks like it could be a campsite. Cobblestones are beneath our feet, and we're sitting at a small circular iron table that can barely fit the two of us. The walls are two stories high—you can't really tell you're still in New York City; we could be anywhere. I felt like that—hidden away—in the billiards room beneath the building, too, when Gabe gave me the tour and told me stories about rumored parties that happened down there during Prohibition, because there are no windows to the outside and the place is practically soundproof. There were framed photos of jazz singers on the walls, along with a deed for the building that looked as if it would disintegrate if the glass in the frame wasn't holding it in place.

It's cozy out here in the garden, to say the least, and something has shifted in the air between Gabe and me. I'm starting to think I didn't peg him right at the reading—that I misjudged what I saw. I'm starting to think he's less interested in me as some kind of love object and more interested in me as a person who will make him feel good—whether that's by sleeping with him or talking feverishly about his work, I really can't tell. But right now I think it's the latter. His eyes widen as he talks about where he was going with this scene and that scene, and how he thinks he needs to plant the killer early enough that the audience will be satisfied to learn that it's really her.

"That's what it is, June," he says, like I'm his student and he must impart this piece of wisdom. "Ask my wife," he says. "She's the one who taught it to me, though I'd never admit that to her." He lets out a laugh that sounds rehearsed, and that's because it is: I've heard him say this very same thing in interviews.

"Is that so?" I ask.

"Oh, definitely," Gabe says, so convinced by his own performance. "You can't throw in a murderer at the last minute. The audience has to see him up close and personal, to really get to watch him and know him. And then, if you can surprise your audience, they'll be satisfied. Sometimes my wife goes back into her manuscripts once they're totally finished and writes a new character who ends up being the killer. Half the reason everyone is so surprised by Rowan's killers is that she's surprised, too. She writes the entire novel being completely open to someone she never saw coming."

He's in love with his wife. It's right there on his face, in his big hands gesticulating when he talks about her.

The deeper we get into the script, the more relaxed I get. And I'm not saying I'm not completely infatuated with him, because I am. He's undeniably one of the most magnetic men I've ever been around, and he's extremely hot. But what I *really* want? What I really want is to be a part of *this*, to be one of these brilliant New Yorkers who walk around with stories in their minds and roles to play and scripts to write and scenes to shoot. I want it so badly I can taste it like sugar. And while I'm sitting here giving Gabe O'Sullivan story feedback with the skills I've honed during the last few weeks reading scripts at WTA, I feel so insanely good.

"So you really think this is too unbelievable, right?" Gabe asks about a scene where the main character's lover shows up unknowingly at his wife's book party.

"Way too much of a coincidence," I say. "Now, if she figured out who the wife was, and then started to stalk her . . . that could work?"

Gabe frowns. "It could, I suppose. Creepy, though."

"Yeah, well," I say with a shrug. "It's certainly the genre for creepy." My phone rings and it makes me jump. "I should get that," I say, fumbling in my bag. "It could be Louisa."

"Go ahead," says Gabe, scrawling what we've been talking about in pencil.

It's a number I don't recognize, but just in case it's Louisa's home phone, I pick it up. "June?" asks an unfamiliar voice.

"This is she," I say, all professional, like how I've heard Louisa answer her phone.

"This is Charles Johnston, from The Slope Playhouse. I'm calling because I'd like to offer you the part of Cecily."

"Oh my gosh!" I exclaim. Gabe looks up from his script.

Charles laughs. "Is that a yes?" he asks me.

"That's definitely a yes," I say, and then I squeal like I haven't done since I was young. I'm barely able to focus as Charles runs through a few details, a rehearsal schedule he'll email me, and some performance dates. I thank him profusely, and when we get off the phone Gabe asks, "Some good news?"

"Oh yes, some good news," I say, my smile nearly cracking my face in half. "I had this audition last night, and I . . . I got the part."

"Oh, wow," Gabe says. "June, that's terrific. Should we go get a drink to celebrate? Rowan could come. Or Harrison. Or whomever you like."

"That's so sweet," I say. "But actually, I think I need to go back uptown. I really just can't wait to tell Louisa in person. I'll be seeing you, though," I say. "Thanks for having me help with the script. It made me feel really good."

Gabe raises a dark eyebrow. "Goodbye, June," he says.

FORTY-THREE

Rowan. Friday evening. November 11th.

I'm running through the West Village among the blares of sirens. I've got my arms around Lila, holding her close and whispering into her ear. Tears are hot on my face; I try to swipe them away, but it's no use. There's crime scene tape on my block. To the first officer I see, I say, "Please let me through," but my breath is coming so fast it's hard to get it out. "Detective Mulvahey is waiting for me," I manage to say. "He asked me to come."

The cop's face is impassive, but he lifts the tape to let me pass.

I round the corner to see June's body on a stretcher. Someone is unzipping an empty black body bag, and I can't help it—I vomit.

"Rowan," says a low voice. I look up to see Harrison and Gabe. I don't know which one of them said my name. They come toward me, and Gabe quickly wraps Lila and me in his arms. Harrison rests a hand on my shoulder and squeezes. It's obvious he's been crying. A glow from a restaurant backlights them, and I see the diners inside staring out the window at our tragedy. A child with fluffy red hair has her face pressed against the window before an unseen adult pulls her away, big hands on her shoulders, tucking the child back into a cocoon of safety, into a world where no one gets hurt, so unlike the real one.

Detective Mulvahey appears behind a car with its flashing lights sputtering red and white through the night air. He looks at all of us. "After Rowan identifies the body, I'll take all three of you to the station for questioning. You should have a lawyer present, so please make arrangements."

What did we do to her? *All of us.* What did we do?

FORTY-FOUR

June. Three months ago. August 10th.

On Wednesday night I'm in SoHo about to have dinner right near Harrison's apartment, at Balthazar. The sky is asleep but SoHo is wide awake. I'm shifting my weight and adjusting my purse, and I'm so insanely excited that my feet feel shaky in my stilettos. I got them at DSW and frankly, they're amazing: four inches high so I'm clocking in at six feet and feeling it. I've got on a chic dress I borrowed from Kai when I went to her apartment for the first time this week, which was a surprise-and-a-half because I turned up to find out Kai lives in an apartment that looks like a museum. Nothing she'd ever said or done before hinted at her being a trust fund kid. She always goes to low-rent places like I do to eat and drink, plus she bemoans our pay at WTA, and I guess it never came up. Or maybe she purposely kept it from me, which kind of feels like a trick, because why act like you have to save money when you don't?

The dress Kai lent me is a conservative Ralph Lauren number, and I picked it for tonight because I think it'll be a surprise; I'm sure Rowan and Gabe probably think I'll show up in something revealing and try-ing-too-hard-to-be-sexy. But tonight I'm *adult, sophisticated June, reader of scripts, haver of things to say.*

Even the models who go stalking by have nothing on my style tonight. (Try going into SoHo once without seeing a model: *c'est impossible!*)

I'm giddy with this night, nervous to double-date with people a decade older than me, but also: kind of ready for it, to try it on for size. And I just feel so good being out in New York beneath the dark sky, like the possibilities are endless. A handsome man in a suit passes me and we catch each other's eyes; a girl in wide-legged jeans and a white top exposing her stomach takes a video of her friend posing near a fire hydrant. A taxi honks at a boy on a bike who swerves onto the sidewalk; a woman holding a baby tells him to be careful.

Our dinner reservations are for nine o'clock. I pull out my phone to check the time and see a text from Sean.

Cutest dog available! Check him out!

There's a link to a rescue organization, and I click. A pathetic-looking Chihuahua mix named Boomer lights up my screen.

He's perfect. We have to get him. Even if we keep killing our fish. I text back with a smiley face. Things have been a little better between Sean and me this week; I can tell he's making an effort to be less controlling about everything, which seems to completely exhaust him. He's shutting his door around eight each night and turning off the light by nine, though I can still see the glow of his computer leaking out beneath the door. But I'm starting to think I can stay.

I look back up from our text exchange. Headlights crisscross the dark, and the glow of shops and phones and people light up the sidewalk. There's just so much living going on here. Each time Balthazar's front doors open, the smell of fresh bread mixes with car exhaust and the smell of trash from a nearby can, and nothing has ever been this perfect.

I glance across Spring Street and see Rowan. She's standing all alone at the crosswalk waiting for the light to turn. A streetlight makes her skin look iridescent, and she's wearing the same pale lip gloss she had on at Gabe's reading. I take a breath, reminding myself this will all be okay. The dinner was her idea, or at least that's how Harrison made it sound. But maybe Harrison was just nervous I'd say no. Agents tell white lies all the time; I've even seen Louisa do it.

The light changes and Rowan steps off the curb. A warm summer gust catches her black silk pants and makes them ripple as she crosses the street. She's a natural beauty, with just the swipe of color on her lips and mascara and nothing else. Her skinny fingers are on her rounded belly again just like at the reading.

She looks up and sees me, and when she smiles, it's a big wide one like she's happy I'm standing there. Or maybe she just loves nighttime, too: the feeling of being young and alive in New York, each night like starting a film and seeing where it goes.

"Hi, June," she says. She steps onto my side of the street and comes right up close like we're old friends.

"Hi," I say.

"I can't believe it," she says with a big exhale. "I'm already so out of breath!" She looks down at her stomach and then back up at me. "Twins," she says, like it's a miracle, and I suppose it is.

"That's amazing," I say. "Congratulations."

"Thanks!" she says. "It really *is* great, it's just I'm only twenty-nine weeks pregnant and I'm out of breath all the time. It's so nuts."

I smile. She doesn't seem to be telling me so I can commiserate or feel bad for her: she just seems surprised by it all. "You must be really excited," I say, because now that I've spent so much time with Louisa, I get it. This week Louisa only took one more day off after her miscarriage, which I thought was insane, but Louisa told me she'd already taken too many days off for fertility treatments. So we just worked side by side all week, and Louisa was in a daze but not enough that I think anyone but me noticed. And she still managed to get everything done.

"We are *so* excited," Rowan says, rubbing her belly clockwise. "We just got the stroller, and we're setting up their nursery, and it's all seeming really close. The babies are coming in October if everything goes okay."

I smile. I don't have much else to say, but I like hearing about it.

"Ladies!" comes Harrison's big voice, making us turn. He's grinning, walking with Gabe. Gabe gets a sly look on his face, hands shoved into his pockets, walking a little slower than Harrison. He's so handsome—they both are. It hits me like a slap that these are the people I'm going to dinner with, and in a way it makes me feel like I've already started to make it in this city: to be respected by other creative people, to be in the world of it, plus tomorrow is my first rehearsal for *The Importance of Being Earnest*, and it all feels sort of surreal.

I watch as Gabe and Harrison come closer. They're placeholders for the real thing, I know that; I already sense I'm probably not going to have some serious thing with Harrison, but I like him, simple as that, and maybe I don't need to overthink everything. They step onto the sidewalk, and Harrison comes close faster than I think he will, and then his arm is around my waist, his fingers curled against my side with more pressure than I'm ready for. We've only had one coffee together since our date to Gabe's reading, nothing else that progressed us forward physically, so this feels quick as lightning and just as dangerous. It takes concentration not to flinch. "Hi," I say, surprise in my voice.

"Hi," Harrison says. He leans in to peck me on the cheek. "You look gorgeous," he says into my ear. I swear I smell whiskey, but I could be wrong. He's been sober three years, so it would be a big deal if he just had a drink somewhere. I look up at him questioningly, but I don't know him well enough to read his face.

Rowan leans into Gabe. He wraps his arms around her and kisses her white-blond hair. "Hey," he says, voice loose. Her head is pressed against his chest and there's a small, content smile on her face. Gabe looks down at her like he's genuinely happy to see her, and his arm is protective when it drops to her waist. It makes me think about how his babies are inside her, and how strange it all is and what it must mean for a relationship to go from just two people to a family of four.

"June, it's good to see you," Gabe says over Rowan's head, and it's almost like they're only there with each other. Rowan looks up and searches Gabe's face, and he looks down at her again and smiles.

"You too," I say back to Gabe. I'm very conscious of Harrison's hand pressing into me, and I'm liking it more the longer it's there. There's a coat of dark blond stubble on his face, and his big blue eyes are rimmed with dark lashes. His dimple puts me a little over the edge—it comes out only when his grin is this wide. "Hey," I say when we lock eyes. He's got my attention; I'll give him that.

"Hey," he says again, and it's so flirty I squirm.

"Should we go in?" I ask.

Harrison nods and pushes open the door to Balthazar. He gives me a secret smile as I pass beneath his arm. Inside, Gabe talks to the hostess, who gets us to a table right away. I think about how when I'm with Kai we always have to wait at restaurants. Not tonight.

Rowan has her head down as we pass the raw bar marked with iridescent clams, and the real bar with a hundred glistening bottles of top-shelf alcohol and decadent wines. We curve between the tables, and people turn to look at her (and at me, too), but Rowan doesn't seem to care. It must be so nice not to care. Rowan and I slide onto the banquette first, sitting opposite each other and closest to the wall, and already the drink lists are waiting. I watch as Rowan's eyes glance over the laminated menu; she has this faraway quality to her, like she's in this world and simultaneously inside another one. She's got a cocktail ring on her index finger, and a small gold wedding band on her ring finger, and the dreamy half smile on her face I remember from Gabe's reading. "I miss white wine," she says to no one in particular.

Mirrors hang behind us. Big golden globes of light hover over the bar. The wooden ceiling is dramatic, and the whole thing is just so exquisitely beautiful it's hard to even put it into words. "So what are you working on?" I ask Rowan. A part of me wonders whether her work is the cause of her distraction: Is she half-inside the world of her current novel?

Rowan looks up and studies me.

"You look distracted," I say. "And it made me wonder if sometimes you're thinking about the people in your books and what they're doing in their world."

Rowan lets out a laugh but it's not at me, it's almost like she's surprised. "That's exactly right," she says as Gabe settles in beside her, Harrison beside me. The guys laugh about something one of them said, and jazz music plays behind us, making everything feel classy and old-fashioned. "Sometimes I even think I'll see my characters out, even *here*, tonight," Rowan says, gesturing at the scene around us. "Isn't that nuts?" She smiles at me. She seems so much kinder than the night at the reading. "It's like I see all these people, and I think one of my characters could turn up as a waiter tonight, or someone at a neighboring table," Rowan says, and then she laughs at herself.

I almost tell her that happens to me with the scripts. But I'm not confident enough yet to say it out loud; she might think my experience pales in comparison to hers, and I'm sure it does: she's working on the same characters and story for months at a time. For me it's a quick immersion, a night or two of reading at most.

"What should we order?" Gabe asks, holding up the menu so close to his eyes he must be farsighted. I can feel Harrison watching me, waiting for me to answer, but then Rowan leans in close across the table like it's just us. "I'm writing this guy now, and he's really possessive, quick to anger, that kind of thing." She gesticulates, her cocktail ring catching the light. "He's going to be the murderer, I'm pretty sure. I mean, he's the obvious choice, so I may change my mind at the end.

But there's something about him that terrifies me, keeps me up at night and everything." She lowers her voice until I can barely make out her words. "He's like any guy we know, do you know what I mean? It's a hairsbreadth difference, isn't it? What someone will do under the right circumstances?"

I swallow. She's kind of scaring me. I feel my body arc toward her—I almost want to reach across the table and grab her hand and tell her I get it, but of course I don't do that. "There was this guy in college I used to date, nothing serious," I tell her. The music is loud enough that I'm not sure if the guys can hear me, because I'm practically whispering. "I think I got out of it just in time. He was like *that*, what you just said: so fast from totally fine to furious." I snap my fingers to emphasize my point: one second fine, one second rageful. "Once we got in the smallest fight and he punched his leg while shouting at me. We were in his car. And when he pulled over I just got out and never called him back or responded to his texts anymore, and I only saw him a few more times on campus and we just ignored each other."

"Good for you," she says, and her voice is loud now, getting the guys' attention. "You trusted your instincts, right? Wouldn't you say?"

"I guess," I say as a waitress brings us waters.

We go quiet and the waitress takes our drink order. Seltzers for Harrison and Rowan, cabernet for Gabe and me. "Maybe that waitress should be your killer," Gabe says with a smirk when she leaves the table, and Rowan swats him.

"What made you want to write?" I ask Rowan.

"Oh," Rowan says with a wave of her hand. The guys watch her. It's so obvious they both find her beautiful. I catch it on Harrison's face as he stares. "I always tell people I write mysteries to get to the bottom of what happened to my father," she says. "He was killed when I was five." My eyes widen. Even though I've read this same thing in her interviews, it's different hearing her say it to me in real life. "And I'm pretty fascinated by what people are capable of, and how you're supposed to avoid the ones who have it in them to do dangerous things. Because how can we really know who those ones are?" She shifts her weight, her pale blue eyes blinking. "But the truth is, I suppose I write to get to the truth of what I'm capable of." She stares at me. "Do you know what I mean?"

I don't really know what she means. My fingers have gone cold squeezing my ice water, wanting her to go on. Gabe leans back in his seat like he's heard it all before. He's watching the side of her face, his big shoulders relaxed.

Harrison's staring, too, and his body has gone tighter, coiled like he'd leap across the table and sit next to her if he could.

"I just mean, what would I do?" Rowan asks. "To protect my family. My mother, say. Or Gabe. Or now." She puts a hand on her stomach. "My babies. I think I'd do anything. And I think most of us would. It's just we don't usually get put in the set of circumstances that test the things we hold so dear. I mean, you might think you'd never kill for anything. But how can you really know?"

A flush of goose bumps sweeps over the exposed skin on my neck and arms. I don't say anything. The waitress comes with our drinks and sets them down. I thank her and take a big sip of my wine. "You're painting murderers like valiant defenders of their family," Gabe says to Rowan, no malice in his voice, more like they always have conversations like this.

"She's not defending them," Harrison says, squeezing lime into his seltzer. "She's saying that none of us have any idea what we'd do if pushed to the limit. Which is true."

"I can say with certainty that I wouldn't kill for certain things," Gabe says.

"Your babies aren't here yet, Gabe, how can you really know?" Rowan asks. She sips her drink, considers her husband.

"Okay, fine, take our family out of the conversation," Gabe says. "There are people who kill out of passion and romantic jealousy."

"And that's what's terrifying," I say, swirling my glass of deep, dark wine, a little too quickly so it almost goes right over the edge. I stop myself in time. "It's so scary because those emotions are everywhere."

"Exactly," says Rowan, locking eyes with me.

I take a swig and the cabernet slides down my throat like medicine. "Obviously women can be violent, too," I say. "But the stats are clear on which gender usually perpetrates intimate partner violence." I don't feel so young anymore; I feel like someone with something to say. "You guys won't ever know what it's like to be a woman entering a relationship without knowing your partner's capacity for violence."

"Bingo!" Rowan says. "And sometimes it doesn't even come out for years. That's what happened to my mom."

She definitely hasn't said that in interviews.

"Should we change the subject?" Gabe asks.

"Would you like that?" I ask back, a challenge in my eyes.

Gabe raises his eyebrows. "I like *you*, June, and I think you're going to be good for my buddy, here," he says, and somehow we all laugh, and we do, eventually, change the subject. Gabe drinks more as the night goes on and gets looser and (admittedly) a little less interesting. But it's sweet how he becomes more affectionate with Rowan.

Harrison does the opposite: he winds tighter and becomes sharper; he starts to ignore Rowan and Gabe and focus on me. Somewhere around midnight, I need to get out of there. I'm ready to be alone with Harrison; I want to see what he says when it's just us, to see how he looks at me, to feel what it's like to kiss him.

"I have an early morning tomorrow," I say, and that gets all of us bemoaning our work schedules (which are benign compared with most New Yorkers', but none of us call each other on that), and then Harrison gets the check and pays the entire bill. At first I think he's showing off, but then Rowan says to me, "He never lets us pay."

"I've made him millions, sweetie," Gabe says with a laugh, his voice slurred with alcohol.

"Yeah, not quite millions, man," Harrison says back.

"Close enough," Gabe says, and there's the tiniest flick of aggression there. But then they both laugh, and Harrison says, "True."

Rowan's staring wistfully at Harrison and I can't really read it. I think she's just tired, but then Harrison catches her glance, too, and he's the one that watches as she carefully gets out of the booth. She seems markedly more pregnant than she did at the beginning of the night. Gabe is off toward the exit door, but Harrison hangs back. "Do you need a hand," he asks Rowan, his head dipped toward her more intimately than I would have expected.

"I'm so swollen and tired at night now," Rowan says softly. Any enthusiasm that was in her voice a few hours ago is gone. I have the odd feeling that I should leave them alone. I head outside to where Gabe is standing on the corner, looking up at the stars like a proper drunk person.

"Hi," I say.

"June!" he says. "Look how clear the night is." He tips his head back even farther. "Usually you can't see the stars like this in the city."

I look up. There's a beautiful, almost full moon and a smattering of stars. He's right: it's clear and gorgeous.

"You know," he says to me, swaying a little. Passersby on the street give him a wide berth. "Harrison is one of the good ones."

"Oh yeah?" I say back.

"Yeah, truly," he says. "He's like a brother to me. There are so many things I've done that I shouldn't have, and Rowan and Harrison keep forgiving me and pulling me back from the edge."

He's too drunk for me to ask what he means; I don't want him telling me a truth he wouldn't have otherwise. I just nod, keeping an eye on him and making sure he doesn't step too close to the curb as he studies the sky.

"How's your revision coming?" I ask, thinking of the two of us days ago on his back patio going over notes on his screenplay.

His gaze falls from the sky and narrows on me. "Rowan read it and tore it apart," he says, features folding. "She said she's not even rooting for the main character." His voice gets angrier when he says, "She doesn't always get that it's the *actor* that determines a lot of that. It's different in her books; she only has words to get the reader on her character's side. But I have the power of Hollywood behind me. Have you ever *not* rooted for Tom Hanks?"

I laugh. "I guess that's true," I say, and then out come Harrison and Rowan. Rowan's face is ashen. "I'm exhausted," she says to me, and then to Gabe, "We have to cab it, my feet are killing me."

We all say things to each other about how we'll have to do it again soon, and it feels real; I have the sneaking suspicion we *will* start seeing each other like this. I watch Rowan and Gabe get into the taxi, and then Harrison turns to me. "Should I get you a cab?"

"What's my other option?" I ask, smiling at him.

He's ready for this moment, for me. He extends a long arm. "See that window right there?" he asks, pointing downtown a block or so. "That's my apartment."

"I've always wanted to check out SoHo real estate," I say. "So I should probably take you up on the invite."

"Oh, that wasn't an invite," he says.

My cheeks burn a little, but he's smiling.

"It wasn't?" I ask.

"Nope," he says. "This is." He comes closer, right into my favorite moment, and kisses me, and his lips are so warm and the kiss is so incredibly sweet and good and I swear I could faint right there, but his strong hand is on my back, pulling me against him. His other hand slips over the back of my neck and it sends chills over my skin. I want everything about this, and the want nearly knocks me off my feet.

"Let's go to my place," he says, and we do.

273

PART III

FORTY-FIVE

June. Three days ago. Tuesday, November 8th.

I'm headed to the coffee shop to meet Rowan, and all I can think about is how awful I think all of them are for doing this to her. This horrible playacting, this sick charade. Harrison and I never even had a fight until this whole thing started, but he's just as bad as Gabe and Sylvie for letting Rowan carry on like this, not remembering Gray. How much longer can they let this go on?

I push open the door to the café and scan the tables.

No. Freaking. Way. What is Sean doing here? Why is he talking to Rowan? I knew we shouldn't have picked this coffee shop—it's his favorite. I hurry toward the table because the last thing I need is him saying something that upsets Rowan.

I get closer to Sean and Rowan and that's when I hear Sean say it: *"Are you even allowed to be out by yourself?"*

Lila lets out a tiny whimper that sears me. Rowan opens her mouth like she's going to defend herself, but she doesn't. Her eyes fill with tears. And then I'm right there, my words slicing the air like a knife. "What did you just say?" I ask Sean.

Rowan looks up and sees me. Her face looks beatific, like she's never been so happy to see someone before. I tug off my earmuffs. "What are you doing here?" I ask Sean.

I'm sure he can't believe I'm on Rowan's side, but that's his own fault for not understanding me, for wanting me to be something I'm not, something he's created in his own mind. A fantasy. And while he was busy building that version of me, he never got to know the real me. The one who would do anything for Rowan and Lila.

"I'm getting coffee, June," Sean says.

I stare at him. He doesn't make a move to leave, so I say, "I'll see you later, *Sean*," and force a smile.

Finally he goes. He doesn't even bother getting coffee, so he's probably super pissed at me.

I sit. "I'm sorry about him," I say to Rowan, unwrapping my scarf and setting it on my lap. "I used to think he meant well and was just overbearing. But now I'm not so sure. Sometimes he worries me."

"You should be careful, then," Rowan says, but I wave my hand like it's nothing. The last thing Rowan needs is to be worried about me. I tap my nails against the table and scan the menu on the wall. I try not to spend money at places like this, though Louisa says I'm getting a raise when she goes on maternity leave next year. I'll be shuttling things back and forth from her apartment, and I've never been so happy that she's old-fashioned and so much of our stuff is on paper, because that way I'll have an excuse to see Louisa and the baby during those three months. The baby's a girl, and Louisa already has a name picked out for her, but she's too nervous and superstitious to tell me what it is, which I totally understand because of everything she's been through.

"I got you a muffin," Rowan says. "I wasn't sure if you drank coffee."

"Thanks," I say. I unwrap it, and I want to eat it, but my stomach is so sick with nerves at the thought of telling her I can't work for her anymore. Trust me, it's not because I don't love her; it's because I *do*, and I can't be a part of Sylvie's egomaniacal game any longer. Even

Louisa thinks it's a bad idea. I get it: Sylvie's top of her field. Sylvie is *the* trauma therapist, she's the Miss America of the PTSD world. But I can't watch them all do this to Rowan, playing along with her like Gray never existed, not telling her the truth about him. The worst is Gabe's mom, Elena, who spends her time nervously fretting about the apartment and barely taking a break from crying (which I totally understand, because Gray was her grandson), but it's hard to watch, especially now that Lila is starting to be awake more and making eye contact.

When I'm in Gabe and Rowan's apartment and Lila locks eyes on me, the world stops spinning for just a second. I can't believe I'm saying this, but I definitely want to be a mom at some point. When Rowan and Louisa talk about babies, I just kind of get it. I mean, not yet, obviously.

"How's she doing?" I ask Rowan about Lila. "I love her little dress."

A smile lands on Rowan's face. The love and pride she has for Lila, I know she would have that for Gray, too, and when I think of her losing him, how they tried to let her hold him and she couldn't do it, I can hardly bear it. I start to cry, I can't help it. When is she going to remember him?

"June," Rowan says. She reaches across the table and takes my hand. "I'm so sorry. I'm so very sorry for what I did to you," she says. She gives my fingers a squeeze, and when she lets go I wish she wouldn't. "What I did was so terrible, and there's no excuse," she says, sounding almost frantic. "I think something's wrong in my brain. Or at least, there definitely was in that moment. I just, I can't even explain it."

You don't have to explain it to me. I understand. That's what I want to say, but I'm worried I'll blurt out the whole truth.

"I was sure that you had hurt the baby," Rowan says in a low voice that I can barely make out over the commotion of the coffee shop. "And I was so terrified I couldn't even think straight," she goes on. "I don't know if I had some kind of mental break or something, or what it was. I'm very, very sorry, June," she says, and I try hard to stop crying, because I don't want her to feel bad about any of this. That's the last thing I want. "It's all I can say," she says. "Even though I know it's not enough."

"I'm sorry, too," I say, barely able to get the words out. *I'm sorry I've played along, that I've lied to you, that I've pretended not to know about your little boy, that I haven't helped you try to remember.*

"You didn't do anything wrong," Rowan says.

"Are you . . . ," I start, because I want to know more about what Sylvie's doing to her, I want to know if Sylvie's close to fixing her. I want to mourn Gray with them; I want to go to the funeral if they have one. I want to take care of Lila when Rowan and Gabe need a break.

A toddler at the next table screams about needing more chocolate syrup in his hot chocolate, and two old women laugh. "Are you getting some good help?" I finally make myself ask. "Like a therapist, I mean? Or some medicine at least?" I feel duplicitous for knowing about Sylvie and acting like I don't—this is exactly why I hate all of this so much.

Rowan looks surprised that I've asked this. "I am," she eventually says. "A trauma therapist named Sylvie whom Louisa recommended, actually. Though I don't know what good it's doing." She shakes her head. "I still can't really remember the birth. Last night I dreamt of that day I collapsed and someone called an ambulance."

I look down at Lila and try not to cry again. "Thank God she was all right," I say, but then I panic, because obviously Gray wasn't all right, and of course I want Rowan to remember Gray, but what if she remembers him right here inside this café, with all of these people around us, without Gabe by her side?

"June, listen," Rowan says, and I can hear the effort it takes her to try to sound like everything is okay, like none of this is the end of the world. "I'm okay now," she says, which cuts right to my gut. She's so very far from okay. "Well, I mean, I think I am," she says. "Nothing like that has happened again, what happened with you that night." She takes a breath, her hand going to her coffee cup. "I've felt more like myself," she adds, like she's trying too hard to convince herself. She takes a sip of her coffee and avoids my eyes.

"Rowan," I say carefully over the sound of beans grinding. "I need some time off from working for you."

"Oh, of course," Rowan says, looking like that was a given, which makes me relieved.

"I want you to know it's not because of what happened," I say.

I can tell she doesn't believe me when she says, "Okay, sure."

I need her to know it's not what she did. "I care about you and Lila so much," I say. "It's more that I need to get away for a little while, and I'd been feeling like that even before everything happened. I'm going upstate to my parents' house."

"Oh," she says, and then, "Where did you grow up?"

"Harbor Falls," I say. I pull off a piece of my muffin and try to eat it like I'm okay, like my stomach isn't so nervous.

Rowan nods like she's heard of Harbor Falls, but usually no one who isn't from upstate New York has. "It's near Saratoga," I say.

Rowan smiles. "Gabe and I went to the racetrack a few summers ago," she says. "It's gorgeous up there."

"It is," I say, not wanting to talk about what it was like to grow up there, because it's too hard to talk about growing up without mentioning my mom. If I sit here and talk about how gorgeous upstate New York is, it feels dishonest in some way, like I'm painting a picture of something that never existed.

"I'm sorry, June," Rowan says.

I feel myself about to cry again. I need to get out of here. "I know you are," I say, and I feel the tears burning the back of my eyes. "And I am, too," I go on, "that everything happened. I really am."

"You didn't do anything," she says again, but I'm standing now.

"I should go," I say, taking my earmuffs from my wrist and putting them on my head. I pack up my muffin and tuck my phone into my pocket while Rowan pats Lila's butt, watching me, seeming nervous.

"Will you be okay getting home with Lila?" I ask, looking down at the profile of Lila's delicate nose and chin.

"Yes, of course," Rowan says, patting faster. "We'll be fine. Thank you for meeting me," she says, but I'm already edging away from them, from these people I love.

"Goodbye, Rowan," I say.

The second I turn away from them, the tears fall over my cheeks. I push through the customers, feeling like I can't catch my breath. I shove open the door and then I'm on the street, crossing it, tears blurring my eyes and seeing the taxi too late, hurrying to get out of the way and just missing being hit. I'm sobbing now. I'm just so incredibly sad for Rowan and Lila that my heart feels like it will beat free of my chest, and then I see Sean. He's standing on the sidewalk, watching me in horror. He comes toward me, careful at first, then extending his arms to me. I feel like I'm going to pass out. I practically stumble into his arms, no other choice if I want to stay standing. He puts his face against my hair and whispers reassurances into my ear.

"Get me out of here," I say, and away we walk, Sean's arm around me keeping me upright.

FORTY-SIX

June. Three days ago. Tuesday, November 8th.

An hour after I see Rowan (and thirty minutes after I finally convince Sean I'm fine on my own) I'm sitting on the stone steps of the New York Public Library waiting for Harrison. The sculpted lions, Patience and Fortitude, tower above me, their stoic grandeur frozen in time. I know what I need to do today, and maybe my timing's off, and maybe it's the wrong day for it. But I'm already a wreck, so why not?

I scan New Yorkers wrapped in scarves and holding coffees, on their phones, listening to music, talking to each other. I don't see Harrison yet. There's a hot dog stand on the corner, but I still don't think I can stomach anything, and anyway I have my muffin from Rowan tucked in a crinkled paper bag. I'm trying to put her from my mind, to focus on this conversation I need to have with Harrison, but it's hard: Rowan's blue eyes feel like they're still pleading with me to understand and forgive her. But there's never been anything to forgive.

I take out my phone and turn the camera on myself to use it like a mirror. I try to swipe away the mascara beneath my eyes. Harrison has never seen me like this, not once since we've started dating, and I don't really know what he's going to say when he gets here and sees me smeared with mascara and snot. I still call it *dating* because that's mostly what we do: we go out. We sleep together but mostly we go on dates and flirt and talk about life and about the industry. He knows almost everything about me, and in some ways, it's one of the most refreshing relationships I've ever had. In other ways, I know I need to end it, because he likes me more than I like him, and that suddenly feels unfair. He's looking for a wife, and I'm not her. I have a feeling he thinks if we take it slow enough that I'll come around, that I'll fall deeply and realize I'm ready to make a commitment. But when I think about any of that I just feel stifled. Yesterday I shot out of WTA like a cannonball after I told Louisa I needed time off, and Harrison was pissed that he heard about that through Louisa and not me. And then he was rude, and we got into an argument, and he seemed to feel the need to apologize profusely, even though it wasn't that bad. I purposely left my cell at home so I could just go out and not feel bad screening his calls, and then he got worried when he couldn't reach me. We worked it out last night when I got back home and called him, and he mostly just seemed relieved I was fine.

I take off my earmuffs and throw them in my bag. The winter sun is warming me up anyway. I'm still in the camera fixing my makeup when I hear someone say:

"Selfie mode. Can't make Instagram wait."

I look up to see Harrison, his smile wide.

"Hey," I say, and then he gets a closer look at me.

"June?" he asks, face falling with concern. "What happened?"

"Sit," I say, patting the steps next to me. He does. I start to cry, and maybe if I was by myself someone would stop to help me, but I've got Harrison here rubbing my back just like I like, because he's actually paid attention during the past few months and knows exactly how to take care of me.

"I saw Rowan," I say when I can catch my breath.

"And?" he asks gently.

"I'm just so sad for her," I say. "I've never been this sad for anyone, ever."

"She's going to remember what happened to Gray," Harrison says, his voice so sure, just like it is at work when something terrible has happened and he has to calm one of his writers.

"When?" I ask, already too shrill. "*When* will she remember?"

"Eventually," he says. His eyes darken; sometimes I think he's just as worried about Rowan as Gabe is. All any of us want is for her to be okay.

"That's not good enough," I say. "And I think Louisa agrees with me," I add, because I feel like I need her backup. I feel like no one will listen to me, because I'm only twenty-two and to be fair: I'm not a mental health professional. "This is all too strange," I say. "Pretending like this."

"Gabe mentioned some therapy for PTSD that Sylvie told him she could try with Rowan," Harrison says, looking down to the shiny black buttons on his overcoat. "It's supposed to work. I googled the crap out of it."

We've all become amateur psychologists these past few weeks. I guess Rowan is lucky to have this many people who love her. Gabe's been keeping her friends updated, but most of them haven't come. Maybe they're scared, or maybe they don't know what to say. Instead it's just me, Gabe, Rowan, and Elena all the time, and it's so obvious Elena doesn't like me. Rowan once told me Gabe's dad had an affair with the nanny, so Elena considers all young women to be potential disasters.

"Harrison," I start, scared to do what I'm about to. "I've been think-ing lately that we should take time off from . . ." I gesture between us, unsure of what to call it because we haven't exactly labeled ourselves the past few months. "From this," I finally say.

His eyes widen, and in that quick flash I can see how taken aback he is. My heart pounds because I understand why he's surprised: everything between us has been so good, and he had no idea I didn't think it was good *enough*, and the longer he stares at me the more I start to doubt myself. Am I really going to throw away the first guy who's truly cared about me in a long time?

"You mean you want to take time off from *us*?" he asks, like it physically pains him to say the words.

"Yes. From *us*," I say. "I could be making a huge mistake." My uncertainty seems to soften him a little—for a second his face goes blank, and I start to feel like maybe he'll be able to take this well, to absorb it calmly and rationally, just like I've seen him deal with so many things at work. But I'm wrong. His eyes go red and misty. He's blinking his dark lashes like he can't believe what I'm doing, that I'm ruining this very good thing that he wanted to take even further. I remember the first time he mentioned marriage, and how hopeful he looked when he asked me if I believed in it, and how he said he did, even though his parents ruined it for each other. That afternoon I made a point of not encouraging the marriage conversation, and instead I steered the conversation to our flawed sets of parents, which was territory we'd already trod.

"Are you serious, June?" Harrison asks now, his mouth not opening all the way, like it's not cooperating, like he wants to keep the words all to himself. He looks like he's going to cry, but no tears come.

"I know it's out of left field," I say, tapping my foot hard against the library's stone stairs, morbidly unsettled, wanting to do this right. "But I know I'm not ready for some big commitment, and I know you are, and I think you deserve someone closer to your age. I mean, oh crap, that's not actually what I meant."

"Then what do you *mean*, June?" he asks. He just looks so sad, and I feel awful; I should have done this weeks ago when I realized where his head was.

"June," he says, and it reminds me of the way my mom used to say my name sometimes, like the very sound of it hurt her brain. It throws me. I take a second, quiet and waiting, and then Harrison says, "I'm just so confused. I thought, it seemed like you liked what was going on, this thing we were doing, and . . ."

"I did—I *do*. But you deserve someone more on your page, someone where you are, someone . . ."

"Someone not like you?" he asks. There's a flush at his hairline, the wind tunnel of New York air mussing up his curls.

"I guess not, I guess," I start, and I try to keep going, but then he's standing up.

"I need to go, June, I'm so sorry," he says.

I stand on shaking legs. "Harrison," I start, "please stay another minute?"

"I can't," he says. "Not right now. I'll get there, I just . . . I really, really like you," he says, unable to even look at me. "And I respect that you're breaking things off. But I don't get it, and I can't just sit here and act like it's okay and that I'm okay. It's going to take me some time, I . . . I'm sorry, I . . . I should go." He turns and looks into the crowd gathered in front of the library taking pictures. Tourists. "I have to get back to the office," he says to no one. He's still not looking at me. He smooths a hand over his long coat, his face becoming neutral again, preparing himself to go back to WTA, the place where we were an *us* just hours ago. "This is gonna be bad," he says softly. And then he turns to me. "I need you to give me space at work. I don't want to let on to our colleagues how serious I thought we were, and how now it's just done. Can we just try to slowly separate, I really, it's kind of . . . well, frankly, it's embarrassing."

"Oh," I say, surprised. I don't get where he's coming from on that. We were office gossip at first, but mostly everyone's moved on. Harrison even stopped coming by my cubicle as much as when we started dating, which thrilled Kai. *I have you all to myself, finally,* she'd said.

"Okay," I say slowly. "I don't think you have anything to be embarrassed about," I add, because I can't quite understand the look on his face. He looks practically shameful.

"Ah, you wouldn't," he says, and I can see the effort it takes to keep his voice respectful like always. "You're young. People your age break up and make up all the time. At my age, it's kind of a bigger deal. At least, it is for me. And before I embarrass myself any more, June, I think I'm going to go." He tries to smile at me. "It was so good while it lasted," he says, but it comes off like he's delivering a tagline he doesn't really mean, like he's in a meeting with producers trying to package a creative project he doesn't actually believe in.

"It was," I say, no idea where to go from here, knowing it's done, and knowing deep in my bones that we aren't going to be able to stay friends. It'll be stilted at work; familiarity gone, conversations brisk, a cold rock in my hand. It'll be like Louisa warned me.

"Goodbye, June," he says, and then he walks toward work. And I just sit there, wondering how much worse this day can possibly get. My phone buzzes with a text from Kai:

Did you end it? Finally? Let me take you out tonight. You name the place.

FORTY-SEVEN

June. Three days ago. Tuesday, November 8th.

That night Kai and I are tucked inside a bar in the West Village right by Gabe and Rowan's apartment. I've had too much to drink, and I'm not a big drinker so I don't have practice at handling it well. The bartender is young, with curly auburn hair, and for the first time in months I think romantically about someone else. I imagine what it might be like to go out with a guy my own age, how much easier it might be.

The bar is dim, with candles lining the tables, and even though I feel awful about today, I'm grateful to be here with Kai, a real friend. "Things were good between us," I say to her. I've only had three drinks but already my words are slushy. "I think he was just surprised."

Kai rolls her eyes. "Don't make excuses for him," she says. "He's intense. Too intense."

"You're intense," I say teasingly, reaching forward to gently tug the long woven necklace she's wearing. "You know you are."

"I *am* intense," she says, taking a sip of her drink. "But at least I use my powers for good."

"You use your powers to get what you want," I say.

"Maybe you're right," she says, pushing a lock of long bangs over the shaved part of her head and behind her ear. "I do seem to get what I want . . ."

I laugh, but she doesn't. We chatter around the edges of things for a while, and I can't stop thinking about Rowan. The more we drink, the more I want to go to Rowan's apartment and see her.

"One more?" Kai asks, and I know I shouldn't have another drink, but I do. "You need someone your own age," Kai says. "Older guys are just so desperate."

"Really?" I ask. "Because you have so much experience with older guys?"

Kai smiles. "For your information, I'm extremely observant. Our entire world at work is older guys."

"True," I say, sipping my gin and tonic. I ordered it because once Rowan told me it was her favorite drink before she was pregnant, and she couldn't believe I'd lived this long without trying one. And now that I'm drinking it, I realize it's completely disgusting. But it was nine dollars, so I suck it down anyway.

"Easy tiger," Kai says as I gulp.

Somehow, instead of the drink quieting me and melting away my stress, it makes me itchy to go see Rowan and tell her about Gray, to somehow make her okay again. The idea of it thrums inside me as Kai prattles on about her girlfriend, Angie, who keeps texting and asking where she is. "I should call her back," she says, her brow furrowing. She dials Angie and says into the phone, "I'm out with June." But then she looks nervous like she's made a mistake. "June and her boyfriend just broke up," she says slowly and clearly, like she's trying not to sound drunk. I don't think Kai would ever have referred to Harrison as my boyfriend, but I think she's trying to convince Angie that I'm not a threat.

They get off the phone and Kai says to me, "I think things with her are over."

"I'm sorry," I say, giving her hand a squeeze.

"She's so possessive," Kai says, which strikes me as ironic because I usually think of Kai as the possessive one, with her friendships and her girlfriend.

"Let's get some fresh air," I say instead.

"Too cold for that," she says.

"Okay, North Carolina girl," I tease. "It's gorgeous out."

"You're nuts," she says as we pay our tab and grab our coats. Outside on the street she slips her arm through mine. "Are you gonna be okay, June?" she asks. I can feel her eyes on my face, trying to figure out what I'm thinking.

"Yeah," I say. "I'm gonna be okay."

"Hey," she says, brightening as we stand there on the corner of Perry and Washington. "You wanna split a cab?"

I shake my head. "I'm gonna walk for a while," I say. "I need the fresh air."

"You sure?" she asks, frowning. I nod, and we hug on the corner. She hails a taxi, and I remind her I'm going to my parents and won't see her until next week.

"I can't believe you're getting a full week off," Kai says as she folds like an accordion into the taxi. "You sure you don't want to split a ride home?" she asks, eyebrows narrowing.

I shake my head and we wave goodbye. I walk south on Washington Street toward Gabe and Rowan's apartment. If I could just see Rowan once more, and really convince her that she has nothing to be sorry for, that none of this is her fault. My head is swirling from the alcohol, but I can see the scene crystal clear: I could just give Rowan, Gabe, and Lila one last goodbye before I go on my trip upstate.

A few sidewalk slabs later my phone rings. I shouldn't answer it because I've already let the battery run down so low, but it's Sean and I know he'll worry if I don't.

"Hey," I say. "What's up? I thought you were with Michalis."

Michalis is Sean's programmer friend who's been avoiding him, but Sean pestered him enough to go talk things through tonight.

He doesn't answer me about Michalis. Instead, he asks, "You all right? You sound drunk."

"Yeah," I say. "I am. But I'm fine. I'm coming home, I just have to stop at Rowan's place."

"Is that really a good idea?" he asks.

"I forgot something there," I lie.

"Okay," he says. "I'm still out, I could come meet you."

"I'm fine, Sean, I—" I start to say, but then my phone officially dies. Crap—now he'll definitely worry. I shiver when I think of this one time when Sean was waiting for me outside Gabe and Rowan's apartment after I finished babysitting. It was eleven p.m., and I can't even imagine how long he must have been standing there, because I'd been working since seven and he didn't know when I'd be off. He's done something like that twice now: the time he came to that theater in Brooklyn after my audition, and then the babysitting night. But I reamed him such a new one when I saw him standing outside Gabe and Rowan's that he never did it again.

I hear footsteps behind me so I turn, but there's no one. Probably being drunk has me a little paranoid. The streets are oddly quiet until a homeless man rumbles past me with a shopping cart. He looks like he's freezing, so I pass him my earmuffs and my scarf, which he takes, smiling at me and thanking me profusely.

I turn onto Gabe and Rowan's street, suddenly sure I can feel someone behind me, their eyes all over me. I walk faster toward the building. A car honks in the distance. I turn and watch a taxi approach, but it changes course and takes a sharp right, and in the back seat I see a girl who resembles Kai. A group of teenagers are coming up the sidewalk in the opposite direction, all of them laughing. I shrug off my nerves and finally I'm at Gabe and Rowan's building, pulling open the front doors. "Hey," I say to Henri. "How ya doing?" I'm trying not to sound drunk, but I don't think it's working.

"Not as good as you, apparently," Henri says, blond eyebrow cocked.

"Rowan and Gabe are expecting me," I say.

"Then go right up, June," he says, his gaze following me just like always. *Ick.*

I take a breath at the elevator bank. I'd take the stairs, but Rowan always has a weird thing about the staircase. I press the button and wait. I really hope they're not mad at me for coming, or that I don't catch them in some awkward argument. Sometimes the tension in their apartment is thick enough to make you want to call it quits. But I never did until today; I *wanted* to stick with them, that's the thing that makes me feel so bad about leaving.

Up I go to the sixth floor. The elevator doors open with a *clank* and I step onto the carpet. I'm trying to seem sober, to make my face go like it would naturally, but I feel a creeping paranoia that I shouldn't be here. I pass the staircase with its iron swirls and tread softly toward their apartment, and then I raise my hand to knock. Heat sweeps over my spine. I need to get out of this down jacket.

Knock, knock. I do it softly at first, but then I hear voices inside, urgent voices, arguing. I know I should probably go but . . .

The voices escalate. The alcohol is hitting me hard. I never should have had that final drink. The hallway outside Rowan and Gabe's apartment seems to twist and turn and blur. I don't think I'm going to be sick, but just in case I sit—I think I just need a moment—and put my head between my knees.

I sit there in the hallway staring at the tan carpet between my feet. Tears spill onto my cheeks. I think of Harrison and the look I saw on his face before he left, how I'd never seen him look that sad before. I think of my parents, and how I'm getting on a train first thing tomorrow, and then I think of Rowan, who doesn't remember Gray, and suddenly everything feels so incredibly dark. It's a combination of the alcohol and the things that make me sad, but suddenly I'm in a way worse place than I've been in for a very long time. I make myself get up. My legs are shaking as I stand. I really should just go home, and I almost do, but then I swear I hear something inside the apartment. I listen closer and I'm sure it's crying. And I assume it's Rowan, so I knock hard. Immediately feet pound toward the door. Is she okay? I hope she's okay.

Gabe swings open the door. He looks like a wreck, standing there in sweats with bedhead even though he doesn't look like he was sleeping.

"June?" he asks, like he's never seen me standing there before.

"I have more to say," I announce. *Oh shit.* I'm way too drunk. I'm not even sure what I mean by it, but I think I mean I want to tell him why I'm really quitting this babysitting job, which is because of this entire charade, but I can't say that if Rowan's in earshot.

"Is Rowan here?" I ask dumbly, peering into the apartment. Where else would she be?

"She's sleeping with Lila," Gabe says, looking understandably confused as to why I'd be here at ten thirty at night.

"Oh," I say. "I heard a woman crying. Are you stashing someone else here?" I'm trying to make a joke, but it doesn't go over.

"Are you all right, June?" Gabe asks. He's no fool. He knows I'm drunk.

Around the corner into the foyer comes Gabe's mother. Birdlike, just as always. It's almost like she floated in, her tiny feet soundless. I look at her face, her eyes as dark as Gabe's, rimmed in red. She's tried to wipe them dry.

"June," she says, her voice full of distaste for me.

"*Elena,*" I say back. I've never called her by her first name.

She doesn't miss a beat. "What brings you here in the dead of the night?" she asks, suspicious, like I'm the harbinger of bad news.

"It's hardly the dead of the night," I say.

Gabe doesn't invite me inside. He just stands there. "What can we do for you, June?" he asks. I hate his tone. It's always different when his mom is around—he's way more professional with me, which makes me feel like he thinks he's doing something wrong when we're casual with each other all the times she's not here.

I try to get my bearings, to feel my feet beneath me so I don't sound too drunk. This wasn't exactly the welcome I was expecting, so I guess I may as well go for it. "I met with Rowan today in a café in my neighborhood," I say. "We talked about what happened. Did she tell you?" I ask. I don't look at Elena, only Gabe. And the way his dark eyes widen, I know this is news to him. Which makes me feel like I have one up on him, like Rowan and I have something important between us, something sacred. "I wanted to talk with her," I say, "to clear everything up, to make sure she knew it wasn't her fault that I can't work here anymore."

"Not her fault?" Gabe asks. Elena's glare is boring into me. She hates me so much. And I realize in that moment that some of it is likely her baggage—her own husband cheating. Humans seem to be both complex and so very simple in how they think: If it happened with her nanny, why shouldn't all husbands be vulnerable to it?

I open my mouth, but nothing comes out. I think back to how stupid I was when I first met Gabe, when I felt that insane crush. Thank God I never tried to get him to do something; thank God I never became the cliché Elena thinks I am. "Look," I say, and now I scan both of their faces, trying to get them to see what I do. "None of this is working," I say, gesturing around the whole apartment. "This charade."

"Did you say any of this to Rowan today?" Gabe asks, his body suddenly rigid, shoulders tight and arched forward like he's ready to pounce on me.

"What? *No*," I say. God, I wish I hadn't had anything to drink tonight. I put a hand on my head and shut my eyes. When I open them,

I still feel a little mixed up. "I'm just trying to say that someone needs to tell Rowan about Gray," I say.

"Keep your voice down," Gabe snarls.

I open my mouth. Tears prick my eyes.

"You're out of your depth," Elena snaps, and there it is: she's cut right to the truth. But even though I know she's right, I can't help but push, for Rowan's sake.

"But she has to remember, and if someone could just take her through it in a safe space—" I say.

Gabe steps toward me. It scares the crap out of me and I jump back, which seems to startle him. He freezes.

"I could watch Lila," I say to him, tears hot on my face. "If you wanted me to, I could watch her and you could be with Rowan when you tell her—"

Elena laughs. She actually *laughs*. "We don't need you to *watch Lila*," she says, like I'm a stupid little girl.

"Why?" I spit. "Because they have *you*? Do you think you're even helping Rowan when you're here, holding Lila and crying all the time?"

Elena recoils like she's been slapped. I bite my lip, not believing what I've said.

"Mom, you need to go," Gabe says. "I'd like to talk to June. Alone." He takes her long camel coat from the rack and holds it out to her. She slides into it, regaining only some of her composure. "Come in, June," Gabe says. Elena shakes her head furiously, her shoulders set as she walks out into the hall. I step into the apartment and she doesn't turn back to look at either of us, and then Gabe shuts and bolts the door.

He turns to me. "June," he says. "What are you doing?"

"I'm sorry," I say. "For what I said to your mom."

He waves his hand. "Not that," he says, his voice hushed. "What's all this about wanting to tell Rowan about Gray? You can't do that, you know that, right?" He's looking at me like the wild card I maybe am. "You could derail *everything*," he says. "Do you understand that? Do you have any idea how terrified I am all the time? It takes everything I have to conceal my panic from Rowan. I walk around this apartment out of my mind with worry that I'm going to lose my wife to the dark corners of her mind. This isn't the first time she's been in a bad place, June, but it's by far the most terrifying. Do you have any idea what the past few weeks have been like for me? I lost my son." His hand goes into his hair, and he stares hard at me. I can't seem to say anything at all. He rakes his fingers back and forth, tugging his hair straight up, and then he growls, "And you come in here acting like you know best, and hey: maybe you're right and maybe Sylvie's wrong. But I'm doing what the professional tells me to do. And if you're not on board, then get out."

I try to swallow down the alcohol that's burning its way up my throat.

"Okay," I say. "I get it."

He gives me a curt nod. "Okay," he says. And then he looks at his watch. "I have to wake Rowan and Lila for a feed in a few minutes. I need you to go. And I need you not to tell Rowan you ever came here, or that we ever had a conversation like this."

"I understand. And I'm sorry, and . . ."

"You don't have to be sorry," Gabe says. "You've helped us, June. You've been here for us when almost no one else could be. We will never forget that, do you understand me?"

It's the best thing anyone has said to me in a long time. "I understand," I say.

He nods. Then he takes a step to the front door and unbolts it. He swings it open and I do something I don't realize I'm going to—I wrap my arms around him in a tight hug. He hugs me back, his muscles softening just a hair. "Thank you, June," he whispers into my ear. "For everything."

I step into the hallway with tears blurring my eyes for the thousandth time today. The door crunches shut behind me, and I imagine Gabe inside his apartment, going to Rowan. I imagine her sleepily waking up, not knowing where she is at first, maybe still dreaming of babies like she told me she always does. I imagine her coming to in the dark room, looking down at Lila, so grateful her little girl is okay, so glad her little girl is *hers.*

I stand there, letting the tears come, thinking I'm alone.

I'm not.

Gabe's mother is there, her back against the hallway's chintzy wallpaper, just out of sight. I hear her shuffle before I turn to see her.

I take in a quick breath. I don't say anything. We just stare at each other.

"What are you doing here?" I ask when I can find my voice.

"Waiting for you, June," she says. Her knotty, pale hands are woven together like she's praying.

I want to leave, to race down the staircase or run past her and catch the elevator, but I'm still too drunk for this night—my limbs don't feel sharp enough to cooperate with my escape ideas.

She moves toward me—just a step at first.

"I have nothing to say to you," I snap. I figure I'll try to move past her to the elevator. She's not saying anything, and even though she's the tiniest thing, the hallway is narrow enough that her standing there makes it too awkward for me to just brush past. So I stay; I wait. I almost consider apologizing for what I said in the apartment about how unhelpful she is with her crying, but then she says, "June, let me tell you what you're going to do," and I laugh, I can't help it—it's so absurd.

"I'm not doing anything you say," I spit out, and now I've pissed her off again. Her lip curls, and she comes even closer. This time she extends her pointer finger. "I've known girls like you," she says.

"Girls like me?" I repeat, and now I'm pissed, too. "You've never known anyone like me, Elena," I say. I stand up taller, dwarfing her, but she keeps coming toward me, and then she says, "Oh, trust me, June, little actress girls like you are a dime a dozen."

"Leave me alone," I say, backing up, because now I do feel like a little girl again, powerless beneath her stare.

"Oh, see, that's where you're wrong," she says, her voice so eerily dark. "*You're* going to leave *them* alone. You're not going to see Rowan, Gabe, or Lila ever again. I see the way you look at them, like you want to be a part of them. I watch you, June. I don't know if you're in love with my son or in love with Rowan or in love with the entire idea of being a part of their broken little family." She considers me, her red-rimmed eyes roving my face. "What is it, June? Was your family broken, too? Daddy left? Mom drank too much? *I can see it in you*," she says.

I stagger back toward the staircase, my hips against it. "Leave me alone, you bitch," I say, because I can't think of a single thing more creative to hurl at her. I step toward Elena so I can get out of here. *"Get out of my way,"* I snarl.

She doesn't.

"If I ever see you back here—" she says.

"You'll what?" I ask. *"I'm not leaving them."*

"You'll ruin them," she says. I shake my head and start to say that I won't, but she's coming at me. "Stay away from them," she practically shouts.

"Make me," I spit back, and she lunges.

It shocks me. Her hands are on my shoulders, digging in. "Get off of me," I hiss, and I'm trying to squirm away, but she just squeezes harder. I turn around as fast as I can and I'm almost sure she's letting go of me, but then I realize she's lost her footing, and the second she regains it she's upon me again, and I don't want to hurt her but I need to get her off me, and then I'm shoving her away and her elbow catches me in my ribs and we twist and turn and I go back, my spine against the railing, and then over and over and I'm backward and she's beneath me and then there's the sound of bone against the railing and I'm falling backward, curving over the rail of the staircase, my head *down, down, down*, time slowing all around me, the cold tile of the basement blurring, coming up to meet me, until I can feel the very first bone go *crack*.

FORTY-EIGHT

Rowan. Friday night. November 11th.

Outside my apartment building in the cold air, the detective stares at Harrison, Gabe, and me like we've all done it to June, like we're the reason she's on a stretcher about to be loaded into a body bag. He must know it was one of us who killed her, because who else? But then he says, "Gabe, have you spoken with your mother since Tuesday night?" He holds up a hand. "And before you lie to me again, I know June came to see you on the night she was most likely attacked right inside your apartment building." He turns to Harrison then, too. "Cozy little group you all are," he said. "We saw you all on the security camera, you know." Back to Gabe. "Your mother, Elena, comes in around seven, and then out in a huff a bit before eleven. There's blood on your mother's coat; it's obvious even from the security footage. Can't wait to get my hands on that coat, to test the DNA. Is she a violent woman, your mother?"

Gabe's brown eyes widen. *"What?"* he asks.

"Your mother?" the detective repeats. "Has she ever been violent with anyone?"

Gabe goes ashen. More people surround us now, a crowd of onlookers, drawn to the tragedy like to a magnet; they seem to press up against us, watching, waiting, *seeing us*. The diners from the restaurants hold hands and to-go bags, huddling on the corner in heavy coats and solemn faces.

I reach out my hand and squeeze Gabe's.

"Or maybe you're the violent one," Detective Mulvahey says to Gabe, like it's a thought that just dawned on him. "Violent mother, violent son?"

I clutch Lila tighter with my other arm. "He's not," I say. "He's never hurt anyone, and he would never hurt June."

"Gabe," Harrison says firmly, stepping toward Gabe as though he can shoulder the detective away from us, as though he can protect us like he always does. But he can't, not now. "You and your mother need a lawyer present," he says. "Don't say another word."

"Now, wait," Mulvahey says to Harrison. "I thought we were all in this together. I thought we all wanted to help figure out *who did this to June?*"

His eyes dart between us; he's so obviously accusing one of us of murder. My mind won't work fast enough, and then I hear a voice call Gabe's name. I turn to see Elena and my mother racing down our block; Elena must have checked her out for bingo, and they probably tried to reach me and couldn't, so they came here. My mother's arm is crooked at an awkward angle, and Elena's gloved fingers are over her wrist. She's practically dragging my mother over the sidewalk.

"Oh *no*," I say.

Gabe turns and sees them. "What are they doing here?" he asks beneath his breath.

"What perfect timing," Mulvahey says, like a satisfied cat.

"Gabe!" calls Elena again, taking in the scene. "Are you all right?" she cries.

"Are they all right?" my mother asks as they get closer, but I can tell something's wrong with her. She has the frantic look she gets when she's confused and doesn't understand where she is.

"Mom," I say, starting to make my way toward them. She stares at me, but I'm not sure she knows who I am.

"Stay here," the detective says, his voice hard.

I freeze. "But, my mom," I say, and I start to cry—I can't help it. Mulvahey doesn't have any mercy on me, and why should he? He waits and watches as Elena drags my mother through the random pedestrians gathered. "Let them through," Mulvahey calls to the officer near the crime scene tape, and as they come close, Mulvahey studies Elena like a portrait at the Met. He can't possibly suspect her of hurting June. She's barely big enough to hurt anything.

"Mom," I say when she's finally to me. I want to wrap my arms around her, but I don't; it'll scare her if she doesn't know who I am. "I'm so sorry," I say, trying to keep my voice calm, to see how far gone she is and not make it worse, "there's been this terrible thing that happened to our sitter . . . and we . . ."

My mother isn't looking at me. She's staring at Lila.

"Where's the other baby?" she asks.

My heart stops. Gabe's hand finds mine.

"Mom," I say. "Oh God."

Her blue eyes are wide and stricken with worry. She looks up at me. "Sweetie?" she asks, like she's not sure if it's really me. "Where's your son?"

"Oh, Mom," I say, and then I wrap my arms around her. I'm holding on to her, but my eyes on are Gabe. He's staring at me, frozen in place. "Gray is gone," I say, tears on my face, my mom and I both shaking. Gabe lets out a long breath and his dark eyes fill with tears. I reach for his hand, holding on to both him and my mother.

"Rowan," my mother says, hugging me so tightly, so perfectly, exactly what I need. "I'm sorry, my darling," she says. "I'm so very sorry about your little boy."

FORTY-NINE

June. Three days ago. Tuesday, November 8th.

My nose is bleeding everywhere. It's hot and gushing over my face, onto Elena's jacket and all over the hand she used to smack me. My nose is broken, I'm sure of it, and I can't feel the elbow that I cracked against the railing. I hate Elena right now—it rages through my feet and into my head. But the sight of all that blood from my nose has startled her—she's frozen in place. Coming over her face is the realization of what she's done, and I use that moment to get myself off the railing and far away from her.

"You almost pushed me over that railing and *killed me*, Elena," I hiss. "Leave me alone, or I'll go back inside that apartment and show Gabe how badly you've hurt me." She looks terrified. She almost seems like she's snapping out of something, like she got carried away and did something she didn't mean to. I have no idea—I just want her to leave. She looks once more in horror at the mess she's made of my face, and then finally she scuttles down the stairs, her tiny feet clapping the marble steps.

Crap, I say to myself when she's gone. I double-check that she's truly left, but on the floor beneath me I see a flash of blond hair and a low male voice that sounds like Henri. Maybe Henri's talking to Elena?

Maybe he was checking up when he heard the scuffle? How did Gabe not hear us? He must have gone back to the bedroom where Rowan was sleeping with Lila. It's so quiet back there. And where are Mart and Mrs. Davis when I need them? Mrs. Davis is usually good for sticking her head out when she hears Rowan and me in the hallway, giving me looks behind Rowan's back like she's trying to telegraph: *Has she remembered the baby yet?* Maybe they're out.

I take a minute and try to clean myself off with the Kleenex in my purse. And then I walk down the hall, and with a trembling finger I press the elevator button. Someone on the floor below says something in what sounds to me like Swedish. Is it Henri? I almost try to find him and see if he can help me get cleaned off, but then I decide against it. The last thing I need is Henri enjoying staring at me in his office, wiping down my face. Instead I step into the elevator and down I go, the thing vibrating and hiccupping over the floors like it always does. In the lobby I spill onto the checkerboard floor. Henri isn't at his post at the desk; maybe he's still upstairs. I'm hurrying across the floor when I see Harrison enter the lobby, color from the cold high on his cheeks.

I do a double take. He's staring right at me, coming fast across the floor.

"What are you doing here?" I ask. I almost tell him that Rowan's sleeping with Lila and he better be quiet if he's planning to go see Gabe, but instead he says, "I need to talk to you."

To me? How did he even know I was here? What happened with Elena has sobered me a little, but I'm still too tipsy to figure this out.

"Is that blood?" Harrison asks, but there isn't concern in his voice.

"Um, yes," I say. "How did you know I was here?" I ask him. Did Gabe call him? "I'll tell you what happened," I say slowly, trying to steady myself. "It was *insane*, actually, what just happened with Elena."

"Gabe's mom?" he asks.

"Yeah," I say. "But I don't want to talk here and Henri will be back soon eavesdropping on us. And I want to talk to you, too, about what happened today with us. Can we please go somewhere?"

"It's freezing out," Harrison says, scanning the lobby. "I don't want to go back out there."

"Fine," I say with a sigh, resigned to doing this all in front of Henri, who will undoubtedly be back any minute.

But then Harrison says, "Let's go down to the billiards room. There's a bathroom down there and we can clean you off."

"Okay," I say. I follow him toward the door leading to the basement. Inside the stairwell I look up to where I was just hanging over the railing five flights above us. I shudder. That fall would have killed me. "Elena just *attacked me*," I say to Harrison as we descend the steps into the basement.

"What?" he asks, a few steps in front of me, not waiting for me to catch up. His feet are pounding the marble stairs. At the bottom he looks back, a quizzical expression on his face. "Seriously?" he asks.

"Seriously," I say. "It was nuts. I went to see Gabe and Rowan because, well, I had too many drinks with Kai in the neighborhood and I guess in the moment I thought it was a great idea to come tell Gabe I think he needs to tell Rowan about Gray."

Harrison whips around. There's shock on his face. "Why would you ever do that?" he asks.

I trot down the next few steps and meet him at the bottom. It's freezing down here. "I don't know, okay? I guess I wasn't convinced that any of this is the right thing, and I was worried maybe Sylvie's wrong—"

"And you know best?"

"You don't have to be rude," I say.

He shakes his head. "Sometimes you seem so mature," he says slowly, like he's realizing the most profound thing. "And sometimes you seem like a child."

"Well, if that's so bothersome, maybe you shouldn't date twenty-two-year-olds," I snap.

He raises his eyebrows and laughs, and the laugh is cruel enough to hit me right in the gut. "Oh God, June, you're probably right," he says sarcastically. "You're very wise."

I put my hands on my hips, aware that move isn't making me look any older. "My youth never seemed to bother you while you were taking me out on the town on your arm."

"Exactly," he says, exasperated. "That's what I can't believe about all of this."

"All of what?" I ask.

"You breaking this off," he says, waving a gloved hand into the cold, damp air of the basement.

"Keep your voice down," I say, because we're right in the stairwell and it's echoey in here. I move past him toward the door that leads to the billiards room and shove it open. "Is the heater broken?" I ask. It feels like it's in the midforties. I wrap my arms around myself, grateful I wore my warmest coat. It's dark down here, and smells like no human has been around in weeks. I can just make out the table in the center of the room. My hand fumbles for the light on the wall—I think I remember where it is, but I keep brushing my hand against the wall and nothing hits. "I can't find the light," I say. He's right next to me now, too close for someone I don't like at this moment. "I can't see anything," I say again, frustrated, because he's just standing there not trying to help me find the switch. My eyes start to adjust a little, and I can make out his shadowy outline. Finally he makes a move to help me. He swipes a hand over the wall and flicks on the switch.

Light floods the room.

There's nowhere to sit in here, so we just stand by the pool table, awkwardly facing off. Harrison has his arms crossed over his chest. The circles beneath his eyes are darker than usual; he gets like this when he's on a big deal at work and can't sleep, or when something is falling through that he really wanted.

"Look, I'm sorry," I say, trying to loosen a little, to bend into this situation, to see it from his side.

He lifts an eyebrow. "About what exactly?"

"That this didn't work," I say.

"It's not that I'm upset that this didn't just *not work* on its own," he says, and he has this stupid smirk on his face like I should know what he's talking about.

"I don't know what that means," I say.

"You weren't honest with me from the beginning," he says. "You used me."

"What are you talking about?" I ask, trying to stall, but he's freaking me out—it's the terminology he's using: because he's not wrong; there *were* times when I was using him for all kinds of things—access to places I never would have gotten into by myself, an entry into a world I wanted deeply to be a part of, a distraction from that rush of feelings for Gabe all those months ago. But mostly I was using him as a friend in a city where I had barely anyone.

He's staring at me, and his face is turning smug, which gives me a knot in my stomach. I look away, my eyes finding the pool table, the impossibly shiny balls stacked inside the triangle. The green fabric on top of the table looks well loved even though I've never seen anyone come down here. "I said I was sorry," I say softly. I can't meet his gaze. The alcohol is making me buzzy and tired; I just want to go home.

He reaches into his bag, and for a second I'm scared he's going to take out a gun or a knife. I know that sounds completely insane, but I hate what's between us right now, the hard edge fizzing in the cold air. There's so much hurt and embarrassment coming from him, and guilt from me, and all of it is like a storm getting angrier by the second.

"I found this," Harrison says, and he's holding out the journal I keep stashed way back inside my desk at work. The brown leather cover matches his gloves.

"What are you doing with that?" I ask. "You snooped in my desk?" I reach out my hand to try to take it, but he snaps it away.

"Yes, I *snooped*," he says. "God, you sound like you're five."

"You're the one who stole a journal from a desk drawer like we're in elementary school," I retort. "You can hardly talk. Give it back," I say. But he doesn't. Instead, he opens it. And right there in front of us is the page where I wrote about what I felt for Gabe that first night at the Playwrights Horizons reading. And even worse, on the next page I wrote that one of the ways I would distract myself was by going out with Harrison to forget I felt like that about someone who was married. And then, because I'm not much of a journal writer, there aren't many other entries—I remember I wrote down a few things going on with work or with Sean, but nowhere in that journal do I start to talk about how I stopped feeling that way about Gabe or how I started to have real feelings for Harrison. "Look," I say. "I only wrote that because I felt really bad for thinking a married person was extremely attractive. But it's not like I acted on it or did anything wrong other than have a fleeting crush."

"And then date me like some kind of consolation prize," Harrison says.

"No, it's not like that," I say.

"It's funny," he says. "I can't tell you how many ways I've lost to this guy before."

"To Gabe?" I ask. I've only seen Harrison take pride in Gabe, to tote him around like a treasured pet. Plus he makes 15 percent of everything Gabe makes, which is a lot, so I didn't exactly think Harrison was harboring any ill feelings toward him.

"Yes," he says, laughing. It's so eerie, him laughing like that, like all of this is funny when it's clearly not funny at all to him. It makes me feel sick. And it's getting harder to breathe in here; there's a thin layer of dust on nearly everything in the billiards room: on the old books stacked on a shelf, a random globe, a pointer stick like they'd have in an old classroom.

"Well, let me rephrase that," Harrison says. "It's not like I care about his big ego and all the ways he gets to be the star and the writer and director and all *those things*. I don't mind being behind the scenes, the agent behind *the Great Gabe O'Sullivan*." He takes a breath here— he's working up to everything like he wants to make sure I understand. He stares me dead in the eyes. *"Rowan was mine first,"* he says, and he lets it hang in the air, lets me really hear it. "She was there one night waiting at the bar, looking indescribably perfect, and we looked at each other. And I swear there would have been something between us if it hadn't been for Gabe and his"—he lets out a barking laugh and goes on—*"his vortex of sex appeal.* I mean, come on, June, that's what got you going that night at the reading, right? The man's sheer sex appeal?"

It sends a shudder down my spine. I don't want to be having this conversation, but there's nothing I can do about it. Something so sharp rips between us that I'm worried he'll stop me if I try to go; he'll make me hear what he's saying whether I want to or not. "It's what got Rowan," Harrison says. "And worse, it's what kept her. She's in love with him. And I've had to watch it up close for years."

"Wow," I say, shaking my head. I let go of a breath. I don't want him to think I'm judging him, because I'm not, because now I know what it feels like to want something you can't have. But I wanted Gabe for a few hours—maybe even a few days—before it simmered back down again. He's wanted Rowan for years and years. I ask, "So then why did you bring me there, to Gabe's reading, if you were so worried about all the ways he pulls women in and makes them want him?"

Harrison shrugs. "I guess I was showing you off," he says.

"At least you're honest," I say.

"Too much therapy not to be."

"Is it working? The therapy?"

"Nope," Harrison says, and he laughs again, and the air changes, and I hate this moment; I want to leave so badly my teeth hurt with the wanting.

"So you're in love with Rowan," I say. "Can we move on now? I really want to get out of here. I'm freezing, and the dust is making it hard to breathe. I'm allergic."

Harrison drops the laugh. "Who wouldn't be in love with her? She's the most appealing creature I've ever met."

I swallow. I almost feel bad for him. "Does she know?" I ask.

He stiffens a little. "Oh, I think she does," he says. "That's the thing with you women: You *like* it, don't you? When a man's eyes are all over you, when they can't get enough?" He brushes a wayward blond curl off his forehead. "You certainly like it, June," he says.

"That's not entirely right," I say. My blood moves through my veins a little faster.

"Are you *sure*?" he asks me. "I've been watching you these past few months. You really are cut out for this actress thing," he says. "You love being in the spotlight."

"I'm not doing anything wrong," I say, moving back a step.

"I think you are," he says. He waves around the journal. "You've wasted months of my life using me to get closer to Gabe. You've been in love with him this entire time. And how messed up is that, that you're the one going to their house to care for their baby." He snaps his fingers. "Oh my God," he says. "Maybe Rowan's not completely insane at all. Maybe you did try to hurt Lila."

My mouth falls. "How dare you?"

"Sometimes real life is stranger than fiction," he says nastily. "Isn't that what storytellers love to say? In fiction, everything has to make sense. Characters' motivations, timelines. There's no room for coincidences."

"If you're done waxing poetic about storytelling, and accusing me of trying to harm children, I'm going to go home now. But for the record, I'm *not* in love with Gabe," I say. "I had a crush that first night we met, like you saw there in my journal when you stole it. And you're right, Harrison, it was all about his *sex appeal*, if that's what you'd like to call it. But then I got to know Rowan, and I care about her, and I am absolutely not in love with her husband."

"So now what?" Harrison asks. "You're just hanging on, trying to be a part of their life? Trying to ruin Rowan by telling her about Gray before she's ready? A little desperate, don't you think?" The back of his hand goes to his forehead and he rubs it quickly, furiously. "I guess I wasn't enough, was I?" he asks. "All those amazing places I took you, though . . . was it worth sleeping with me for that kind of access, June?"

I gasp. "I'm done here," I say, making a move to get past him.

"You're not," he says, and then he grabs my arm.

"Ouch!" I say, and I see it register on his face, but I can't read the look I see there. It's almost like he's scared of how far he's gone, and for a second I think he'll let me go. "You're hurting me," I say when he doesn't.

"You hurt *me*," he says. "You played me like a pawn." He shakes his head as if he can't believe how despicable I am. "I've tried moving on from Rowan so many times," he says. "And every time I end up with women like you. Self-involved, immature, deceitful. There are so many women like you and not enough like Rowan."

I hold back tears because now he's said the thing that breaks me, the thing I fear is the most true: that I'm not shiny and good, that I'm just *untalented, selfish, unlovable June*. I start crying, choking over the words as I say them: "Did you ever think maybe you're not good enough for her, either? Did you ever think that Gabe is just *more* than you—that he's everything Rowan wants and you aren't?"

I barely mean the words even as I say them. I'm just so hurt. Harrison's features shift into something terrifying, and I open my mouth to take back what I've said, but then his arms are coming at me, his gloved hands at my throat, pressing against me. *Tighter, tighter.* The room spins. The green of the table whirls together with the reds and yellows and oranges of the billiard balls. I'm slipping somewhere I don't want to go—but I can't get a breath in, the dusty air barely makes it down my throat with him squeezing it so hard. My knees buckle beneath me and down, down I go, onto the floor, everything growing darker, darker.

FIFTY

Rowan. Friday night. November 11th.

I unwrap myself from my mother's arms and turn to my husband. "Gabe," I say. I put my hands on his face. I think of June, about how much she loved Lila, of how scared she must have been to know all of this about Gray when I didn't remember him, and the way she kept taking care of us anyway. "I remember Gray," I say to Gabe, and his entire being lifts in a way I've never seen before, and it reminds me that marriages are full of new things. "You remember him," he says, his voice cracking.

Harrison backs away from us, leaving us in our own shared tragedy.

I hold Lila closer, bouncing her gently but staring only at Gabe. "I do," I say. "And I'm so sorry I forgot him. I'll never forget ever again."

Gabe shakes his head. He can barely speak, but he manages to say, "I love you."

I say it back, and he pulls our daughter and me inside his arms. I close my eyes. I want to stay here forever—I don't want to open my eyes; I don't want to see June inside that bag, taken away from us.

The detective finally leaves us alone. Maybe we're such a sad group, he realizes we're not even capable of bolting. Harrison comes back over to us and launches into full agent mode, robotically telling us we need a lawyer, but on closer inspection I can see his face has fallen, the side of his mouth hanging low, his eyes red. He cut himself shaving today, maybe, because there's a spot of blood on his neck.

The police lights scatter across the night sky. The sound of cars racing down the West Side Highway mix with the sounds of cops and emergency personnel talking over their radios.

Emergency workers flood the scene; I keep expecting them to put the three of us in handcuffs, but no one does. We just stand there, useless, Elena watching my mom and me with a drawn expression on her face, Harrison getting downright furious when Gabe doesn't seem to be listening to his advice.

Neighbors have come out of their homes, from other buildings and from our own. Henri is standing there with our neighbor Mart, both with their arms crossed over their chests like they've seen this all before, like babysitters have long been buried inside this very building.

"What have we done to June?" I ask against Gabe's chest.

"I don't understand what happened to her," Gabe says, pulling away from me. "I don't get how she was down there for three days and no one found her. It had to have happened that night she was here, at our place, trying to talk to me about . . ."

His voice trails off.

I tip my chin up to look at him. "About what?" I ask, already scared to go near the answer.

"She always wanted to tell you about Gray. She was convinced what Sylvie was doing was wrong and unfair to you. And it's not like I was one hundred percent sure on the right thing to do . . ." He shakes his head. "That night, she was drunk when she showed up at our apartment. She came when my mom was here and we were both pretty hard on her, we told her it wasn't her place to tell you and that if she wasn't on board she should get out and not come back."

I imagine it unfolding: June fighting on my behalf, Gabe scared and questioning himself, Sylvie, me. "I did this to all of you," I say, but it barely holds weight in the air. Even I know it's more complicated than that. Gabe wraps his arms around me again. I close my eyes, and when I finally open them I look for Harrison, thinking I should comfort him, too. But he's nowhere. I scan the crowd, but I see only my neighbors. Maybe it was all too much for him, losing the girl he loved, seeing her lying there like that. There are firemen on the scene now, too, and I'm distracted by their large presence and the way they talk to the police officers like this isn't an emergency, like a dead person in a basement is just something they see all the time.

I scan the crowd again. Harrison is gone.

Paramedics and other emergency personnel block my view of June. They seem so busy, flitting around her. Now the uniformed men with the black body bag move closer and I can hardly bear it. Lila whimpers, and I want to use it as an excuse to go somewhere else, anywhere but here, but I don't. I make myself watch. June was here, in my home, and then she died. She was babysitting my baby, dating my friend, taking care of *me*. I make my eyes follow the men, but instead of stopping next to June's body and putting her inside the body bag, they move toward our apartment building.

"Where are they going?" I ask Gabe. He's watching as Elena carefully leads my mother away, all of us worried this is too much for her in her fragmented state. Tears are still streaming down Gabe's face, but his arm is slung around my waist and there's a looseness to him I haven't felt in weeks. He turns back to see the men with the black bag on the steps of our apartment building.

"To the basement," Gabe says. "That's where he is."

I open my mouth to ask what he's talking about, but then Mulvahey is suddenly next to us. "Are you ready?" he asks. "I'd like you to identify his body."

I turn to look at Mulvahey's face, but it's too hard to make out his expression in the dark with the police lights flashing, making everything feel chaotic. "Sorry, what did you say?" I ask.

"He's not carrying a picture ID," Mulvahey says, impatient now. "And I'd rather get this process started now rather than have everything held up at the morgue. I've got his name from his credit cards, but I'd like your eyes on him to make an ID, since you seem to be the only one who's ever met him."

A shake starts in my legs. I lean into Gabe. "I think I've misunderstood something," I say, my voice barely making it above the noisy scene around us. My hand presses against Lila, grounding me to real life, making me stay here.

"Who's down in the basement?" I ask.

FIFTY-ONE

June. Three days ago. Tuesday, November 8th.

I'm on the floor of the billiards room and Harrison is still on top of me, shouting, "Do you get it now? Do you understand what you've done?" I'm fading in and out, praying he'll just take his hands off my neck and let me breathe again.

There's a clatter on the stairs. Someone's coming to help us; someone has heard Harrison shouting—someone knows something bad is happening down here.

Gabe? One of the neighbors?

If we didn't shut the steel door at the very top of the stairs, someone in the lobby could still hear us down here. It could be Henri; it could be anyone.

Please, help me.

"I didn't want to do this to you," Harrison says, his voice strangled and wild, and when I snap open my eyes I swear I see the craziest thing: Sean's face, contorted and rageful, his arm lifting, his Swiss Army knife glinting.

I close my eyes again—I can't seem to keep them open.

Was that really him?

I force my eyes to open, to try to see him again, and there he is: *Sean*. Not in my imagination—I'm almost sure of it. His Swiss Army knife flies high into the air above us. Is he here to help me? He is, he is. He's here to help.

"Get off of her!" he screams. And then down he goes onto Harrison, but Harrison's too fast; he turns and pounds against Sean's ribs, and Sean's going down now, they both are, onto the floor, the knife between them.

FIFTY-TWO

Rowan. Friday night. November 11th.

"Sean is dead, Rowan," Gabe says, his eyes roving my face like he's trying to make sure I'm all right. "He and June were both down there together in the billiards room."

"*What?*" I ask. "But is June, I thought June was . . ." And then I turn to the stretcher, and I swear I see a flicker of movement between the people around her, strapping things to her, fussing over her body. I swear I see June's slender wrist move from her side to rest gently on her stomach.

I sink to my knees, clutching Lila. "Rowan," Gabe says, bending, helping me get back up. "Rowan?"

"I thought," I start to say, but instead of explaining anything to him, my feet start carrying Lila and me in the direction of June. I can feel Gabe behind us, calling my name, but I don't stop. Through the warm bodies I go, trying hard to be polite and say *excuse me* and not push them aside. Hot tears are on my cheeks. Maybe because there's a newborn on my chest they all let me pass, no one restrains me, and then I'm right there at the stretcher, so close I could reach out and touch my beautiful babysitter.

"*June,*" I say. The word is magic on my lips.

There's dried blood in June's hair and caked on her hands. Blankets cover her. She smells like she was the one who died down there, and I have to fight my stomach not to get sick. "June," I say again, and I can't help it, I want to be strong for her but I can't stop crying. "Are you okay?" I ask softly. I reach forward and take her bloody hand. And unlike in the café that morning, this time I don't let go.

She can't meet my eyes. Her gaze is vacant as she stares down at her fingers, and it's hard to tell if she even knows I'm here. In the minutes since I saw her lying on the stretcher the paramedics have put an IV line into her arm and an oxygen mask on her face. They're barking orders to each other, and then one of them says to me, "Do you know her?"

"Yes," I say. Gabe is right there by my side, staring at June. "We know her," I say. "She's our babysitter."

The paramedic nods. "You can ride with her to the hospital," he says. "That way she won't be surrounded by a truck full of strangers. But I'll need you to step aside for the moment while we stabilize her."

Tears are all over my face and my legs are shaking. I back into the crowd of people, and from this angle I can see Harrison: he's near the front of the ambulance, talking with Detective Mulvahey. I see Louisa and Sylvie right there with him—Sylvie must have called Louisa when I got the call from the detective in her office. Louisa's crying, her hand on her pregnant stomach. Sylvie is hanging on Harrison's words. Gabe guides me toward Sylvie and Louisa and I let him, even though I don't want to leave June. "Sean was stalking her," Harrison is saying to the detective. "He was *obsessed* with her. She told everyone that." Harrison looks at all of us to confirm it, and so does Detective Mulvahey.

"She told me sometimes he worried her," I say. "I need to comprehend this, to know what happened to June six floors below where I've been living and breathing for the past three days while she lay trapped. "You're sure Sean's the one who hurt her?" I ask.

"It certainly looks like it," Harrison says. "She must have tried to fight him off and thank God she did."

Detective Mulvahey stares at me. "There are only June's and Sean's fingerprints on the knife. There's a partial of June's thumb on the handle along with four neat fingerprints. She only held it once, likely to defend herself, and then never touched it again."

"Oh God," Louisa says. "She told me things about Sean, how intensely protective he was of her . . . but . . ." Louisa looks down at her hands. The detective stares at her face like he's trying to read something important there, but Louisa doesn't say any more.

"June is nearly catatonic," Mulvahey says. "She's concussed and severely dehydrated, though the paramedics seem convinced she'll make a full recovery. She may come to in the hospital and be able to tell us what happened, but it wouldn't surprise me if she didn't remember anything about what happened in that basement. We see it all the time."

Sylvie nods along to the detective. "All the time," she chimes in, looking almost reverent, and maybe she is: maybe there's beauty in the flawed way the mind protects us.

"The wounds found on June are consistent with an attack," the detective goes on, "and Sean received a single stab wound, likely inflicted by June in self-defense. Forensics is down there now, but it looks like June got ahold of Sean's knife and used it once to stab him in the abdomen. He bled out, and she was too traumatized, concussed, and injured to crawl and get help. Rowan, I'd like to take you down there now to ID the body."

The last thing I want is to see Sean dead. "I'll do it," I mumble.

"When June is well enough, she'll be questioned," the detective says.

"We shouldn't push her," Harrison says, an air of authority about him, clearly not afraid of the detective. "She's obviously beyond traumatized."

Sylvie's nodding again. Trauma: her bread and butter.

"He could have *killed her*," Harrison says. "And I feel terrible. I should have stayed with her that night rather than leave my girlfriend all alone in that building waiting for her deranged roommate to pick her up." His face folds like he's an actor in a play. Louisa's staring hard at him. I've never heard him use the word *girlfriend* to describe June.

Gabe's eyes cut to Harrison, and I can't read his face. Harrison goes on: "I'll be the one to take care of her. I'll be the one who gets her back on her feet. I owe her that, at least."

No one else says anything, and the air is too quiet between us.

"I'll identify Sean's body now, if you're ready," I tell the detective. "And then I'd like to be the one to ride with June to the hospital."

"I'll go with her," Harrison says. "It should be me."

I open my mouth to argue that that's not right, but Gabe is already at my side, pulling me toward our building. "Let's get this over with," he says.

FIFTY-THREE

Rowan. Friday night. November 11th.

Down the steps Gabe and I go, following the detective. Cops bump into us on the stairs, apologizing when they see Lila against me. In the billiards room, the stench is enough to make me sick, and Mulvahey tells me the only reason it isn't diabolically worse is because it's been so cold down here. My eyes blur at the bright lights, crime scene tape, and the big sheets of plastic fluttering just like you see in the movies. A forensics team moves through the room like wild animals at a kill. There's a knife in a plastic bag, and the overhead lights catch the blade and send the reflection somewhere past my retinas and deep into my brain to all my tragedies. I flash back to the knife that was used to kill my dad lying there on the bedroom floor and I think of my mother, pulling me close. I think of Lila, and what I wouldn't do for her, and finally I can move again, across the floor, past the knife, past the pool table until I see him: huddled in the corner, slumped over himself, next to a bucket and cleaning supplies. *Sean.*

The forensics team slides to the side so we can move closer. Detective Mulvahey is right behind me as I stare at Sean. His round face is just as

I remember it, his hazel eyes still open. I shake my head—I can hardly believe he's lying there like that, or that he hurt June.

"It's Sean," I say, shaking, unable to take my eyes off him. He looks so young, like a scared little boy. Gabe's hand is on my back, and him being there steadies me like it used to. "I'm positive," I say, my voice stronger.

FIFTY-FOUR

Rowan. Friday night. November 11th.

U p we go into the night air. I adjust Lila's knit cap over her ears, my fingers trembling from seeing Sean. I'm heading toward the ambulance, but they're shutting the doors.

"No!" I cry out, picking up my pace. I can see Harrison in the ambulance, his eyes holding mine until the ambulance doors slam shut. Louisa is still outside on the street, looking stricken as Sylvie rubs her back and says something I can't make out.

The ambulance's engine revs and something inside of me becomes animalistic. I'm sprinting now, shoving through the crowd, pounding on the back of the ambulance. But it starts pulling away. "Wait!" I cry out. And then that same paramedic I spoke with spots me in the rear-view mirror. He stops the ambulance and gets out of the driver's door. "Get in," he says gruffly. Gabe catches up to me. The paramedic makes his way to the back of the ambulance and starts to work the handle. He swings open the doors, and I see Harrison too close to June's gurney, the paramedics off to the side. June seems to be more awake than before, and she looks agitated, but it's hard to tell because the oxygen mask is over her face. Gabe climbs into the back of the ambulance first, and then he reaches out a hand and pulls Lila and me up.

Up and in we go. June is moving erratically, like her limbs are trying to get free from the blankets. I go right to her as the ambulance starts driving again. Harrison runs a hand over his hair. "Leave her alone, Rowan," he says. "She's clearly not okay."

I don't leave her alone. I put my hand on her arm. "It's all right, June. We're all here with you." June's trying to lift her arm, but it's like she doesn't have control of her limbs. "You got hurt," I say carefully. "And I know you don't remember what happened, but we're going to be with you the whole way. I'm not leaving you, June."

Finally June gets her hands to cooperate, and in one swift movement she rips off her oxygen mask. Her lips are the same purple-blue shade as the bruises on her neck. A paramedic approaches her carefully, his eyes on the monitors. She tries to speak to me, but her voice is crackling like a scratchy record. I can't understand her. So I bend closer, Lila still strapped to me, both of us nearly crushed against June. My ear goes closer to June's lips so I can understand.

"Harrison strangled me," she whispers. *"And then he stabbed Sean and left us for dead."*

A scream rises in my throat like a banshee waiting to be set free.

My fingers start to shake, and I almost lose it right then and there and blow June's cover, and then Lila's squirming against me and I think about Gray, and I think about the woman I was before my children were born, and even though I didn't know love like this, I knew secrets and mysteries and everything people are capable of when they're pushed beyond their capacity, when they're desperate. Harrison's eyes are dark, his skin sallow, his fingers gripping onto the side of June's makeshift bed. I keep my face very, very still, and then I think of how I would write this scene if I wanted my heroines to stay safe.

I take a breath, feeling my lungs inflate like balloons, and I'm struck with a clear memory of being pregnant with Lila and Gray, when it was so very hard to get a full breath in because they were jammed against my ribs. I remember it perfectly.

"She's not making any sense," I say to everyone in the ambulance, using every ounce of control I have to keep my voice neutral. Harrison's eyes are all over me, trying to read my face, to know what I'm really thinking: his specialty. "I really need to feed Lila," I say, more confident now, and then I fumble around for my phone, like I need it to check my feeding app, but Harrison arcs toward me and I'm terrified I'm not fooling him. My confidence starts to slip, and my fingers are fumbling as I fire off a text to the detective. Harrison reaches out toward me.

She remembers everything. Harrison did it. Get him out of this ambulance.

I'm about to press send but we fly over a pothole and my phone clatters to the floor.

"Let me get that for you," Harrison says.

"*No,*" I say, frantic as the phone slides beneath June's gurney. I've got Lila on me, and Harrison is already bending beneath it. But then Gabe lurches forward and somehow snatches it up. I see him stare down at the screen.

Does he see what I wrote? I can't read his face. He taps the screen and then pockets the phone.

I feel like I'm going to be sick. "Gabe?" I ask. Did he press send? "Can I have my phone back?" My voice is shaking.

Gabe turns to me. "I'll hold it for you till the hospital," he says. His gaze is hard, locked on mine. I can't argue with him or it'll come off as too suspicious. "Is that new writing?" he asks me slowly.

We're quiet for a moment. June's eyes are closed now.

"Um," I stall.

"On your phone," Gabe adds, impatient. "Is it new stuff?" His voice is more gentle now. He pats the top of his daughter's head, his eyes on me.

"Yes," I say, my mind racing. "I was about to press send on a message to Dave," I say, picturing my agent in his Brooklyn apartment, wondering what he would ever say if he knew we were living a scene from one of my novels.

"I think it's been sent," Gabe says, holding my gaze. And that's when I know.

I reach forward and take June's hand. She squeezes, or tries to, her grip is so weak.

Harrison's eyes dart between Gabe and me.

The ambulance lurches to a stop and everything goes quiet. Harrison is looking down into his lap, a tiny vein pulsing at his temple, and then we're zooming forward again.

The air feels deadly.

My baby girl nuzzles her head against me. The lights flash, and it feels like a sign from God. Sirens blare.

"What's going on?" Harrison asks as the ambulance careens right and pulls over to the side of the highway.

Police lights are everywhere—even though they're behind us we can see them scattering through the night. And then a cop car pulls in front of us, stopping mere feet from the bumper.

The paramedic places the oxygen mask back on June. But her green eyes open, and they never leave mine.

The back doors of the ambulance swing out to Detective Mulvahey and a squad of police officers, weapons raised.

"Exit the vehicle, Mr. Russell," Mulvahey says to Harrison. Harrison protests, a slew of curse words. But he does what they say—he gets out, Gabe staring in disbelief as they handcuff him against the truck.

"June," I say softly, moving closer to her still body. "It's all over now." I tuck a piece of blond hair behind her ear. "You're going to be okay. I'm going to make sure of it." I lean forward to embrace her. Gabe's arm is around me as I hold my little girl and June tight against me, my makeshift family safe at last.

EPILOGUE

June. One year later.

I'm standing behind the curtain, about to take the stage. The house lights are still up on the rows of seating in the tiny black box theater. I peek through a gap in the curtain, and I can make out my new friends from acting class, and of course Louisa, Rowan, and Gabe. Elena's watching Lila tonight back at their apartment. I still babysit once a month, mostly to stay connected with Gabe and Rowan and because I love Lila so much. I don't need the extra money as much as I used to, because Louisa started her own agency and she pays me pretty well for an assistant position. Nearly all of Louisa's clients followed her from WTA to her new shop. She's bringing on another agent next month, and we're looking for office space; but for now it's just her and me, so we work from her apartment. Sometimes during work, we sneak out and play with her little boy, Nate, while the nanny makes lunch, just because we can.

I wrote the one-woman show I'm about to perform tonight. I'm not Shakespeare or anything like that, but my stuff is kinda funny. I don't think I ever realized I could be funny on stage; I was always so drawn to the drama. But I feel lighter on stage when I'm making people laugh, and it's an escape from everyday life, and from everything that happened this past year. It's an escape from waiting for the news about Harrison's sentencing; and it's an escape from the reality that Sean is dead, and how much I feel like his dying is my fault. I know I didn't kill him myself, but I dragged him into my mess, and I'll have to live with the crushing guilt of setting into motion the night of his death. When the cops tried to find Sean's family, we learned he didn't have one. I guess he was trying to make one with me, and realizing that awful truth nearly killed me. My mom came to stay with me for a few weeks after I got out of the hospital, and Sylvie has been working with me every Friday for the past year. Finally the nightmares and flashbacks have stopped, but there are things I don't think I'll ever shake, like my guilt, or the memory of Sean and me cold and shaking on the floor where Harrison left us to die, Sean bleeding out as I tried, delirious and in vain, to help him. I can't quite remember the time that passed after I realized he was dead. I remember slipping in and out of consciousness, and the irrational, incessant thought that I couldn't leave Sean there alone; I just couldn't.

I exhale. I close my eyes and do one of Sylvie's breathing exercises that helps me get out of that basement and back into the present moment a little easier. I open my eyes slowly, try to focus on my surroundings, the sights and sounds and smells that anchor me. I can see the audience scurrying around, taking seats, scanning programs, unwrapping mints, taking sips of water, and generally looking excited and pleased to be here.

I feel a little calmer when I see Rowan. She definitely looks happy. I can see it on her face: the dreamy half smile, her hand linked with Gabe's. Gabe's dark brow is furrowed with the serious artistic expression he wears at events like this, because that's part of who he is: *Gabe O'Sullivan, writer, creative powerhouse.* He's also Lila's dad, and Rowan's husband, and the person who buried his son after a Catholic funeral in a cathedral in Rowan's hometown. Maybe all of us are more things than we can count.

The lights flicker, warning the audience that the show will start soon. I get the same buzz I always get right before I go on. I have a feeling that Louisa, Rowan, and Gabe are going to love this play. It's my fourth night performing it, and it's gone well each time, the laugh lines getting the reaction I hoped for. There's so much more artistic control in writing my own stuff. And I'm making progress: last month I signed with a small acting agency. It's not as prestigious as WTA, but Louisa really respects my new agent, Cherise. And Cherise has more expertise in the theater versus film and TV, and it turns out the theater is where I feel more at home.

Home.

What a word. I've started going upstate every month for an overnight at my parents' house. Sometimes it's good, and sometimes it's not. But it's my family: the only one I've got. My mom and dad have come to every opening night of my performances, and I can always make out the precise ring of my dad's chuckle from the audience. It's gotten to the point when I write now, I know the lines he'll find funny, and sometimes when I get writer's block I imagine writing only for him, and I find it's easier to keep going. On opening night this past weekend, my mother brought me a bouquet of red roses. Her hands were shaking when she gave them to me.

The lights dim in the house. I take a breath, my opening lines running through my brain.

The spotlight goes up, blazing down upon me.

I take a deep breath, and then I smile.

I'm on.

ACKNOWLEDGMENTS

My biggest gratitude goes to all readers, especially those who identified with any aspect of this story. I'm thankful that the conversation around maternal mental health is becoming increasingly open and that awareness is expanding around infertility, miscarriage, stillbirth, traumatic birth, maternal mortality, and postpartum depression and anxiety. If you need help as a new mother, you can always start by asking an OBGYN or primary care doctor. You are not alone.

I'm thankful to my editor Carmen Johnson, who understood this book from our very first conversation. I always rely on your keen eye and your talent as an editor, and even more so with this book. I am very grateful to be one of your authors.

My agent, Dan Mandel, is even more wonderful than Rowan's fictional agent, Dave. There is no one more capable, wise, supportive, encouraging, and kind.

Thank you to everyone at Amazon Publishing and Little A. I enjoy every step of the process of working with you, and your dedication makes these books sing. Thank you especially to Jeff Belle, Emma Reh, Michael Schuler, Amy VO Snyder, Kristin Lunghamer, Erica Mena, and Adrienne Krogh, and to Zoe Norvell for an unbelievably beautiful cover. Thank you to Jennifer Mullowney for an author photo that feels like me.

I'm grateful to all of my friends and family—they know who they are. After writing the early days of motherhood in *The Break*, I feel especially grateful to my closest friends during my first son's early years, Kate Brochu and Maria Manger.

Thank you also to a group of very creative women from my twenties who surrounded me at a clothing shop where I worked as a salesperson, who always made me feel as if I could do anything, especially Stacia Canon, Jenna Yankun, Jen Cohn, Asli Filinta, and Nesha Russell. From that same era, writers Micol Ostow, Kristin Harmel, Alecia Whitaker, Taiia Smart Young, Sara Polsky, Anna Carey, Allison Yarrow, and Noelle Hancock were so encouraging that they made me believe I could write fiction, and I am so grateful. Thank you also to writers Jen Calonita, Kieran Scott, Melissa Walker, Fiona Davis, Mary Kubica, Mary McCluskey, and Kimberly Rae Miller, and to all of the writers in my community, especially Fran Hauser, Jimin Han, and Isabel Murphy, and to the young writers I meet each year through our library's writing contests. Thank you to the editors from whom I learned greatly along the way: Brenda Bowen, Alessandra Balzer, Kelsey Murphy, Sara Sargent, Jennifer Kasius, Lanie Davis, and Sara Shandler.

Thank you to all of the readers, reviewers, librarians, booksellers, bloggers, and bookstagrammers who spent time in these pages. It's exciting to hear people talking about the world of books and characters as if they're real, and I am very grateful to anyone who spends their time and their money to read one of my novels. Thank you.

Thank you to early readers who gave me such great feedback: Chrissie Irwin, Artika Loganathan, Megan Mazza, Tricia DeFosse, Caroline Rodetis, Janine O'Dowd, Wendy Levey, Brinn Daniels, Annie Manning, Molly Hirschel, Antonia Davis, Liv Peters, Lauren Locke, Nina Levine, Ally Reuben, my aunt Joan, and my amazingly supportive sister-in-law, Ali Sise. Thank you to Dr. Audrey Birnbaum for her keen editing and attention to detail. Thank you especially to my dad and my uncle Bill, who read early drafts and talk at length with me about character and plotlines. My favorite part about each book is the moment I send them both a draft. Thank you to my mom, a therapist who specializes in trauma and who helped me with specific trauma-related details. Thank you to my closest friend from childhood, social worker Erika Grevelding, who read an early draft and let me pick her brain about the therapist-client relationship and real life versus fiction. Thank you to OBGYN Jessica Salinas, who has been a friend since college and who helped me navigate some of the details of Rowan's birth experience. Thank you to postpartum doula and lactation consultant Alexandra White, who gave me such thoughtful advice on the early postpartum days and beyond. Thank you to my brother-in-law, Dr. Roby Bhattacharyya, and my sister, Dr. Meghan Sise, for giving me such wise feedback and encouragement. Thank you to Stacey Armand, whose sharp sense of books is invaluable to my writing. Thank you to investigator James Castiglione, who has fielded calls from my uncle Bill and from me to discuss crime scenes in my books. All mistakes, as always, are mine.

Thank you so much to Zibby Owens, who is the godmother of many, many books and certainly of mine. How lucky I am that we met.

Thank you to all of my friends who show support in so many ways. Special shout-out to Kinga Gartner, Felipe Osses-König, Antoine Sanchez, Josh Laka, Johnny Pallotta, Rob Caldwell, Heidi Rojas, Jamie Greenberg, Sarah Webb, Sarah Mottl, Heather Trotta, Katelyn Butch, Ali Tejtel, Jesse Randol, Gabriela Hurtarte, Tracy Weiss, Bianca De La Cruz, and Patti Osborne. Thank you Raj, Artika, and Nikhil Loganathan for your friendship to my whole family. Thank you to the following pals who have been there for me since I was a teenager and only dreamed of writing and working in entertainment: Caroline Moore, Jessica Bailey, Megan Mazza, Kim Hoggatt, Tricia DeFosse, Claire Noble, J. J. Area, Erin Lutterbach, and Mike Bolognino.

Thank you so much to my children's incredible teachers, and to all of my teachers, especially the ones who encouraged my writing: Mrs.

Harrison, Mrs. Orr, Mr. Bedell, Dr. Danaher, Mrs. Betro, Mrs. Kuthy, Dr. Pilkinton, Shannon Doyne, and Siiri Scott.

Thank you so very much to my family, including all of my aunts, uncles, and cousins. Thank you to Linda and Bob Harrison, and to my loving and supportive in-laws: Ray, Carole, Christine, Tait, Walker, and Josey. Thank you to my awesome brother, Jack, and his wife, Ali, and their amazing kids: Jack, Darcy, and Schuyler. Thank you to the incredible Bhattacharyya family: my brother-in-law, Roby; my niece, Rose; and my nephew, Owen; and to my sister, Meghan, who is my best friend, closest confidant, and every-day phone call. Thank you to my kind and loving parents, Jack and Mary Sise, who read every word I write. I am so lucky you are mine.

Thank you so much to Lorena, whom I love like family, for making me laugh, and for loving our family beyond anything I could have ever foreseen on the day she came into our lives.

Thank you to my husband, Brian, who is, even after all these years, my true love. Thank you to my children, the absolute loves of my life: Luke, William, Isabel, and Eloise. I'll love you to the stars and back forever.

ABOUT THE AUTHOR

Photo © 2022 Jennifer Mullowney

Katie Sise is the Amazon Charts bestselling author of *Open House* and *We Were Mothers*. Her novels have been included on best-of lists by *Good Morning America*, the *New York Post*, E! Online, PureWow, POPSUGAR, and *Parade* magazine. She is also a jewelry designer and television host and has written several young adult novels, including *The Academy*, *The Pretty App*, and *The Boyfriend App*, as well as the career guide *Creative Girl*. She lives with her family outside New York City. You can visit her online at www.katiesise.com.